Three Hours

'*Three Hours* is both a gripping thriller and a beautiful
meditation on the nature of family, friendship, courage and
unintended – lethal – consequences. Superb' Kate Mosse

'*Three Hours* is one of the most exhilarating reading experiences I've
ever had. Rosamund Lupton takes a dark, painful subject and turns it
into a novel full of hope and compassion. An amazing achievement'
Emma Healey

'This is a stunner of a book. Staggeringly good' Jane Fallon

'ASTONISHING. Powerful, terrifying, heartbreaking' Emma Flint

'Propulsively plotted and full of vivid characters who earn our
concern, *Three Hours* held me in its eloquent grip' Emma Donoghue

'So gripping, intelligent, timely, affecting and moving' Marian Keyes

'Utterly breathtaking and dazzling' Jenny Colgan

'Will chill your blood and break your heart by turns – a
masterclass in suspense' Cara Hunter

'Rosamund Lupton's best book yet, and that is high praise. A monster
story for our fractious historical moment. Chilling, suspenseful,
humane and brave' William Landay

'An incredible, unbelievably powerful book. It's taut, it's appalling, it's
uplifting, it's extraordinary. Simply stunning' Dinah Jefferies

'This is an incredible novel: a heady combination of elegant writing,
nuanced characterization, deep emotion and heart-stopping tension'
Elizabeth Brooks

'*Three Hours* is exceptional – at turns hearbreaking, warm, terrifying,
perceptive and grippingly page-turning' Kate Hamer

'I read *Three Hours* in two days, in awe. It's breathtaking. A modern rumination on the issues that divide 21st-century life, a celebration of refugees, of mental health, of love and hope and bravery. I loved it more than I can say' Gillian McAllister

'Beautifully written, emotionally note-perfect and nail-bitingly tense. It's brilliant' Tammy Cohen

'*Three Hours* is about hate crime, but what rings out from its pages – what is likely to stay with you long after you've read that magnificent last line – is love. I wanted to read *Three Hours* slowly to savour every beautiful word, yet it is so compelling that I couldn't put it down. This one is destined for the bestsellers list, I reckon, and rightly so. It is phenomenal' Fiona Mitchell

'It's mind blowing. It's a horrifying story but told with such compassion and humanity. A large cast of characters and yet you feel genuinely emotionally engaged with each one . . . Amazing' Francesca Jakobi

'*Three Hours* is a brilliant novel – moving, relevant and honest. Rosamund Lupton takes us through the story of a siege in an English school, building on the tension and our emotions as the story speeds to its conclusion . . . An exceptional and heartbreaking read' Jenny Quintana

'Lupton tells her story with searing beauty and unbearable tension. Exquisite. Compassionate. Painful. Fantastic. A work of powerful imagination that wears its intelligence lightly. Don't read this if you want to be able to put it down' Kate London

'*Three Hours* has a voice all of its own. Character and plot leap out at you from the first line. Rosamund Lupton makes you race through the pages with her irresistible storytelling. Impossible to stop until you reach the poignant end' Jane Corry

'*Three Hours* is phenomenal. Absolutely glorious, heart-rending and gripping!' Gytha Lodge

'Exceptional. I'm in awe of Rosamund Lupton' Sarah Edghill

'*Three Hours* is incredible. Haunting. Heartbreaking, relentless, beautiful' Abi Daré

Three Hours

ROSAMUND LUPTON

VIKING

an imprint of

PENGUIN BOOKS

VIKING

UK | USA | Canada | Ireland | Australia
India | New Zealand | South Africa

Viking is part of the Penguin Random House group of companies
whose addresses can be found at global.penguinrandomhouse.com.

First published 2020
001

Copyright © Rosamund Lupton, 2020

Extract from 'Burnt Norton', *Four Quartets*, by T. S. Eliot,
reproduced courtesy of Faber and Faber Ltd

The moral right of the author has been asserted

Set in 12.59/14.9 pt Dante MT Std
Typeset by Jouve (UK), Milton Keynes
Printed and bound in Great Britain by Clays Ltd, Elcograf S.p.A.

A CIP catalogue record for this book is available from the British Library

HARDBACK ISBN: 978–0–241–37449–8
TRADE PAPERBACK ISBN: 978–0–241–37450–4

www.greenpenguin.co.uk

For Felicity Blunt

an inspiration and an exceptional person, thank you

PART ONE

*And you? When will you begin that long
journey into yourself?*

Rumi (1207–1273)

I.

9.16 a.m.

A moment of stillness; as if time itself is waiting, can no longer be measured. Then the subtle press of a fingertip, whorled skin against cool metal, starts it beating again and the bullet moves faster than sound.

It smashes the glass case on the wall by the headmaster's head, which displays medals for gallantry awarded in the last World War to boys barely out of the sixth form. Their medals turn into shrapnel; hitting the headmaster's soft brown hair, breaking the arm of his glasses, piercing through the bone that protects the part of him that thinks, loves, dreams and fears; as if pieces of metal are travelling through the who of him and the why of him. But he is still able to think because it's he who has thought of those boys, shrapnel made of gallantry, tearing apart any sense he'd once had of a benevolent order of things.

He's falling backwards. Another shot; the corridor a reverberating sound tunnel. Hands are grabbing him and dragging him into the library.

Hannah and David are moving him away from the closed library door and putting him into the recovery position. His sixth-formers have all learnt first aid, compulsory in Year 12, but how did they learn to be courageous? Perhaps it was there all this time and he didn't notice it; medals again, walked past a hundred times, a thousand.

He tries to reassure them that even if it looks bad – he is pretty sure it must look very bad indeed – inside he's okay, the who of him is still intact but he can't speak. Instead sounds are coming out of his mouth that are gasps and grunts and will make them more afraid so he stops trying to speak.

His pupils' faces look ghostly in the dim light, eyes gleaming, dark clothes invisible. They turned off all the electric lights when the code red was called. The Victorian wooden shutters have been pulled shut over the windows; traces of weak winter daylight seep inside through the cracks.

He, Matthew Marr, headmaster and only adult here, must protect them; must rescue his pupils in Junior School, the pottery room, the theatre and the English classroom along the corridor; must tell the teachers not to take any risks and keep the children safe. But his mind is slipping backwards into memory. Perhaps this is what the shrapnel has done, broken pieces of bone upwards so they form a jagged wall and he is stuck on the side of the past. But words in his own thoughts grab at him – *risks*, *safe*, *rescue*.

What in God's name is happening?

As he struggles to understand, his thoughts career backwards, too fast, perilously close to tipping over the edge of his mind and the blackness there; stopping with the memory of a china-blue sky, the front of Old School bright with flowering clematis, the call of a pied flycatcher. His damaged brain tells him the answer lies here, in this day, but the thoughts that have brought him to this point have dissolved.

Hannah covers Mr Marr's top half with her puffa jacket and David covers his legs with his coat, then Hannah takes off her hoody. She will not scream. She will not cry. She will wrap her hoody around Mr Marr's head, tying the arms tightly together, and then she must try to staunch the bleeding from the wound in his foot, and when she has done these things she will check his airway again.

No more shots. Not yet. Fear thinning her skin, exposing her smallness. As she takes off her T-shirt to make a bandage she glances at the wall of the library that faces the garden, the shuttered windows too small and too high up for escape. The other wall,

4

with floor-to-ceiling bookcases, runs alongside the corridor. The gunman's footsteps sound along the bookcases as he walks along the corridor. For a little while they thought he'd gone, that he'd walked all the way to the end of the corridor and the front door and left. But he hadn't. He came back again towards them.

He must be wearing boots with metal in the heel. *Click-click click-click* on the worn oak floorboards, then a pause. No other sounds in the corridor; nobody else's footsteps, no voices, no bump of a book bag against a shoulder. Everyone sheltering, keeping soundless and still. The footsteps get quieter. Hannah thinks he's opposite Mrs Kale's English classroom. She waits for the shots. Just his footsteps.

Next to her, David is dialling 999, his fingers shaking, his whole body shaking, and even though it's only three numbers it's taking him ages. She's worried that the emergency services will be engaged because everyone's been phoning 999, for police though, not for an ambulance, not till now, and maybe they'll be jamming the line.

When I am Queen . . . Dad says to her, and she says, *When I am Queen there'll be a separate line for the police and ambulances and fire service*, but she can't hear Dad's voice any more, just David's saying, 'Ambulance, please,' like he's ordering a pizza at gunpoint, and now he's waiting to be put through to the ambulance people.

It was the kids who started the rush on 999 calls, not only directly but all those calls to mothers at work, at home, at coffee mornings, Pilates, the supermarket, and dads at work, mainly, but some at home like hers, and the parents said: *Have you phoned the police? Where are you? Has someone phoned the police? I'm coming. Where exactly are you? I'm on my way. I'm phoning the police. I'll be right there. I love you.*

Or variations on that call, apart from the *I love you*; she's sure all the parents said that because she heard all the *I love you too*-s. Dad said all that. She'd been in the English classroom then, where phones are allowed. Not allowed in the library, left in a basket outside, switched off. David is using hers.

She's trying to rip her Gap T-shirt to make a tourniquet for Mr Marr's foot, but the cotton is too tough and won't tear and she doesn't have scissors. She only wears this T-shirt in winter under something else because everyone wears Superdry or Hollister, not Gap, not since lower school, and now she's in front of loads of people, including the headmaster, wearing only her bra, because her clothes have had to turn into blankets and bandages, and she doesn't feel any embarrassment, just ridiculous that she ever minded about something as stupid as what letters were on a T-shirt. She wraps the whole T-shirt around his foot.

Click-click click-click in the corridor. The door doesn't have a lock. She goes to join Ed, who's pulling books out of the bookcase nearest to the door, FICTION W–Z, and piling them up against it.

Why's he just walking up and down the corridor?

She tries not to listen to the footsteps but instead reads the titles of the books as they use them to barricade the door: *The Color Purple* by Alice Walker, *Trainspotting* by Irvine Welsh – *click-click* – *The Time Machine* by H. G. Wells – *click-click* – *To the Lighthouse* by Virginia Woolf, *Godless in Eden* by Fay Weldon, *The Book Thief* by Markus Zusak. She imagines bullets going through the books, leaving splashes of purple, a wrecked time machine, a smashed lighthouse lamp, and everything going dark.

She returns to Mr Marr while Ed continues adding more books to the large heap against the door. As she kneels next to him, Mr Marr's eyes flicker and catch hers. Before he was shot Mr Marr told her love is the most powerful thing there is, the only thing that really matters, and as she remembers this she digs the palm of her hand into her T-shirt bandage covering his foot to staunch the bleeding.

But the word *shot* lodges in her mind, cruel and bloody, making her nauseous. *Shot* isn't written down or spoken so she can't cover it up with her hand or shout it down and she wonders what a mind-word is if it can't be seen or heard. She thinks that consciousness is made up of silent, invisible words forming unseen sentences and paragraphs; an unwritten, unspoken book that makes us who we are. Mr Marr's eyes are closing. 'You have to stay awake, Mr Marr, please, you have to keep awake.' She's afraid that if he loses consciousness the silent invisible book of him will end.

The footsteps sound louder again alongside the library wall, coming back towards them. She has to try to be calm, has to get a grip. Dad says she's resourceful and brave; George in *Famous Five*, Jo in *Little Women*. Never a pretty girl, especially not a pretty teenage girl, she has developed a sturdy character. Rafi says she's *ya amar*, like the moon, but she doesn't believe him.

Ed has moved on to FICTION S–V, trying to stay out of the line of fire if he shoots, throwing books on to the pile from the side. There's many more books at the bottom, new ones sliding down from the summit to the base.

The footsteps get to outside their door and stop. She holds her breath, hears her heart beating into the silence, then the footsteps walk past.

★　★　★

Daphne Epelsteiner, the fifty-five-year-old drama teacher, has loved the school theatre since it was built five years ago for its practical beauty and sensitive aesthetic. Designed to look as if it's an organic part of the woods surrounding it, it's formed of two connected cedar boxes. The larger box houses the generous stage, auditorium and foyer; the smaller one has a rehearsal room, dressing rooms and two props rooms.

Now she loves the theatre because it is safe. There are no windows for the bastards to shoot through. The walls are only faced with cedar, beneath is mortar and concrete; a budgeting and fire issue. There are fire-exit doors at the back leading directly out into woodland, but the headmaster was concerned about vandals and thieves breaking in from the woods so the fire doors are exceptionally strong and robust. (Thank the Good Lord for vandals and thieves and budgeting and fire issues and the headmaster.)

Teenagers are hiding under the seats in the auditorium, a few under the stage itself. She can hear them talking to one another and doesn't silence them, not yet. They don't need to be quiet until she gives the signal.

Five teenagers are hiding in the barricade left over from last year's performance of *Les Misérables*, because no one knew what to do with it and Daphne couldn't bring herself to throw it out. It looks finished on the outside, but in the cavernous interior rough-sawn wood and half-hammered-in nails scrape at them; they breathe in dust and flecks of old paint. Twelve others are hiding behind a theatrical forest, saplings felled last week from the woods around the school and stored four deep backstage.

Just over half an hour ago a police car was shot at near the gatehouse, they think he was firing from the woods. Then three minutes ago they heard two shots in Old School. So there must be two of them, maybe more.

Old School is linked to them by a corridor, which ends in doors to their foyer. She has left these doors open and feels their openness as a coldness on her back, a terrible vulnerability. But what else could she do? The theatre is the safest place in the school, virtually unassailable, like a huge panic room. The children and teachers in Old School must get here and be safe too; then she'll lock the doors. But leaving them open might be jeopardizing the safety of her students here in the theatre, which is why she must hide them, as best she can, until everyone in Old School can join them – or until it's clear that they are not able to – and only then will she lock the doors.

Something might well go wrong. The thought nags at her, throbs inside her chest. What if she doesn't reach the doors in time? She could be shot, a decent chance that she will be. She's pretty sure that the doors are impregnable once you lock and bolt them, like the ones at the back, they are security doors, but they're not likely to be bulletproof. She just hopes she'll be shot after, not before, she's locked them.

Her young colleague Sally-Anne, all corkscrew auburn curls and pink cheeks, is acting as lookout in the foyer and will let her know by WhatsApp the moment that their colleagues and students – or the gunmen – are coming their way. Although mobile reception in the theatre is patchy, every part of it gets Wi-Fi.

'Okay everyone in the barricade?' she asks the kids in the *Les Mis* prop, her voice sounding extraordinarily jolly, she thinks, as if she's calling out something in a panto. There are some valiant yes-es. For a moment, she remembers the barricade last year in the triumph of a production, Enjolras holding his red flag aloft, the students on the barricade so courageously idealistic and heart-breakingly naive. It stabbed you in the solar plexus when the parts were played by genuine teenage students, rather than adults in a West End production.

'You're doing brilliantly,' she says to them.

She is missing four students: Dom Streeter, Jamie Alton, Rafi Bukhari and Tobias Fern. She's least worried about indolent Dom, who texted her at 8.20 saying he was running behind, most probably from beneath a fuggy duvet. She imagines him idly pedalling his bike along the road and seeing police cars at the turning to the school; not allowed any further.

Jamie Alton was here earlier this morning but left at 8.15 to get the witches' cauldron from the CDT room in New School, which means he's safe, surely it does, because New School is right next to the road, easy as pie to evacuate everyone in New School, so no need to panic about Jamie.

Rafi Bukhari didn't turn up at all this morning and he hasn't texted. She has a huge soft spot for Rafi, nearly all of them do; everything he's been through, and that smile and quick intelligence. Those liquid dark eyes, like a gazelle. Extraordinary, kind, beautiful boy. But he's survived a boat in a storm and people smugglers; he has survived Assad and Daesh and Russian bombers, for heaven's sakes; of all these children, the adults too, he knows how to look after himself.

But Tobias Fern. Anxiety for Tobias feels heavy and unwieldy, like a squirming toddler refusing to be put down, a feeling that is the opposite of Tobias himself: tall and slim, self-contained and private, a boy who only just tolerates being touched. Tobias sometimes loses track of where he's meant to be and has been found wandering around the school campus with his noise-cancelling headphones. But he was looking pale yesterday, she commented on it to him, urging him to get a good night's sleep, so she can allow herself to hope that his mother's kept him home today and in all the chaos her message hasn't got through.

No WhatsApp message from Sally-Anne in the foyer.

She goes backstage to check on the kids hiding behind her forest. Some are covered by evergreen spruces and are surprisingly well camouflaged, but others are sheltering behind deciduous leafless trees and their clothes and pale faces shine through.

'Birnam Wood! You need to have make-up. Dirty faces, please.'

The woodland parts. Saplings are laid on the floor.

She hands out make-up cases. 'Make each other's faces grubby; browns and greens.'

They hurriedly put make-up on each other's faces, fingers clumsy. Joanna starts on her friend Caitlin, neatly using a brush. Daphne thinks about telling Joanna just to slap it on, this is not the Make-up Design module of a GCSE drama exam, but suspects this is how Joanna is coping so will leave her be.

'You're in a safe place here,' she says to them all. 'There's no windows and the doors are extra strong. There's no way they will get to us.'

'But you haven't locked the doors to the corridor, have you?' Luisa asks. Her twin brother, Frank, is in the library in Old School.

'No,' Daphne says. 'I haven't locked them. Right, once your make-up's done, put on your costumes.'

Their costumes for *Macbeth* are brown hessian tunics, which are used pretty much for every production in some form or another. For *Macbeth*, they're tied with rope round the waist as tunics. They'll blend better behind the trees than colourful hoodies and T-shirts.

'Are we going to rehearse?' Joanna asks.

Mother of Mary, is Joanna even on this planet?

'Maybe later,' she says to Joanna.

'Are Anna and Young Fry safe?' Josh asks. 'Have you heard?'

Seven-year-olds Anna and Davy, nicknamed Young Fry, are playing the Macduff children but weren't due to be here till before their cue, in over an hour's time.

'They were doing art in New School this morning,' she says. 'So they'll have been evacuated.'

'You're sure, Daphne?' Josh asks her.

'Yes, easy to evacuate New School.'

They all call her Daphne, which started when they were much younger because her surname is long and complicated, so they called her 'Miss Daphne', and then as they got older they dropped the 'Miss', and for heaven's sakes, what does it matter what they call her? But it does. It's like they trust her not to be separate from them, to level with them.

'What about everyone else in Junior School?' Antonella asks.

'There will be a contingency plan,' Daphne says, making it up as she goes along, not levelling with them, because what possible contingency plan can there be for everyone in Junior School, a remote building at the end of the drive, a mile from the road and help? She's tried ringing colleagues in Junior School but nobody has answered. Focus on these children right now, because they're the only ones you can help.

Boys and girls are changing in the same room, which wouldn't normally happen. A few are clearly embarrassed and she's heartened because they can't be that afraid if they're able to be self-conscious; though teenagers can probably be self-conscious in any situation.

'Once you're changed I want you behind the trees again. Become Birnam Wood! Method act a woodland!'

A few smiles. Brave kids.

She helps the last few camouflage their faces, the ones whose partner's hands were shaking too much to do it.

'Won't be long now till the police are here,' she says, because surely the police will help them soon. 'This is just me being ultra-cautious; my OCD kicking in.'

She hides them behind the rows of saplings, then goes to the props rooms. The first one is locked and Jamie Alton has the key but the second larger one is unlocked and filled with more saplings. She drags them backstage. The bark splinters into her hands and they're heavy. Last year, when their house was flooded out, Philip had called her a trooper and now she's acting out that part because she doesn't know what other part she can play that will be of any use to the children.

They are well hidden behind the trees, surprisingly so. There's a good chance that if her plan goes wrong and the gunmen come in and just have a quick look, they won't be seen. A really good chance.

She goes from the auditorium to the foyer. This evening, two students were meant to stand by the auditorium doors, handing out *Macbeth* programmes to parents and staff.

There's a bar area in the foyer and security doors to the glass corridor that links to Old School. A hundred feet long, the corridor goes through the woods and was designed so that people could come and go from the theatre to Old School without getting wet, and she'd been snarky about it – *has no one ever heard of an umbrella?* – but now it means escape and safety.

She'd hoped to see children and teachers running along the glass corridor through the woods to the sanctuary of the theatre. But the corridor is deserted, snow falling all around it. There are no lights shining at the other end from Old School; the door shut and the school in darkness.

There's just Sally-Anne standing watch at their open doors holding a nail gun. She doubts a gunman will allow Sally-Anne near enough for her to fire nails at him but admires her pluck. Good grief, she's using her grandmother's war words; there's a whole vocabulary to go with this new character she's playing, although she's starting to feel that this is her most real self; that how she has been to this point was a just a read-through for who she is now.

'Anything?' she asks Sally-Anne.

'No. How are our kids doing?'

Daphne wonders if she imagined the stress Sally-Anne put on 'our', signalling where Daphne's responsibilities should be; pointing out that the safest thing for their kids would be to lock the doors of the corridor their end and block off the means of escape for everyone in Old School. Sally-Anne could be holding the nail gun not because she's plucky but because she's protecting herself with the only available weapon. She's worked with Sally-Anne for nearly four years, but you don't know a person, she realizes, including yourself, not until the everyday is stripped away. Sweet young Sally-Anne could be anyone at all; colleagues who've worked together for years, friends, can be turned into strangers with one another.

'Do you think the theatre is really that safe?' Sally-Anne asks.

Because if the theatre isn't 'really that safe', then they cannot offer a haven to the other teachers and students and so can lock their doors without any guilt.

'Yes I do,' she replies.

'Good,' Sally-Anne says. 'We'll wait then, as long as we have to.'

'Birnam Wood have make-up on,' Daphne says. 'I wanted them to splodge on some camouflage but Joanna made up Caitlin like a wood nymph.'

Sally-Anne half laughs.

'You think a nail gun will do any good?' Daphne asks.

'We can always hope. Might slow them down. I thought we should rig up the brightest lights and if we see the gunmen shine the lights in their eyes. It'll blind them for a bit; buy us a few more minutes.'

Daphne likes the symbolism of blinding with light and feels ugly for doubting her.

2.

9.20 a.m.

Beth Alton is driving her Prius *like a bat out of hell, Mum,* down the country road, skidding on ice, righting the car and foot flat down again. School in lockdown. Told by a PTA group text, not Jamie. Hasn't heard anything from Jamie. One hand holds her mobile to her ear, other on the steering wheel. Jamie still not answering; pick up, pick up, pick up.

You don't let me drive like this, Mum, even on a farm track.

You're a learner.

Dad's going to be seriously unimpressed if you dent it.

I know.

Pretend it was someone in Waitrose's car park again.

It was.

Jamie's laughter.

All in her head.

His number goes through to message again: 'Hey, it's Jamie, leave me a message.'

'Jamie, sweetheart, it's Mum again. Are you okay? Please ring me.'

Why isn't he answering?

Her mobile rings, a jolt of hope, but it's her husband, Mike, that's displayed.

'Anything?' Mike asks.

'No.'

'You know what he's like with his mobile,' Mike says.

'But he'd phone, with this happening he'd phone us.'

'I meant he forgets to charge it,' Mike says. 'Or leaves it somewhere. He was doing the dress rehearsal this morning, wasn't he?'

Why does that matter?

'He'll be in the theatre,' Mike says. 'Safest place in the school. No windows. Like a bunker.'

'Yes,' she says. 'Yes, that's where he'll be.'

Thank God for Zac and even Victor, who she loathes but now forgives, because Victor and Zac are the reason that Jamie's in the theatre, they're the friends who persuaded him to join in the production of *Macbeth*, otherwise – she doesn't want to think about otherwise. Safest place in the school.

'I'm getting the train, should be at the station in an hour, but the snow's making things slow.'

He's in Bath, meant to be at a conference.

'Okay.'

She ends the call. No missed call or message from Jamie. But he's in the theatre, safe, Zac there too; all of them together.

It's just props, Mum, wasn't like I had to audition or anything.

Props are really important. And Zac's doing the technical side too, isn't he?

Yeah, lights. Victor is Macbeth.

Props are just as important.

As the main part? Seriously, Mum?

To me, yes.

Heart soft as a baby bird.

Is that from that TV series?

And I try to give her a compliment.

She looks up Zac's number on her mobile contacts, swerving into the snow-covered verge as she takes her eyes off the road. She presses dial, two wheels on the verge, the car tipping at an angle. As Zac's phone rings, she remembers Jamie's first day, joining in Year 10 after being bullied at his mean, strict school for the previous three years – not sporty like his older brother, not resilient. The other pupils at Cliff Heights School had looked so relaxed in their scruffy clothes, so confident, arms casually flung round each other; Jamie a stiff wooden pin, as if still wearing a blazer and balancing a cap. Then he'd made two friends, Victor, older than Jamie but new like him, and Zac, the same age, who'd been at the school since Reception, a warm-hearted, easy-going boy who'd clap his arm round Jamie's shoulders and say 'Jamester!' and Jamie would look startled but pleased. Zac's text nickname for him was 'J-Me' and Jamie loved it, still uses it for his Twitter, Snapchat and Instagram. Jamie's never become as outgoing and confident as Zac, the unchecked cruelty at the previous school leaving a legacy of vulnerability.

Zac's phone goes through to message.

'Zac, it's Beth, Jamie's mum. Are you with Jamie? Is he okay? Can you ask him to ring me?'

She hangs up and rights the car, jolting back on to the road. She didn't think to ask Zac if he was okay.

She hasn't seen much of Zac recently, not for ages, because Jamie hasn't seen him outside of school, at least not at their house. Yesterday she was actually worried about that.

She's nowhere near the school yet, but there are police cars blocking the road so you can't even see the school or your child running down the driveway towards you – because that's been the spooling film of fantasy all this time, that he will run to you and you will be there and that's the end of it.

Other parents' cars are just stopped any old how along the verge. No one is wearing coats, one father still in pyjamas; everyone running to their cars to get to school. Beth hurries towards the police, surrounded by a group of parents. A man is shouting at them, 'Why aren't you in the school? Why aren't you doing anything?' Other voices as she tries to push her way through:

'Armed police are coming.'

'There's been shots inside Old School.'

'Are any children hurt?'

'A few minutes ago.'

'Has anyone been hurt?'

'I thought he was in the woods, by the gatehouse.'

'Must be more of them.'

'He's in the corridor.'

Beth, a slender five foot two, not a pusher or shover, is at the front, elbows outwards, facing a police officer. 'I have to get to the school. My son's in there.' A right of entry, because who can argue with that? The police officer looks at her like everyone else here has said the same thing.

'We're asking relatives to go to The Pines Leisure Centre, outside Minehead. Do you know how to get there?'

But how can she possibly leave him?

'A police officer at the leisure centre will update parents with information.'

She's torn between not wanting to leave the place where he is and wanting to be told he's okay; that he's safe. She walks back to her car, the icy ground slippery under her shoes, other parents also returning to their cars.

She hadn't noticed the snow falling, covering her hair and shoulders, but as she drives away, the snow melts, dripping down her neck inside her collar, off her sensibly cut hair and on to her hands, and she feels like she's abandoning him.

The trees and roads and hedges are being covered in snow, making the familiar landscape unrecognizable.

A text buzzes from Zac.

> Hey Beth, J-me went 2 CDT room 2 get cauldron

He's not safe in the theatre with Zac and his friends. Not safe.

★   ★   ★

In the library, Frank is in the alcove furthest from the door, crouched under a Victorian table that's bolted to the floor, one hand pressing his mobile against his left ear as he talks to his mum. He has his mobile and laptop with him, even though they're not allowed in the library, jittery if he's away from his technology. His other hand is over his right ear to try to block out the sound of the footsteps. They make him feel breathless, like they are hands squeezing his throat. His twin sister, Luisa, is in the theatre, safe.

Feeling a coward, treacherous, he pretends to his mum that he's almost out of charge and ends the call, because at some point it stopped being her comforting him and turned into him comforting her and he just couldn't do that any more. He hands his phone to Esme, crouched next to him.

There are thirteen of them in here and to start with it had been almost fun in a weird kind of way, it was all *Code red!! Lockdown!!* like they were starring in a Netflix series, but now Mr Marr's been shot and footsteps are walking up and down and it's something that makes you terrified and small and huddled into yourself.

He looks up at the shuttered windows, too narrow for a person to get through and too high up. Even if they could fit, it wouldn't do any good. There were gunshots earlier near the gatehouse – back when it was all dramatic and exciting and not frightening, before it really began – so there's another gunman out there, maybe more than one, and no cover on the lawn. Frank thinks of deer running and a sniper picking them off, and hunches down, as if he can make himself even smaller, as if that will help.

Hannah is with Ed and David; they're helping Mr Marr and talking to the ambulance people and piling up books against the door. He hates himself for not being brave like them. A nerd, he says to himself, a computer nerd, what do you expect? Furious with himself. Hannah is splattered in blood and just wearing a bra and he's never seen anyone so impressive in his life before. He's had a crush on her since Year 7, something delicate and gentle and secret. Other boys wouldn't understand, they don't think she's pretty. Rafi does though; Rafi thinks she's gorgeous. Lucky Rafi.

Hannah checks Mr Marr's head wound. It's not bleeding as much but he's getting paler.

The footsteps have stopped for almost a minute, he's just standing still in the corridor. What is he waiting for?

On her phone David is saying 'but how soon?' and 'he needs help right away', like he doesn't trust them to get an ambulance here as fast as they can.

She hardly has any charge left and all the time David talks to the 999 people the percentage left for Dad and Rafi ticks down, which sounds a bit 'last dance on the *Titanic*' but on this ordinary school morning is true; she'd called goodbye up the stairs to Dad, didn't kiss him, didn't even see him.

In the corridor, he's started moving again, coming closer towards them: *click-click click-click*. Why couldn't he have worn trainers and been stealthy? She'd choose stealthy over this, like some deadly kind of tinnitus. He must've bought boots with metal in the heels specially. Must've known it would make people feel like she does. Arsehole.

David hands her back her phone. 'Sorry,' he says because there's no charge left. 'They didn't say when the ambulance will get here.'

There's a mobile being handed round at the back of the library and maybe they should take it but surely the ambulance will get to them as quickly as possible, surely you don't need to chase up an ambulance when your headmaster's been shot; and people also really need to talk to their parents.

She doesn't notice Frank coming over until he's crouching down next to them. He has a laptop with him; she'd never had him down as a law-breaker.

'There might be something on the news that'll tell us what's happening,' he says. 'Maybe about help coming.'

'Brilliant,' she says to him.

Tap-tap go Frank's fingers, confident once he's at a keyboard, a different person. He must have 4G on his laptop because there's no Wi-Fi in here, part of Mr Marr's drive to get them all to read books in the library.

He brings up *BBC News 24* with the sound muted, as if the

gunman in the corridor might forget about them if they make no noise. Hannah can see from the screen that all the news is about their school. Even the bit at the bottom, running like a tickertape, which normally has other news, is just about them.

... shots in the school grounds ... 47 secondary school children and 7 members of staff known to be still in the school ... 140 junior school children and their teachers are unaccounted for ... unconfirmed reports of an explosion at 8.20 this morning ... police not giving more information ...

'Junior school's okay though, right?' Ed says.

'They're a mile away from the road,' Frank says. 'And surrounded by woods. So the gunmen probably don't even know they're there.'

Frank seems newly bold to Hannah, crouching close to her and Mr Marr.

'Anything about a rescue?' David asks. 'An ambulance?'

'No,' Frank says. Hannah thinks he sees her disappointment. 'But I was being stupid before. I mean, the police aren't going to say on telly, are they? They'll keep it secret.'

'What about the man in our corridor?' Ed asks.

'Not yet. But it'll be the same thing; they won't say.'

An aerial picture of their school comes up on the screen.

'Must have a drone with a camera,' Ed says. 'A local journalist maybe. Or someone's sent it to them.'

It's weird to see school from above, blurry with snow, and to know that they're there, right now, inside a news photo. The photo of the school has arrows and captions. At the bottom of the photo is NEW SCHOOL, by far the largest of all the buildings, with ROAD next to it; lucky people in New School, they had an escape route. Further up the photo, half a mile away from the road and an escape route, through the woods, is where they are: OLD SCHOOL. A little away from OLD SCHOOL they've marked THEATRE. Even further up the map, deep into the woods, POTTERY ROOM. And at the top of the photo, almost in the sea, a mile from the road, is JUNIOR SCHOOL. A dotted red line shows the private drive that links up all the buildings.

Hannah hopes that if Frank's right about the gunmen not knowing where Junior School is that they're not watching TV, but it's general information, it's on the school prospectus even. Hopefully they haven't done their research. Hopefully they just grabbed a gun on the spur of the moment. And on the spur of the moment will just fuck off again.

There's a number to ring 'if you have any information' ticker-taping along the bottom of the screen. Hannah supposes it's to keep the story going, little titbits added to keep it fresh and spicy. Because Frank is right, the police won't be telling them anything.

She's holding her phone tightly, even though it's out of charge, like it still connects her to Dad and Rafi, and she knows that's ridiculous but doesn't loosen her grip.

Frank is searching through news sites; all of them are about their school, not like the usual news, all slick and organized, but hurriedly put together. On one site, there's a male reporter she recognizes talking straight to the camera, as if directly to her.

'Could this be a terror attack?' he asks. 'We're going now to our terrorism expert, David Delaney.'

She looks up at the skylight. Snow is falling down on top of them, smothering the daylight.

*　　*　　*

In the theatre, Daphne and Sally-Anne get a WhatsApp message from Neil Forbright, the deputy head, who is alone in the head-master's office in Old School.

> We can't get to you. You must lock the doors

'What do you think?' Sally-Anne asks.

Daphne thinks their young deputy head is astonishingly brave. 'We must do as he says.'

She closes the security doors across the entrance to the glass corridor, then locks and bolts them. Everyone who was critical of Neil Forbright will have to see his courage now, even that wretched father of his, who Daphne could cheerfully throttle. But Daphne has seen Neil's courage for the last year, because teaching with depression is impossibly hard and he managed it on and off for months. Not bravery like this though; because Neil hasn't only locked himself out of safety – only! – but is shouldering the burden of that decision so she doesn't need to. But it's her fingers that locked the door, slid the bolt across, and her hands feel treacherous.

Neil often comes round to theirs for pasta and a chat; other staff trapped in Old School are friends too. And the teenagers. Dear God. She's known many of them since they were young children in junior school. And now she's locked the doors against them and left them with a gunman.

Neil didn't say if anyone was hurt and he would have told them. Surely he would? She hurriedly WhatsApps him.

'I'll wait here by the doors,' Sally-Anne says. 'In case something changes. In case they can get to us.'

'Good plan,' Daphne replies, because she wants to believe something will change, but fears that if it does the likelihood is that it will be for the worse.

But worrying's no use to anyone in Old School, Daphne, no use at all. You just have to get on with it; put your best foot forward for the children in the theatre until this terrible thing is over; shove to the back of your mind this terrible anxiety about the people in Old School and the missing children and everyone in Junior School and this new love for your husband that keeps inappropriately pressing itself forward. *Right then*, a phrase she has never used before, suspicious of people who used it, right then, she must keep everyone calm; keep them busy. They came to school this morning thinking they were going to be doing a dress rehearsal of *Macbeth* so that is what they are going to do.

She claps her hands, forces her voice to be loud and strong.

'Tell your parents that you're safe in the theatre, if you haven't already, and that you're turning your phones off – then all mobiles off, please.'

Phones aren't allowed in the library but the students in Jacintha's English classroom will have their mobiles with them. She thinks that, like her kids in the theatre, they'll be phoning their parents first, poor loves, of course they will, not yet siblings or friends, but they most probably will. If bad news happens, she doesn't want her kids in the theatre to get it.

They all protest about turning off their phones. She raises her voice above the hubbub of theirs, but keeps it calm.

'We are going to rehearse *Macbeth* – Joanna, that was absolutely the right thing to suggest earlier – and I don't want phones pinging.'

Amazingly, the kids seem to buy this bit of normality, her usual rule, and turn their mobiles off, though she doubts it will last for long.

'Finish off your costumes and keep your faces as they are. Zac, Luisa and Benny, lighting and set, please. Once you're ready, refresh your lines.'

No WhatsApp reply from Neil. She opens her copy of *Macbeth*, playing her part in this charade, and reads the opening; the same opening Shakespeare's King's Men would have read four hundred years ago.

Macbeth

Act 1, Scene 1

A desolate place.

Thunder and lightning. Enter three WITCHES

The kids had brainstormed ideas for 'A desolate place', sitting in a safe, warm rehearsal room. Tim wanted a shopping mall and Daphne liked the idea, Princesshay Shopping Centre being her idea of Dante's fourth circle of hell, but Luisa said, 'Desolate actually means bleak, abandoned and forsaken, not Zara and Lush.' Josh came up with a windswept moor, but that was 'a bit Heathcliff 'n' Cathy', and then Rafi Bukhari suggested Aleppo.

'But does Syria have any link with *Macbeth*, really?' Luisa, ever the realist, asked.

'You don't have to be literal in your staging,' Daphne said.

'Aleppo's mentioned in the play,' Rafi said. 'In Act One, the First Witch says, "Her husband's to Aleppo gone".'

Daphne had never noticed that the poor sailor cursed by the witches was on his way to Aleppo and she was struck by the similarity to Rafi and his brother's journey, also cursed and tempest tossed, in the opposite direction.

And now Benny is projecting a photo of a bombed street in Aleppo on to the back wall of the stage. It looks like an urban moonscape: collapsed chalk-white buildings, black shadow spaces where rooms and people should be, whitened cables and wires trailing down into the street that is piled high with chunks of houses. The streets in this photo are deserted but the original has a father holding his baby, her legs and small feet covered in white dust, but they'd edited them out; too much for children in the audience, for parents too, but the pair still hover there for Daphne.

She has never fully engaged with the photographer's point of view before but looking at the photo now she realizes that the picture was taken looking down a street, and right off into the distance to other streets, and in the photo there is not one building that remains a building, not a room left intact; that the horror of this picture is that there is nowhere left to run.

Her mobile vibrates with a WhatsApp message from Neil. She reads it, appalled.

* * *

An eight-year-old boy is hiding in a shed; he has a stitch in his side from running, faster than he's ever run before, and he's still out of breath. The wooden door isn't closed properly, because he's scared of the dark. The cold creeps in through the gap. His red woolly gloves are wet with snow and freezing cold so he takes them off. There are canoes stacked up on the walls on special hooks and at the very back there's a wooden rowing boat like Ratty's in *The Wind in the Willows*. He can leave the door open just a tiny bit and if the man comes in he will hide in the rowing boat.

But the man has a gun.

He has to shut the door but it's going to be all right because he's got his mobile phone and its screen will glow in the dark, like the rabbit night light he had when he was little. He opens his mobile and puts it on the ground with the screen shining up at him.

He shuts the door, trying not to make any noise; then he grips the bolt, bumpy with rust, and pushes it across.

On his screen there's a picture message of a frog and another one of a bowl, like a cereal bowl, full of sweets, and a message but he doesn't read it because he's seen that his battery level is 15%. He left his farm game running otherwise the animals run out of food and get hungry. He looks again hoping it will say 50% or even 25% but it's still 15%.

If the man with the gun comes he'll need his phone to get help. He closes the game, saying sorry to the chickens and pigs for not feeding them, and turns off his phone.

The smell of the shed is stronger in the dark: something rotting and damp wood; dank, dark smells that make him feel sick. He hears blood rushing in his ears, his limbs are shaking, he feels tears wet and warm on his cheek, like weeing yourself. Stupid arms, stupid legs, stupid tears. Eight's too old to cry. He must be brave. Brave as a Barbary lion. Brave as a Bengal tiger. Brave as Sir Lancelot.

3.

9.25 a.m.

In the library, Hannah smells cigarette smoke. No one in the library is smoking. It must be coming through a gap in the door; the top part because most of the doorway is covered by the mound of books. He's just outside. Is he taking fast drags or slow ones? What will he do when he finishes?

Mr Marr is trying to talk but she can't make sense of what he's saying. She bends her face closer to his as if his words lose their shape and meaning as they travel the distance between them. But it's worse now because she can hear how hard this is for him, the rasping of his breath as he struggles to speak. Perhaps he sees that he's upsetting her because he stops and his eyes meet hers as if it's him who's worried about her, rather than the other way round.

Frank hands her his laptop which is on a news channel. A presenter is talking about them. It's the presenter Dad says wears too much lip gloss and that the news isn't a cocktail party and she shouldn't talk about people being killed while showing off so much. He means showing off so much cleavage though he wouldn't say that to Hannah in case he embarrassed her but she knows exactly what he means. Dad's normally pretty laid-back about that kind of thing, but he really doesn't like lip gloss and low-cut tops on newsreaders. Distracting, he says. She thinks that people probably like to be distracted when the awful things are on.

Frank gives Hannah his headphones. 'You're live now, Face-Timing,' he says.

'You're sure you don't want to?' she asks and Frank nods.

26

She puts on the headphones and looks at the screen.

Bloody hell, she's on telly. Instead of the map of the school there's a picture of her in a box; the presenter with the cleavage and lip gloss is talking about her –

'We have a pupil at Cliff Heights School . . .'

She and Dad are going to find this hilarious tonight, when they watch it on TV. *Of all the presenters in all the world . . .* Dad'll say to her.

'I'm Melanie,' the presenter says. 'What's your name?'

Even though the gunman in the corridor knows they're in here, she keeps her voice quiet.

'Hannah Jacobs.'

She sees that on TV they're blurring her out below her face, so that you can't see the blood, or maybe it's the bra, maybe that's just too much cleavage for TV, although definitely not the cocktail-party kind. She finds this a little funny. She imagines someone getting out a pot of Vaseline or lip salve and smearing it over the lens. But in here nobody takes any notice of her just wearing a bra, when yesterday it would have been shocking and unthinkable.

'Our headmaster has been shot,' she says. Totally shocking, totally unthinkable. 'He's bleeding and he's very pale and cold. We need to know when an ambulance will get to him. He's in the library by the door.' Surely they're giving it an armed escort or something, surely they'll get help to Mr Marr.

'Okay. My producer is finding out now.'

'Thank you.'

'Are you okay, Hannah?' Melanie asks.

The smell of the cigarette is making her nauseous. She imagines Dad's arm around her, his terrible French accent, *Courage, mon brave*.

'Yes. It's not me who's hurt, it's Mr Marr who's hurt.'

'Can you tell me what's happening?'

Maybe the gunman is watching this on his phone as he has his cigarette. The arsehole smoking gunman *knew* to charge up his phone fully this morning, probably brought a juice-pack with him. If he's watching this on his phone she's not going to show him she's afraid and she's definitely not going to give him any information. She looks at Melanie in her lovely safe TV studio.

'I don't think that's a very good idea,' she says. 'Do you know when an ambulance will get here?'

'I'll let you know as soon as I do. We've heard it all began with an explosion . . .?'

Like the explosion was the beginning of a story: 'What's the story in Balamory?', 'Postman Pat and his black-and-white cat.' She's being sarky about Melanie – *Your fault, Dad, you prejudiced me against her.*

'A teacher's told us that they were warned about a possible explosion in the woods at 8.20, the reason for the amber alert,' Melanie says. Hannah imagines the producer's voice in Melanie's discreet little earbud giving her info.

'Yes.'

'The school is right in the middle of the woods?' Melanie asks.

So not a CBeebies TV story but old-style Grimms' Fairy Tale woods: a huntsman taking Snow White into the deep dark woods to kill her, to return with her lungs and liver; a girl in a red cape being stalked by a wolf through the trees.

But the explosion in the woods an hour ago wasn't the start of the story; a prologue maybe, an introduction; not the beginning. Because it began – whatever 'it' is and it's not a story, not to any of them inside it – it began when someone shot their headmaster in the corridor of their school. That's when life as they'd known it before ended and something else began and reset time. Because she thinks the something else is measured in lifespans and how long Mr Marr has left to live, maybe how long all of them have left, started at that moment.

'Did you hear the explosion?' Melanie asks, because for her the starting point is neutrally impersonal. But the police might need to know more about the explosion, it might be important.

'Yes. We were in the woods . . .' she says.

She sees Mr Marr looking at her, keeping his eyes on hers, and she finds it comforting; she thinks he knows that.

She remembers running through the woods with Rafi, holding hands tightly, cold, numb fingers together, so she could feel his bones, like two in-love young skeletons; which is morbidly weird but frankly she is a weird person and at a party four months ago told Rafi one of her weird (but not morbid) thoughts and wanted to grab the words back again because she had this huge crush on him. But he understood. Understood her. And it had been like their minds were touching.

The in-love bit isn't true, not for Rafi anyway, because he is charismatic and has an extraordinary story and so that kind of thing happens to him on pretty much a daily basis; but it was unique for her – she touched a boy's mind and he touched hers. She hasn't ever told him she loves him.

Fuck's sake, back to the woods, Hannah. Quarter past eight, but wintry dark, making you want to press a switch and turn on the lights. Rafi's hand was pulling her along, helping her go faster, so she wouldn't be late for English and he wouldn't miss the start of the dress rehearsal. She'd left her puffer behind yesterday in the common room but she didn't want to slow down. Rafi must have heard her wheezing because he stopped running. She sounded like an old man, not a gentlemanly one but a gross one who smokes sixty a day, huffing around in a tartan dressing gown.

'It's so quiet,' she said, blaming the quietness of the woods for Rafi being able to hear her sixty-a-day old-geezer wheeze.

A cold touch on her face and she saw snowflakes, most getting caught in the trees, and it seemed for a moment that it was just her and Rafi alone in the dark tree-limbed world.

Then Rafi abruptly turned away from her. 'Have to go,' he said, hurrying away with his long-stride walk, a slight limp in his right leg. She wanted to tug him back to her, call after him, but made herself still and quiet. Every time Rafi left her she thought he'd seen what everyone else saw: a weird plain plump girl with too-pale skin and too-red hair and now with an old-geezer wheeze and totally undeserving of him.

'Nobody can make you feel inferior without your consent,' Dad had told her last week; 'Sensible lady, Eleanor Roosevelt.' She thought Dad trawled wise female sayings to make up for her lack of mother, though he really didn't need to and Eleanor didn't help as she watched Rafi disappear round the bend in the path.

She remembers the woods closing in, the trees treacherous, as if moving stealthily towards her once she was alone; remembers the loss of Rafi in the hand he'd been holding, colder than the rest of her. She'd shoved her hands into the pockets of her puffa jacket but couldn't get her fingers warm. She'd looked up at the snowflakes, doing skittish dancing above the trees, most too weightless to fall, and saw a glint, vividly bright in the dull winter sky.

She should have remembered the glint before; should have told Mr Marr. But after the glint there was so much else.

'I think someone may have been watching us,' she says to Melanie.

'Watching you . . .?' Melanie says like she's a lip-glossy parrot – *You were right about her, Dad* – but this is on TV and the police may watch and it might be important.

'There's a high ropes course in the woods for Outdoor Ed; really high,' she says. 'We don't use it in the winter. But someone was up there because I saw something glinting, like binoculars.'

Birdwatchers had gone up there last summer term and the PE teacher had spotted them because of their glinting binoculars and '*read the twitchers the riot act*'. But how likely was it to have been a birdwatcher on a freezing November morning?

'How much longer till there's an ambulance?'

'I'm sure help will be with you as soon as possible. Can you remember anything else?'

Is Dad watching this? The thought of him watching her makes

tears start; her face tightens. Frank's phone is on 12% charge and she's afraid it'll run out before she gets a turn. She smiles at the screen in case Dad can see her.

'So you thought someone might be watching you,' Melanie says. 'What happened then?'

It's warm in the library, the Victorian cast-iron radiators blasting out heat as usual, but the memory makes her shiver. Frank must notice because he asks in a whisper if she's okay.

'Hannah . . .?' Melanie says.

Courage, mon brave.

Her trainers were leaking. The cold wet of the bracken seeped into her socks. Her fingers stung with cold. Her wheezing was getting worse. She stopped and put her fingers to her lips, trying to use her breath to warm them. She turned, just in case Rafi was coming back towards her, hoping.

A brutally loud noise, an assault of sound startling birds out of the trees, as if their branches had been shaken, sending them wheeling up into the sky. And then gone. The air still, the woods quiet, the birds back in the trees. Nothing to prove it had ever happened. She'd thought it hadn't been that loud. She was upset about Rafi and pathetic about the woods and had jumped at a loud noise. It was probably someone fooling around with fireworks or a farmer with a pigeon-scarer thing; something like that.

Taking her fingers away from her mouth, the cold air sharp against her damp skin, she'd looked again for Rafi and seen a thin pall of smoke moving between the snowflakes and the trees.

'I heard a loud noise,' she says to Melanie. 'And then I saw some smoke, but I didn't think it was anything bad. Just a pigeon scarer or something and a bonfire.'

'Really . . .?' Melanie asks, like she would have thought *Clearly a bomb!* and not think of normal things to explain it, like a bonfire and pigeon scarer. But being fair to lip-glossy Melanie, it's not her fault that Hannah didn't tell anyone.

Before Mr Marr was shot, she'd said sorry to him for not realizing and telling him because if she had maybe everything would be different. He told her other people had heard it too and not realized. One teacher had complained about some kind of rumpus in the woods; 'Rumpus, like *Where the Wild Things Are*,' Mr Marr had said, trying to make her smile, because he's kind and knew she felt bad about not telling him and that she was afraid. It wasn't just that he reassured her, it was that he took time with her; even with everything else going on, he took time to do that.

Then he'd put his arm around her to hurry her away from the front door and said, 'Love is the most powerful thing there is, the only thing that really matters.'

And now he's lying shot in the head and the foot. He's still watching, keeping his eyes on hers, but as if it's getting harder for him. Frank is at the back of the library again and she doesn't blame him for leaving the area by the door.

'You said *we* earlier?' Melanie says. '*We were in the woods?* So someone else was with you?'

The producer must be talking into Melanie's little earbud again. She imagines all the people behind the scenes finding things out; maybe looking things up about her, looking at her Facebook page and Twitter and Instagram. *You've got to make it all private*, Dad was always on at her. *Any nutter can look you up.*

'Your boyfriend is Rafi Bukhari?'

Should have listened to you, Dad.

'He's a Muslim from Syria?'

'Tell the ambulance to hurry.'

She smiles at the screen again in case Dad is watching then she ends the FaceTime call with Melanie and takes off the headphones.

On Frank's laptop, Melanie's mouth is opening and closing as she speaks, tiny on the laptop screen and far away and not connected to her and the others trapped in school, because that's the truth. When she was talking to Melanie, even though she didn't much like her, it stopped her from feeling like they were totally alone.

Mr Marr has closed his eyes and she doesn't think he's still conscious.

She's been imagining an ambulance with paramedics hurrying to the rescue, blue lights winking, siren calling – *I'm here I'm here I'm here* – but they can't get to Mr Marr because of the gunman in the corridor and another one in the woods, and she thinks she knew that, secretly, all along but just wanted to believe help was coming for him. An armed escort had felt unlikely even as she'd thought it to herself. And even if that is what's going to happen, they're miles from any city so how long will it take? She's frightened it will take too long.

'We're almost out of 4G data,' Frank says, coming back towards her holding his anorak. 'Not enough for FaceTime or the internet. Just emails now.'

He's so cold. He must be lying in snow. Why's he lying in snow? A game with Reception children? He must have just fallen asleep. His muscles are frozen, unable to flex, so his whole body jerks with the shivering. He opens his eyes. Hannah is bending over him. Not a game. His mind an island thick with fog. He tries to move. Can't move. Try harder. Still nothing; as if the command and control centre in his brain has been disconnected. Why's he thinking of a command and control centre?

It's the soldier in you. Not too late to join me and the boys in the Paras.

I'm forty-five years old and a pacifist, Rob, he tells his older brother. *And you've been dead for fifteen years.*

But for a moment his brother reaches across from his single bed in their new foster home to Matthew's and takes his hand and the dense fog thins a little.

He's in the library. Something terrible has happened. And he just fell asleep and left them. What's happened?

Hannah moves and in his line of vision he sees that she's covered in blood. Please God let it be his and not hers. Must be his surely because she looks afraid but not in pain. She's just wearing a bra and she must be so cold, much colder than him. He's got someone's clothes covering him, he can glimpse the edge of a coat, and he must give it to her but he still can't move.

He sees Frank wrapping an anorak around Hannah and is grateful to him.

What the hell's happened?

A flashback to this morning; a dealer flicking memories in front of him, no control of them. Putting the bins out in the dark. Crushing down the stiff black bin bags. The car iced up. Hands cold on the ice scraper. The print of a fox in the deep frost. The coldest day for five years. Snow forecast. Everything normal apart from the cold.

Lighting a fire in his office, the wood catching. Warmth taking the chill off the large Victorian room. Nothing to alert him.

An image spikes through his semi-consciousness: little hands are playing with clay, snow falling around them. But the young children aren't in coats. They are inside the pottery room. It's snowing outside the windows and one of the children looks up at it. Huge glass windows with no shutters: no protection. In the woods. Far from help.

Questions not memories barge their way into his mind, sharp-edged and brutal.

Are the children in the pottery room safe?

Did junior school get out?

Who is safe? Who is missing?

What in Christ's name has he allowed to happen?

4.

8.15 a.m.

An hour and sixteen minutes ago

From the top of the high ropes course he watched the school. He was the *deus ex machina, apò mēkhanês theós,* ἀπὸ μηχανῆς θεός; the god from the machine that nobody expects.

Earlier, he'd watched parents taking their children into Junior School, the gate in the fence left open for busy drop-off time. The school started early, 8.10 drop-off, 8.15 registration. And then the ant parents had left again in their ant cars, going along the drive to the road a mile away.

And then it was quiet.

It started to snow, just a few flakes, and he knew before the ants because the flakes weren't yet reaching the ground. But he was prepared. His hands were in gloves and he didn't feel cold. The man next to him cursed, but he ignored him.

In an hour, give or take a minute here or there, the headmaster would be shot and that would be a starting gun – he liked the economy, the violence, the aptness of that – and everyone would realize, if they hadn't already feared it, if they were a bit slow on the uptake, that their lives and stories weren't their own; and all the different stories he'd set in motion would play out at the same time, the simultaneity generated by him.

And he was trying so damn hard to be serious, but he was playing a game, *a fucking game*; he was a croupier, using hours and minutes as counters, and none of the ant people knew that they were on a roulette wheel, a wheel of fortune, wheel of fate, *rota fortunae, Bhavacakra*, with him about to turn it.

Movement in the woods below. He trained his binoculars and

35

saw the back view of two teenagers running, holding hands. In another part of the woods, a class of young children and a teacher were hurrying along a path towards the pottery room. But he didn't leave his place; not yet. Everything was set up, everything planned.

Before the starting gun, there would be a little alert. Perhaps the teenage couple would see, perhaps not. Didn't matter. It was just a warning, a tap at the door; a joke.

⋆   ⋆   ⋆

A class of seven-year-olds, coats buttoned and zipped up against the freezing weather, raced through the woods, some breaking into a skip, jostling and laughing, with Camille Giraud, their sixty-year-old teacher, leading the charge along the path. She'd been ferrying them in a school minibus from Junior School to the art block in New School, the distance judged too far for little legs, when she'd asked them if they'd like to make clay acorns and now the minibus was parked at the side of the drive and the same legs that were too little to walk far were running and skipping, because clay was magic and part of the enchantment was the pottery room in the middle of the woods.

One of the skipping girls said she was frightened of the pottery room because it was like a witch's house! And then a boy grabbed hold of the story, embellished it, and the kiln was the witch's oven! Roasting children inside to eat! And they were all enjoying the quiver of fear because Camille was with them and it was just the pottery room and a kiln which had baked their clay-coil snails; fun to be a little afraid. And then it started snowing, a few flakes but enough to banish the witch and her oven, the children screeching the word 'SNOW!!' as though it was a visiting deity.

Camille had an odd sensation, a chill that wasn't the snow; a feeling of being watched. Perhaps Lily, who'd been fearful of the witch's house, had felt something too, which had prompted the

36

image; something not quite right in the woods. But Camille knew her artistic nature could make her overly sensitive, so she ignored the sensation and listened instead to the children planning a snowball fight, a snowman and an optimistic igloo for break time.

★　★　★

Rafi Bukhari's hand was holding on to Hannah's as they ran through the woods, helping her to run faster and because he loved touching her; her beautiful red hair and pale skin and her kindness; *Angels are bright still*. His best friend, Benny, would say, *Wow, man, you're so fucking deep*, and he'd say back, *Hey, bro', you're so fucking shallow*.

The rhythm of his feet hitting the path as he ran, then Hannah's a moment later, thudding out an iambic pentameter; his friends would say, *You really are fucking weird, bro'*, and they'd be right but Hannah was equally weird and they were united in their shared weirdness, a normality of two.

His mum and dad were fluent in English but never used words like *fucking*, *bro'*, *chrissake*, *hench*, *peng*, *wanker*; they'd be shocked, but his older brother, Karam, would have learnt it all immediately.

His thoughts were full of Hannah and the luxury of worrying about being late for your school dress rehearsal. He'd brought his dad's copy of *Macbeth* from Syria but had never seen it performed. And now he had a part! He wished he could tell his dad. He heard Hannah wheezing and pulled her to a stop. A white snowflake landed on a fiery gold strand of her hair and for a moment he saw the beauty of it.

'Have to go,' he said, then he turned from her and ran towards Junior School, because his younger brother was terrified of snow – not stopping for even a moment to explain to Hannah, and later he'd wonder if it was because he thought she understood or because responsibility for his brother trumped everything and this was a kind of selfishness and smallness in him because he wasn't able to incorporate Hannah too.

'Snow is a PTSD trigger for Basi,' Dr Reynolds had said, but for him and Basi *trigger* meant a gun, a real trigger on a real gun; men holding guns, their dogs barking and snarling; just the word *trigger* making memories jump alive again. So he and Basi had their own word – *hole*. Because the present was the floor you trod on, all fine and oblivious, and then – BAM! a hole – and you fell down into the past.

He saw the tarmac drive which wound through the woods ending in Junior School, but the path would be quicker.

He jogged, not slowly but not flat out; Basi had become quicker to recover in the last few months and he felt guilty for wondering how long he'd need to spend with Basi, if he'd still make it back in time for his cue.

The percussive roar of an explosion, ripping the air around him, cutting inside his memory as if it was flesh and could bleed, and he was falling into the past.

His dad was running, carrying toddler Basi in his arms, his mum and older brother ahead of him, yelling at him to run faster but he couldn't hear them, just saw their mouths, because the sound waves had torn his eardrums. He fell as another building was hit.

He was under the rubble, calling for Baba and Mama, but his mouth was dried with dust and he couldn't make any sound. It was four hours until he was pulled out by his parents, his right leg broken, but lucky; Baba's hands bloody from digging for him, two of Mama's fingers broken by her search through the rubble.

He was struggling to breathe under the rubble but at the same time he was pressed against an English oak tree, its trunk soft with moss. He thought of the face of a stranger who'd been kind because that's how he could clamber back to the present. Today it was the judge, his beard flecked with salt, talking to him all through the first night on the boat, and Rafi came fully back to the English woods with snow falling.

He walked towards the flames being extinguished by the snow, charcoal smoke smudging the sky; then the wind blew the smoke into his face, stinging his eyes, smarting at the back of his throat. Pulling his hoody over his mouth and nose, he went closer. A twisted, blackened piece of metal, the size of a lunch box. A small bomb, nothing like the ones in Aleppo, but a bomb. The tree close to it had pieces of shrapnel sticking into its trunk. The lower branches were charred and, as he watched, fragments of blackened bark fell with the snow to the ground. He couldn't see anyone else in the woods.

Fuck's sake, it's just your PTSD! You're still in the middle of it, numb-nuts! His rational mind had to be aggressive and swear to get his attention because he had the six-pack version of PTSD with what Dr Reynolds called hypervigilance and delusions, a kinder way of saying psychosis. But delusions didn't sting your throat, phantom smoke didn't smart into your eyes.

He ran flat out towards Basi, his lungs hurting as they pulled in the freezing air.

The woods thinned and he saw the Junior School building and playground in front of it; the pirate ship playset with swings and a slide, and a huge old tree with parts of its roots exposed. Basi had shown him the houses they'd made for their Lego minifigures in the roots; tiny twig roofs.

Junior School had more security than the rest of the school, with a link-wire fence around the playground and building, barbed wire at the top, the suggestion and ugliness disguised by clambering ivy. The secretary always took ages to open the locked gate, huffing and puffing and complaining and making him sign something; every time; like she didn't already know who he was.

No time.

He ran at the fence, leaping as high as he could, one foot hitting against it, bouncing against it, while his left hand grabbed the top through the ivy and his right helped swing him over, the barbed wire tearing his hands as he vaulted it.

As he ran through the playground to the building, he saw a hardback book on a swing, protected from the falling snow by the pirate ship canopy. The illustration on the cover of the book was a woodland in snow and looked so like the real school woods in snow that for a moment he paused, then ran to the door.

The secretary busybodied after him down the corridor; she must have seen his ninja-vaulting from her office window.

'Tell Mr Lorrimer I need to see him straight away, please,' Rafi said. 'It's an emergency.'

Then he ran to Basi's classroom.

Just before circle time Basi Bukhari was looking at their scarecrows on the windowsill, waiting for springtime to guard the allotment, when he saw snowflakes. Everyone else in his class saw the snow too and ran to the windows, shouting, 'Snow! Snow! Snow!' But Basi was sick. Mrs Cardswell didn't get cross with him, just with Samantha, who said it was gross. Mrs Cardswell told everyone else to go to the reading room and then Miss Price came because she was his teacher when he'd first arrived and still came to be with him when he was upset. But he was falling down the hole and no one could reach him. And then he heard Rafi's voice.

'S'okay, Little Monkey, I'm here, you're safe. It's all okay.'

'Snow.'

'I know. A hole.'

'The worst hole.'

'I've got you now.'

He put Basi on his lap.

'The judge. Remember him in the boat? I was just thinking about him. His long grey beard with all the salt in it?'

'He gave me a lemon, because I was seasick.'

'Yes. He did. And it helped, didn't it?'

Basi opened his eyes, fixed them on Rafi as he came back to the classroom and his brother.

'His last lemon,' Basi said.

'That's right. I have to go and see Mr Lorrimer for a minute but Miss Price will look after you and then I'll be back, I promise.'

Rafi hurried to Mr Lorrimer's office. It would be too dangerous to take Basi through the woods, the bomber might still be there, but this building wasn't safe, he'd just got in without any problem. Junior School was at the top of the cliffs with a path leading down to an out-of-bounds beach. He'd gone to the beach last summer, a big group of them playing music and laughing, making more noise than they needed; challenging someone, claiming something. Too hot in the sun, they'd drunk beers and smoked in the cliff's shadows and no one had seen; maybe the beach.

He arrived at Mr Lorrimer's office. Miss Kowalski was with Mr Lorrimer and she smiled at Rafi as Mr Lorrimer started on about irregular visits during school hours. Rafi interrupted, trying to sound adult and calm.

'There was an explosion in the woods, near to the path.'

'You're saying there was some kind of bomb?' Miss Kowalski asked, but she was worried about him, not about a bomb; she didn't believe him.

'Probably firecrackers or something,' Mr Lorrimer said, irritated. 'Someone pissing around.'

Pissing because Lorrimer was annoyed with Rafi, and because he was sixteen so Lorrimer could use words like that. With the little kids, he probably would have said *messing*.

'I heard it and saw it,' Rafi said. 'Afterwards I checked and found a container, the size of a lunch box, and there was shrapnel in the trees. It was a bomb.' Trying not to speak too quickly, to sound mature, so he'd convince them. But he could see his reflection on their faces – a teenager with PTSD who imagined things that weren't there.

'A lunch box?' Mr Lorrimer said.

'Was anybody hurt?' Miss Kowalski asked, but without urgency, just saying this because she had to, like she knew that nobody was hurt because there hadn't really been an explosion.

'No.'

'Was anyone with you when you saw it?' Mr Lorrimer asked.

'No.'

Mr Lorrimer looked down at his paperwork, so Rafi would get the message that he was wasting his time.

'This building is very safe,' Miss Kowalski said patiently. 'No one can hurt Basi here.'

And even if he didn't have PTSD, they would still find it hard to believe him because around them were books sorted out into reading age and coloured crayons in pots and small coats on pegs, each with a photo of the wearer above. It was so gentle and organized that it felt safe.

'Perhaps you'd like to go home for the day,' Mr Lorrimer said, not knowing their foster mother wasn't there today. The house was in West Porlock, only three miles away, and if he could take Basi there he would, but to get there they'd have to go through the woods, on the drive or the path, and the woods weren't safe.

'I need to talk to Mr Marr,' he said, sounding too loud in the quiet room.

They were silent, Miss Kowalski with that patient quietness of teachers, Mr Lorrimer with annoyance, and all the time they were patient and annoyed Basi was in danger. He'd just have to take Basi and run. But what about the photos above the small coats? He'd have to take all the children to the beach, but he didn't know how he could do that.

Mr Lorrimer hadn't picked up the phone on his desk so Rafi got out his mobile. Mr Marr always took his calls. Should've done that straight away; he'd wasted time.

★　★　★

Through his office's large sash windows Matthew Marr saw that it had started to snow, the first time in years. Opposite him was his young deputy head, Neil Forbright, huddled into his chair, looking cold despite the fire Matthew had lit in the grate, and

Matthew worried that Neil should have taken more time off, had again come back to work too soon; a pattern for the last year. His mobile vibrated, 'Rafi' displayed, and he picked it up.

'There was an explosion in the woods, Mr Marr,' Rafi said. 'About fifteen minutes ago, maybe less.'

'Has anyone been hurt?' he asked.

And in the few moments before Rafi replied, fear blew inside him, a barely perceptible spasm in his face, a gust of adrenaline speeding his heart and breathing; and that physical reaction meant that he didn't dismiss what Rafi told him, because he had felt a presage of something appalling.

'No,' Rafi said. 'But I heard it and saw flames and smoke.'

Matthew put the phone on speaker so Neil could hear.

'I found the remains of it,' Rafi continued, 'a burnt-out container bent out of shape, the size of a lunch box. And there was shrapnel in the trees.'

Rafi was trying to sound calm, but Matthew heard the boy's fast breathing.

'Did you see anyone near the explosion?' he asked.

'No, but I didn't look, just ran to Basi.'

Matthew thought that Rafi's explosion probably had an innocent explanation – a bonfire that had an aerosol can and a lunch box burnt inside it; bits of bonfire floating up and getting caught in the trees looking like shrapnel to Rafi. He suffered from severe PTSD, which would transmute a small bang with an innocent explanation into a bomb. He imagined Rafi hearing a loud noise and seeing flames and PTSD taking his mind away from the woods and back to Syria; the horrors there.

Tonya, his secretary, came in from her adjacent office, and he thought she must have heard some of their conversation.

'Two teachers have phoned in,' Tonya said. 'Complaining about a loud noise in the woods. They think it's kids messing around with firecrackers.'

That's what Rafi's explosion most likely was, firecrackers and a bonfire.

'I'm at Junior School,' Rafi said. 'But they don't believe me. I have to get Basi, all of them, to safety. They can't stay here, Mr Marr.'

It could well be, most probably was, PTSD that had convinced Rafi it was a bomb, when in fact it was, as the teachers thought, kids fooling around. But what if Rafi was right? A thousand-to-one shot – but what if? At Columbine, teachers had thought it was firecrackers not bullets to start with; just a prank.

'We have to get them out,' Rafi said.

Matthew remembered the schoolroom in the Dunkirk camp, plastic crates on the mud floor as seats and desks, the other two volunteer teachers also in wellies and hats. Two filthy boys walking towards him, the older one looking angry, his dark eyes and mouth forming a surly expression, until he got closer and Matthew saw that he was fearful and defensive. One hand was holding tightly on to his little brother's, his other holding a battered copy of *Macbeth*.

At fourteen Rafi had brought his six-year-old brother all the way from Syria to France. He'd told Matthew about their journey, fragment by fragment, over the last two and a half years; his love and responsibility for Basi gluing the fragments together. If Rafi thought Basi was in danger then Matthew had to help him, had to give him the benefit of the doubt. And Rafi did have first-hand experience of bombs; the only one of them that did.

He took the school's emergency plan from his bottom right-hand desk drawer.

'Can you ask Mr Lorrimer to speak to me, please, Rafi?'

He turned to Neil.

'I'm grading the incident amber, instigating the school emergency plan and evacuating Junior School,' he said, a little alarmed by what he was saying. 'I want the rest of the school to stay inside school buildings and not go anywhere near the woods until the police give us the all-clear.'

Neil picked up the phone to call the police; under the emergency plan the deputy head was in charge of liaison with the emergency services.

Lorrimer came on the phone and Matthew thought that his lack of hurry, his deliberate keeping him waiting, was to let him know how busy he, Lorrimer, was and that he resented being handed a student's mobile phone.

'I am activating the school's emergency plan. I want you to evacuate Junior School,' Matthew said without preamble. In retrospect that was a mistake, he should have prepared the ground a little.

'You believe Rafi Bukhari?' Lorrimer sounded dumbfounded. 'It's just kids fooling around, Matthew, and—'

Matthew interrupted. 'You are to evacuate all the children and staff to Fulmar beach immediately.'

There were a hundred and forty children in junior school between the ages of four and ten, plus ten members of staff. When Matthew had planned junior school's evacuation drill he'd imagined a heatwave in the summer term drying the woods to tinder and a fire started by a careless smoker or picnicker. The Junior School building was surrounded on three sides by woodland so the children would escape by evacuating down the cliff path to Fulmar beach, from where they would be rescued by police launches and coastguards; they had life jackets kept ready for just such an eventuality. He'd never imagined a freezing day at the end of November, with snow falling.

He heard the sound of a door closing and guessed that Rafi had been ushered out of Lorrimer's office; then Lorrimer came back on the phone again.

'I know how much you care about Rafi,' Lorrimer said. 'That he's something of a son to you. But he has mental illness and is surely therefore not reliable? I understand that this is something you might feel you need to do to help him feel safer, but it's snowing, the cliff path down to the beach will be slippery, it's not safe, some of the children have asthma and—'

'Yes, they are vulnerable young children. You're isolated there. It's a mile to the road, half a mile from us down a drive through woodland. Your building is not adequately secure. If

45

the school is under attack, if there is any possibility of that, then we need to act swiftly. You have a route out, but a route that could be closed off. If it turns out to be a false alarm, which I'm ninety-nine per cent certain it will be, you can bring them all back again for break.'

Opposite him Neil was talking to the police. Tonya was telling receptionists there and in New School to lock the doors.

'You've seriously graded this a code red?' Lorrimer asked, and Matthew imagined Lorrimer opening his office door and looking at Rafi and wondering how a teenager could wreak such havoc in his junior school.

'Amber at this stage,' Matthew replied. 'But amber still activates the emergency plan. Do you know if any children or staff are missing?'

'The Year Threes were picked up as usual by Camille first thing to go to the art block in New School, so they aren't here.'

The children in Junior School were taught art and sport in the facilities of New School, minibuses took them to and fro. He would get confirmation from New School that they had safely arrived.

'Please send this morning's electronic register to the school secretary,' he said.

'I'll get it sent to Bethany, then.'

Lorrimer wasn't using the emergency protocol when people went by their role not name, so that roles could be reallocated if necessary. Bethany was off this morning.

'Find your Emergency Plan document and use it,' Matthew said. 'Tonya is acting the role of school secretary.'

Lorrimer, like the rest of the senior management and governors, had a hard copy of the Emergency Plan in his office as well as on e-format. Matthew had scrutinized it many times, usually as a tick-box exercise rather than as a document they'd ever need to use. But after a terrorist atrocity, or any violence against a school, he'd find himself redrafting it in the middle of the night, the insomniac periods of anxiety when the responsibility for so many children weighed heavily.

'Take the emergency mobile and keep us updated as best you can,' he told Lorrimer.

He'd tested mobile reception on the cliff path when he was planning the fire drill and no mobile network covered the path. Vodafone got patchy reception on the beach; so the emergency phone was on a Vodafone network.

'And what should I tell my members of staff?' Lorrimer asked.

'That this is just a precaution; that we are doing it to avoid a very small likelihood of risk, but to take it seriously. I know that Margaret and Peter have children in upper school. You can tell them that the rest of the school is not in full lockdown at this stage but students and staff will be staying inside until the police say it's safe.'

'Right.'

He could imagine Lorrimer's own explanation to the teachers; a neurotic headmaster making a ludicrous judgement call.

'Head of New School is liaison for parent queries and information. Tell Junior School's secretary to automatically forward calls to her before evacuating the building.'

He put down the phone. Tonya turned to him. 'I've sent out the amber alert.'

It would have gone out as a group text, email and WhatsApp to all members of staff. It would also go on to classroom smartboards as a code, known only to teachers.

'Thanks, Tonya. We need an up-to-date register of all children and staff.'

A key part of the emergency plan was that his office would collate a central register of everyone on site and anybody who was missing.

A knock on the door and Donna, Old School's receptionist, came in.

'I've locked the doors securely. There's something you should know. I'm so sorry, I was going to say, to tell you, but I phoned maintenance first instead . . . It's the CCTV camera. The one on the gatehouse, that connects to my monitor so I can see who's coming up the drive? The thing is, it wasn't working this morning. I went and had a look just before eight, just after I got here, and someone's splattered yellow paint all over it, the camera. I thought it was just kids with a paintball.'

'Well, that's the most likely explanation,' Matthew said. 'It's probably nothing.'

And it probably wasn't anything. It could easily have been kids with a paintball gun, besides which the drive going past the gatehouse and camera wasn't the only way into the school. Because as Matthew knew, but hadn't fully appreciated until now, the school's border was insecure. The extensive school grounds, mainly woodland, only had a post-and-rail fence separating them from the road and neighbouring land. On foot, anyone could simply climb over the fence. So the paint-splattered camera wasn't necessarily significant; but he felt a frisson of anxiety shift inside him as a weight was added to the side that said he wasn't being paranoid.

* * *

In the pottery room, the children were making acorns from clay, small fingers patting and moulding the cupule shape, and Camille was pleased to see that although each of them kept glancing through the windows at the wondrous snow, checking it was still really there, they were working with quiet concentration, the feeling of the clay on their fingertips absorbing.

Coming here was mining something precious from a time-tabled day, a sanctuary from hectic technological demands, where important quieter things had a chance to be noticed. In here there was no Wi-Fi or whiteboards or computers, not even any phones as the younger children weren't allowed them at school and hers was switched off in her jacket pocket.

Despite the huge windows, she'd had to turn on the overhead lights. When it had first been built the trees would have been further away, but over the last century the woods had crept steadily closer.

A little while ago, she'd smelt bonfire smoke, not the lovely tangy earthy smell of wood burning, but something with a chemical bite in it. She looked out of the window and saw a line of black smoke moving between the trees.

5.

8.38 a.m.

Rafi said they were all going to play a game outside and they put on their coats, not one class at a time like normal, but all squashed together. Rafi got things out of the big cupboard and put them into black bin bags and Mr Lorrimer looked even crosser and said it was a fool's errand, but Basi didn't know what that meant.

Some of the Reception children and Year Ones were crying because Mr Lorrimer was cross and because some of the teachers looked really worried and they were missing circle time.

Rafi called out, 'Who likes playing hide-and-seek in the snow?' and he held Basi's hand tightly as he said that, because he knew Basi was frightened of snow; and the little children stopped crying because everyone liked playing hide-and-seek and everyone liked playing in snow, apart from Basi.

'Who's the seekers?' Mani asked, and Rafi said, 'The sixth-formers!' Everyone thought it super-cool the sixth-formers were playing with them. And then Rafi said, 'We're going to win because we're going to the beach where they won't be able to find us and we're going to go quickly so we get a good head start.'

'Which beach?' Mani asked.

'Fulmar beach,' Rafi said and people were excited because no one had been there before, because it was out-of-bounds.

Basi and Rafi had played hide and seek lots of times on the Journey and they always hid together.

Some people started putting on their welly boots, but Rafi

said they didn't have time if they wanted to get hidden, so they went outside in the snow just wearing their indoor shoes, even Samantha in her Lelli Kellys. Rafi asked teachers and the older, stronger children to carry the big black bin bags and they all said yes, but Rafi didn't ask Mr Lorrimer.

In the car park, there were just the teachers' cars because all the parents had gone. On the other side of the car park was the gate at the top of the path that went down to the beach. They weren't allowed through the gate. Mr Lorrimer had to unlock it. Some of the boys heard him swearing.

When they got through the gate, Rafi knelt down so Basi could get on his shoulders for a piggyback ride, which they also played a lot on the Journey, because he got tired and because his shoes had holes in the bottom. Rafi's did too, but he said his feet were toughened up. It was still snowing but Basi was okay because Rafi was with him, holding tightly on to his legs, and he could bend down and put his face against Rafi's hair.

'How long till the seekers come?' Sofia asked.

'Not long,' Rafi said. 'But if we hurry we can get hidden.'

'But where can we hide on a beach?' Mani asked and Basi had been wondering that too.

'We could bury ourselves in sand,' Sofia said but Basi thought that was a silly idea, nobody had brought a spade or anything.

Rafi stopped walking and shouted out really loudly so everyone could hear, 'The cliffs jut out so we're going to hide in the overhang. It's a great place because when the seekers come searching for us, they'll look down at the beach from the top of the cliff and won't be able to see any of us.'

'What's an overhang?' Sofia asked and no one else knew either. The teachers probably did but they were all on their phones, trying to get a signal, but they couldn't.

Rafi opened his mouth and stuck his front teeth right out over his bottom lip and chin and made everyone laugh, and then he pointed to under his sticking-out teeth and said 'overhang', which sounded funny because his teeth weren't in the right place to talk. 'We are going to hide on the chin.'

★　★　★

In Matthew's office, Neil put down the phone to the police, wired with anxiety, his fingers tapping one after another on the desk. 'A police car's close, he'll be here soon; just one officer though, their cars aren't double-crewed any more, because I asked. She said it's an initial response and he'll report back, and if necessary try and contain what's happening as much as possible.'

Tonya put down the phone to Gina Patterson, designated head of New School.

'Camille Giraud isn't in the art block. She told Gina she was taking the children to the pottery room, but we think she must have switched her phone off because she's not picking up.'

The pottery room, in the middle of woodland, was accessible only by foot.

'We could put the siren on,' Tonya suggested. They'd installed a lockdown siren two years ago, a different sound to the fire alarm.

'Too far away, they won't hear it. I'll go and let Camille know,' Matthew said. 'In the meantime, keep trying to call her.'

'I'll go,' Neil said, fingers still drumming.

'Your role is liaison with the emergency services,' Matthew replied. 'You need to stay here.'

'Four children in that class are off sick,' Tonya said, looking at the register. 'So Camille has sixteen children with her.'

Matthew left his office, walking along the corridor towards the front door. Behind him the corridor used to end in a blank wall but now there were doors to a glass corridor leading to the theatre. He'd thought about evacuating everyone in Old School to the theatre but the glass corridor was too exposed to the woods and any possible threat there.

This had been the original school building, with just forty students when it was founded in the 1920s as part of the Progressive School Movement, but it had quickly expanded, so an existing building half a mile away had been converted into a junior school; and then New School had been built on the other side of the road to meet demand. In the last two decades a sports hall, music block and art block had been added on to New School. The doughty sisters who'd founded the school would be astonished.

He walked past the library, where sixth-formers were making a racket. He'd instigated a 'no mobiles or laptops' rule in the hope some of them might read a book but it clearly wasn't working, nor were they in the least worried by the amber alert, which could well be the right reaction; and then on past Jacintha Kale's English classroom, the usual hum of a lively discussion inside.

It was all so normal; even the feel of the floor under his shoes, the grooves in the wood worn smooth with running footsteps thumping down on to the floorboards. *Don't run!* teachers would call and he'd wish it was a command that could apply to him. He felt the kids' energy under his feet.

The dark-green walls had every year's framed photo of those responsible for the worn floor; the numbers increasing over the years, their clothes and hairstyles changing from the 1920s to the present day, but the children's faces all had a similar expression, smiling and open, not imagining danger. At the end of the corridor, near the front door, there were black-and-white photos of young soldiers, boys barely out of the sixth form, who'd gone off to fight and die in the Second World War. As Matthew got older those boys' faces seemed to get younger. Had war seemed unimaginable to them as they'd raced with thudding footsteps along this corridor a year or so before? *Don't run!*

He often thought about those boys as he walked along this corridor, thought they had fought and died for the next photo of school children, and the next and the next; that a school like this one, progressive, non-religious and open-minded, which had a bursary fund to take in refugees – Jewish children smuggled out of Poland, children from Sarajevo decades later, now Rafi and Basi – a school that was genuinely tolerant and liberal, was only possible because they had fought for it. That's why their photos were the first you saw as you came into the school. Medals of three of them were displayed outside the library.

'A little maudlin, isn't it?' the deputy head before Neil had said, missing the point that a great relaxation of spirit, liberalism and openness was something hard-won; something to be remembered; commemorated.

The man had been an imbecile. The kids got it, though. Running footsteps often abruptly halting.

He passed the doors to the empty drawing room, used for music recitals and parents' evenings, and reached Donna at the reception desk. The Gothic-Victorian front door had been bolted top and bottom with the original iron bolts, more secure he thought than the more recently added Banham.

'I know Tonya asked you this, but is there anyone you might have let in that you didn't know? Or who seemed off in any way?'

Donna shook her head. 'No one.'

'You're absolutely sure?'

'Yes. I spoke to Serena in New School, and she's the same. We've been racking our brains, just in case. But there's nobody. This far into term no one is new any more, staff or kids, we know everyone.'

'Thank you.'

He needed to be certain he'd made the right call to keep everyone, apart from the children and staff in Junior School, which had special circumstances, inside the school buildings.

'Can you lock the door behind me?' he asked Donna.

'But it's not safe to go out,' she said, looking afraid.

'I'll be fine. This whole thing has most probably been a huge overreaction on my part. But I want to tell Camille in the pottery room what's going on. Why don't you go and wait in Jacintha's classroom? Not be on your own. I'll phone Neil to let me in again.'

He went outside and waited till he heard Donna bolting the

door behind him, then walked quickly over the lawn. He hadn't paused to get his coat and the air was startlingly cold. A low stone wall surrounded two sides of the lawn, edged with evergreen Christmas Box becoming whitened with snow.

No one was outside apart from him, children still in their first lesson, most of them not yet even aware there was an amber alert. He looked back at Old School with its mellow bricks and ornate chimneys and gargoyles, the lawn powdered white and the woods stretching off into the distance, with snow falling between the trees; like walking through a Christmas card. Inconceivable in this tranquil scene that there was a threat to the school. What was conceivable was that he would look – or actually was – paranoid and panicky; adjectives that hardly topped the list of desirable qualities in a head teacher.

He should have spoken to Rafi for longer, had a more detailed conversation with him. Rafi genuinely believed he'd seen and heard an explosion, but Matthew should have ascertained more facts. Lorrimer had said Rafi was '*something of a son to you*'; he hadn't known it was so obvious, thought he'd hidden this paternal love for Rafi; but Lorrimer was right and perhaps it meant he'd believed Rafi too quickly.

It was Neil, as well as Rafi, who'd convinced him he needed to act urgently, because right from the start Neil had taken the threat seriously, believed that something terrible was happening to the school. Yes, because Neil suffered from depression, barely controlled by medication, and probably shouldn't be back at work. Because in his depressed state the world was a hostile and frightening place, with dark catastrophe closing in. He was mentally primed and waiting for something bad to happen.

The terrible coincidence was that he also felt paternal towards Neil. Just these two people, he didn't go around feeling paternal willy-nilly. Everyone else had the normal kind of headmasterly attention, shared equally among them, but Rafi and his young deputy head were different; perhaps it was because he didn't have children and his paternal love needed an outlet. But whatever the reason, love makes you biased, makes you behave illogically.

He saw flashing blue lights in the distance, getting gradually bigger. A police car was coming up the tree-lined drive, still a long way from him as it approached the gatehouse. The police car didn't have a siren on; maybe because the police driver knew that it was someone, him, overreacting, or just because they didn't put a siren on in a school.

Rafi's PTSD, Neil's drumming fingertips, and here they were with the school under amber alert and a police car coming up the drive. Lorrimer would be vindicated. Bloody hell. Lorrimer. He would think the photos of those boy soldiers maudlin too.

A gunshot. The sound spliced through the iced air.

The police car had skewed off the side of the drive, stationary.

He had no recollection of dropping to his knees. He crawled towards the low wall on one side of the lawn, sheltering under it. He thought the shot had come from the woods, near to the gatehouse.

His instinct was to run crab-style back inside Old School, still close to him, to safety; quickly replaced by his need to reach the pottery room and make sure the children were safe and didn't go outside where a madman was shooting. His third instinct, inculcated into him by seminars on safety and by insomniac run-throughs of worst-case scenarios, was to make sure essential information was relayed as quickly as possible. He dialled Neil on the emergency number.

'Someone's fired a gun. The police car was shot at. Near to the gatehouse. Put me on speaker. Tonya, put out a code red alert now. Neil, put on the siren.'

A second shot. On the phone he heard Tonya scream, she must have heard it too.

'Evacuate New School immediately. Get them on to the coach and minibuses and teachers' cars and get them away, sitting on each other's laps, on the floor, just get them out. Everyone else follow the emergency protocol. If the room has curtains or blinds or shutters, get them down. Lock all doors that have a lock. Keep everyone down on the floor, below windows and away from the doors. Put desks up against doors and windows. Turn off lights and smartboards. All phones turn off ringers.'

The school lockdown siren wailed into the frozen air. Anybody outside would get into a building as quickly as possible. Anyone who couldn't get to the shelter of a building would hide, and then phone to let them know where they were.

He stood, the length of him exposed, and ran from the lawn across the drive towards the woods and the pottery room. At any moment he expected to hear the shot. Expected to feel it. He was a coward, he realized, because he was terrified. He reached the edge of the woods and headed into the dense interior. It was snowing more heavily and he prayed the snow would obscure him as he ran. He was wearing a dark-blue jumper and brown chinos; he didn't know how conspicuous that made him. He felt totally conspicuous.

He was away from the siren now, quietness around him. He used to think the ancient woods had a living pulse, beating back through time to charcoal workers cutting trees every fifteen years for iron smelting, so that sunlight could reach the woodland floor and continue the rhythm. And then the violent dissonance of those shots and the pulsing rhythm was stilled.

Footsteps cracked on frozen twigs. He listened again. Someone was near him. The gunman had come after him. He crouched between two hawthorn bushes. He'd already turned off the ringer on his phone, now he turned off vibration.

He ran from the hawthorns to a copse of rowan trees, pressing himself against their trunks, and then he was running again towards the pottery room. He'd thought he was pretty fit, but his muscles ached and his breath was laboured and it felt impossible that he could keep up this pace but he kept running to the next copse of trees; sprinting, hiding, getting his breath back.

Lone wolf, the expression coming into his head because that's how he imagined him as he ran, a human finger on a trigger with a wolf's face. But maybe there was more than one; a pack of the bastards.

He reached an oak, its bark covered in dense moss, surrounded by tall holly trees. He pressed himself between the oak and hollies. He couldn't hear the footsteps, but maybe the snow was muffling his sounds.

Why would anyone do this? *Madman*, he'd thought earlier, *lone wolf*, but was that true? What if this was a terrorist attack? But why would terrorists attack this small, non-religious school in Somerset, miles from anywhere?

He saw the path that led to Junior School and ran along it, the snow heavier now. After a hundred yards it forked, the smaller fork leading to the pottery room.

As he raced towards the pottery room, sweat running down his face, he saw children through the windows, their small hands working with clay; one child looked out of the window, up at the snow.

Through the huge pottery-room windows Camille Giraud saw Matthew running – *running* – towards the pottery room and knew, a wire vibrating inside her, that something was terribly wrong. He came into the room, so much larger than everyone else, his hair and shoulders covered in snow, and he was out of breath.

He turned off the light, making the room abruptly dark. He whispered to her, 'Code red,' and then turned smiling to the children.

'What are you making?' He was still out of breath, his words sounding strange to her, but not to the children.

'Acorns! Acorns!' they all chanted, thrilled by his unexpected arrival.

'Wonderful! We'll make a display of them in Old School. Camille, you said there was a problem with a tap?'

They went into the tiny bathroom; her squashed up against the basin, him against the loo; children's murmurs next door, a boy

58

laughing; no one questioning their headmaster as impromptu plumber.

'There's a gunman in the woods,' he said.

'A gunman?' She couldn't take it in.

'It's too dangerous to evacuate them through the woods. Until the police arrive you need to keep them all here. Get them on the floor. Have you got a phone?'

'Yes. What will you do?'

'I think the gunman might have followed me. It might be me he's after. I'm not sure. I think I make you a target.'

'So, you need to leave.'

'Yes.'

'Be careful.'

She went back to join the children, Matthew behind her. He waved goodbye to the children, hesitated by the door for a few moments, and then slipped out.

Camille went to get her mobile out of her jacket pocket but there was only the keys to the minibus, a bag of Jelly Babies and a packet of Kleenex. The phone that she seldom used was in her handbag, which she'd left under the driver's seat because she didn't think she'd need it. Didn't think about the phone. Should have thought. How could she have been so irresponsible? She hurried to the door to call to Matthew, but he was already out of sight.

The children's heads were bent as they went back to their clay, their hair shiny despite the absence of the overhead lights; all oblivious as they made their acorns.

The dark trees outside the windows looked malevolent to Camille, hiding threat. The glass windows turned into weapons.

'We're going to make a house out of our tables,' she said to them.

6.

9.01 a.m.

They arrived at Fulmar beach. Miss Kowalski's phone made a cuckoo sound and Mr Lorrimer's phone pinged – *ping! ping! ping!* – with messages. Miss Kowalski read her phone and did a little scream, then put her hand over her mouth like she could put the scream back in again and started crying and Mr Lorrimer said 'Fucking hell', and the children all laughed because it was such a bad word and if they laughed it would make it funny he'd used a bad word, but Basi just looked down at the beach which had snow footprints not sand footprints. Other teachers couldn't get reception on their phones, so they all looked at Miss Kowalski's and Mr Lorrimer's phones, and Rafi did that too.

'Everyone run under the cliffs as quick as you can!' Mrs Cardswell shouted, like she'd got all excited about the game. 'Each form will hide all together. My form with me, please!' But the sea and the wind were too loud. So Mr Lorrimer, who had a big booming voice, shouted it too and they all ran under the cliffs, the teachers hurrying them along, like the teachers all really, really wanted to win.

The cliffs made a roof over them. The teachers emptied all the bin bags they'd been carrying and they had life jackets in them.

Basi was still looking down at their snow footprints because he didn't want to look at the sea. But the sea was shouting at him:

Wa-Hush, Wa-Hush, Wa-Hush.

Wahush meant 'monsters' in Arabic; the sea was telling you that it had monsters inside it.

Miss Kowalski said, 'We've got a big treat today. We are all going to go on a real lifeboat! And maybe a police boat too! And then the seekers will never find us!'

And everyone apart from Basi was laughing, because all the grown-ups were playing, the lifeboat people too, even though it was a little bit like cheating.

Rafi was holding a life jacket and he started putting it on Basi. It felt all rubbery and damp and he hated the smell and the cold heaviness.

'Remember the piñata in Alexandria?' Rafi said, because he could tell Basi didn't like the life jacket and he wanted to make him smile. And it was really funny. There'd been a shop selling little life jackets for children and babies. An old man had said something to Rafi, but really quietly so Basi couldn't hear. He thought what he'd said had made Rafi angry because Rafi got a stick from the back of the shop and hit a little life jacket and hit it and hit it. The shopkeeper got angry too and Basi started to cry, then Rafi said, 'It's a piñata, Little Monkey!'

'Are there sweets inside?'

'No, it's a terrible piñata.'

And they'd laughed because it was funny Rafi thought a life jacket could be a piñata and because they'd been naughty and were afraid of the shopkeeper.

'We ran so fast, didn't we?' Basi said.

'Super-fast.'

When they'd got their breaths back they found another shop. Before they went in he told Rafi the old man had lied, life jackets are never piñatas, they never have sweets inside. It was the first time he could tell Rafi something important he didn't already know. The shop had been selling balloons too, maybe that's what had got Rafi muddled. Rafi looked at the life jackets in the next shop really carefully, but he didn't hit any of them, and then he bought Basi a Yamaha one, which was red and grey and used up almost all their euros but it was the best kind you could get.

The school life jacket was yellow. Rafi pulled it up over his head, snagging it on his ears, and it hurt.

Rafi made sure Basi's life jacket fitted properly and wouldn't come off over his head. They were safe now under the cliffs, he was pretty certain of that. Nobody had followed them along the path, nobody had seen them. He'd done it. And boats would soon be coming.

He tried his phone again but there still wasn't a signal. Miss Kowalski had shown Rafi her text messages when they'd got to the beach, like he was a member of staff too: *code red*; *gunman in the woods*; *police car shot at*.

'Rafi? You need to put on your life jacket.' Basi was tugging at him.

'I'm sorry, Little Monkey, I can't come with you.'

'Then I won't go.'

'You'll have Miss Price looking after you and Mrs Cardswell and you'll be with all your friends.'

'I don't want to play any more.'

But he knew Basi had already guessed this wasn't a game.

'It won't be anything like the Journey, I promise.'

'No. You have to come too.'

'It'll be a very short boat trip with nice English policemen who'll look after you; special boat policemen. Please will you be brave and go on the boat?'

'They're shouting at me, the monsters, *wa-hush*, *wa-hush*, listen! Can you hear?! It's worse than a hole!'

He was breathing too fast, eyes dilated, terrified.

Rafi listened to the waves crashing on to the beach and understood Basi's terror and knew that this was the worst thing he'd ever done to him.

'Remember the princess in Milan, Basi? Do you remember her face?'

Trying not to rush Basi, he talked about the beautiful woman in Milan station, who'd been so kind to them. When Basi's breathing slowed, he took his hand and led him over to Miss Price, who was doing up life jackets on a group of children.

'Rafi, I don't know how to thank you. If it wasn't for you—'

'Look after him, for me.'

'But—'

'I'll be fine.'

She didn't argue; evacuating them bought him a bit of trust, he thought, deserved or not. He passed Basi's hand over to hers, but Basi tried to hold on to him.

'It's a *Have-To-No-Arguments*,' he said to Basi. 'Okay?' He waited and then Basi nodded and stopped trying to hold on.

He kissed him on the top of his head, his silky hair soft against his lips, saw the pink raised scar along his cheek, his long curling eyelashes, tears at the ends like beads. He told him to be brave, that he loved him, and then he ran back towards the cliff path.

Being apart from Basi felt like a physical severing but they'd all look after him and he was in a proper life jacket, not one made out of foam that soaked up water and drowned children faster. An old man had quietly warned him. Not thinking about the effect on Basi, he'd picked up a stick and bashed a tiny life jacket so that the foam spilled out and everyone could see it was an evil trick, and not to buy one, and the shopkeeper had yelled at him but he hadn't cared and then he'd seen Basi crying as he hit the life jacket. *It's a piñata, Little Monkey!* The balloons probably gave him the idea, like it was a party shop, but they were sold for keeping phones dry at sea.

It was snowing more heavily as Rafi sprinted up the path to get to Hannah, his feet sometimes slipping as he struggled to get purchase.

* * *

Matthew walked back towards Old School, his phone's ringer switched on, bashing against branches, snow falling inside his collar and down his neck, wanting to draw the man after him, away from the pottery room – if it's me you're after, you bastard, then come and get me, but leave the children alone. No point shouting this in your head so he shouted it at the woods, 'Come and get me! You bastard!' The noise startled a flock of fieldfare thrushes that scattered into the sky. But then there was silence, no one behind him.

His phone rang,

'Matthew? Are you okay?' Neil asked.

'I think the gunman was following me in the woods, almost to the pottery room.'

'Can you see him now?'

'No. If he comes back . . . They don't even have a lock on their door, Neil, nothing. And no shutters.'

'The police are treating this as a major incident and sending in armed officers and everyone else they think is needed. I'm sure they'll make the pottery room a priority. Everyone in junior school has got to Fulmar beach and the coastguards have been alerted. We've accounted for everyone apart from Tobias Fern and Jamie Alton. The policeman who was shot at isn't hurt, he's in the gatehouse. I'll wait by the front door for you.'

'Thank you, Neil.'

He was grateful to Neil for rising to this crisis, for taking it so impressively in his stride, but not hugely surprised. He'd always seen Neil's strength of character, had thought him a person who, if it came to it, would step up to the mark; thought too that Neil probably didn't know this about himself nor that courage wasn't the same thing as robust mental health.

He'd read that Winston Churchill suffered from depression. A historian suggested it was his depression that meant he saw the evil in Hitler, the true threat he posed, long before anyone else; as if depression had already adjusted his eyes to the darkness so that he could see the danger it contained; Neil's drumming fingertips.

As he neared Old School he saw Tobias Fern on the lawn

holding his flute, wearing his noise-cancelling headphones; he must have heard the siren even with the headphones, but it probably just terrified him, made him withdraw further into his private world.

'Tobias?' The boy startled. Matthew tried to take his hand but Tobias winced away from him; he hated being touched. So, instead, Matthew held his arm a little way from Tobias, as if holding the air around him, and Tobias understood and moved quickly with Matthew over the snow-covered grass in front of the school.

It was suddenly quiet; Neil must have switched off the siren – it had done its job in alerting everyone and its screech would just induce more panic. Shutters were pulled across all the windows, no lights shining out, the facade of the school no longer welcoming.

He knocked on the door. Neil quickly let them in.

'You found Tobias,' Neil said to him, his relief clear. 'I've told Tonya to wait with Donna and Jacintha, she has her laptop and phone with her. Once the major incident response people arrive they'll set up a command and control centre and organize things from there. I'll see you in your office.'

Then he was leaving the reception area and striding briskly along the darkened corridor.

Matthew bolted the heavy door, glad of its heft. It took a little while for his eyes to become accustomed to the gloom. Tobias had visibly relaxed, his hands no longer covering his headphones, though he kept his headphones on.

'Mr Marr?'

He hadn't seen Hannah in the shadows by the door.

'You should be in your classroom, Hannah.'

'I heard something in the woods earlier, a really loud noise, and I saw smoke. It was an explosion, wasn't it?'

'Probably, yes.'

'I'm sorry, I should have told you. If I had—'

'Teachers heard it too and didn't know what it was either. Mr

Benson complained about some kind of rumpus in the woods – *rumpus*, like *Where the Wild Things Are*.'

'I don't know where Rafi is,' she said. 'I keep phoning him but he's not answering.'

So that was the reason she was by the door – waiting for Rafi. Or perhaps she was on her way out to find him; he wouldn't put it past her. 'Cliff Heights School's very own Romeo and Juliet', staff called them, but the teasing epithet, the sarcasm implicit, was more about the adults and a certain wistfulness.

'He's fine, Hannah, he just doesn't have any reception. He evacuated everyone in Junior School down to the beach, coast-guards will be on their way to pick them up.'

She smiled, eyes shining, her relief luminous in the darkened space.

'Love is the most powerful thing there is,' he said. 'The only thing that really matters.'

Was it appropriate for a head teacher to be saying this kind of thing to a student? Yes, he thought, this was exactly the time and place for it to be appropriate. And he loved Rafi Bukhari too and his relief that he and his little brother were safe, while not making him glow, was none the less something light inside him.

'Let's get going,' he said and they started walking along the shadowy corridor, Tobias lagging a little behind. He was thinking about love, that it was such a vital thing, like gravity or breathing.

His phone rang and he answered it.

'Mr Marr? PC Beard here. The copper who got shot at.'

'Are you all right?'

'Fortunately, the bugger missed. I'm in your gatehouse. I phoned the main school number, spoke to someone called Tonya. She gave me your numbers. Mr Forbright said you went to warn the teacher in the pottery room?'

'Yes.'

'You mustn't go putting yourself at risk like that. You have

66

a police officer here. So, it's my job not yours to do anything like that.'

'But you're not armed either and—'

'It's my job and besides it's much more exciting than dishing out speeding fines to tourists and there aren't many of those in November.'

Matthew guessed him to be in his fifties; imagined a bit of a paunch from evenings with mates in the pub. He liked him.

'Mr Forbright said you thought the gunman was following you. Probably the same nasty bugger who shot at me. Any idea where he went?'

'No.'

He walked round the bend in the corridor with Hannah and Tobias, towards the library, English classroom and his office.

The sound of something behind them. Matthew hung up the phone and listened.

A door being closed.

Which door? A classroom door? No classrooms behind them. It must have been the door to the drawing room, which was empty. Surely to God the drawing room had been empty.

Tobias, with his headphones on, hadn't noticed but he saw Hannah stiffen, afraid.

Someone had been hiding all this time, locked with them inside Old School.

Footsteps behind them.

'Go into the library, quick as you can,' he said.

Hannah hurried into the library but Tobias either hadn't heard him or wouldn't be hurried. He put his arm around Tobias, trying to get him to hurry, but Tobias flinched at being touched and stood stock-still.

The footsteps continued, getting closer.

A click. The cock of a gun.

He put himself between the gun and Tobias.

He pushed Tobias's earphones away from his ears and whispered to him, 'Go into the library now.'

Tobias walked through the open library door; he wasn't sure if Tobias was doing what he was told or just getting away from being touched and having his headphones removed.

He turned to face the man behind him, because going into the library might draw the man into the library too.

A black balaclava covered his face, eyes looking out of slits. He was pointing a rifle, another gun strapped to his chest. The guns rigid and inhuman, the man rigid too, as if his guns and his body and his hate were all the same terrible thing.

Matthew took a step backwards, against the wall now; his head by the display case of medals.

'Please . . .' Matthew said, dropping his mobile on the floor, betraying his fear. 'Talk to me. Tell me why you're doing this.'

The man looked back at him and said one word.

Matthew recognized his voice.

And the one word explained everything.

A moment of stillness, as if time itself was waiting.

He thought he saw his finger move, maybe imagined it moving.

The bullet travelling faster than its own sound.

Those boys dying so that this wouldn't happen.

Their medals turning to shrapnel.

The benevolent order of things destroyed.

Another shot. Hannah was pulling him inside the library, she must have waited by the door; a habit of waiting by doors. Brave girl. Why didn't he know about this courage of his students?

She's bending over him now and time must have passed, but how much time? He doesn't know. Can't tell. She's saying to him that help is on the way and he can tell that she's lying, that she's being brave for him and Jesus Christ it should be him being brave for her. He should be brave for her. She's by the door; the most dangerous place. He must tell her to move away from him and the door. And he must tell her the gunman's name, he must warn all of them. And he must find out about the children in the pottery room and if the junior school children have been rescued. Again and again he tries to speak; Hannah bends down closer to him, trying to understand, but it's no good, he can't make the words and he feels part of his consciousness fragmenting into blackness, forgetting who the gunman is and the word he said, knowing only that it is all his fault.

7.

9.34 a.m.

Beth Alton arrives on the outskirts of Minehead; country lanes have given way to roads and traffic lights. Her mobile vibrates and she grabs it. But it's a PTA group message, not Jamie:

> **Matthew Marr shot, wounded in library.**
> **No children hurt.**

The word *yet* hovers there. Yet. Yet. Yet. And she feels guilt that she can only think about *yet* and not about Matthew Marr, not until she knows Jamie is safe.

She parks on the snowy pavement by The Pines Leisure Centre, other cars parked erratically in front of her. As she opens her car door, another PTA message buzzes on her phone.

> **New School evacuated!!** ☺

So, that mother's child is safe. What about other people's children? Is there a terrified emoji, for Christ's sake? These women, these women. She's never understood them, never been an insider and now especially not.

Parents are running through the open glass doors of the large modern leisure centre. Beth doesn't run because she feels too far from Jamie as it is, five miles away through the snow.

You worry too much about me, Mum.

Not any more. I don't care if you flunk your A levels or go to university, none of that matters.

She says after we've all traipsed off to St Andrews.
And I don't mind that you're not outgoing and not very confident.
Jeez, thanks, Mum.
Sorry.
I'll phone you when I go off to university.
More than you do at the moment?
I live with you, why should I phone you?

She's imagining his voice, of course she is, but she's using old con-versations between them, his words and phrases just rejigged to fit.

She remembers how when he was born he simply took up a different place inside her, everyone and everything else making room for him, shifting around him, so that he is always with her, even when he's physically not here.

Inside the glass doorways of the leisure-centre foyer a group of parents have phones open showing messages from their chil-dren, evacuated from New School.

'In the coach, they were sitting on each other's laps.'

'On the floor in the minibuses.'

'Ten of them were squashed into Mrs Fenwright's car.'

'Maddie was in Mr Johnson's boot, and it's just a regular boot.'

And the parents who know for sure their child is safe start talking about Matthew Marr, able to feel the horror of it, but she can't, not yet.

At the far end of the foyer there's a police officer with a clip-board, a shifting, pressing group of parents around him. Rumours hum through the parents – his clipboard has a list of names that's been scanned across; if your child has been evacu-ated, their name is on the list, *in their own writing*, you can then go and wait for your child to be brought to the basketball court. If your child hasn't written their name, you go to the cafeteria.

People are shoving to get to the list and Beth is trying too, but is pushed back. Parents who have seen the list are either hurrying through to the basketball court, their footsteps fast and light, their breathing changed, like a long exhalation, or to the cafe-teria, not breathing, or breathing very slowly, as if holding your breath could change the reality you're inhabiting, their footsteps slow and heavy, carrying an unaccustomed weight.

'Where's the CDT room?' she asks a woman in front of her. 'My son was going to the CDT room.' But the woman doesn't turn. She spots a woman she recognizes, a mother who knows everything, chairs the charity committee and is a parent-governor. 'Do you know where the CDT room is?' But the woman just shrugs, as if she doesn't know anything any more. A father in a Mumford & Sons sweatshirt turns to her.

'The CDT room is in New School,' he says.

New School has been evacuated. Jamie crouched in a boot or squashed up ten to a car and got out. And soon she will read his name, in his own writing, and she will remember helping him to do cursive writing, the hours and hours they spent on it together, and so she will see 'Jamie' with the 'e' at the end remaining a little lopsided, a difficult join, and she'll run through the swing doors to the basketball court and wait for him.

Fear leaves her body, muscles relaxing but skin prickling as if the tension lingers there on the outside of her body before dissipating into the warm air in the foyer.

Told you, Mum, you worry too much.

You're right.

Do I still have my get-out-of-jail-free card for A levels and university?

Absolutely.

* * *

In the theatre, Daphne gets up on to the stage and claps her hands. She's tried not to think about Neil's WhatsApp message, to concentrate only on the kids; not possible, so she's been hiding her feelings and wondering how good an actress she really is.

'Right! Two minutes, everyone! Zac and Luisa, get ready for thunder and lightning; Benny, projection. My three lovely witches, positions, please.'

And for a moment a buzz goes through them all, a moment when 'two minutes' to curtain-up generates adrenaline.

The kids' faces are still in camouflage make-up in case gunmen storm the theatre and they have to hide. Sally-Anne is standing sentinel at the locked security doors that lead to the glass corridor, one hand holding her phone, the other the nail gun, with the forlorn hope that the kids and teachers can still reach them, as if something will change.

She sees Tim, who plays Macbeth, sitting in the wings, dragging on a cigarette, quick deep drags like he can find some magic potion hidden at the bottom. She goes over to him.

'How's our leading man?' she asks.

'Thing is, shouldn't be me doing the part,' Tim says. 'I knew that but my parents, they're so proud. Didn't even tell them about Victor, that he was first choice, and much better than me.'

Tim is worried about his acting! How marvellous is that? She loves these kids. Absolutely adores them.

'He's brilliant, isn't he?' Tim says, looking at her.

'He's very talented,' she replies.

For a second or two, she remembers her swell of pride in Victor, a raw natural talent like nothing she'd ever seen in all her years teaching. First term in her class she'd give him notes – a bit of vulnerability here, more nuance there – and he'd just do it, perfectly, first time. But he'd had to leave when his parents couldn't pay the fees.

'You're very talented too,' she says to Tim. 'You'll storm it.'

'Really?'

'I have absolute and total faith in you. Go knock 'em out.'

'Thanks, Daphne.'

Miranda, playing Lady Macbeth, sashays over to him, still doing her sex-kittenish act, even though it's never tempted Tim away from his girlfriend, let alone that the school is under attack. She thinks Miranda spectacular right at this moment. Miranda slides herself down next to Tim.

Daphne's mobile buzzes with a WhatsApp from Sally-Anne

73

in the foyer, who's just received an update about the people in New School and a message from a junior school teacher. She leaps to her feet and claps her hands, soles of her feet and palms stinging with adrenaline.

'Listen up, everyone! I've had some good news. Everyone in New School has been evacuated and junior school are safely on Fulmar beach, waiting for boats to pick them up. Rafi got them out.'

A cheer goes up, the kids momentarily elated. Jamie Alton went to New School to get his cauldron, so he's definitely evacuated too, blessed, blessed cauldron. Anna and Davy, her little Macduffs, were also in New School, so are also safe, and all the other junior school children are safe too, because of Rafi; a huge hoorah for Rafi, wonderful boy.

'So Anna and Young Fry are all right?' Josh asks.

'Yes.'

'What'll we do without them when we get to Act Four, Scene Two?' Joanna asks.

'We'll think of something.'

But even if the young children were here – thank you, Lord Jesus, that they're not – she would have stopped the rehearsal before this scene. The other murders in this play aren't so terrible, committed off stage and adult to adult, but the murder of Macduff's son is on stage, right in front of you, the murderer stabbing the little boy as he holds him on his lap. Then, in their production, the little girl runs but is caught by a murderer in the wings, because Macduff had all his *babes savagely slaughtered*. She'd faff about this play's themes and various interpretations and then she'd get here, to its terrible black heart, and know it was a play about raw evil.

My children too? . . . My wife kill'd too . . . all my pretty ones?
Did you say all?

* * *

74

In the woods, Rafi Bukhari has stopped running to check his messages but his thumb has got too cold to be recognized on the touch ID so he has to key in his passcode and he's wasting time, wasting time. He skips hurriedly through voicemails from friends and teachers, still nothing from Hannah. But she doesn't ever leave voicemails, only talks on the phone when there's a voice talking back to her. She'd told him that the night they'd first properly spoken to each other at a party. Before that, they'd hung out with different people, were doing different subjects, and he'd been shy of approaching her.

He's running again, flat out, towards Old School.

At the party, she'd been sitting on a sofa, and he'd sat next to her and she'd jumped. And then he didn't know what to say to her, didn't have a clue. *Idiot.*

'Do you think we wake up every day the same old self?' she said. 'Or do we have a choice but we don't realize that? It might be just habit that makes us the same self as yesterday even if that's not who we want to be at all?'

He just stared.

'Oh shit, you think I'm totally weird.'

This girl.

'I think that's what mental illness is,' he said. 'I think it takes away the choice. You're stuck being someone who isn't even really you. And you should know that the not-really-me has PTSD and I'm genuinely weird in a psychotic way. You're beautiful.'

She glanced away from him, deflecting what he'd told her as untrue, and it was a week before she explained she was turning away from him calling her beautiful, dismissing that, not his PTSD.

'Jesus, Rafi, what kind of horrible person did you think I am?'

'Yeah, but I still wanted to kiss you.'

'So, it was always a totally superficial physical thing for you?'

'Totally.'

At the end of the party, everyone else fuzzy with drunkenness

75

and tiredness, they'd felt sharpened, wide awake, and they talked about calling each other later that night, not wanting their conversation to have an ending, and she told him that she never left a voicemail, because she could only talk to someone if someone was talking back to her. Weeks later, she said it was because she might say something stupid and he could hear over and over again what an idiot she was.

He stops to phone her again, wiping the snow off his screen, keying in the passcode, but again it goes straight through to message.

'Hey, it's Hannah . . .'

She must have run out of charge, that's all, doesn't mean anything bad. Can't mean anything bad.

As he pockets his phone he feels someone behind him; a sensation that makes his back feel exposed, as if he's missing clothing, and then the wind drops for a few moments and he hears footsteps and breathing.

The man behind him is just a delusion. He has PTSD and is hypervigilant and highly stressed and this man doesn't exist. And even without PTSD as an excuse, he cannot trust himself to know what is real.

His love for Hannah is a delusion too.

No, that's not true.

There was an explosion and you didn't warn her, didn't help her, didn't even think about her until you got Basi to the beach.

He's running again over the snow-covered earth, his feet no longer beating out an iambic pentameter but a criticism over and over, *you left her*, and the boy holding her hand and the man he was becoming, around the bend in the path, have disappeared.

★ ★ ★

In the foyer of The Pines Leisure Centre, Beth Alton's eyes are playing tricks or she's in too much of a hurry and reading the list of children's names too fast because if she slows down surely this time she'll see Jamie's name.

And you tell me not to rush things, Mum.

I know. But I meant homework, not—

More haste less speed, you say.

Please don't tease me right now, Jamie.

Well, someone needs that job, Mum.

She just has to be more logical, not dart about but start at the top and work down, because it's not like this list is in alphabetical order, any kind of order, just children writing their names down in a biro that's running out, and then changes to a thick pen, and they didn't have anything to press on which means it's all a bit wonky and so easy to miss Jamie's name.

Her phone keeps buzzing with calls and messages from her parents and sister and Theo at university; but she doesn't answer. Another text from Mike.

> Is he evacuated?

She hesitates but cannot pretend any longer.

> No

The police officer holding the list looks at her with kindness. 'If you go to the cafeteria on the first floor, police officers are updating relatives who still have children in the school.'

She feels weak for clinging on to hope when all the time the police officers in the cafeteria might have important information about Jamie, which conflates in her mind into being something that will help him if only she knows what it is.

The large cafeteria has no windows. Built in the interior of the leisure centre, it looks down over the swimming pool and a children's play area, emptied now, everyone sent home apart from them. At the twenty or so tables parents have phones pressed to their ears as they talk to their children, others just gripping phones, willing them to ring; the air so tense that Beth thinks she can see wires criss-crossing the room, threading through the parents, winding tighter.

Another text from Mike.

> Will ask Mum to drive over and check our answerphone

Their house mobile reception is unreliable so they often have to use the landline to call someone at home and Jamie might think that she's at home. But surely he'd call her mobile too?

A police officer comes over to her. 'Can I have your name, please?'

'Beth Alton. My son Jamie was meant to be in the theatre, but he left to get a cauldron from the CDT room in New School.' Why's she telling him about a cauldron? 'But he wasn't evacuated. His name isn't on the list.'

'Yes,' the police officer says, 'I have a record of your son.'

'You know where he is?'

'Sorry. I meant that we know he was supposed to be in the CDT room.'

'Does anyone know where he is?'

'I have no more information, I'm sorry. I'll let you know as soon as I do.'

She is made of damp cardboard and is folding in half. She doesn't know how to keep standing, so she sits at a table of strangers.

You okay, Mum?

Yes, course I am. It's you that needs to be okay.

Jamie is four years old. She is in bed with flu. She hears his foot-steps on the stairs, a chink of the china mug on a plate as it wobbles. He sets the mug in its swimming saucer down on her bedside table. 'Tea,' he says and clambers in next to her, his little body pressing close to her.

*

Some of the parents are shivering though it's too warm in here. A teenage member of staff, wearing a Pines Leisure Centre sweatshirt, gives his phone charger to a mother, helps her to plug it in. 'No problem,' he says. The mother sits on the floor, holding her phone as it charges.

Beth feels something at her feet. A child's party balloon is under the table with '4' on it; she must have seen this balloon, not realized she'd seen, attuned only to Jamie so that she'd thought of him bringing her tea. This room is usually used for children's parties with easy-wipe Formica tables and linoleum on the floor. She's been here before with Jamie and Theo years ago, for birthday teas, parents all chatting, the children's hair wet from the swimming party.

A commotion. Three parents are with a young woman police officer who looks outnumbered. The older male officer is coming to her aid.

'The TV says armed police have arrived.'

'I can't comment on that.'

'The TV bloody well has so why can't you?' a suited man says.

'I'll find out, sir. Please, calm down, I'll find out.'

'But what if the children are hostages?' a mother asks. 'What if he starts firing when the armed police go in?'

'Safety of the children is their absolute priority,' the woman police officer says.

The suited man steps away from her. 'Yes. I'm sorry. Of course. I really am sorry.' As if he needs to get back in her good books, because if he's in her good books then the police will take better care of his child.

A man in his mid-twenties, too young to be a father, too old to be a brother, barges through the swing doors of the cafeteria on the phone. He looks at the room full of parents. 'They're still on Fulmar beach,' he says. 'My fiancée just told me. She said boats are on their way but the weather's really bad and held them up.'

At the far end of the cafeteria, junior school parents' voices cluster and grow frantic.

'What if he goes down to the beach? There's no other way out.'

'But he's in Old School, in the corridor, he's nowhere near the beach.'

'There might be more of them.'

'What does your fiancée say?'

'I only spoke to her for a few seconds, there's a helicopter flying over the beach, you can't hear to talk.'

'That's good though, isn't it? The helicopter. They're making sure they're all right.'

The young man looks too energetic to be in here, toe tapping on the floor, thumbs tapping at his phone, like he could spring away at any moment. The folding-in-half parents have had all their energy leached away by terror, can barely sit upright.

Something presses into Beth's side; the edge of a laptop. Sitting next to her is a man in pyjamas, who has his laptop open flat on his lap. For a moment, she's embarrassed to be so close to a man's pyjama crotch; tiny taboos continuing. On his screen is a news channel, a girl is talking to a presenter, blurred out below her face. She's asking how long the ambulance will be. The girl's called Hannah. She gives an uncertain smile directly at the camera and the man in pyjamas puts his fingertip on to the screen, touching her face.

'They keep showing it,' he says. 'She's in the library.'

'She's with friends,' Beth says. 'Your daughter, Hannah, she's not on her own.'

'No. Your child . . .?' Hannah's father asks.

'Jamie. No one knows where he is.'

How can that be? How can nobody know?

'I think he must be hiding.' And as she says this, the image crystallizes. Jamie is hiding and he can't phone her because he can't risk making any noise in case he gives his hiding place away.

★   ★   ★

In the theatre, the start of the dress rehearsal has been postponed. Someone, Daphne doesn't know who, doesn't matter, switched on their mobile and got a message from a friend in Jacintha's classroom and now they all know. Their headmaster has been shot and is lying wounded in the library. Matthew, that kind, charismatic, extraordinary man; she still can't fully take it in.

Jacintha must have shared Neil's WhatsApp message with her kids; Daphne and Sally-Anne hadn't shared it with theirs, had wanted to protect them, but perhaps that was wrong of them. Daphne hasn't told them she already knew, because she doesn't want them to stop trusting her.

Neil's message said that Mathew is still conscious, that he's been wounded in the head and foot, but the bullet can't have hit his head, must have hit something else first, which is lucky, Neil said.

Still conscious. She's been holding on to it tightly. *Lucky.*

She claps her hands. 'Luisa and Zac, thunder and lightning, please.' But Luisa doesn't move, her camouflaged face pinched into green and brown streaks of anxiety. Her twin, Frank, is in the library and she's staring at her phone, waiting for him to ring her or reply to her texts.

Tobias is in Old School too, Neil told Daphne that, and although terrified for him, she's glad he's not on his own. Tobias was meant to be playing his flute in tonight's performance; a soundtrack for the good and noble characters. She and the kids had debated whether Macbeth was allowed a few of Tobias's flute notes at the beginning of the play, before he's turned wicked. Later, Tobias's flute was to have been the soundtrack to the little Macduff boy being murdered.

Sally-Anne has remained in her position at the locked doors to the glass corridor, phone and nail gun to the ready, determined in spite of everything that the people in Old School will still escape to the theatre; there's a kind of courage in her hopeful-ness that Daphne admires but cannot share, because it's impossible with a gunman in the corridor – a gunman who's prepared to shoot, who has shot Matthew – for any of them to reach the safety of the theatre.

'We carry on, everybody,' she says, her voice loud with far more confidence than she feels. 'We rehearse this play and we do not let the bastards stop us. Okay, everyone? We carry on!'

A few nods, everyone apart from Luisa looking at her now.

Still conscious.

'Zac, thunder and lightning, please.'

Lucky.

Zac claps his hands, a quietly human noise, not the ear-splitting, heavens-in-outrage thunder, but they could hardly have a loud bang at the moment.

'Witches, please . . .!' Daphne calls, because they haven't heard Zac clapping and have missed their cue or because they're too shocked to carry on.

Zac strobes a bright light across the stage for lightning, the same light that Sally-Anne plans on shining into the bastards' faces if they attempt to storm the theatre.

Sophie and Tracey walk on to the stage, hunched with upset and fear, poor loves, but the third witch, Antonella, strides out with attitude. All three have goosebumps despite the central heating.

She can't see the expressions on their faces because they are wearing black balaclavas. They have black sashes over their hessian tunics, with the Daesh insignia in white; in this production, the witches are terrorists radicalizing Macbeth.

It was Rafi who asked for them to be called Daesh, the pejorative for Islamic State. She doesn't know if it was Rafi who had the idea that this was a play about radicalization; a group had come to Daphne with it, excited by the idea. She'd thought it was fantastic. The witches lure Macbeth in and start the corruption of a man into somebody evil. The murders won't happen for a while yet, all the witches are doing here is planning to meet Macbeth upon the heath, a seventeenth-century dark web.

Dear God, what if the gunmen actually are Daesh terrorists? And storm in here and see themselves shown as witches? Being portrayed as weird sisters won't go down well with Daesh.

Oh for heaven's sakes, be rational, Daphne. Why would terrorists attack their non-religious school in the middle of the countryside?

But someone wicked has. Someone has shot Matthew Marr and is terrifying the children and staff in Old School.

On stage the three girls start the play, shakily at first but gradually sounding less afraid, the nursery-rhyme rhythm of the opening familiar and calming, as if by performing the words and actions they've rehearsed they can find a safe space.

Was the man who shot Matthew a good man once? If so, how was he corrupted? She wants to know what they are up against; the evil they have to contend with.

Rafi told her once that for him it isn't Macbeth and Lady Macbeth who are the frightening characters, but First Murderer, Second Murderer, Third Murderer, men without names; unknown killers in the darkness.

PART TWO

To think of time – of all that retrospection,
To think of to-day, and the ages continued henceforward.

Walt Whitman, *Leaves of Grass* (1855)

8.

9.38 a.m.

Three miles from the school a helicopter lands on a snow-covered field. It is fifty-three minutes since a gunman fired at the local police officer as he drove towards the school; twenty-two minutes since the head teacher was shot.

Detective Inspector Rose Polstein gets out of the helicopter, running under the still-spinning blades, snow whirling around her, slapping her face, billowing her dress and hair, stinging her ears. Before she gets into the waiting Land Rover Discovery, she's sick, attributing nausea to the bucking helicopter journey and morning sickness, not nerves. She puts a mint into her mouth and gets inside the vehicle. Simon Letwynd, working for Bronze Commander, drives her towards the command and control centre near to the school, set up a few minutes ago. She and Letwynd have never met each other. Snow scuds against the windscreen, tyres only just gripping.

In a major incident, command is structured into bronze, silver and gold tiers, with roles allocated by task not rank. Rose thinks the impersonal metallic system is not only practical but helps foster a sense of rational order being imposed over something chaotic; hard metals a bulwark against unknowable extremes.

'How many children and staff are still in the school?' she asks. Since getting into the chopper she's had limited communication.

'Our current information is seventy-one in three locations – Old School, the theatre and the pottery room,' Letwynd says. 'Plus one hundred and twenty junior school children, between four and ten years old, hiding under the cliffs on Fulmar beach with ten

87

adults. The beach is accessible only by the school path and by sea. High winds and snow have delayed the rescue boats. We have a helicopter flying over the beach and there's no sight of a gunman.'

Letwynd will have been briefed en route to the school as well as during the few minutes after arrival.

'Any change to the situation in Old School?' she asks.

'The gunman is still in the corridor and hasn't fired again. The head teacher is badly wounded in the library with thirteen sixth-form students. We've been unable to get medical attention to him; paramedics are standing by. There are a further twelve sixth-formers and three members of staff in a classroom further along the corridor and the deputy head, Neil Forbright, on his own in an office on the same corridor.'

'Any kids still missing?'

'Rafi Bukhari, sixteen, and Jamie Alton, seventeen.'

'What about the children in the pottery room?'

'In the middle of woodland. Pedestrian access only. Large glass windows. A class of sixteen seven-year-olds and their teacher. We have no communication with them. Armed teams are on their way to get them out.'

Rose feels sick again, winds down the window, the icy air blowing against her face although she's already shivering hard. *Take a breath, Rose, for fuck's sake. Take a breath.*

'The rest of the hostages are in the theatre,' Letwynd says. 'Twenty-two kids and two teachers.'

Rose doesn't correct him, doesn't say that they are only hostages if the gunmen want to use them as bargaining tools, if the gunmen actually have an interest in keeping them alive.

She believes an understanding of psychology is crucial in effective police work and eight years ago took time out from the police service to do a degree in psychology, followed by an MSc in investigative forensic psychology at London South Bank University, before rejoining and rising rapidly to Detective Inspector. At thirty-one years old, she's widely regarded as an exceptional police officer.

Her role in this attack is to predict what the gunmen are going to do next and help other officers find out who they are, using her expertise both as a detective and as an investigative forensic psychologist.

'The theatre has security doors and no windows,' Letwynd says. 'Safest place in the school. The vast majority of students and staff were evacuated from the New School complex, situated near to the main road. There are other outlying small buildings, but they are simply storage sheds and so forth, not occupied apart from the gatehouse, where PC Beard has taken refuge.'

'He's unharmed?'

'Yes. Just his radio damaged. He spoke to someone in Bronze Command on his mobile. He described the sound of a rifle and said it definitely came from the woods, but he didn't see the shooter and can't tell us anything more. The windows in the gatehouse are bricked up so he can't see anything. He apologized for not being able to help and said not to waste any resources on him. We'll get someone to his family when we can but we're already stretched. We've told him to stay put in the gatehouse.'

'Good.'

'The CCTV camera on the gatehouse was painted over early this morning, so even if we can get hold of the footage it won't give us anything on the shooter.'

'Do we know what kind of weapon was used to shoot the head teacher in Old School?'

'From Neil Forbright's description of the sound in the corridor, it was also a rifle.'

'We still only know of two shooters?'

'Yes, the one who was hiding in Old School and another who fired from the woods at PC Beard's car. Neil Forbright told us that the head was followed through the woods. The timings suggest this gunman shot at the police car and then followed the head. We've started searching for him using surveillance drones and helicopters but we're being hampered by snow and by press and sightseers, who've got drones in our airspace.'

'You're telling them to get the hell out of the way?'

'Less politely. I heard you trained in the States on school shootings?'

'Six months. Always had an interest.'

A horror, more like, that the same thing could happen here; and with terrorist attacks on the increase in Europe, a fear that a school would be a target.

'Anything on phones?' she asks.

'We're working with mobile phone companies, but it'll take time.'

'And vehicles?'

'We're using drones to check the school car parks for a vehicle not belonging to staff or sixth-formers.'

'Can we secure the perimeter?'

'We're attempting to, but it's huge and open.'

Her phone rings; it's Stuart Dingwall, a senior officer in the South West Counter Terrorism Intelligence Unit, a colleague who she knows well and likes.

'We'll be there in five, Stuart,' she says. 'Anything to suggest a terrorist attack?'

'Nothing that's been on our radar. My team's been speaking to evacuated teachers and to governors and the school has a robust Prevent policy; they're all certain that no students have been radicalized.'

'An outside attack?'

'I think it's a stretch but I'm not discounting it.'

'Anything more on the explosion in the woods?'

'A student saw it and informed the head and deputy head. It sounds rudimentary; a small amount of low-grade explosives. Possibly a pressure-cooker bomb, made from that article, "Make a Bomb in the Kitchen of Your Mom".'

The article came out a few years ago and gave any wannabe bomber step-by-step instructions to whip up his or her very own bomb. It could be deadly if the bomber had powerful explosives, but not in this instance.

'If it is a terrorist attack, then it's not a sophisticated one,'

Stuart continues. 'A couple of rifles, an ineffectual home-made bomb and some paint on a CCTV camera. It seems amateur.'

'Yeah, let's hope so.'

But she feels disquieted because why set off a bomb in the middle of the woods? All it did was alert the police to a possible attack. It doesn't make sense.

'Something feels off to you?' she asks Stuart.

'A little, yeah.'

'We're almost there.'

Through the driving snow, she sees mast-mounted infra-red CCTV cameras and antennae sticking up from police mobile command and control vehicles. They are parked next to rapid response paramedic vehicles, behind them cars and vans belonging to armed police and counterterrorism. The emergency vehicles have arrived recently, no snow yet accumulated on their roofs and windscreens.

The emergency drills are paying off in this impressively fast deployment and Rose realizes that the drills are as much about the logistics, how to implement an as-fast-as-humanly-possible response, as about what to do once they're there.

'Relatives are at a leisure centre five miles away. We have two police officers with them,' Letwynd says.

He parks the Discovery and she gets out. 'You left in a hurry?' he says, noticing now that she's wearing a dress without a coat. Because her coat, gloves and scarf are all on a chair in St Michael's hospital maternity department. There was a 'Turn Off Your Mobile' rule, which she'd obeyed, but kept her pager on – nothing about pagers in the rules –

School attack. A chopper waiting.

Too urgent and too warm in the hospital to stop and think about her coat; bloody freezing now.

There are three mobile command and control vehicles next to each other, each with an on-board generator for power, able to

91

receive and view footage from remote deployable static cameras, body-worn cameras, helicopters and UAVs. They have advanced communication systems for instant sharing of data and video.

The briefing is being held in the first vehicle, occupied by Bronze Command, then Rose and her team will occupy the one on the left-hand side. She guesses the third is for the heads of armed units or counterterrorism, perhaps both.

While Gold Commander is in overall command and sets the strategy (basically: rescue the kids and staff, arrest the perpetrators, secure and preserve evidence) and Silver Commander is the tactical adviser on how to achieve that, it is down to Bronze Commander to actually implement the plan. Gold Commander and Silver Commander are both off site, but Bronze Commander is the person on the ground and has been assigned officers, including armed officers and specialists.

As Rose hurriedly walks with Letwynd, she passes the Trojans – BMW SUVs with yellow stickers marking them as armed response vehicles. She can feel the heat from their still-warm engines. Nobody's inside, their gun safes emptied of Glock pistols, Heckler & Koch assault carbines and SIG Sauer automatic rifles.

'They're doing a dress rehearsal of *Macbeth*, apparently, the kids in the theatre,' Letwynd says.

'You're kidding?'

'No.'

'How fucking amazing is that?'

She wonders for a moment how many stories are playing out here simultaneously, connected by time and place.

A middle-aged black woman, who's also hurrying towards the command and control vehicles, holds out her hand.

'Dannisha Taylor, hostage and crisis negotiator,' she says. Rose takes her hand, notices its warmth and strength.

'DI Rose Polstein.'

Rose opens the door of Bronze Command's command and control vehicle and they go in.

★

It's almost as cold as outside, snow tracked across the floor. Computer systems are being set up, two screens already operational, the vehicle crowded. Bronze Commander, a man in his fifties with red hair and florid face, sweating despite the freezing weather, is pinning a large plan of Old School up on the wall. Rose, like virtually every other officer, has never met him, doesn't know his name, but he'll be referred to by everyone as Bronze Commander, keeping things as simple as possible. He points at the plan of Old School.

'He's in a long interior corridor with an L-shaped bend. There are no windows or skylights and no other access short of digging a bloody tunnel to him. So no way to mount a surprise attack. If we attempt to storm the Old School building, he will have time to open fire before we take him out.'

So that's why he chose Old School, Rose thinks, rather than New School which had many more students and staff, because he could seal himself and his captives away from both the road and escape, and from the police.

'Given these facts,' Bronze Commander says, his hand slapping the plan of Old School on the wall, as if angry with the layout, 'we only go in if he starts firing.'

A young woman staring at a monitor, wearing a headset under a hijab, puts a hand up to request silence and everyone falls quiet.

'UAV's picked up the second gunman,' she says.

They cluster round her screen. The picture from the police drone, a UAV, starts fuzzy, snow falling and branches of a tree obscuring part of the image, but she adjusts the digital zoom and the image becomes clearer: a man in army combat fatigues, his face hidden under a black balaclava, pointing a gun. She moves closer in towards the gun; stills will be taken and blown up later, but even at this distance it's clearly a semi-automatic. The gun is braced against his right shoulder, a finger on the trigger. Ammunition belts are looped around him.

'Move the drone out,' Letwynd says.

'Jesus,' someone whispers.

In front of the gunman is an old brick building with large windows. The pottery room. Half a row of what look like clay tiles have been formed at the bottom of the windows. Someone's hands are putting in more tiles, crouched down so you can't see a face. The tiles are protection, Rose realizes, the teacher is trying to protect them. The gunman is standing ten feet or so from the pottery room, his semi-automatic trained at the windows and their soft clay tiles.

For a few seconds, there is silence in the crowded vehicle; the air seems to alter, to grow damp and heavy.

'The children aren't visible, they are probably crouched down, perhaps underneath tables,' Bronze Commander says, 'but he's tall and his weapon is powerful. With that trajectory, he can kill them from where he's standing. We must now assume that the gunman in Old School also has a semi-automatic.'

Rose thinks that the original rifle shots were a deliberate misdirection, so that they wouldn't see this was a more sophisticated and brutal attack.

'Two messages have just been received by the BBC,' an officer says. 'First message, if they see police they will shoot the children. Second message, if anybody tries to escape they will be shot.'

Rose hears orders being given to armed officers on the ground to pull back; to wait.

'How will they see us? Surveillance drone?' Letwynd asks.

'Probably,' Bronze Commander says. 'There are still numerous drones above the school, which could belong to the press or sightseers, but the attackers may also have one up there. We need to clear them. At present, our snipers are too far away from the pottery room and visibility is too poor to take him out cleanly. We risk wounding him before killing him and if he puts any pressure on the trigger he can inflict multiple civilian casualties. It would also tip off his pal in Old School, who'd open fire too. Until the drones are down we cannot risk going any closer; not unless we have no other option. Detective Inspector Polstein, what's your opinion?'

94

Jesus, is that all the time she has? Fuck.

'This is on the fly, with little to go on,' Rose says.

'Your best guess?' Bronze Commander says.

Get it together, Rose. Focus.

She separates herself mentally from the noise and activity, her brain finding its space for concentration, emotions pushed aside. In the US, she'd spoken to people who'd been involved in school attacks, including local law enforcement officers, FBI officers, students, teachers and psychologists. But none of those attacks, on the face of it, were anything like this one.

'This is not a typical school shooting, when shooters go on the rampage from the off, killing as many as possible,' she says. 'They have only shot at two people, both of whom are adults, and significantly haven't fired again after shooting the head teacher. There are two interpretations of this. The first is that they want to enter into negotiation, which means they are prepared to release the children. If this is the case, they may have demands that they want to make, probably using the BBC, as they have phoned a warning message to them. The second interpretation is that they want us to think exactly what I just outlined, and are playing for maximum airtime.'

'Publicity?' Bronze Commander asks.

'Yes. They want this story playing out live, everyone glued to their TVs and tablets and phones, with the shooters as the stars of the event. They want to be trending on Twitter and TV programmes interrupted with updates. The longer this goes on, the bigger the audience. Any attack that is unfolding live attracts very large numbers.'

'And when their audience is big enough?' an officer says.

'We hope they make demands and don't start a televised tweeted killing spree?' Bronze Commander says and Rose nods.

'The two adults they've shot at are both figures of authority,' she says. 'A police officer and a head teacher. I know that we're already investigating anyone who has a personal grudge against the school, but it's also possible that these authority figures may represent something – a political system, a religion, a country even.'

'So, a terrorist attack?' Bronze Commander asks.

'It's a possibility, yes.'

There really should be a different noun to *terrorist*, she thinks, especially when they attack children; *inadequate cowards* springs to mind. Evil bastards too, of course, but also cowards. At moments like this she realizes that she really went for her job out of rage.

'I think that one of the gunmen is highly manipulative and if we do negotiate he will attempt to play us,' she says. 'We've seen that with the misdirect of using rifles when they have semi-automatics.'

'One of the gunmen?' Bronze Commander asks.

'It's unlikely there would be two manipulative people working together – one would be dominant, the other subordinate. Even if it's a terrorist attack with a defined goal, we cannot treat the gunmen as a single unit.'

Dannisha Taylor, lead hostage and crisis negotiator, joins the discussion. 'I agree with Detective Inspector Polstein. Their personalities and individual motivations will be different, and they'll need different negotiating tactics. But it will be difficult to establish a communication channel.'

A priority for the tech teams, working with mobile companies, is to get the gunmen's mobile phone numbers and any other comms data.

Rose studies the gunman outside the pottery room. His build is obscured by the webbing and weapon, he could be scrawny or muscular, slim or heavy, impossible to tell; his face is obscured by the black balaclava, just his eyes showing through the slits in the fabric. She remembers a description from *Macbeth* which she did at school many moons ago, 'false face'.

'If they have a surveillance drone watching us, who's flying it?' an officer asks.

'The gunman in Old School?' Letwynd suggests. 'No one knows what he's doing in the corridor.'

'And the gunman outside the pottery room could have an earpiece under his balaclava,' another officer says. 'For a mobile or walkie-talkie.'

'I'd guess at a two-way digital radio, harder for us to monitor,' Bronze Commander says. 'There may be more gunmen, but these two bastards haven't been shy about being seen so I'm hopeful that there aren't. The weather's set to get worse, a storm's moving our way and visibility may well become atrocious, so we hunt as hard as we can now.'

Alongside the physical search of the school by police surveillance drones and helicopters, counterterrorism units are monitoring internet chatter and they are getting info on all mobiles operating within the school campus.

'Will they react to seeing a helicopter?' an officer asks.

'They know they can't be taken out by a helicopter,' Bronze Commander says, 'nor can children be rescued, unless it lands. So they won't be bothered by a helicopter.'

'What about PC Beard? Does this change anything for him?' another officer asks.

'No. As far as we know there's no gunman anywhere near him,' Bronze Commander says. 'And the gatehouse is secure. He should stay put.'

Rose turns to the three police officers who have been assigned to her from different divisions in Avon and Somerset Constabulary, an area covering almost five thousand square kilometres, including Bristol where Rose is based. None of them have met before nor worked in the school's area. She managed to speak to them briefly en route.

'Are we getting anything on number plates?'

'Trying to with UAVs,' DS Thandie Simmonds says. 'But most of the plates are obscured by snow.'

'Tell them to try and get partials. And we need to look at cars

97

parked within a mile; but no one goes close. Columbine shooters booby-trapped their cars. And I want to know everything we
get on that message to the BBC.'

'If either gunman starts shooting, we go in,' Bronze Commander says. 'Until then we try every option to avoid civilian
casualties.'

★   ★   ★

In the pottery room, the children are underneath the eight
tables that sixty-year-old Camille Giraud pushed together. She's
given them each a fat chunk of clay and they're making cups and
bowls for their house while Camille makes clay tiles to stop flying glass. The children in their house haven't seen the gunman.

The first row of clay tiles are stuck to the wooden window
frame and if she moulds the next row just right they should stick
to the first row. She's been crouching down but now she needs
to stand because otherwise she can't reach to do the tiles. She
unbends, her knees clicking. As she stands she sees the man in
the balaclava through the window, pointing his gun at her. She
pushes the clay tiles against the window, not looking at the
man's eyes in the slits in the balaclava, but instead remembering
Jemima; how beautiful she'd been. Her smile. It was her smile
that was beautiful, so completely artless, so unaware of its
power; dazzlingly lovely. And meant for her. That was the miracle of loving Jemima. That this woman had loved her back. And
not because Jemima had a husband, although she had, but
because anybody loving Camille was surprising to Camille and
that Jemima did was something she daily didn't believe. The
man in the balaclava shifts his gun, as if feeling the heft of it; it's
pointing pretty much at her mouth.

Up until now, she didn't mind the idea of dying at all. If there
was a heaven, an afterlife, which Jemima believed in, then they'd
be reunited. She'd imagined Elysian fields. Or their first kiss,
played over and over, the joy of it repeating. But it would be too

98

much. She'd need to take a quiet calm walk in those Elysian fields, which hopefully would be English like Jemima, with bluebells and cabbage whites, and then return to Jemima's kiss. And then she'd imagined just reliving the bits she loved and misses the most now, tea in bed together, the feel of her softly warm against her back when she woke up, the smell of Jemima's perfume as she came in through the front door; the sound of her voice saying Camille's name with more love and affection than either of her parents had ever used. And if there weren't any Elysian fields, a heaven, an afterlife, then that would be okay too because she wouldn't have to buckle under the weight of grief any more; the loss would stop eating at her. She wouldn't have to hold it together all day until she could get into the house and crumple next to the front door, arms round her knees.

But the children.

Clearly, obviously, they have to live and that means she must too, because it's up to her to keep them safe.

She bends down under the tables. 'Do you think your house should have pets?' she asks, giving them each more clay.

The children will not die. That simply cannot happen. And she will make sure they're not afraid.

9.

9.49 a.m.

Neil Forbright, the deputy head, stands at the locked door of the headmaster's office. The fire has gone out in the grate and the large Victorian room is cold as well as dark. An email comes in on his phone from Frank in the library, sent to him and Jacintha: Matthew is still conscious. He's only realized today that Matthew is like a father to him, that he relies on his kindness and belief in him. His actual father would say Neil looks for a top dog, because he is not. His father believes that humans are pack animals. For a moment, he thinks absurdly about Elsie, his elderly Labrador rescued from the pound, and wonders who'll feed her and let her out this evening.

His phone rings. 'Mr Forbright? It's PC Beard.'

'Do you know if the children in the pottery room are safe? If—'

'Sorry, I'm still stuck here in your gatehouse and don't know anything, but the high-powered lot running this will be doing everything they can to help them. Your school secretary, Tonya, told me your head teacher was shot?'

'Yes.'

'And the gunman, he's still in the corridor?'

'Yes.'

'I've been to your school before with my wife, watched your plays when you open them up to the public. *Les Mis*, last year. Point is, I've been in your theatre and it's very secure. So we need to get you all to the theatre.'

'It's not possible.'

'Can you describe how you'd normally get to the theatre?'

'It's really not possible.'

'Please, can you just tell me?'

He's clearly not going to give up.

'To the left of Matthew's office, the end of our corridor has doors, and they open on to a glass corridor which goes to the theatre.'

'Matthew's office is where you are?'

'Yes.'

'And what about Tonya? She said she's in Old School.'

'Yes, in Jacintha's classroom. It's to the right of Matthew's office.'

'How many other people are in Jackie's classroom?'

'Jacintha.'

It's important Jacintha's name is said properly because if she dies, then the last few times people speak her name they have to use the right one, the one that she is loved by. At the moment, her A-level English class are reading poems, the beautiful ones, she says, that are soothing in cadence and imagery; and for a short while she'd put her phone on speaker and he'd listened to her reading aloud:

'I know a bank where the wild thyme blows,
Where oxlips and the nodding violet grows,
Quite over-canopied with luscious woodbine . . .'

He can see how poetry might help. His thoughts are daisy-chaining, one to the next, to get away from the gunman in the corridor; mindfulness, which he's been told to practise, is the opposite of daisy-chaining and is about physically inhabiting the present moment, actually remarkably easy to do with a gunman outside your door; every hair on your arm, every breath, every sound and smell is magnified and it's appalling, hateful, shocking, and he'd rather daisy-chain to Jacintha's bank of wild thyme for a little while, for a reprieve. *Be a man*, his father says to him.

And all this takes place inside his head in a second, his thoughts absurdly fast, not daisy chains but fibre optics, because that's the other thing that happens when you're in a building with a gunman, time changes, so that your inner self moves too quickly, an insect trapped in a jar, frantically battering wings against the glass.

'There's twelve sixth-form students and three members of staff,' he says. 'Tonya, Jacintha and Donna, the school receptionist.'

'And the head teacher is in the library?'

'Yes. With thirteen teenagers.'

'And the library is where exactly?'

'The other side of the corridor, opposite Matthew's office, Tonya's office and Jacintha's classroom, running almost the whole length of our part of the corridor.'

'That's everyone?'

'Yes.'

'Righty-ho, I'll let you know when I've got a plan to get you all out.'

He hangs up. *Righty-ho*, he actually said that, and for a moment Neil thinks of the photos of the boy soldiers and imagines PC Beard rowing a little boat to the beaches of Dunkirk; a leaky bathtub, because there's not a snowball in hell's chance of getting to the safety of the theatre.

He listens to the footsteps again; they are outside the library and coming back towards him. When his phone rings, he thinks it's PC Beard again, back with more nonsensical optimism, but it's a woman's voice, young and serious, part of the 'high-powered lot', he guesses.

'Mr Forbright? My name's Detective Inspector Rose Polstein.'

'Are the children in the pottery room safe?'

He thinks there's a pause before she speaks, a fumbling.

'We are doing everything we can,' she says.

'And junior school?'

'Boats are on their way, we'll evacuate them as quickly as we can.'

'What about Rafi Bukhari and Jamie Alton?'

Lorrimer had phoned Tonya from Fulmar beach, his voice chastened, to pass on the information that Rafi had left. It was just before Matthew was shot and he's glad that Matthew doesn't know.

'I'm afraid we don't yet know the whereabouts of either boy,' Rose says. 'Has the school received any threats?'

PC Beard hadn't asked about who might be doing this, just focused on his nonsensical plan to rescue them; he likes PC Beard for that.

'No, at least none that I've been told about,' he says. 'But I've been away, off sick. I'm sorry.'

His catch-up meeting with Matthew had barely begun when Rafi phoned from Junior School.

'Do you think it's possible the school, or a person in the school, could be a target for terrorists?'

He wants to think the question ludicrous – but what would Daesh make of him? They'd stoned gay men to death in Raqqa and thrown them off buildings; beheaded women for not covering themselves top to toe. He has gay and lesbian colleagues who are married, a transgender student, and no one bats an eye, that's the thing, nobody bats an eye and girls can wear miniskirts and boys a tutu if that's what they want, because what you wear doesn't matter, it is you who matters.

And they're in the middle of woodland without even a proper fence; so an easy target.

'You told a police officer earlier that you don't believe any of your students have been radicalized?' Rose Polstein says.

'No. We have safe spaces for debate, democracy in action through the school council, everything that's required; but tolerance is an integral part of the school. It's why we don't have a uniform here and the students are free to practise whatever religion they choose, or none. We have no head boy or girl and no prefects; every member of the school is equally valued and the children are respected by the staff as well as the other way round. We foster tolerance and mutual respect from Reception through to our sixth form.'

He looks at Frank's email on his phone.

Mr Marr is still conscious. We are all ok. We have barricaded the door with books.

He thinks of the kids in the theatre rehearsing *Macbeth*; Jacintha and her class reading poetry. They have clearly also fostered courage. He wants to say that he is extraordinarily proud of them, but how will that be helpful?

'Do you check what students are doing on the net?' Rose Polstein asks.

'We get alerts if anyone visits an inappropriate site but most of them have 4G and when they get home we can't keep an eye on them. But we have equipped them to resist extremism.'

'One of the students, Rafi Bukhari, is a refugee?'

'Yes.'

'How long has he been at the school?'

'Just over two and a half years.'

'How did he come to be here?'

'Matthew, the head, met him and his brother at the Dunkirk migrant camp, they were unaccompanied vulnerable children. There was a huge amount of red tape, lots of barriers, but Matthew managed to bring them here.'

Matthew had gone as a volunteer teacher to the Dunkirk camp for the Christmas holidays and then spent months waging a one-man campaign against bureaucracy to get Rafi and Basi to England; sponsoring them himself, finding foster parents, getting them a bursary to come to this school; feeling guilt for the unaccompanied children he'd had to leave behind. Neil has sometimes suspected Matthew just hid the boys in his boot and drove them here himself.

'The Bukhari brothers are from Syria?'

'Yes.'

'They're Muslims?'

Neil thinks these questions are suggesting something ugly.

'It was Rafi who knew what the bomb was and warned us, nobody else had a clue. He made sure the juniors were evacuated.

He and his brother came to England because their father and older brother were murdered; they wanted to be safe.'

Outside his door, the footsteps are coming closer, as if they have followed Rafi and Basi here, the terror they fled.

'Poor boys,' Rose Polstein says and her tone is softer; she must've had to check.

'Do you know why Rafi left the beach?'

'Probably to make sure his girlfriend was okay.'

⋆   ⋆   ⋆

Rose thinks for a moment about Rafi Bukhari, evacuating Junior School then coming back to make sure his girlfriend was all right. Stupid bloody boy; stupid bloody brave boy.

She is now in her own command and control vehicle with her team of three: Detective Sergeant Thandie Simmonds, a black woman who's young to be a DS; quietly spoken Detective Sergeant Amaal Ayari; and Detective Constable George Hail, the most junior member of the team. She would have liked time for proper introductions, a bonding cup of coffee, but they are getting to know each other on the hoof. Young DC George Hail looks nauseous, his freckles vivid against pallid skin, and she hopes he isn't horribly out of his depth. Their job is to liaise with other officers and feed back to Rose, as well as endeavouring to collect any information she asks for.

Her conversation with Neil Forbright is on speakerphone so that they can quickly share and follow up any new leads.

'I need to ask you about people who may have a personal grudge against the school,' Rose says. She has a list of names that Neil has already given the police, and they are being investigated by other officers, but she wants to check for herself.

'What can you tell me about Mark Henley?'

She expects Neil to tell her he's said all this before, but to his credit he doesn't.

'Mark was a maths teacher here; he shouted at the kids,

belittled them by reading out test results, that kind of thing. Didn't fit the ethos of the school. He was sent on a retraining course but his behaviour deteriorated.'

'And after that he was fired?'

'Yes.'

'A year ago?'

'Yes. He stopped teaching after that, went into business, I think.'

'What about Jed Soames?'

'A PE teacher. He flirted with a girl in Year Thirteen and secretly asked her out. One of her friends came to me. He resigned before he was fired but we wouldn't supply a reference. She was eighteen, so a grey area legally but not morally. That was nearly two years ago now.'

'What was his reaction to not getting a reference?'

'He tried to sue, sent Matthew and some of the governors abusive emails, but then he stopped the legal proceedings. I don't know why.'

'There've been three students expelled in the last five years?' she asks.

'Yes. Simon Shawcross, Victor Deakin and Malin Cohen. Simon was found dealing Spice eighteen months ago. We give second chances to users of drugs, but not dealing. We reported him to the police.'

'And Malin Cohen?' Other teachers have told the police about Malin's aggression; Malin Cohen is the one name that's been put forward, reluctantly, but put forward all the same.

'He was expelled a year ago for attempting to punch a pregnant teacher. A student grabbed him in time. It was an immediate expulsion. Malin has always had behavioural issues but Matthew tries to see the best in a young person, give them a chance to redeem themselves.'

'How did Malin react to being expelled?'

'He became uncontrollable. We had to have three male members of staff escort him off the premises, threaten him with the police. Hold on a minute.'

'Are you okay? Mr Forbright . . .?'

'He's outside again, right outside the door.'

Rose presses the receiver to her ear to block out the other sounds around her. Neil Forbright must be holding the phone away from him, because she can hear a clicking sound. Footsteps, she thinks. She has a sudden glimpse into what it is like to be on your own, a gunman's footsteps just the other side of a door. She admires Neil's calm, his quiet courage.

'Those are the gunman's footsteps?'

'Yes.'

'Can you tell me about them?'

'He just walks up and down this length of corridor, apart from when he has a cigarette break and then he sits right up against the library door; the kids in the library could smell the smoke. Does that tell you anything?'

'Possibly, yes.'

She can't share most of the information she has, but she will talk to him about the footsteps, because she thinks he's owed that at least and because he might help build a profile.

'I think that he's either deliberately trying to intimidate you—' she says.

'Because we are less likely to fight back?'

Oh Jesus, please don't let them fight back. There might have been a chance for some of them against a rifle but not against a semi-automatic.

'You really mustn't attempt anything yourselves, do you understand, Mr Forbright? We don't know what weapons he has.'

'Right . . . And the other reason?' Neil asks.

'It could be that he gets bored easily, he's walking up and down to keep moving, to keep himself psyched.'

'That helps actually. Makes him seem less in control.'

'What can you tell me about Victor Deakin?' she asks; the last in the list of expelled students.

'Victor joined the school in Year Eleven and was expelled just over seven months ago.'

'Why was he expelled?'

'I don't know, I was off sick again at the time; depression. I'm sorry.'

'Did Mr Marr say anything to you about it?'

'Just that he'd left. If it wasn't an ongoing issue, then he wouldn't have bothered me with it. Matthew tries to take as much off my plate as he can. But Victor wouldn't have minded being expelled. It was his parents who made him stay here after GCSEs, Victor wanted to go to college. He felt he was being infantilized, his words. He didn't want to be here. Hold on . . .'

Neil Forbright must be holding the receiver a little way from his ear again, because she can just make out the footsteps.

'Mr Forbright . . .?'

'I'd forgotten. Earlier, I heard footsteps going down the corridor, not just our stretch, but further, all the way to the front door. The only time they've gone that far. But I don't think they were the same as these, I think they were lighter. I heard the front door. It's heavy, makes a clang. Then footsteps came back and I think they were heavier.'

'They swapped over?'

'I think so, yes.'

'When was this?'

'Just after Matthew was shot.'

'Thank you, Mr Forbright, you've been very helpful. Let me know if there's anything else you think of.'

She ends the call.

'The BBC warning was from a burner phone,' DS Thandie Simmonds says. 'Not traceable. The tech guys say he must have removed the battery. They're trying to find the last position it was used.'

'Anything on the voice?' Rose asks.

'He used a voice-changer app. They've got some background sounds that they're working on.'

'Thanks, Thandie.' She turns to DS Ayari. 'Amaal, can you look into the significance of today's date?'

She's using their first names to create intimacy because in this high-pressure situation they need to feel a personal relationship with one another to function best as a team.

'Look out for anything a terrorist would ring in his diary,' she continues to Amaal. 'Anniversaries, religious holidays, birth dates of martyrs and leaders, and the number – day, month and year, both ways, American and English.'

The cowardly inadequate bastards do so love their special dates.

★　★　★

The wind makes the bolt on the shed door do shivery rattling and the dark creak. The eight-year-old boy is shuddering with cold, his knees knocking into his chin as he huddles; his fingers are numb. There's a keyhole in the shed door with no key and a little bit of light like a magic wand comes through it.

The smell of the shed presses against his face, the rotting smell, but he can smell poo too, so an animal's in here. He loves all animals, even the ones most people don't, like rats. Maybe there's a rat in the shed and they will become friends and he'll take him with him in his pocket, like in the *Indian in the Cupboard* book, and no one will even know he's there and he'll feed him bits of cheese at lunchtime.

He thinks he hears a scrabble in the darkness. 'Ratty?' he says quietly, in case the man is listening outside. 'The man can't hurt us. I've bolted the door.'

He turns on his phone and shines his screen around the shed but he can't see a rat; he's probably shy and hiding. He has 7% charge. His phone animals haven't been fed for ages and they'll be really hungry so he'll just quickly feed them, it'll only take a tiny bit of charge. And then he must turn off his phone and be brave as a Barbary lion, as a Bengal tiger, as Sir Lancelot and the little mouse in *The Gruffalo*.

★　★　★

In the leisure centre cafeteria, Beth Alton has texted Zac five times but he hasn't heard from Jamie. Her phone keeps ringing and each time she jolts with hope but it's Mike or Theo or her parents, and she quickly answers because leaving it ringing means it's engaged for Jamie; she speaks for just a few seconds then hangs up. She holds her phone tightly, as if it is Jamie's hand.

The smell of old coffee and burgers is getting stronger as the room heats up. She wishes there was a window. She doesn't even know if it's still snowing; totally separated from Jamie.

More parents of the trapped children have joined them, but the noise level remains almost mute. Two journalists tried to blend in with arriving parents but were spotted immediately by the police officers; although the right age, the journalists' bodies were too relaxed, their walk too easy, their faces too healthy. They were hustled out and since then a police officer has stood guard by the doors.

At the tables, the parents are isolated units; a brief exchange of information or sympathy, that's all; even couples, pressed against one another, seem locked into this separateness.

The stillness in the large room, the terrible inertia, is broken by the young man – Steve, Beth has discovered, the fiancé of a junior school teacher, Chloe Price – who's pacing fast up and down between the tables. She thinks of Jamie hiding on his own, and wishes there was someone who loved him and he could think of her and feel less alone, less afraid. And it can't be her; she's not enough, just his mum. He needs magical teenage romantic love and he had that once, but lost it, and that will make this even harder for him. And she shouldn't even know about it; she has no right to know about it.

There's something I have to tell you, Jamie.

Sounds ominous . . .

I found your diary.

You must have looked pretty hard.

I was changing your bedclothes.

Under the mattress?

I lift the mattress up so that the bottom sheet is good and tight, more comfy.

For God's sake, Mum. I told you to leave my room alone, that I can change my own bedding. Did you read it?

I'm sorry.

You had no right.

I know.

Fucking hell, Mum.

I know, there's no excuse, I know that, but I could tell you were unhappy. And I kept asking you but you kept just saying you were okay.

She'd thought if she just knew what was making Jamie unhappy she could lead the conversation into the right area and he'd confide in her.

In his diary, she'd read about his romance with Antonella, pages covered in beautiful drawings of a girl's face, often just her blue eyes with long black lashes, and poems written alongside the drawings. He's always loved to draw, not cars and dinosaurs like other little boys, but multicoloured intricate flowers and randomly coloured rainbows and then a girl's beautiful blue eyes. And then, after three months of drawings, 'It's over' in biro, his anguish clear in the jerky writing.

Theo hadn't talked to her about girlfriends but he wasn't vulnerable like Jamie, probably treating the girls badly rather than the other way round. And a little part of her was glad that she could help Jamie.

But whenever she attempted to talk about relationships his head had just bent lower, shoulders hunching towards her, and he'd found an excuse to leave the room.

Once she'd been able to make it better for him – giving a hug, reading a story and witch-hazel on bruises. But the terrible thing about your teenager being unhappy was that he doesn't want your help and however much you love him, show him you love him, it just doesn't make that much difference.

Can you say something? Jamie?

You've already read all about it so what's there to say?

I really am sorry.

All those hinty conversations about girls.

Yes.

She hears him give a quiet laugh, resigned, and she's forgiven.

He'd use the word *hinty*, would laugh like that, would forgive her. She's known him since he was a few moments old, the time it took the midwife to hand him to her, and she knows what he would say to her.

Around her, parents are starting to talk to one another; tendrils of conversation branch outwards, so that groups at a table are talking and now a subject is seized upon – Who's doing this?

Beth can't think who would do this, but people are pitching in, some searching on their phones and iPads and laptops.

'News sites are saying it might be a terrorist attack.'

Maybe they think if they understand what's happening they are somehow less powerless to help their children.

'Islamic State.'

'That's what they're saying on Twitter too; that it's an Islamist terror attack. Thousands of people are tweeting that.'

Their skin prickles with the words, sweat between shoulder blades, a terror under the conversation.

'But why would ISIS come here?' a mother asks, because they are just becoming more frightened, seeing their children in greater, unimaginable danger.

'On the news, they're asking about the school's Prevent policy,' a father says. 'Look . . .'

He turns his laptop to the room. On *Sky News*, the anchor is talking to a counterterrorism expert: 'Cliff Heights School, like every school, has to have a Prevent policy by law . . .'

'He's saying it's kids at the school doing this,' the father says.

And this is less frightening than ISIS terrorists with machetes and guns, posting beheadings on the internet, who speak a different language, who cannot understand English and their English children.

'The terrorists are kids at our school?'

'That's what he's implying. Yes.'

'What difference does it make?' a mother says. 'Matthew Marr's been shot and the gunman might shoot children in Old School and there are junior school children hiding for their lives.'

And she's right, they all know she's right, and can no longer believe radicalized students are any less frightening.

'They mean those Muslim brothers, don't they?' another mother asks.

'The refugees?'

'We don't know anything, we don't know—'

'Who made sure they were refugees?'

'Was any kind of check done on them? To prove who they say they are?'

Beth thinks that the cafeteria is becoming ugly, fear peeling away their clothes and skin, exposing something that should be hidden. Most of the parents had welcomed the refugee brothers, cleared out cupboards for clothes for them, donated books and toys for the younger one, held raffles to raise money. She's shy in a crowd, not as confident as the other mothers, but she has to say something now because this isn't right.

'Those boys wouldn't hurt anyone,' she says, but her voice isn't strong enough to be heard, as if every part of her is diminished, but she carries on, 'We shouldn't blame two children who—'

'What about the Parsons Green tube attack?' a father says, interrupting. 'The attacker was in foster care, just like the Bukhari brothers.'

'Are the foster parents here?' a mother says. 'Anyone? Is anyone here foster parents to the Bukharis?'

A moment of silence in the cafeteria.

'I think they were planning on seeing their daughter in Cardiff,' a woman says. 'The mother said something about it last week at a coffee morning.'

They might not even know yet, Beth thinks, but once they do they'll hurry back, terrified as all the parents here are terrified. Mike is still on the train, slow because of the snow.

A woman in sportswear holds her iPad up to Beth.

'Islamic State train teenagers then send them over here, pretending to be refugees; a *Trojan Horse*, that's what they're called. I'm sorry if you find that hard to believe.' So she did hear Beth earlier in her quiet attempt to stand up for the boys.

'You're *researching* this nonsense?' Hannah's father says, appalled. 'As if those poor boys haven't been through enough.' Beth likes him for it.

'The older one is sixteen. More than old enough to be a terrorist,' the mother in sportswear says. 'And the other one isn't too young,' she continues, her finger on her iPad. 'They have taught *five-year-olds* to be terrorists.'

'Oh, balderdash,' Hannah's father says. 'Rafi and Basi ran away from terror. Most of their family was murdered. They just want to be safe.'

'Your daughter is the older boy's girlfriend, isn't that right?' a woman asks.

'Yes, she is,' Hannah's father says. 'And I didn't like that, not one bit, I'll admit that because what father likes his daughter having a boyfriend, if we fathers are honest? But if it has to be someone, I'm glad it's Rafi, and that's what I'm going to tell her. When this is over.'

'So, she's safe, your daughter, then, he's not going to shoot her, is he?'

'My daughter's in a class with Rafi and she likes him,' another father says. 'So, I don't think it's those boys. But it could be *connected* to them. ISIS or ISIL or Islamic State, whatever the hell they're called, they could've found out that the school took them in and now our children are being punished. Like a country who takes in refugees, it makes you a target.'

'But how would ISIS even know?' a mother asks.

'There was that article in the local paper, wasn't there? When Matthew Marr went to the Dunkirk camp. And when the brothers came to our school.'

'And that goes online. So, they'd find out that way,' a mother says.

'And then they could've looked into the school further, found out about the smoking and drinking and sex, and they wouldn't like that.'

'None of us like that,' a father says. 'But it's what teenagers tend to get up to.'

'But ISIS punish people for unmarried sex and for drinking, don't they?' a mother asks. 'For not being modest even, for not covering up.'

'Here, nobody minds what the girls wear,' another mother says. 'I mean, in the summer, their clothes are really skimpy . . .'

'And the school has gay staff and nobody minds, but they'd mind,' a father says. 'They kill men for that.'

'We felt so pleased with ourselves, didn't we?' a mother says. 'For choosing this school. For our liberal values.'

'Always said that lax was the word for it,' a suited father says. Next to him, a much younger woman in jeans, second marriage, Beth guesses, puts her hand on his arm but he continues. 'Girls in ridiculously short skirts, boys in whatever they like too, transgender and gays all at the school. In your face. It would antagonize them.' His young wife tries to intervene, but he shakes her arm away from him. 'If the school had made them obey a few rules of normal decency, Charlotte would be safe.'

★   ★   ★

In the theatre, despite the kids' faces being camouflaged in case they have to hide in a hurry, and the gunman being only a few hundred metres away, they are miraculously rehearsing. And yes, lines are being fluffed, cues are missed, but it's as if the kids are holding on to this one strand of continuing normality with Daphne prompting and encouraging and keeping the rehearsal on track.

Sally-Anne is still at her place by the foyer doors, standing guardian with her nail gun, in case everyone in Old School can run down the corridor to safety; as if that is still possible.

The actors are starting tedious dialogue about Norwegians but Daphne's grateful for tedious Norwegians and dreads the violence that's coming. Why hadn't she chosen a different play? A comedy. A musical. *Oliver* would be fantastic right now, all that ensemble singing and dancing, but no, she'd pushed for *Macbeth*. And not only because Rafi Bukhari had brought his father's copy from Syria but had never seen it performed – not only that, as she'd made clear to the committee deciding on the annual school production, no, not just that; she'd thought they should do this play because of its universal themes which every young person should have as part of their cultural heritage. Yes, she'd spouted all that utter claptrap. What universal themes, for heaven's sakes? Murder, tyranny, terror? Which of them, apart from Rafi and Basi, had any of those things as a theme in their lives?

Sophie, Antonella and Tracey, her three witches, are waiting in the wings. The girls have taken off their balaclavas and their sashes with Daesh insignia. It's not imaginative any more to portray the witches as Daesh terrorists because what if it is Daesh attacking the school? The girls in their sashes would be murdered first. And if the gunmen are Daesh but can't get in – the theatre's mercifully solid walls and security doors – then they don't want to imagine, more than they have to, the terror in Old School.

The three girls are waiting for Zac to hit a gong for thunder, a compromise between an inappropriately loud bang and an inadequate handclap, but Zac doesn't do anything, is just sitting there, holding his phone. Daphne claps her hands loudly and the witches go on to the stage. Sophie and Tracey are taking their cue from Antonella and no longer huddle, but are attempting to stand tall; good for you, girls.

As they begin their lines, Daphne goes to Zac at the back of the auditorium. Luisa is next to him and she can hear their argument as she approaches.

'I hadn't even noticed he wasn't here,' Zac says. 'Not till his mum phoned me the first time.'

'But why's she asking you?' Luisa asks.

'Are you all right, Zac?' Daphne asks him.

'Jamie's mum hasn't heard from him; keeps texting me in case I have.'

'But he was in the CDT room in New School,' Daphne says. 'He was evacuated.'

'No. He didn't get to New School. Nobody knows where he is.'

Daphne feels terror for Jamie.

'He'll have heard the siren,' she says, because surely he would have done, the racket it made, enough to wake the dead, he must have heard it. 'So, he did what he's meant to do, which is hide. And that's what he'll be doing now.'

'You're meant to tell,' Zac says. 'You're meant to hide then tell. He should have phoned, said he's okay.'

'Maybe he doesn't have his phone on him or it's out of charge,' Daphne says, comforting herself as much as Zac, but it's not working because she still feels terror for Jamie and guilt because she should have known this before, should have been worrying about him all this time, even if worry doesn't do any good.

'Why's Jamie suddenly your responsibility?' Luisa asks Zac. 'I mean, what are you supposed to do about it?'

Since hearing about Frank in the library Luisa has hardly spoken but it's as if possessiveness of Zac animates her.

'He was my friend,' Zac says. 'And hey, mission accomplished, he's not any more or I'd know where he is, I'd know if he's okay.'

Luisa looks startled. Zac has never called her out on it before, but Daphne had noticed the countless small slights that a couple can inflict on a former friend who isn't wanted by one of them. Jamie had been stoic and sad, just getting more anxious about his props.

'It wasn't me,' Luisa says. 'Victor was the reason you stopped hanging out. Because of that thing at the after-party at Easter.'

It astonishes Daphne that even with this happening, Luisa can think about some teenage drama at a party. Zac seems equally taken aback.

'Fuck's sake,' he says to her. 'We've got a fucking gunman in the school, Jamie's mum can't get hold of him and neither can I and you're worried about whose fault it is I'm not friends with him? About some stupid thing months ago?'

Luisa looks shocked; Zac never gets angry, never shouts. 'Victor left ages ago,' Zac continues. 'And I knew Jamester was lonely but still didn't . . . Should have been a better friend.'

'Frank hasn't emailed me for ten minutes,' Luisa says; the twin whose nerdiness used to embarrass her. They sit stiffly side by side, then Zac puts his arm around her and she leans a fraction into him.

On stage the witches continue.

FIRST WITCH   *Here I have a pilot's thumb,*
Wrecked as homeward he did come.

THIRD WITCH   *A drum, a drum;*
Macbeth doth come.

Oh hellfire, Daphne thinks, the tedious Norwegians have finished and the violence is about to start; a spreading evil that leads to children being murdered and men not being able to walk at night, and the world turning dark even in daylight.

10.

9.58 a.m.

A police surveillance drone, with a live feed to a screen in Rose Polstein's command and control vehicle, keeps watch on the gunman outside the pottery room. Their teacher is still putting in her clay tiles. It's been an hour and thirteen minutes since a gunman shot at the police car, forty-two minutes since the head teacher was shot, and no more shots have been fired. The gunman in Old School continues to walk up and down the corridor. There has been no more communication with the BBC or anyone else.

'Why aren't we just going in there and rescuing the kids?' Thandie asks. 'Why the hell aren't we doing that?' Energetic, athletic and impatient, Rose bets Thandie regularly goes to a gym and beats the hell out of a punchbag.

The answer: because the gunmen threatened to shoot the children if they see police and there are still drones above the school. They must wait until the gunmen cannot watch them from the sky and even then there are no guarantees.

Because looking at the plan of Old School, which they all have, the corridor has no windows or skylight to surprise him and take him out before he can open fire; because the windows in the library and English classroom are too small for the kids to escape through; because he almost certainly has a semi-automatic and if the police storm the building, how many will he kill?

And because the children in the pottery room have no means of escape, are corralled into a single place with large windows, and he most definitely has a semi-automatic pointed at them. The police marksmen will have to shoot a part of his brain, the medulla oblongata, so there's no involuntary muscle movement and he can't press the trigger; but the medulla oblongata is only 3 cm by 2 cm. The marksmen have to get closer, and they can't, not yet, not until they know they're not being watched.

And because the safest way for this to go would be a negotiation so that the captives are set free, unharmed.

'We have our job and we leave the armed units and everyone else to do theirs,' Rose says to her. 'We have to trust in their skills and experience; trust they know what they're doing; that's how this has to work.' Jesus, she's turned into her former boss, who was a patronizing bastard, but it's true. 'We have our own job to do,' she repeats.

In order to predict what the gunmen are going to do next, and whether they can negotiate, they need to know who the gunmen are. A list of suspects with a grudge is being winnowed down – anybody the police have been able to speak to, anyone who is definitely not at the school – and they are left with three names: Jed Soames, the disgraced former PE teacher, and the two expelled sixth-formers, Malin Cohen and Victor Deakin.

Detective Constable George Hail ends a phone call with other officers who are working off site. George is less nervous now, his round face almost pink again as he's got stuck into the job.

'Jed Soames has been found at his ex-wife's. Malin Cohen's mother said he was at work in the local café, but he's not there and hasn't shown up for the last two weeks. There's a girlfriend they're trying to track down and an incident in the States that's being checked out.'

'Thanks, George. And Victor Deakin?' Rose asks.

'He isn't at college but his first class isn't for another ten minutes. They can't get hold of his parents. His mother has a Mini convertible. There's a Mini convertible parked in Junior School car park.'

'They're making the Mini a priority?' Rose asks.

'Yes.'

But it could easily belong to a member of staff. Throw a stick at a car park and it probably hits a Mini or falls on to the convertible roof.

Police drones are photographing number plates in the school car parks and the surrounding area, but nearly all are partly or fully hidden by snow and slush; maybe they'll get lucky and get a partial match.

But the attack might not be motivated by a personal grudge. The more Rose has found out about this school, with its strikingly liberal ethos, the more she's feared it could be a target for terrorists.

'Amaal, did you find anything significant in today's date?'

'Not yet. I'm checking lesser-known nut-job anniversaries.'

'We've got through to Rafi Bukhari, the boy who saw the explosion,' Thandie says to her. 'He's in the woods.'

'Thanks.' She takes the phone, puts it on loudspeaker.

The sound of the wind howling through trees; she thinks she can hear branches creaking and she feels the disconnect between herself with her screens and her computer, her bottle of mineral water, the safe interior of this purpose-built vehicle, and what is happening outside.

'Rafi, my name is Rose Polstein. Are you okay?'

'Fine.'

'You saw the explosion in the woods earlier?' she asks.

'Yes.'

'Did you see anyone?'

'No. But I didn't look.'

A loud gust of wind and it's hard to hear him.

'Rafi?'

'I just ran.'

'Do you think someone could have been hiding?'

'Maybe.'

The bomber could have been hiding close by and used a garage door opener or key-fob to detonate the bomb. Or he might have been nowhere near the woods, the bomb being detonated with a timer; an alarm clock or a kitchen timer would do it.

'Do you know if Hannah Jacobs is safe?' He sounds very young to Rose. 'Are junior school on the boats? Please, I have to know.'

'Junior school are getting on to the boats now and we're flying a helicopter over the beach to keep them safe. I'll let you know when they're away. I don't know about Hannah, I'm sorry.' The identity of the captives is not her area of responsibility; her task is to help find the identity of the gunmen, help negotiate and predict what they are going to do.

'Sorry. Gotta go,' Rafi says to her.

She guesses it's because she's answered the only two questions that matter to him, and because he's saving precious charge on his phone.

'Be careful,' she says, about to add more, but he's hung up and in the sudden quiet she feels that she is skimming surfaces, gleaning information and imposing rational thought, but far from the heart of what is happening here.

★ ★ ★

Rafi is running and phoning Hannah again, each time the same vertiginous desperation that she'll answer him, but again she doesn't. She's run out of charge, that's all, or she saw it was him and doesn't want to talk to him, because she hates him for abandoning her; hopefully that's why. He rings her landline, because maybe she's safely at home by now and the landline won't show it's him so she'll pick up. The answerphone clicks on. Not at home.

As he runs on towards Old School, the gatehouse now in sight through the trees, the wind drops for a few moments and he hears the rustle of an anorak. His rational mind that's paid attention in therapy says *Fuck's sake! It's just your PTSD!*, but the frightened part of him that hasn't paid any attention tells him to run and he races to the gatehouse, a hundred feet away through the woods.

Spruce trees have grown right up against the back wall of the gatehouse and he squeezes between the wall and the trees; his heart's pounding away like a punk band drummer and his chest's going in and out like a demented pigeon's and then he sees a fishbone pattern of bricks in the back wall and it calms him that over a hundred years ago a person built this detail. In Arabic, *Daesh* sounds like the word to crush and trample; builders and architects are the absolute opposite of Daesh.

He's listening, but the wind's picked up again and around him everything's creaking and rustling, too noisy to hear an anorak. There's a CCTV camera on the gatehouse wall; he can just see yellow paint under the covering of snow.

He edges round the gatehouse and sees a police car skewed at an angle to the side of the drive. The windscreen has a bullet hole and around it are thousands of cracks, like dense spiders' webs, clouding the glass, but he can just make out that the car is empty. The police officer is probably inside the gatehouse. It's safe in the gatehouse, thick walls and no glass windows. Like the theatre. That would be the safest place to go to. Hannah would think to go there. She's sensible, she'd think to do that. Benny was doing the dress rehearsal this morning.

He phones Benny. After two rings Benny answers.

'Rafi? You okay, bro'?' He hears the warmth in his best friend's voice and then other people in the background and Benny saying, 'It's Rafi!', and people are calling out to him, saying, 'You on a boat, Rafi?', 'You'll miss your cue, bro'!', 'Hey, Rafi, you're missing the fucking dress rehearsal.' But they all sound frightened.

'While you're on your boat trip, we're rehearsing *Macbeth*,' Benny says.

'Is Hannah there?' he asks, no time to explain about not getting on a boat.

But Benny can't hear him over the wind and he has to shout, 'Is Hannah there?' and he's afraid that the man after him, who isn't even real, will hear him shout.

'No, she's not. Sorry.'

'D'you know where she is?'

'No. You okay?'

'Yeah. Gotta go.'

She could still be on her way home. Who'd know? Her first lesson was English and Charlotte does English too and he has her number in his contacts so he texts Charlotte.

> It's Rafi, do u know where Hannah is?

Moments later Charlotte texts back.

> Am in Mrs Kale's classroom but she's not here. Think in library w Ed Frank & other people

In Old School. In the library. Not safe. He sprints through the falling snow towards Old School.

Before his father and brother were murdered he didn't think someone he loved could die, as if him loving them meant that couldn't happen, even in Syria with bombs exploding and evil let loose, even there. After it happens, you know there's a price tag attached that's unpayable so you don't love anyone new. But he'd thought in England it was safe to fall in love.

He reaches Old School and crouches down. The friendly building has turned hostile, the shuttered windows looking blankly back, the bricks rough against his cheek, a gargoyle mocking him as he stoops beneath it.

He hears a twig snap. Above him, brick dust falls with the snow so that the snow is turned orange. The wall has been shot at; he's been shot at.

And his rational mind says, *Fuck's sake! It's not a bullet hole, it's just a crumbly old building is all, and you just imagined a twig snap because there are no fucking twigs here, just like there was no man in an anorak. You are highly stressed and hypervigilant and paranoid with delusions.*

And his fearful, irrational PTSD self tells him to run again and already he's running, around to the side of the building. There's a PE equipment shed, next to the side wall of Old School; a gap just wide enough for him to hide.

★　★　★

Inside Matthew Marr's head, a rising tide takes away memories and he is trapped on a spit of land. He knows that he recognized the gunman in the corridor, but his name has washed out to the encroaching sea, a sea that is blood or cerebral fluid, pieces of medals and bones on the sea floor.

The gunman spoke one word and that word explained everything but the sea has covered it over.

High above him, a kite without a string, is a single brightly coloured memory of the day with a china-blue sky, Old School bright with clematis, the call of a pied flycatcher, and the answer is here on this day but he cannot take hold of it.

The children in the pottery room are in danger, but he no longer knows the reason. He tries to ask Hannah, bending down close to him, but he cannot form the words. He thinks he hears a helicopter.

Through a gap in the shutters lights from a helicopter slice into the library, and Frank thinks that help must be coming, but then the lights go and they are in almost darkness again. As the sound of the helicopter fades they can hear the footsteps. Frank's mobile is down to 3% charge and they've agreed to use it only for an emergency now.

At the back of the library Tobias has his earphones on, his hands held tightly over his earphones as if he can double-block out what's going on as he rocks to and fro. Tobias is different from all of them, has been since Reception. They're all protective of him. Esme puts her hand on Tobias's to comfort him, but he flinches and she takes her hand away.

Mr Marr's face is paper white and his eyes keep closing, like he's finding it really hard to stay conscious, and then he forces them open again. Hannah and Ed are next to him. The ambulance people are emailing them what to do, but she isn't sure it's helping. Sometimes he makes sounds, like he's trying to speak, but no one can understand.

Their friends in the English classroom along the corridor feel like they could be a mile away. They have three adults with them and no one is hurt and everyone has phones and Jacintha is reading them poetry. She has typed up poems and sent them to Frank's laptop, as if poetry can help; maybe it can but not when your headmaster is so badly injured and so close to you, at least it can't help Frank right at this moment. The people in the English classroom have desks to barricade the door, not tables that are fixed to the floor with old Victorian bolts.

His phone rings and he doesn't recognize the number so he answers, in case it's the police, in case it's help on the way.

The wind in the background is really loud and it takes a few moments before Frank can hear Rafi talking to him. And he's annoyed because Rafi is not the police and is using up charge and how did he even get his number? And then he hears what Rafi's saying. He's not on a boat being evacuated to safety, like everybody thought, but is at the back of Old School looking for Hannah; of course he is, all chivalrous in shining armour, winning his spurs in the stories of old, and Hannah will be so amazed and thrilled and he's the person that has to tell her that her boyfriend is in fact a knight.

'Hannah, it's Rafi on the phone. He's looking for you. He's outside Old School.'

He said it all kind of deadpan but everyone turns, though it's not him they're looking at with amazement, it's Rafi, who obviously can't see them, but Frank can.

'Tell him I've been evacuated,' Hannah says. 'Tell him I'm safe.'

Oh, it's all too fucking selfless. No, untrue, unfair. He's jealous, is all. Jealous, jealous, jealous; and it's not just of Rafi making

126

Hannah glow like that – seriously, she's glowing like she could take off, like she's got rocket fuel burning inside her – no, it's jealousy that you could be brave like that, like Hannah and Rafi. Do people who are going to be heroic have a kind of radar for one another before they actually prove it, because what are the chances of the two of them being like this?

'Hannah has been evacuated,' he says to Rafi, who thanks him, sounding so happy, and then he hangs up; 2% charge left now.

Though clearly Rafi was *already* heroic because he brought his little brother from Syria to England when he was only fourteen, all those awful things that they had to escape, which he hardly ever talks about but they all know it was bad. He's crying now, for Rafi, because putting his nasty jealousy to one side, Rafi is really great and he's had a terrible time and he does things like put everybody's phone numbers into his contacts, because he's friendly to everyone, and then some arsehole shit-face gunman is probably going to kill the girl he loves, who he's come back for, is probably going to kill all of them, has already badly wounded Mr Marr who was the person who rescued Rafi in the first place.

He didn't tell Rafi about Mr Marr, just couldn't. Crying too because he's afraid and isn't a hero and because he can never make Hannah glow like that and if he dies today then he'll never have the chance to become braver and better and meet a girl a bit like Hannah and make her look like she's got rocket fuel burning inside her.

★   ★   ★

The wild relief is energizing and Rafi is standing, wanting to run, shout – *She's alive! Safe!* He'll go to the theatre and be with his friends – Fuck! Join in the rehearsal! He remembers when all he and Basi had in the world, which was basically his pocket, was fifty euros, a laser pointer and his dad's battered copy of *Macbeth*, treasured because it belonged to Baba and because it was where they were going, the land of Shakespeare, so it was a double talisman.

She's safe, she's safe, she's safe!

There's a direct route from here to the theatre, but even for-getting his phantom PTSD pursuer, the psychotic illusion in his head who snaps invisible twigs, he might be spotted by the real gunman in Old School.

The woods aren't far from here and there's a small winding path through the trees which comes out at the back of the the-atre. There's a fire-exit door and his friends will let him in.

He hears the sound of a helicopter and he sprints to the woods, hoping that the helicopter will be a distraction if the gunman looks outside. Glancing up through the snow, he sees the yellow POLICE flash on the helicopter. Snow eddies and whirls around the helicopter, and for a moment it twists round and round in the sky as if it's losing control, and then it rights itself.

He reaches the woods and the trees feel safe to him, hiding him. His phone buzzes – a text from Detective Inspector Rose Polstein.

> Junior school safely evacuated on boats.
> Where you should be. When this over
> expect bollocking.
>   Find somewhere to hide and stay there
> till we can get to you. For that bollocking.

He loves this police officer, this Rose Polstein, for telling him, for keeping her word, as if it's her doing that Basi is now safe.

He tries to ring Basi but it goes straight through to message. Maybe there's no reception on the boat or he's run out of charge because he's been feeding all the animals that live inside his phone. For once he agrees with Mr Lorrimer that Basi should only use his phone for emergencies, but for Basi his animals are an emergency.

He sends him a text:

> I love u 🐿

This evening, when everything is safe – because this is England and things will be safe again, safe is the normal everyday here – he'll read Basi a story as usual. He imagines Basi sitting on his lap, the comfortable warmth and weight of him, and he'll tell him that he knew Miss Price would look after him, and the other teachers and the coastguards, the police, everyone. People to fear in other countries, who'd set dogs on them and beaten them and stopped their boat from landing, weren't like that in England. He knew people would take care of Basi; that's why they'd risked so much to try and get to England; that's why Rafi could leave him.

He'll text Rose Polstein when he gets to the theatre, tell her that he's okay.

Snow is falling more heavily, covering everything white, and the woods look beautiful to Rafi. Even when he imagined his phantom pursuer earlier he felt safe in the woods, the trees protecting him, but Hannah is afraid of them.

'*Hansel and Gretel, Snow White, Little Red Riding Hood – all English people are scared of woods.*'

'*What about when you got older? "Lord of the Rings"?*' he'd said.
'*Cool trees.*'

'*Not trees, Ents who speak Entish.*'

'*"Game of Thrones"?*'

'*Fucking weird trees with faces.*'

'*Shakespeare's comedies. You can be a different gender in the woods.*'

He remembers Hannah's eyes as she smiled and nodded, her long shining hair falling in front of her face. He's told her Syrian folk tales and she's told him her fairy tales, and they sound completely crazy, both sets, when told to the other, and no wonder she's afraid of woods – little children being abandoned and following breadcrumbs, a cannibal witch with children in a cage, a wolf waiting on the path.

This morning they'd met up before school started, like every other morning, to go for a walk in the woods, because they wanted to be alone together, although Hannah says *alone together* is an oxymoron, and they'd lost track of time and had to run and then it had started to snow.

He hasn't tried phoning Hannah again because he just wants to be happy that she's safe; because that is enough.

*   ⋆   ⋆

In the leisure centre cafeteria, Beth Alton has one hand holding on to the edge of the Formica table, as if she needs to keep hold of something, everything physically precarious, her other hand holding her phone that Jamie doesn't ring.

The large room around her has come more into focus. On the far side, at the tables of junior school parents, a mother tries to rock a baby to sleep, her movements jerky; a father has a toddler on his lap who's watching cartoons on an iPad, headphones much too big for him. It's only when she sees how young the junior school mothers and fathers are that she realizes how long ago it was since Jamie and Theo were that age; since she was. It goes in a blink, she wants to say to them, warn them, all of it, just a blink.

The older male police officer asks a group of junior school parents to go with him. Beth watches them leave the room, footsteps springy with relief. She assumes that these elect parents have children who are now safely evacuated, what other reason could there be for them to leave? Elect, why did she think that? As if there was some kind of Calvinist salvation and the cafeteria is purgatory. Do Calvinists believe in purgatory? Or is that just a Catholic thing? She absolutely believes in purgatory now, knows first-hand all about purgatory, and it has a linoleum floor and Formica tables and no windows and a phone that doesn't ring. Doesn't ring.

Calvin, Mum? Really?

His voice is smiling and it feels so real that for a moment he's here in this terrible place.

At the table next to Beth there are two mothers who are clearly friends, clutching at each other's hands, both manicured, so that their long shiny nails in different bright colours interweave, their faces pale. She can't hear what the dark-haired woman is saying, but she catches 'Antonella' a few times; so, she is Antonella's mother. She feels fury, hot and urgent, with this manicured woman as if it's her fault her daughter broke up with Jamie. Wrong. Wrong. She just wishes Jamie was still in love and happy, so that he'd have that to hold on to while this terrible thing is happening.

Steve, the young man, holding his mobile, raises his voice: 'My fiancée is on one of the boats with the children, they've got away.'

The room quietens instantly, as if for a moment it's all their children who are safely on boats. And then questions erupt from junior school parents whose children are on the boats, and the parents whose children are still in danger feel the contrast.

'Milly's terrified of the sea,' a young mother says, crying.

'They're being very well looked after,' the woman police officer says. 'The boats are very stable and they're all wearing life jackets. The lifeboat men will take good care—'

'We never go on seaside holidays,' the mother says. 'We go to the Dordogne. There's a river and Milly likes rivers and she's been canoeing with the school on an inlet, but the sea really frightens her.'

Beth doesn't want to listen; doesn't want to feel blazing outrage that this woman can be talking about her Dordogne holiday and canoeing when Jamie is hiding and in danger.

You worry too much about me, Mum, you really do.

I know. You're right. But now I am really worried and it makes all those other times seem so stupid.

Worrying that his ex-girlfriend, this Antonella, had broken his heart, and him being lonely and too shy and not confident, and none of those things matter to her, not one bit. And never will again.

II

10.10 a.m.

The police still do not know if the gunmen intend to make demands and negotiate or if they are waiting for a yet larger audience, perhaps for more countries around the world to wake up and follow the siege (*siege* the word being used by the media).

Four drones, all operated by off-site amateurs hoping to cash in by selling photos, malfunctioned because of the snow and crashed to the ground; but there may be more above the school. A severe weather warning has been issued; the storm is closing in with blizzarding snow and strong winds which will hamper the search. It will also make flying helicopters virtually impossible and impact their hunt for a possible third gunman.

Hopefully, there's no third attacker to be found and Rafi is safe. But Rose will keep her word and give him a bollocking when this is over for not being evacuated with junior school, for adding to the stress of their job, for being so bloody inconsiderate. Do you have to be sixteen to be so idiotically, wonderfully courageous like that? She wonders if she or Jonny would leave safety and return to face a gunman on just the supposition that the other might be in danger. She thinks that they would, but it's hardly likely to ever be put to the test. *Jesus, Rose, focus.*

Stuart Dingwall, senior officer in counterterrorism intelligence, comes on the line.

'Rose? Stuart. One of our surveillance UAVs found the remains of the bomb and sent us footage. It's pretty much covered in snow but there's enough to confirm our guess that it was a pressure-cooker bomb; but not powerful. Two teachers heard it and thought it was firecrackers. A girl on TV said she thought it was a bonfire and a pigeon scarer. What I don't understand is why set it off in the first place? Do you have any idea? Because logically I can't think of a reason.'

Rose has wondered that too, because apart from Rafi, it didn't frighten anyone, if that's what it was meant to do; all it did was alert the school and the police. But she now believes the woods were significant.

'I think the school was meant to go into lockdown,' she tells Stuart. 'The bomb made the woods appear dangerous so that the decision was made not to evacuate children and staff through the woods but to stay inside school buildings. One gunman was already hiding in Old School. I think that the other gunman, who shot at PC Beard from the woods and then followed Mr Marr through the woods, wanted to reinforce the idea that the woods were too dangerous for the children and staff to go into. Again, he was keeping everyone inside buildings; corralling them inside.'

'And junior school would have been a soft target if they'd stayed inside their building.'

'Exactly. Pure bad luck for the bombers that it was Rafi Bukhari who saw the small explosion and knew what it was and got junior school evacuated; probably the only person in the school who'd do that. But I don't think our bomber necessarily banked on it being seen by anyone – it's a large woodland, and classes were about to start so most people would've been inside.'

'But if nobody saw the explosion, shooting at PC Beard from the woods would make the point that the woods were dangerous.'

'Yes. I think the explosion may be part of some kind of game we don't yet understand, that links to the rifles as a misdirect. I think it tells us something about the mindset of one of the gunmen.'

'And you're working on the mindset?'

'Yes.'

She ends the conversation.

'Victor Deakin hasn't turned up to college,' George tells her.

133

'And there's no sign of Malin Cohen either. Teams are en route to all suspects' houses.'

'I've got an evacuated teacher on the line,' Amaal says. 'Gina Patterson wants to talk about Victor Deakin, one of the boys who was expelled.'

Rose puts the phone on speaker.

'Gina, my name's Detective Inspector Rose Polstein. What can you tell me?'

'We all just thought it was for his EPQ, what Victor wrote, but maybe it wasn't. Maybe that's why Matthew expelled him, maybe it's Victor doing this. I mean I don't think it is, I can't believe that, but he only joined us in Year Eleven and most of our kids have been at the school for years, since Reception, so we know them really well and they absorb the school ethos, but Victor—'

'What did Victor Deakin write?'

'It was a rape fantasy. He said it was for his EPQ, extended project qualification, which was on sex offenders. He told the teacher who found it that he was just getting into the mindset of a sex offender. His tutor confirmed he was doing an EPQ on that. He said he just chose the name Sarah because it was a common name. But there's a girl called Sarah in the year below.'

'Her surname?'

'Jensten.'

'Did Sarah and her parents want him gone?'

'No, they believed him. He wrote to them, to Sarah and her parents, to apologize for any upset he might have caused. I saw the letters. He was genuinely sorry.'

'But he was still expelled?'

'No. Matthew let him stay on condition that Olav Christoffersen, head of IT, had daily access to his laptop and his tutor could conduct random searches of his study area. Victor said he understood. Most of us thought Matthew was being too harsh, all teenagers have things on their laptops they'd rather keep hidden, but Matthew said he was being careful.'

'And then?'

'I don't know. Matthew didn't talk to us about the expulsion. It was the summer term so we were frantically busy, focusing on our GCSE and A-level students, too busy to pursue Matthew about it. But what if Olav found something on Victor's laptop? What if that's why he was expelled?'

'Did Olav Christoffersen say anything?'

'No, but he wouldn't. Olav's very circumspect, never gossips. And like I said, we were all really busy so we just accepted the decision and got on with our jobs.'

'Do you know if Victor is friends with Malin Cohen?'

'They live close to each other, but I didn't think they were friends. Victor's off-the-chart bright, Malin struggles academically. But I suppose it makes sense. If any of this makes sense, Christ. Malin's a thug. Always has been. An uncontrollable temper.'

This corroborates what other teachers have told them.

'Is there anything that's happened recently that's been strange, even a small thing?'

'Well, there was something, I suppose, but it was three months ago now.'

'Can you tell me?'

'One of the gardeners saw a man outside a maintenance shed. There's a tractor and trailer, tools, that kind of thing. But nothing was stolen.'

'Is the gardener here today?'

'No, he works part-time in the winter.'

'Did he say what this man looked like?'

'No, I think he just saw his back. It was in the school holidays, so not a student. But like I said, nothing was stolen so we didn't take it any further.'

'Where is the maintenance shed?'

'Just off the drive in the woods, near the high ropes course.'

'Is there anything else you can think of at all?'

'Just some silly pranks. In the last few weeks, someone cling-filmed the stools together in the science labs; someone put glow-in-the-dark slime inside the girls' toilets in the art block; someone rang Old School's doorbell really loudly and then ran away again before we could see who it was. That's all.'

'Thank you.'

She ends the call.

'Sarah Jensten was evacuated from New School,' Thandie tells Rose.

So, if it's Victor Deakin and he's aiming the attack at Sarah Jensten, then he's been extremely careless. But Neil Forbright told them that Victor didn't want to be at this school in the first place, so there's no obvious reason for him to have a personal grudge against the school.

'We need to talk to the school's head of IT, Olav Christoffer-sen, as soon as possible,' she tells George.

'A junior school teacher just phoned in from one of the boats,' Amaal says.

'Are they okay?' Rose asks.

'Reception's terrible. They're getting the teacher to text.'

★　★　★

In The Pines Leisure Centre cafeteria, Steve, the energetic young man, is shouting into his mobile phone: 'Can you hear me . . .?! Chloe . . .?' Beth Alton imagines the noise of the sea and the wind, a young teacher straining to hear her fiancé's voice.

You know, Jamie, I don't mind that you didn't talk to me about Antonella.

Mum . . .

You're seventeen and boys of seventeen don't talk about those kind of things with their mothers.

He's growing up, growing away, and she's been trying to hold on to him, holding him back, she realizes, trying to make him her little boy again. Perhaps it's because he's her younger child, she wasn't like this with Theo. But Jamie should grow up; that's the right and natural order of things. He should grow up.

She sees Antonella's mother on her own. Her friend with painted nails must've gone to the loo but won't take long; will dash into a cubicle, not locking the door, not washing her hands, doing up her zip with one hand as she runs back, other hand holding her phone, suddenly hopeful of news in the few minutes she's been absent.

Beth goes over to her. 'I didn't know whether to come and say hello. I'm Jamie's mother, Beth. Beth Alton.'

Antonella's mother doesn't smile; no one smiles in this room, no social niceties here, but she doesn't react at all.

'Jamie Alton is my son.'

Antonella's mother looks perplexed. 'I don't know anyone called Jamie.'

Did Antonella keep you a secret from her mother like you kept Antonella a secret from me?

But teenage girls talk to their mothers; especially pretty mothers with long glossy hair and nails.

'I'm sorry,' the woman says. 'But I really don't know your son.'

Does Antonella do this to you? Pretend you don't even exist any more? Is that why you've been so unhappy?

'Jamie was Antonella's boyfriend for three months, up until the end of June.'

There, putting it down on the table, so she can't look away from it, can't look away from Jamie.

'Her boyfriend is Tim Makeston,' the woman says. 'Has been for two years.'

I don't understand, Jamie . . .? In your diary . . .

You thought it was real. Antonella and me. I never said it was real. It wasn't meant for anyone else to read.

So, it was a fantasy.

That sounds porny and it wasn't.

All those beautiful drawings; more of a dream.

No, it wasn't, I'm sorry. I'm really sorry.

He's been lonelier than she thought; the sharp cutting of unrequited love in so many hidden ways. And now he's hiding alone, most probably terrified, without even remembered love to comfort him.

There'll be someone else, sweetheart. When you go off to university there'll be so many lovely girls, and you'll fall in love again, with someone who'll love you back.

Yesterday, this morning even, she'd have felt jealous, threatened, by such an imaginary girl. She'd had no idea then of the love she had for Jamie, had assumed it was possessive, grasping, but the make-up of her love is not like that at all.

Antonella's mother is leaning closer towards her, two mothers sharing a confidence. In a minute, she will put her manicured hand round Beth's garden-rough one.

'Maybe your son just had a crush on her. I know lots of the boys do.'

Not boasting, but giving an explanation for Jamie, perhaps understanding his vulnerability. She's kind. Is her daughter kind? Beth thinks probably not, because what teenage girl with lots of boys who have crushes on her is kind?

'Her boyfriend, Tim, isn't that special. I really don't know what she sees in him.'

As if she is softening the blow and if it were up to her she'd choose someone different, Jamie perhaps, for Antonella.

'Tim's the reason she is in the theatre and not evacuated,' she says. 'She doesn't even like acting.'

Was it because of Antonella that Jamie wanted to be part of the production? A beggar-my-neighbour game – Jamie there because of Antonella, Antonella there because of not-very-special Tim.

Zac and Victor were in it too, Mum. My two best mates, remember?

Yes, sorry.

Didn't know Zac would get a Velcro-girlfriend and Victor would leave, did I?

You must've felt lonely after that.

Must be exhausting, Mum, being in a paddy about me all the time.

I'm not, but—

I'm not a complete loser all the time, you know.

Of course you aren't. I never thought that. And you carried on, didn't you? You didn't give up.

Exactly. I'm a trooper. And what about my A levels? My party?

In his bedroom above his desk is a piece of paper pinned to the wall with '100%' written in his beautiful calligraphy and she'd been both heartened at his ambition for his A levels and worried that he'd fall short, because though some kids do get 100 per cent in their A levels they work far harder and are cleverer than Jamie; she's feared disappointment, sadness. Next to it, an elaborately drawn '18', although his eighteenth birthday is almost a year away and she's been worried about that too, that his imagination would outstrip whatever party he gave. Or maybe she didn't want to think about him becoming an adult before she had to. Mike had been irritated with her for not seeing the positive.

As if parties and grades matter now, as if anything matters now apart from him being alive and safe and able to live the rest of his life.

Steve has put down his mobile and is speaking too fast, a shake in his voice, as if his fiancée's feelings have physically transferred themselves to him.

'A little boy in her group is missing. He didn't get on to any of the boats. Chloe thought his form teacher, Mrs Cardswell, had him, but his form teacher thought Chloe was looking after him. It wasn't her fault, I kept telling her that; a girl had an asthma attack and—'

'What boy?'

'Which class?'

'In Chloe Price's class?'

'Is the girl all right? The one that had an asthma attack?'

'Yes.'

'You're certain it's a boy?'

'Do you know his name?'

'Basi Bukhari,' Steve says.

'Oh, thank God. I'm sorry. I'm sorry.'

★   ★   ★

In the shed, eight-year-old Basi Bukhari is standing because it's less cold than sitting on the floor, which is all damp and icy, but his legs are getting wobbly with being tired and frightened. His hands and ears sting with cold. He tries to pull his sleeves over his hands but they're too short, so he hunches his shoulders together so the sleeves will reach.

When they all got to the beach it was freezing, the wind picking up the icy cold of the sea and throwing it at their faces and hands and any part of them where their clothes had got untucked.

Rafi was looking at Miss Kowalski's phone, with other teachers looking at it too, but he was just listening to the sea shouting that it had monsters inside it – *Wa-hush, Wa-hush, Wa-hush!*

Sometimes it pretends to be blue and friendly but it drowns people.

Rafi put a life jacket on him and they joked about the piñata in the shop in Alexandria and he thought it would all be okay because Rafi was with him and it was okay if Rafi was with him.

He told Rafi he needed to put on a life jacket too, but Rafi didn't say anything and he didn't want Rafi to say the next thing, because he knew it would be a bad thing. He said he didn't want to play any more, though he knew, really, that they weren't playing. And then they argued, Rafi saying he'd be safe and him saying he needed Rafi to come with him, so it wasn't a real argument, just him trying to stop Rafi leaving him. Rafi has never left him.

'But they're shouting at me, the monsters, *Wa-hush, Wa-hush,* listen! Can you hear? It's even worse than a hole!'

'Remember the princess in Milan, Basi? Do you remember her face?'

'No.'

'She was in the station, remember?'

'We pretended the station was a palace,' he said because maybe if he kept Rafi talking he wouldn't leave.

'Romanesque,' Rafi said because he is going to be an architect when he's older, like Mama, and knows the names of every-thing. 'With a piazza and columns and friezes.'

'And there were benches made of marble.'

'That's right.'

'But we had to go into the bit that had ropes around it. The migrant bit.'

'And when people went past I told you to watch out for their briefcases,' Rafi said. 'Because you were at the edge and they could bash into your head.'

'I thought you said "brief faces" not "briefcases"!'

'That was brilliant of you, because that's what they were like; lots of brief faces. And then the princess stopped.'

'We don't know for sure she was a princess.'

'I think that she was.'

'Me too,' Basi said, because she probably really was, and he was only arguing before because he wanted to keep Rafi talking.

'And she gave us money,' Rafi said. 'So we could buy new clothes and train tickets. Do you remember what you got?'

'Blue trousers and a shirt with cowboys on it from the shop in the station.'

'Zara Kids,' Rafi said.

'And lots of pants and socks.'

'We had a good wash and we got changed.'

'And we put our old clothes in the bin,' Basi said, 'because they were really smelly and horrible.'

'We looked so smart and smelt so nice that no one thought we were migrants any more.'

'Two princes out for a stroll together.'

'A couple of regular brothers having a latte together.'

'You had the latte and I had the choco frappuccino,' Basi reminded him.

'That's right. Remember her face?'

'Course.'

★

In the shed, Basi thinks Ratty is making scuffly noises, telling Basi he's there with him.

'Her eyes were bright blue, Ratty, and her skin was like caramel, and so was her hair, like a princess; like the station was her palace. Her face was all shiny with tears and she said she was sorry but I don't know why she said that.'

And then after he and Rafi had spoken on the beach about the princess in Milan station, he'd felt a bit calmer, and Rafi must have thought that meant he was all right because he took him to Miss Price. And they spoke really quietly so all he could hear was the sea shouting. Miss Price held his hand but he tried to pull away and still be with Rafi. Then Rafi said, 'It's a *Have-To-No-Arguments*, okay?'

Rafi had only said 'It's a *Have-To-No-Arguments*' twice on the Journey. *Have-To-No-Arguments* means Rafi is talking for Baba and Mama.

Basi nodded but that can mean you understand, not that you agree. Mr Lorrimer says he is *a slippery character*. And he thinks he was being slippery then.

Rafi kissed him.

'You are as brave as a Barbary lion,' Rafi said. 'And a Bengal tiger.'

'Brave as Sir Lancelot,' Basi said. 'And the little mouse in *The Gruffalo*.' If he could just keep thinking of more brave people and animals, on and on, Rafi wouldn't leave him.

'Brave as Odysseus,' Rafi said. Basi tried to think of another brave person or animal, but he was being too slow.

'Brave as Basi Bukhari,' Rafi said. 'I love you, Little Monkey.'

Then he turned and ran back to the cliff path.

Miss Price held his hand and asked if he'd like to stay with her or go and be with Mrs Cardswell and all his friends. And he thinks he said he'd like to be with his friends, or maybe he didn't say anything, because he was listening to the sea shouting at him.

And then Miss Price took her hand away from his because

Milly was wheezing, like she couldn't breathe properly. She took off Milly's life jacket to check her coat pockets for her puffer. His hand felt lonely and afraid.

Wa-hush, Wa-hush, Wa-hush.

Miss Price called to the teachers, 'Does anyone have Ventolin?' But the wind and the sea were too noisy and then Miss Price shouted, 'A CHILD NEEDS VENTOLIN!'

Wa-hush, Wa-hush, Wa-hush.

People falling from the boat and the monsters in the sea holding on to them and pulling them deeper and deeper and not letting them back to the air. A little girl fell in wearing armbands, and her mama and baba both jumped in after her and they drowned as well. Rafi held on to him, really tightly, and didn't let him go. When people were pushing hard and he thought he was going to fall into the sea, Rafi held on to him.

Wa-hush, Wa-hush, Wa-hush.

He could see Rafi walking quickly up the cliff path.

He ran after him but nobody noticed because they were all helping Milly.

The cliff path was slippery and he was worried about so many things. He was worried about Miss Price being cross with him for running away and not telling her first. She'd never been cross before but she'd never shouted before either. Maybe she wouldn't even know, because everyone else in his class was with Mrs Cardswell, their form teacher, and she probably thought he was with Mrs Cardswell too. And he was worried about Milly, but then he remembered that Lucas always has an inhaler in his coat pocket, and one in his trousers pocket too, because his mother says she's a *worrywart*, so Lucas would give Milly his inhaler. Mostly he was worried about catching up with Rafi, because he was going as fast as he could, faster than he'd ever run before, but Rafi was running too, and getting smaller and smaller. He shouted at him but the wind just stole his words away before they got to Rafi.

He got a stitch in his side and it was hard to run in the life jacket, because he couldn't move his arms very well. The snow was blowing against his face, the cold was biting his cheeks and the trees by the path were all twisted and bent over because the wind had hit them so much.

He got to the gate and had to climb it because it was locked. It was covered in snow and ice and his feet kept slipping and his life jacket made him clumsy and his stitch really hurt. From the gate, he saw a light on inside Junior School and he thought that Rafi might be inside.

He ran towards Junior School across the slippery car park, past all the teachers' cars which had snow over them and looked like snow cars. Through his classroom window he could see Rafi! He knew Basi would be frightened of the sea so he'd waited for him!

He ran towards Rafi but when he got closer to the window he saw the man inside was much taller than Rafi. The man's back was towards him, so he couldn't see his face. He had a big gun and belts of bullets and at any second he might turn round and see Basi looking at him through the window. He imagined Rafi saying to him, *Duck down and keep still, Basi, still as a statue, then find somewhere to hide.*

He ducked down and tried to take off his yellow life jacket, because it was too easy to spot, but he couldn't undo it in woolly gloves, so he took his gloves off and they fell on the snow. Then he managed to take off his life jacket.

He heard a sound like a stone being thrown on to an icy puddle, lots of stones, and glass breaking, but he kept still as a statue till his knees hurt from crouching, and when he stood up a little bit he couldn't see the man inside any more.

The window was smashed and the scarecrows they'd made were all shot with pieces of window sticking into them. Lucas's mum had given Basi some of Lucas's old clothes for his scarecrow because he didn't have his own old clothes. There were bullet holes in his scarecrow, through his clothes and through his face, so he didn't have a face any more.

He ran away as fast as he could, slipping on the ice in the car park, hiding behind the snow cars. He saw the boatshed and the door was open a little and he ran inside.

Remembering the man has made him frightened all over again; he pushes his face into the crook of his elbow, burrowing into his anorak, like he can hide from the man and not hear the breaking glass any more.

Think of a kind face, that's what Rafi tells him to do when he's really frightened. All on his own, he thinks of two! The Soup Sisters in the Dunkirk camp. One had crinkles round her eyes when she smiled, so her whole face was a smile, and her sister had a thin, stern face but when she smiled at him it was like her face was a lamp switching on. The Soup Sisters mean he's not going to be sick any more.

When they were in the camp they thought about Mr Marr's kind face, but Mr Marr's face doesn't work now because they see him for real every day and Rafi says you have to use your memory and imagination, like opening a storybook in your mind, the best unexpected bits, and going there for a little while.

He remembers there's a rowing boat at the back of the shed – he'll hide inside it so that if the man gets in he won't see him. He turns on his phone so he can see his way.

He has a missed call and a message from Rafi!

> I love u 🐿

He only has 4% charge left. Rafi calls it 'juice' and says you mustn't run out of juice, but Rafi doesn't have animals inside his phone. Basi's the only person in junior school who's allowed a phone at school and Mr Lorrimer doesn't like it, but Mr Marr says Basi can always talk to Rafi if he wants to.

Even with the light from his phone, he's still bumping into things, but he gets to the rowing boat, with its smooth curvy sides, and he clambers in.

He reads Rafi's text again then turns off his phone. It's even darker further from the door inside a boat.

He mustn't turn it on again and phone Rafi back, mustn't do that. Because the man with the gun might be outside and shoot him.

He's got to keep on being brave like a Barbary lion and a Bengal tiger and Sir Lancelot and the *Gruffalo* mouse and Odysseus. And then Rafi had said, 'Brave as Basi Bukhari.' And he's trying really hard but he doesn't know how much longer he can be brave.

★ ★ ★

In the woods, the path has almost disappeared under the snow when Rafi sees the theatre and the fire-exit door at the back. He's stopped checking behind him because there was never anybody after him; nobody shot at the wall above his head or broke a non-existent twig; his damaged mind just imagined it all and his phantom pursuer belongs back in the past with Assad's men and Daesh and the gangs in the camp.

He wonders where his friends have got to. Whenever they rehearse *Macbeth* he hears his father's voice again because, for Baba, Syria was a *suffering country under a hand accursed*, that *sinks beneath the yoke. It weeps, it bleeds*; Bashar al-Assad, Russian bombers and every single person in Daesh was *a devil damned in evils*. And when they made plans to leave, Baba had said that they had no choice, because their country was *no longer their mother but their grave*. But then Baba and Karam were murdered – *each new morn, new widows howl, new orphans cry, new sorrows strike heaven on the face* – but Baba wasn't there to say that any more and there was only enough money left for him and Basi to escape.

Baba had liked other playwrights, especially Saadallah Wannous, but Shakespeare was his go-to guy for quotes.

He should have said Birnam Wood to Hannah, when they were talking about trees. Why didn't he say that? The coolest woods in literature and stage are the trees marching to Dunsinane Hill and defeating Macbeth; not real trees, of course, or

Ents, but soldiers using trees to camouflage themselves. But even so, the trees march. He loves that. Maybe that's why Baba loved the play so much, for its ending. They are using trees from these woods in their production. Daphne has a whole load backstage.

His mobile vibrates with Basi's rhythm – *rat-a-TAT-tat, rat-a-TAT-tat* – a rhythm they'd set up in the camp; a secret code between them.

He answers the phone, having to shout above the noise of the wind.

'Little Monkey, are you okay?'

'I'm almost out of juice.'

Basi breaks down sobbing, as if he can't get enough air to breathe.

'What's wrong?'

But Basi doesn't speak, just breathless hiccuppy crying.

'One elephant, two elephants, count your breaths, that's it, slowly, three—'

'I left the beach. I wanted to be with you.'

Rafi feels sick; his hand holding the phone is shaking.

'You didn't get on the boat?'

He's shouting at Basi, like he's angry, but it's because otherwise Basi won't hear him above the sound of the wind. Basi's voice is very quiet.

'No. I didn't.'

He tries to sound calm so Basi won't know he feels sick and his hands are shaking.

'It's all right. Don't worry. I'll come and find you.'

'There was a man with a gun. He shot our scarecrows.'

'Did the man hurt you?'

'No. I kept still as a statue and then I hid. You have to be careful of the man.'

The connection ends. He dials Basi but it goes to voicemail.

He hurriedly phones Rose Polstein. Someone else answers, but then he puts Rafi through to Rose.

'My little brother, he's not on a boat.'

He's now running through the woods towards Junior School.

'We just heard. I'm so sorry, Rafi. Did he say where he is?' Rose Polstein asks.

'No, and he's run out of charge, but he saw a man with a gun shooting at the scarecrows which are in Mrs Cardswell's classroom window, and then he hid, so he must be in Junior School.'

He's having to yell above the wind and run at the same time and it's making him breathless.

'Did he describe the man?'

'No, just said he had a gun.'

'Do you know what time he saw this man?'

'I think he left the beach just after I did. So I think maybe about nine thirty.'

Basi came after him and Rafi didn't know. He never turned round to look. Even though Basi's a fast runner, he's much smaller than him and would have taken longer to get to the top of the path.

'We only know of two gunmen, Rafi, and neither of them is now anywhere near the Junior School building. I want you to find a place to hide and then stay put till this is over.'

'Okay.'

He ends the phone call with Rose Polstein and keeps running. He'll hide when he's found his brother.

Basi is frightened, but he said he wasn't hurt. And Rose Polstein, who he trusts, doesn't think there's a gunman near Junior School any more. Besides, surely they wouldn't spend time looking for one little boy?

It's all right. Don't worry. I'll come and find you.

He remembers, suddenly and vividly, men with guns and dogs pushing Basi and him face down into the sand on the beach by Abu Qir harbour. They were separating the refugees into three different groups. He'd squashed up tight to Basi, put an arm around him, as if they were just one person lying on the sand. One of the men had put a gun between them, using it to prise them apart. Rafi had bunched Basi's damp T-shirt into his hand and held on tightly and the man moved on to the next group and they hadn't been separated.

The last time he ran to Basi through the woods it was barely snowing; now the trees and path are covered in white. Only half a mile to Junior School. He will get to him soon.

*　*　*

Rafi will find it really funny that's he's inside a boat inside a shed because they've been in a boat before and in a shed before but not at the same time! The boat was really squashed and Rafi had to stand on one leg so Basi had room to sleep, but the shed in the Dunkirk camp was nice; Rafi called it their castle because it had a bolt on the door. His friends call places *homey* when they play 'It' and he always thinks of their castle-shed when they say *homey*.

In the camp, the girls and the women slept in nappies and the boys had bottles, because it was too dangerous to go out at night if you needed to wee. In the day Rafi had to leave their castle-shed-homey to get food and they had their own special knock – *rat-a-TAT-tat*; *rat-a-TAT-tat*.

'But why can't you just say it's you?' he asked Rafi.

'I think there's a place giving out food.'

Which wasn't an answer; Mr Lorrimer would say that was *slippery*. Once when Rafi had gone out someone had knocked, *THUD THUD*, not *rat-a-TAT-tat*, *rat-a-TAT-tat*. He didn't unlock the door and then he heard men's voices shouting but they'd gone away again. Later he heard *rat-a-TAT-tat*, *rat-a-TAT-tat* and knew it must be Rafi and when he'd opened the door. Rafi was there with the Soup Sisters. The smiley-eyes sister held his hand all the way to their soup kitchen, and they stayed with him and Rafi, even when the food had all gone, so that nobody would hurt them.

Rafi's a really fast runner. And he'll be here soon and then he'll be all right.

12

10.17 a.m.

'I've checked with all other units,' Thandie tells Rose. 'There's been no sighting or indications of a third gunman.'

They all want to believe there are no more gunmen; that Basi and Rafi are safe.

'It must've been one of the two gunmen we know about who Basi saw in the Junior School building,' Thandie says. 'He shoots at the first copper to arrive then follows the head teacher through the woods. The head goes to the pottery room but the gunman goes on through the woods to Junior School and hunts for children, which is when Basi coming up from the beach sees him.'

'But Junior School was empty so he went to the pottery room?' George asks.

'Yes. There was still a class of young children left to terrorize.'

'What I don't understand,' George says, 'is why didn't he shoot the head teacher in the woods? Why allow him to come back to the school?'

'I think this was very carefully planned,' Rose says. 'But the plan didn't include the headmaster leaving Old School to warn anyone in the pottery room, because they didn't predict anyone being in the pottery room. I think the gunman followed the headmaster, hoping he'd return and they could continue with their original plan.'

'Because shooting him in Old School would cause more terror to the children and staff?' Thandie says.

'Yes.'

'The tech teams have got mobile phone numbers that are on

in the theatre and Old School,' Amaal says. 'The numbers have all been matched to kids and staff, as well as PC Beard's personal number that's on in the gatehouse. They've got one number in Old School which doesn't match students or staff, so must be the gunman's. They're trying to trace an ID.'

If they find out who he is, Rose has a chance of predicting what he's going to do. But the gunman in Old School will be using a burner. He won't use his own mobile; not going to make their life easy like that. Bastard.

She watches the feed from the police surveillance UAV above the pottery room and can just make out the teacher pushing her clay tiles against the window; protection against flying glass but useless against bullets. The teacher's name is Camille Giraud, Rose has found out. Camille's colleagues say that she's sensitive and artistic; their surveillance footage shows that she is also brave and indefatigable.

It's snowing harder, making it more difficult to spot a hostile surveillance drone. Rose had hoped if one was watching from the sky snow would get into its motor or blades and bring it down, as happened with the amateur drones, but apparently not; not if they've got one of near-military grade.

It's been an hour and two minutes since the head teacher was shot, and there have still been no more shots, no further threats, no demands. *What are they going to do next, Rose? What do they want?*

Rose didn't choose to study investigative forensic psychology because she was fascinated by criminal minds (unlike her fellow students, though Rose graduated top of her year); the minds she finds fascinating belong to composers, artists, playwrights, poets, engineers and architects and to people who have done extraordinary, but uncriminal, things – flown to the moon, landed a plane on a river, filmed a turtle for two years. She isn't even *interested* in the criminal mind, she's interested in people who work a nine-hour day and then volunteer in the evening, by the serious way children play, by teenagers' restless newness and inventiveness. But understanding criminals' minds, their cruelty, selfishness, viciousness, is necessary to help the people who do interest her, who matter to her.

'We've got a mobile phone number match and a match to a number plate,' Amaal says. 'Same person.'

And Rose's first thought is, why not use a burner? Why use a car that can be traced to you? It feels off to her; again this feeling that one of the gunmen is playing them.

*   ★   ★

In the theatre, Daphne wants to believe it's not true, that there's been a ghastly, ridiculous mix-up. But it is true. Victor Deakin's mobile is being used in Old School; his mother's car is parked in Junior School's car park where it has no business to be. Daphne knows this because she argued with Detective Sergeant Amaal Ayari, the gentle-voiced policeman who told her – no, she'd said to him, you must've made a mistake! A terrible, terrible mistake! You don't know him. I do. He'd never do this!

The mobile. The car.

Detective Sergeant Amaal Ayari and his colleagues haven't made a mistake.

The gunman who shot Matthew, who's terrorizing everyone in Old School, is someone Daphne has taught, who she's hugged – *Well done, Victor! Fantastic performance!* Whose hair she's tousled, as she does to all of them, just can't resist when she's walking past and they're sitting down – *Daphne, please, took me ages this morning*; *Gerroff*; *OMG, you're like my mum! My granny!* – but Victor just stood up and gave Daphne's hair a quick ruffle back and made her laugh; a young man who charmed her totally.

Who is he when he isn't acting? This man in Old School with a gun?

There'd been a phone call from him in April, out of the blue one evening, saying he'd had to leave because his parents couldn't pay the fees. He'd asked her not to intervene and get herself in trouble over him; and she'd thought it was just like him to be thoughtful towards her. She'd petitioned Matthew anyway to give him a bursary – he was midway through his A-level course and she'd just cast him as the lead in the school play – but Matthew had been intransigent, had told her the subject was off-limits, and she'd had the weirdest feeling, right before she was outraged, that Matthew was sparing her feelings. What had Matthew known?

She'd thought her seeing the best in people, particularly young people, was a good thing, something to be proud of, in a teacher especially. But it's nothing to be proud of. Children and colleagues are in danger and she's afraid she's a part of it.

Detective Sergeant Ayari had gently but firmly insisted that she told the kids about Victor and asked them for any information. They are sitting on the stage, shocked that it's a former student, one of them. Two girls are whispering about fancying him, feeling guilty for that now, dirtied by it. She hears Josh talking about 'that Rohypnol thing'. Tim says, 'Fuck's sake, that was a joke.'

'The police want to know who his friends were,' Daphne says.

'Loads of us were his friends,' Tim says. 'Thought we were. Fuck.'

'But nobody close,' Tracey says. 'When you think about it, he went to parties and gatherings but he DJ'd, not really part of it, just making sure we all listened to his music, and he wasn't anyone's real friend, was he?'

'He was Jamie's,' Antonella says. 'But Jamie dumped him, didn't he? Wouldn't have anything to do with him.'

Jamie is missing and Victor is murderous.

'I'm sure Jamie is safely hiding somewhere,' Daphne says, not sure, a shake in her voice. *Get a hold of yourself, they're all looking at you.*

'The police asked if he's friends with Malin Cohen,' she says.

She'd taught Malin in junior school and hoped he'd grow out of his behavioural problems, but a year ago he'd tried to punch a teacher and been expelled.

153

'God, no, Victor would never hang with Malin,' Josh says. 'Too fucking mental.'

'Yeah, right,' Antonella says. 'And Victor . . .?'

'Perhaps they were friends secretly, then, or some shit; or became friends after they left here.'

'In a way it's good it's Victor,' Luisa says. 'When you think about it. Victor's really fucked off with Mr Marr for not letting him stay here. Gone bloody mental about that. God. But he hasn't got anything against anyone else, has he? Frank's done nothing to him. He's never even spoken to Frank. Wouldn't talk to someone like Frank. And Malin too, if it's him too. This is just against Mr Marr, against adults.'

'I think you're right,' Daphne says. 'Victor and his henchman' – *henchman*, new words for Victor now – 'I think they've done what they came to do. So we just need to wait it out. And while we do, let's continue the rehearsal.'

'Seriously?' Tracey asks.

'Yes,' Daphne says. 'We're not going to let them stop us. We will pick up from where we left off. Duncan, Lennox, Malcolm and Donalbain on stage, everyone else ready for your cues.'

Behind her, Zac is walking up the steep banked steps of the auditorium, fast, as if he can outpace his thoughts; reaching the top and no way out, so back again; and as he gets closer Daphne sees his body shaking as if he's in freezing water.

★   ★   ★

Dannisha Taylor, lead hostage and crisis negotiator, has joined Rose's team in their command and control vehicle. She's sitting close to Rose and Rose is grateful both for her composure and for her lemon soap smell, which is helping to relieve her nausea. Dannisha has told her she has five children at home, five, bloody hell. There's something reassuring about being close to Dannisha.

Rose will use her training and experience in forensic psychology to assist Dannisha with negotiation. She has briefed Dannisha on what they know so far about Victor: he wrote a violent rape fantasy that he managed to explain away; he is off-the-chart bright; he was expelled from the school but they don't yet know the reason; he didn't want to be at the school in the first place.

Now they have Victor's mobile number, Dannisha has a channel of communication.

Dannisha types a text.

> Can we talk?

'Nothing confrontational and not giving away that we know who he is,' Dannisha says. 'A place to start.' Rose nods and Dannisha sends the text.

'Do you think he knew we'd find out who he is?' Dannisha asks.

'Yes. He's using his own mobile and his mother's car is parked in Junior School's car park. If it wasn't for the snow we'd have found out his identity sooner.'

'He could be tremendously idiotic,' Dannisha says.

'I'd go for tremendously arrogant. I think he wants us to know who he is.'

'Yes, I agree with you.'

There's a live feed to their command and control vehicle from the police team outside Victor Deakin's house. Rose is glad they had the foresight to dispatch teams in advance to all the suspects' houses, not wasting any time, especially in appalling driving conditions. A neighbour has told them that Victor's parents are away, a riding holiday in Chile. Rose thinks Victor Deakin planned this for when there were no parental eyes on him.

She watches the screen and for a few moments she isn't in the cramped police vehicle but hurrying along an icy path, a shortcut across the lawn, footprints in snow; other officers are at the back of the house. The sound of a battering ram against the door. A burglar alarm shrieking. Then footsteps, lots of footsteps, doors banging, voices. They're in.

Perhaps they'll get lucky and find a journal or letter outlining what Victor Deakin intends to do and the name of his accomplice; or failing that, perhaps he's confided in someone and they will find something to lead them to that person, or maybe he's been seeing a therapist and they'll find a note of an appointment, a contact number, and she'll be able to get a psychiatric evaluation. But if that isn't the case, if they don't get lucky, no journal, no confidant, no therapist, then it's Rose's job to help find the ID of his accomplice and predict their behaviour.

Her team and other officers are talking to Victor's teachers and fellow students, anyone that can help. Under normal circumstances the gunman's identity would not be made known, but nothing about this is normal and they have to find out everything they can about Victor Deakin as quickly as possible.

'Who's computer forensics lead at the house?' she asks.

'Lysander Kiehl,' Thandie tells her.

Rose is glad it's Lysander, his surname redundant not only because of his extraordinary first name, what were his parents thinking, but because of his reputation as being mind-blowingly brilliant on computers. Getting into Victor's computer and what he's been doing online is a way of getting inside his mind; it could well be Lysander who finds out what Victor Deakin intends to do.

On Dannisha's phone Victor has marked the text as read.

'Okay, let's try calling him,' Dannisha says.

She phones Victor Deakin's mobile; all calls are on speakerphone. The call goes through to message but he hasn't recorded a message, just silence, wrong-footing the caller.

'You said he didn't want to be at the school for sixth form?' Dannisha asks.

'That's right. Neil Forbright said Victor thought it infantilized him,' Rose replies and she thinks the word is telling.

'I've got a lad in the theatre,' Amaal tells Rose. 'He knows something about Victor but he's in a state. Name's Zac Benton.'

'Thanks.' She takes the call. 'Zac? My name's Rose. You all okay in there?'

'Yeah.'

He's breathing too fast; she needs to calm him.

'You're rehearsing *Macbeth*?'

'Yeah.'

'Where've you got to?'

'Duncan's palace in Act One.'

His breathing sounds a little slower.

'You've got something to tell us about Victor Deakin?' she asks.

'I don't know. I hung out with him and Jamie for a bit, but that was ages ago.'

'Jamie Alton?'

'Yes.'

'Can you tell me anything you know about Victor? Can you do that, Zac?'

'Jamie was Victor's friend but then he wouldn't see Victor any more. Said Victor was psycho. And now Jamie's missing.'

The boy's voice is jumpy and his breathing too fast again; so his fear is for Jamie not himself.

'I didn't make sure Jamie was okay. I'm his friend, used to be really close to him, but . . .'

'We're doing all we can, Zac. I promise you that. Do you know why Jamie called Victor psycho?'

'It was after this thing in Exeter, at Halloween.'

'Can you tell me about that?'

'Yeah. Victor threw a brick through a shop window. Jamie said he'd brought the brick in his messenger bag, that he'd planned it, but Jamie didn't know anything about it till it happened. The shop alarm went off. Jamie told Victor to run away, but he wouldn't, even though Jamie kept saying the police would be there any minute. Victor peed through the broken window but Jamie said the police can't have known about that because they didn't charge them.'

'Was that what upset Jamie? Vandalizing a shop and getting arrested?'

She thinks there's more to this.

'Victor made it look like it was all Jamie's fault, but in a

157

mind-fuck way – sorry. He told the police not to be hard on Jamie, not to blame him, that he was older and took full responsibility for it. Jamie said the police lapped it up. They didn't believe Jamie when he said he'd had nothing to do with it, they thought he was pathetic and Victor was this really decent guy protecting him.'

'And Jamie stopped being friends with him?'

'Yes. Said I was right about him, because Victor had done all sorts of weird shit, Jamie just hadn't really seen it before.'

'What kind of weird shit?'

'There was an after-party at Easter. Victor said he'd got Rohypnol and was going to put it into Aysha's drink.'

'Is Aysha at your school?'

'Yes, but she's been evacuated – because I wondered, when I heard about Victor – anyway, I got angry with Victor about the Rohypnol, but he said loads of girls fancied him so he didn't need to use Rohypnol, said that was why it was a *fucking joke*. Jamie had believed that, most people did. But the thing is, I knew Aysha didn't like him.'

'What happened?'

'I told Aysha and she left the party. Even if it *was* a joke, it was a sick joke. But after the shop thing, Jamie saw what he was really like.'

'Did Victor have other friends at school?'

'Yeah. But nobody close, nobody he stayed in touch with after he left apart from Jamie, and then not him.'

'What about Malin Cohen?'

'Not when they were at school but maybe after they both left, I don't really know.'

'Do you know how Victor gets hold of people?'

'Snapchat mainly. I was on his group Snapchat for a bit, before he left.'

After ten seconds, a Snapchat message disappears.

'Did you screenshot any of them?'

'No. Sorry.'

'Do you remember any?'

'Not really, they were just weird. He used the Face Stealer app. Like, where you can merge your face into someone else, like Einstein or Hitler or whatever? There was one where he had shark teeth where his mouth should be, black holes instead of eyes. Freaky. Sometimes he used WhatsApp too, with a voice-changer app, like for a joke. Will you find Jamie?'

'We'll do everything we can, I promise.'

She ends the call with Zac.

An update comes through from a police officer at Victor Deakin's house. This briefing is going to all personnel. In the background, they can hear drawers and cupboards being opened; the room's being ransacked.

'We've found ammo for a semi-automatic and ingredients for a pressure-cooker bomb,' the officer says.

'What about a laptop?' Rose asks; because she's pretty sure that whatever Olav Christoffersen, the IT teacher, found on Victor's laptop got him expelled.

'Just a desktop in his bedroom.'

'Have we got hold of Olav Christoffersen yet?' she asks George.

'He was evacuated and is driving home. He's not answering his mobile.'

'Do you know what car he drives?'

'A Renault Clio.'

'So he'll be going slowly in this. We need to send an SUV after him and get him on the phone.'

*   *   *

The air in the library has changed; it is staler, like you're breathing in other people's fear. A shutter that isn't properly secured bangs against a window as the wind gusts outside and Hannah startles. They are all jumpy with fear. The sound of his footsteps and his phone ringing, but he doesn't answer it. Then the phone stops and it's just his footsteps.

The last of Frank's mobile charge was used up on letting Tobias call his mum; they cannot talk to anyone outside the library now.

Mr Marr has lost consciousness again, as if he's slipping in and out of two worlds, Hannah thinks, but he was always so fully present in this one, the captain of the ship, and she knows he's trying to stay with them, knows how much effort it probably is for him just to keep breathing.

The ambulance people keep telling them what to do by email, and they're making sure Mr Marr is warm, that his airway is clear, that he's still in the recovery position, and it feels comforting that they're doing everything right, even though they can't really help him at all, and she thinks the ambulance people understand that and are telling them all this to help them as much as Mr Marr.

He's big, that's what Hannah thought when she heard it was Victor Deakin. Six foot and heavy; so, what will happen if he shoves the door?

FICTION A–C and FICTION D–G are the latest door fortifications; Mrs Ramsay joined by Jo March, Elizabeth Bennet, Jane Eyre, Maggie Tulliver and Dorothea Brooke; all those women with their many sisters and friends and enemies and poor-choice husbands barricading the door. But how substantial will they be against Victor Deakin if he tries to get in?

Frank's twin, Luisa, emailed him a little while ago from the theatre, all happy, saying, 'It's good news because you're not the target, he's done what he came for.' Like shooting Mr Marr was the end of it, so they could all relax and soon it would be over. But he hasn't got what he came for because he's still in the corridor. And what does it mean, getting what he came for – shooting Mr Marr? Because that means he's a cold-blooded would-be murderer, or hot-blooded, temperature of his blood not really the issue, what matters is that he's willing to kill and if he's tried to do it once, then she thinks he'll do it again, she thinks that's what he's building up to as he walks up and down, imagining it, like Christmas Eve and putting out your stocking, getting all excited.

No one's said it yet but they feel the huge distance between the people who are safe in the theatre and everyone in Old School with the footsteps, especially all of them in the library with Mr Marr's poor white face, his injured head and foot, and blood soaking into the floorboards and the rug. Nobody who isn't here will ever understand, just Rafi, when before none of them could really understand him.

'Mr Forbright's emailed,' Frank says. Brave Frank with his laptop is still near to her and Mr Marr, still near to the door. 'He says the police want any information we have on Victor Deakin.'

There's silence as people wonder what information they have that can help. Hannah didn't know Victor Deakin, just saw him around. He wasn't a loner though, wasn't creepy – well, clearly he's completely fucking creepy, but not the kind of creepy that gives you warning he is going to shoot someone.

Dad would call him *a nefarious fiend, a degenerate devil*; Great-Grandpa's words would be called into use. Dad thinks words are like watches, you hand them down to the next generation and use them on special occasions – *Stupendous! Balderdash!* – and words for monster men too – *unholy scoundrel, diabolical*. Great-Grandpa was in the war, when they had to coin words with bigger meanings.

Esme at the back of the library says, 'He went on the school surf trip but went too far out, wouldn't come back, so wasn't allowed again.'

Hannah thinks of salty air and waves and escape.

Other people are pitching in with sports he does, as if putting together his personal statement or sports BTEC, because what does it matter that he abseils and goes free running and rock climbing? Why couldn't he have free run between two really tall buildings and missed or fallen off a cliff face or surfed into the open ocean and never come back? But he's here. Just outside the library.

And how did he even get a gun? It's not like Somerset is Alabama, not like you can just pop into a supermarket and stick a gun in your trolley with some ammo. How's he done that? How did he know how to do that? Her thoughts are sounding high-pitched in her head, getting panicky; she's got to keep calm, she must be brave and undaunted like Maggie Tulliver and Jo March and Elizabeth Bennet, but she's just plain terrified Hannah Jacobs looking at a pile of books against a gunman.

She thinks of Rafi – the flashing joy that he'd come for her, loves her – and for a little while, despite everything, she feels euphorically happy, weightless, floating above the library and the nefarious fiend in the corridor. But Mr Marr is bleeding and the footsteps are outside and she feels weighted down all over again by fear and shock and just the horror of it, really, the terrible awfulness, like the footsteps flatten her.

Rafi must be okay, must be, because he's out in the woods, not here in the library with the diabolical man, and yes, there were shots heard in the woods earlier, but they were near the gatehouse, and the woods are huge, and Rafi can hide and be safe.

* * *

It's snowing harder; the wind's making the trees bend like air has muscle. Snow has covered the path and Rafi cannot find his way back. There's nothing familiar, everything blanketed white.

He turns and runs in the opposite direction. Surely he'll find a landmark he recognizes and then the path. The wind blows snow at his face, making his eyes smart, and he feels tears and he thinks of Mama, as if the tears came first, before he thought of her, but that's not true because she's always there, and he thinks love lives inside his face, behind his eyes.

Not enough money for her, just him and Basi; ten thousand

euros each to go via Italy, the safest route, the people smugglers said. And oh for fuck's sake, people are bored of this story, all that tugging misery, and you get fed up with desperate people and he gets that, he really gets that, because he'd rather binge-watch a series on Netflix or listen to Spotify or play Xbox or hang out with his friends too, who wouldn't?

But sometimes he tells parts of his story, and Hannah and Mr Marr and Benny and some of his other friends have listened. He hasn't told them all the details, because some things Assad and Daesh did no one should have in their heads. They know he had to leave his mother behind but he hasn't told anyone that on the Journey he'd sometimes thought she was with him; that he'd felt her hand in his as they ran from gangs or police with dogs and rubber bullets; heard the sound of her voice, gentle and quiet, encasing the shouts of men, softening them with her love for him. A woman's shape near, but not too close, and she was there; and then the woman would turn or they'd get closer and she was too old or had short hair or was too tall and how could he ever have thought she was his mother? It was just him and Basi and he had to keep his six-year-old brother safe, that was all that mattered.

For six months looking after his brother was this huge responsibility, yes, but it was also protection against his own grief and loss. Getting to safety in the UK was not an unshouldering of a burden, it was sudden exposure to his own childishness and wanting Mama.

Right from the start Mr Marr had understood. In the Dunkirk classroom, he'd checked with Rafi about Basi: 'Do you think he's up to learning some maths today, Rafi, or maybe a story?' Small things. Important things. And in England he must have spoken to his foster parents, or perhaps they understood too, not to strip the responsibility of Basi away from him, because it is also the skin that protects him.

He left Mama, but he loves her. He left Hannah, but he loves her too. He is someone who leaves the people that he loves.

But he will get to Basi. He just has to find his way through the woods.

★   ★   ★

Basi is getting colder. If he leans against the side of the boat his shivering makes the boat shiver too, and the oars make a rattling sound, like the wind against the door. He hopes Ratty isn't as cold as him; fur is probably warmer than an anorak.

We've done much worse, Little Monkey, Rafi will say when he gets here, and they have done worse but Rafi was with him.

He wishes he could light a fire to keep warm. Mama and Rafi burnt rubbish when they slept outside, broken chairs and tables and things that had once not been rubbish at all. They were waiting for buses to take them out of east Aleppo. The day before, the buses along the road had been like his plastic snake with different joints that wiggle and each joint was a bus, but he'd been too ill to go, so they waited one day, and then there weren't any more buses. Lots of people wanted to get warm by their fire so they all budged up but there wasn't enough room for everyone. He was still ill so he got a good place.

Rafi will be here soon and then he'll rub his arms and his legs and do hot potatoes and they'll do some star jumps and get warm together.

★   ★   ★

The wind is strengthening and the snow getting heavier. Coastguard and police rescue boats with the junior school children and staff have arrived safely further down the coast and Rose feels a moment of relief from nausea. She thinks of Basi, and Rafi, who is responsible for their safety, somewhere out there in the snow, and the nausea returns. The worsening weather is hampering their efforts to search for a third gunman and to spot any hostile surveillance drone.

164

She looks at the feed from the police surveillance UAV above the pottery room; she can't see the teacher at the window – perhaps she's looking after the children inside.

A police imaging specialist took a still from earlier footage of the gunman, blew it up large, and saw the antenna of a two-way radio protruding from the top right-hand pocket of his army cargo trousers, the earpiece most probably hidden under his balaclava, confirming how the gunmen are communicating.

Victor Deakin hasn't taken Dannisha's calls or answered her texts. A police SUV is looking for Olav Christoffersen.

Lysander, lead computer forensics officer, phones from Victor Deakin's house. His call is going to all senior officers.

'Victor Deakin ordered *The Anarchist's Cookbook* from Amazon and downloaded a PDF of "Make a Bomb in the Kitchen of Your Mom" from *Inspire*, the online magazine for Al Qaeda.'

'Anything on guns?' an officer asks.

'I'm sending everyone the emails now. Victor arranged to meet a man four weeks ago in London. His email address is an alias – we're trying to unpick it and it looks like it's most probably Ukrainian. The week before this meeting Victor made three withdrawals of £2,000.'

Six grand, a lot of cash, but Dad drives a new Jeep, Mum a new Mini convertible, holidays in Chile; a teacher's told them a rumour about the family losing all their money, a rumour that is patently false. Their son clearly had a fair whack in the bank to go shopping for rifles and semi-automatics.

'Did Victor do all this on the regular net?' Rose asks Lysander.

'Yes. A Gmail account. Google searches. *Inspire* is easily found on a basic Google search, with a PDF download on how to make a bomb, open to anyone. *The Anarchist's Cookbook* has an Amazon sales ranking and blurb telling you that it has illustrated chapters on the home preparation of weapons and explosives. It probably provides the ingredients on a dropdown menu.'

'How hard was it for you to access his computer?' Rose asks.

'No security at all, and it auto-filled his passwords on every site.'

'Too easy,' Rose says.

She thinks of the rifle shots to misdirect them away from the semi-automatics.

'I think the obvious information could be a decoy for what he didn't want found,' she says.

'I'll look for what he's hiding,' Lysander says.

And it's not just the rifles, it's using his own mobile, not a burner, his mother's car parked in full view. Rose thinks he enjoys playing them; likes being cleverer than they are.

'I think Victor Deakin wants to feel superior and in control of us,' she says to Dannisha. 'I think we could use that. We play to his ego.'

'Okay, let's try,' Dannisha says. She types

> I really want to know all about you Victor.
> Tell me why you want to do this.

Moments later Victor texts back.

> You wouldn't understand moron

> Can you explain it to me?

> Waste of time you're all cretins fucking retards

> I'd really like to hear what you've got to say.

> Just said, waste of fuckin time cretin

> I want to know what's going on inside your head.

> Yeah right, like you'll get it

He's texting back quickly now, caught up in it.

> You're clever then?

> Don't fucking patronize me

Rose types and Dannisha nods.

> Have you got Jamie Alton?

> Would you like to know?

> Yes. Will you tell me?

> Ok

Twenty seconds later another text from Victor.

> Not yet

They wait, but no more texts come through. Rose's team have been focusing on their own work, not allowing themselves to be distracted, and Rose is impressed with them.

Thandie puts down her phone. 'Malin Cohen's ex-girlfriend said he'd been loaned a motorbike by a mate.'

A motorbike is easier to hide than a car. Perhaps you could get a motorbike to go off-road on trails through the woods.

'They're retrieving Victor's mobile phone data,' Amaal says. 'Not the content but the numbers. We should know who he's been contacting.'

*   *   *

It's as if the cafeteria has been holding its breath and with the news that it's Victor Deakin, not terrorists, attacking the school,

167

the room has exhaled. Hannah's father's face is no longer pinched tight, his fingers uncurled a little.

And Beth cannot endure their relief, the sharp contrast to her own feelings.

Hannah's father must realize because he looks at her with kindness. 'It's not good news for you?' he asks; an unselfish, thoughtful man to even notice. She shakes her head.

'I'm sorry,' he says.

Has Victor hurt you, Jamie?

She cannot bear to think of him hurt. She wills her phone to ring. The windowless cafeteria is closing in on her. Ten minutes till Mike's train gets in. When she told him about Victor, he made a sound like a cushion being plumped up, a sigh of feathers against air, as if someone had held him up and punched him in all directions, but he didn't want her to know.

Mike's mother's small car can't get through the snow, so he's asking a neighbour they barely know to break in through their kitchen window. Jamie could still have left a message on their home landline; hope a soap bubble, untouchably fragile.

'Victor Deakin's just getting revenge,' the father in the Mumford & Sons sweatshirt is saying. 'He shot the headmaster for not letting him stay at the school. But he's got no reason to hurt the children.'

This has already been said but it's as if repeating it will give it more solidity, make it more valid.

'The police will make him see that, won't they?' Antonella's mother asks, colour back in her face. 'They'll reason with him that it's nothing to do with the children.'

Other voices join in, 'Of course they will.'

'He'll let them go.'

'He's got no reason to punish the children.'

'They're not a target.'

But Jamie is a target. He's got a reason to hurt and punish Jamie. It was the 31st of October, early evening, when she got a call from the police in Exeter saying Jamie had been arrested. Jamie, who'd never even had a detention at his previous, strict school, who's never even given in his homework late.

When she and Mike arrived at the police station, Victor and his father had already left.

They talked it all through that evening, Mike and Jamie and her, glad that Theo was at university, so their attention could be entirely on Jamie; all of them were shocked because she and Mike had liked Victor too – *liked him!* They said Jamie had to stop all contact with Victor; and Jamie, feeling utterly betrayed by his friend, agreed. Victor had left the school months earlier, so no reason that Jamie needed to ever see him again.

I'm so sorry, sweetheart. I never thought he was violent, never imagined he could be dangerous.

Me neither, Mum, and I was his friend.

I should have told you to ease away from him; should have warned you to be careful.

She sees Victor as a caged snake, and the cage door opening.

Around her a conversation has started about why Victor had to leave. A father is saying it's because his parents couldn't pay the fees and the school wouldn't give him a bursary, which Beth already knows.

'No, that's not true. He was expelled,' a mother says, a parent-governor and chair of the charity committee, who up until a few minutes ago had been mute with fear. 'It was nothing to do with the fees. That was the story he put about and people believed it but it wasn't what really happened.'

But that's what Jamie thought and other people Beth knew at the school too, not that she knows many people, but they all said the same: the house and cars were being defaulted on and repossessed; it was the fees.

'Doesn't matter,' a father says. 'Whatever the reason he had to leave, he's got nothing against our children, that's the important thing.'

'He was expelled for writing rape fantasies,' the parent-governor says. She pauses a moment, not meeting anybody's eye. 'We were told during a governors' meeting. But not in any detail. He'd gone by then, wasn't allowed back on to school property, so we thought it was over. We never thought, any of us, that he'd attack anyone. Hurt anyone.'

Beth should have made friends with this woman, not been intimidated but made herself into a confidante, because then she'd have been suspicious of Victor and would have protected Jamie; would have known she had to do that.

'Do you think he's a danger to the girls?' Hannah's father asks. 'Do you think he's going to harm one of them?'

The room has constricted with tension, this new information pulling them taut, tendons in hands and shoulders and necks tightening.

The young female police officer comes towards her. 'Mrs Alton?'

'Yes.'

'Detective Inspector Polstein would like to speak to you. There's a car for you downstairs.'

'Has something happened to Jamie?'

'I don't have any information, I'm sorry.'

She goes with the police officer; the air too heavy to breathe.

As they walk down the stairs, Beth feels the chill and sees through the windows that it's snowing heavily. It's been snowing all this time. She should have known it was snowing and this cold before, should have realized that Jamie might be outside and frozen. She tells him to wear a coat, but he hasn't, not for years, just a hoody.

On the way to the exit, they walk past a room with a clear Plexiglas wall alongside the corridor. Inside a pregnant mother sits on the floor, rocking to and fro; nobody going to her. Just outside, a young father is playing with a toddler, winding up a clockwork Postman Pat van. He sets the Postman Pat van going along the corridor and the toddler chases it. The toddler is laughing; the father's face is so white that she thinks he'll pass out. She recognizes him, but cannot place him.

Press are gathered outside the leisure centre glass doors, a crush of them with cameras and sound booms, a police officer standing guard. She's ushered away from them, to a goods entrance at the back.

★ ★ ★

In the library, Matthew Marr is losing his vision and each breath is harder than the last. He wants to do something, anything, to help the kids but he cannot move or speak. He forces himself to stay conscious, to stay with them. His hearing isn't damaged; he can hear the footsteps walking up and down, up and down, and someone is talking about Victor Deakin.

Fragmented images wash ashore on to the part of him that is still able to remember: a vicious rape fantasy; a diary on a computer.

He feels anxiety for Jamie Alton but doesn't know why.

He sees again that day with the china-blue sky, Old School bright with flowers, a bird calling. Darkness clouds around it, hiding something. He tries to go nearer – *Come out! Come out! Show yourself!* – but whatever it is retreats further into the darkness and he knows only that it evokes terror and guilt in him.

★ ★ ★

Beth Alton is in a police Range Rover, driving through heavy snow. She is in the back, like she's a child or a prisoner. She remembers going home from the police station in Exeter, Mike driving, her in the passenger seat, Jamie in the back, utterly bewildered and so hurt by Victor, and she wished she'd told Jamie to swap places with her.

It was Halloween and they'd driven past houses with skeletons dangling from front doors, ghosts and devils in porches and windows; the more frightening the house, the more welcoming to children, and she remembers the paradox.

When they got home, their conversation about Victor continued, punctuated by the doorbell ringing. Mike wasn't in the mood for trick-or-treaters but she and Jamie handed out Quality Streets. She looked at the mothers of little witches and superheroes standing close to their children; easy to keep them safe at that age when they are still within touching distance. Jamie's phone kept pinging with Snapchats and WhatsApp messages from Victor, which Jamie didn't answer.

As it got later the kids got older and the masks turned into a Hannibal Lector, a Munch Scream, a devil.

I heard you on the phone that night, Jamie. You were talking to Zac and you were saying, like you were laughing, 'He's a psycho!' and Zac would have thought you were smiling, from your voice, but you weren't.

No.

Victor's mask was his face.

Deep, Mum.

Don't tease me, Jamie . . .

Sorry.

I thought you'd see more of each other, you and Zac; become close friends again.

Like in Year Ten?

Yes.

I'm in the sixth form, doesn't work that way any more.

But if Zac had been your best friend again . . .

I'd be safe now?

Yes.

Zac's not like Captain America.

No. I know. I'm not being logical.

Never been your strongest suit.

No. Please ring me, Jamie. If you can. Please.

A message from Mike on her phone – the neighbour broke in, there's nothing from Jamie on their home answerphone.

Jamie isn't hurt. He's still hiding, that's all, still hiding, and in a building, not outside in the snow, which is why he can't even text her because a glowing screen might give him away. And he doesn't wear bright clothes any more, so that'll mean he's less conspicuous.

A gust of wind batters the police Range Rover. Out of the window, the snowflakes are thick and frenzied, each one an insubstantial feather, weightless, but massed together they are piling on to trees, fences, hills of grass and ploughed fields, everything weighted down and smothered; the landscape being suffocated.

★   ★   ★

The storm has hit, a white-out and gale-force winds making flying the police helicopters virtually impossible but the pilots want to keep searching the woods for more gunmen. A police SUV has found Olav Christoffersen, who'd pulled over on the side of the road, unable to drive further through the snow; he's getting into the police vehicle and will be on the line any moment.

'Not yet' was Victor Deakin's last text and there's been nothing further from him about Jamie Alton. Rose thinks he'll be enjoying the suspense.

'Olav Christoffersen is on the phone,' George says, his face pink with relief at accomplishing his task.

Rose takes the call, putting it on speaker.

'I'm so sorry, I started driving home. Not thinking straight. I always turn off my mobile when I get in the car, just habit. To be safe. So stupid. I just didn't think—'

'Mr Christoffersen—'

'It's Victor Deakin?' Olav Christoffersen says. 'You're sure?'

'Yes, we're sure. I need to know about the events leading to Victor's expulsion.'

'You know about the rape fantasy, which he said was part of his EPQ?'

173

'Yes.'

'After that Matthew asked me to search his laptop. Victor had given permission but even so I was reluctant – I'd believed him about the EPQ and I'd never searched a student's laptop before, we're not that kind of school.'

His Scandinavian accent is more pronounced as his anxiety comes through.

'I found a journal and more rape fantasies about other unnamed girls.'

In the background Rose hears a heavy vehicle rumble past, muffled by snow.

'Have you still got them?'

'I deleted the fantasies immediately. It was an emotional reaction, shouldn't have done. Matthew told me that too. But I, well, I just couldn't bear it for those girls, what he said about them, to still exist, even in type on a laptop.'

'What can you remember?'

'They were sadistically violent. But it wasn't just that. Just. My God. It was the way he referred to the girls, like they were disposable, like toys for him.'

'And his journal?'

'The entry that disturbed Matthew most was typed by Victor the same day he'd written apology letters to Sarah and her parents. In his journal, he said Sarah should be grateful for his attention, and he was outraged at having to apologize. He called Sarah and her parents worms plus a whole load of expletives.'

'Can you remember any of his exact words, including expletives?'

' "A load of fucking worms think I should fucking grovel to them, fucking cunts." That was one line. And then more of the same. Violent, vicious.'

'Do you remember the letters he wrote to Sarah and her parents?'

'Yes. He was very apologetic, said he regretted it all terribly, hated himself for causing upset. He was charming and self-effacing. The letters were totally believable, that's why I hadn't wanted to search his laptop, because I'd read the letters. Matthew was shaken by the difference between his journal and the letters. Said in his entire teaching career he'd never had a student that convincing and manipulative.'

'And he expelled him?'

'Yes. I'd deleted the rape fantasies so we didn't have any evidence to take to the police. We also knew how credible and persuasive Victor could be. We were worried that Victor's parents would go to the governors, who we knew would support Matthew's decision, but even so it would draw things out. But the parents didn't appeal, just accepted it straight away. Matthew met them and they promised they'd take him to a psychologist, keep a close eye on him. Matthew told me he'd make sure wherever Victor went next knew about him, off the record if it breached privacy rules. But a local sixth-form college took him anyway. He must have been very persuasive when they interviewed him. I'm not sure that he even went to a psychologist. I've thought about this, and I can't imagine him agreeing to see one.'

He's right. There were four letters found in Victor's bedroom, all of them asking why Victor hadn't shown up to his appointments; written to Victor not his parents because he was over sixteen.

'How hard was it to get into his journal on the laptop?'

'Extremely. He had a highly sophisticated firewall and complex encryption. He probably okayed the search to Matthew because he didn't think an IT teacher would get through it, but I worked in IT for a defence contractor before becoming a teacher.'

So why no firewalls or encryption on his home computer? It adds weight to her belief that Victor wants certain things found by the police; that he's trying to orchestrate this police investigation as much as he is the attack itself.

'He's exceptionally bright,' Olav Christoffersen says. 'I'm not sure if you've been told that already. Not only in IT and his other

A-level subjects, but across the board. He taught himself ancient Greek and Latin for fun.'

'Thank you, Mr Christoffersen. You've been very helpful. Let me know if you think of anything else.'

'Yes.' He starts weeping. 'I'm so sorry. We knew he was wicked, but we never suspected, Matthew and me, that he'd get a gun, attack the school, never even imagined it.'

He hangs up.

Intellectually her focus now has to be on Victor Deakin, her mental energy directed at him but – and this is important to Rose, crucially important to her – only so she can help the children and staff held captive in the school. Deakin doesn't matter, they matter. It is for them and for their families that she is doing this job, why they are all doing their jobs, and she finds herself wanting to tell Victor Deakin this: it is not you who counts, it is the people you're terrorizing who count, everybody else around you, everyone apart from you, you little shit.

Rose runs through the PCL-R checklist to diagnose Victor. In an ideal world she would have a structured interview in scientifically controlled standardized conditions, but with his journal, the rape fantasies and with what the kids and teachers have told them about Victor Deakin she has enough and needs must when the devil drives; and this is surely when the devil drives. There is a score from 0, 1 or 2 for each category on the checklist. For the planned rape with Rohypnol and for the rape fantasies he scores 2 in the categories 'callousness and lack of empathy', 'shallow affect' (superficial emotional responsiveness) and 'sexual promiscuity', as defined by attempts to sexually coerce others into sexual activity. From his laptop journal, maximum marks for the categories 'grandiose estimation of self', 'lack of remorse or guilt' and 'failure to accept responsibility for own actions'; while the letters to Sarah and her parents and lying to the teachers gain him top marks for 'pathological lying', 'glib and superficial charm' and 'cunning and manipulativeness'; for vandalizing the shop in Exeter full marks for the categories 'poor behavioural controls', 'high levels of irresponsibility' and 'juvenile delinquency'. His extreme sports show a 'need for stimulation/proneness to boredom' and 'being overly impulsive', while at this moment he is flaunting his 'criminal versatility' and she could carry on but he has reached 30, the number that makes the diagnosis.

'What do you think?' Dannisha asks, but Rose is sure that Dannisha, who heard the conversation with Olav Christoffersen, has reached the same conclusion.

'Victor Deakin is a psychopath,' she says.

As Thandie sets up an on-screen briefing, Rose remembers the response of a scientific journal to Dr Hare, an expert in criminal psychology, when he sent them brainwave patterns of psychopaths. The journal returned them to Dr Hare saying they couldn't possibly belong to real people.

The children and teachers in Old School are up against someone who challenges our notion of what it is to be human.

13.

10.45 a.m.

The door of the command and control vehicle swings wide open, banging against the wall. Snow and icy wind blow through the vehicle, scattering notes on Rose's desk, chilling her legs and cheeks as she begins the on-screen briefing to Bronze Command and team leaders.

'Victor Deakin is a narcissistic psychopath,' she says. 'He is ruthless, has no empathy or conscience. Psychopaths can kill for perceived slights and for kicks. Victor isn't attacking the school in retaliation for being expelled and being upset about that, at least not in the sense that his life suffered as a consequence, but because someone had the temerity to do that to him. Matthew Marr had the audacity to get rid of him. He is also adept at manipulation.'

The journal demonstrated that he was enraged at being crossed, a young man whose ego made him infinitely superior to the 'fucking worms'; the letters showed he could play the penitent convincingly enough for teachers to believe him, including very experienced teachers.

'Kids and teachers have also told us that he's into extreme sports,' Rose continues. 'So thrill-seeking is a part of what drives him. But psychopaths get bored quickly, which is why he is pacing up and down the corridor, keeping himself going, as well as enjoying having power over the people he's terrifying.'

'Bored?' Bronze Commander asks, sounding astonished.

'Psychopaths have been known to stop halfway through a killing spree out of sheer boredom.'

'Is that likely to happen here?'

'I think that's one reason why Victor got himself a partner; someone to keep him hyped, giving him hits of adrenaline to keep going.'

'Did none of the kids suspect he'd do something like this?' an officer asks.

'I very much doubt it.'

Psychopaths are not the sinister outsiders keeping to the shadows, but often charming, likeable and outgoing. And they enjoy, revel even, in their deceptions. A few are homicidal.

'With a psychopath, it's a totally different negotiation than with any other kind of person,' Dannisha says. 'We cannot establish a connection based on any kind of rapport. I cannot appeal to his conscience or to any sympathy for what he is putting the children through, even young children. Instead, we have to play to his belief in his own superiority, he needs to feel in a position of dominance. Detective Inspector Polstein has already helped with that, which is why he responded to our earlier texts.'

'We're still waiting for him to tell us about Jamie Alton?' Bronze Commander asks.

'Yes. He'll be enjoying making us sweat, having that power,' Rose says.

'Do you think it was Deakin who shot the head teacher?' Bronze Commander asks Rose.

'No. If Neil Forbright is right, and I think he is,' Rose says, 'Victor Deakin wasn't in Old School till just afterwards, when he swapped places with his accomplice. But I'm certain that it's Victor Deakin who's the orchestrator of the attack.'

'Why swap places?'

'I think Deakin came to check up on his accomplice, to make sure he went through with it, and that was part of the plan; possibly it was a form of remote coercion because his accomplice knew Victor would be coming to check up on him. Then once he was inside Old School, he chose to terrorize people in a centrally heated building where he could stride up and down, enjoying the power, not stand out in the cold.'

'And he told his accomplice that there were children in the pottery room,' Bronze Commander says. 'Because he'd followed the head teacher there earlier.'

'That's the logical conclusion, yes.'

'Any more leads on Deakin's accomplice?' Bronze Commander asks.

'Malin Cohen was arrested nine months ago in the States for serious assault,' an officer says. 'His father got him a good lawyer and he was still under eighteen then so they just kicked him out of the country.'

'Victor and Malin Cohen met each other,' another officer says. 'I've spoken to an evacuated teacher who saw them together in a pub five months ago.'

'You said at the beginning of this, Inspector Polstein, that the dominant one, who we now know to be Victor Deakin, is trying to get as much attention as possible,' Bronze Commander says. 'And that he might just be playing for time to maximize his audience?'

'Yes, and knowing what we do now about Victor Deakin, that is a highly likely scenario.'

'And when he's got his audience? Do you know what Deakin intends to do?'

'There are two options. Both are as a result of him being a psychopath. The first is that Victor being a psychopath actually works in our favour because psychopaths rarely commit suicide. According to teachers he's extraordinarily bright, so smart enough to know that if he opens fire police will kill him. It's possible that he wants to have the power that he has now, and the spotlight of media attention focused on him, but doesn't want to die so will eventually give us his demands for how to end this peacefully.'

'And the second option?'

'The worst case is that he wants to massacre as many people as he can in front of a vast audience and it's worth dying to accomplish it. He will commit mass murder to get fame; he thinks a monstrous event will guarantee his name a place in posterity.'

At Columbine High School, Eric Harris wanted fame. That

was it pretty much. To be a bigger badass than the worst murdering badasses to date, to kill more, to inflict more carnage,
and he was hyped and ready to die to achieve it.

The briefing ends.

⋆ ⋆ ⋆

Snowflakes are almost blinding against the windscreen of the
police Range Rover. The vehicle hits a patch of ice, Beth Alton's
mind and the car skidding together, and she hears Jamie aged
five counting the seconds.

One banana, two bananas – how many bananas?

Ten, then you shout, 'Ready or not!'

You can also count in giraffes, Mummy.

You can.

Victor hasn't found him. He can't have done. She keeps forgetting to breathe and feels it like a scream building inside her.

They've skidded into a snowy bank. The police driver gets
out and Beth gets out too, to help him, to hurry him, but he tells
her to get back into the car. She thinks this will make things
quicker so she does as he says.

⋆ ⋆ ⋆

Neil Forbright stands at the locked door of Matthew's cold, dark
office, listening to the footsteps in the corridor, intimidating,
unrelenting, and realizes that for months this was the sound of
his depression, but now the threat and his isolation are real.

If the police attempt a rescue, which means shooting dead
Victor Deakin, he'll have time to open fire before they bring
him down. The kids in the library don't call him Victor Deakin,
but 'the gunman', as if he has forfeited the right to a name. Neil
thinks they are right and will follow their example.

Which room will he choose? Neil prays to God it'll be this
one, but fears it will be the English classroom, their barricade of

desks giving way and Jacintha's poems turned bloody with bullets; he cannot think of dead children and staff, he simply cannot, so he thinks instead in cowardly metaphors. Or he'll choose the library first because Matthew is in there, and he'll want to finish the job of murdering him and because the library has the greatest number of children.

But Matthew may already be dying, and he can't be with him.

He unlocks the door, because if the motherfucker with the clicking heels starts firing, he's going to ignore the police's instruction to 'stay put', and go out and tackle him. *Motherfucker*, when was the last time he'd used that word, any aggressive pejorative adjective, against anyone but himself? Anger is a new emotion and he welcomes it; like a freak gust of wind, abrading his fear so that he feels clean of it.

He is deputy head, responsible for the children in this school, and must step up to the mark.

But how can he overpower a man with a gun? He's not armed, nor is he strong and athletic. How can he help them?

⋆ ⋆ ⋆

In the library, the shutter is banging and banging as the wind outside builds. Mr Marr has lost consciousness again. Hannah is checking his pulse, which is getting harder to feel.

Everyone is quiet, listening to the shutter and the footsteps which are coming back towards them. *Click-click click-click*; does he know that his footsteps are like time beating? The footsteps stop outside their door.

If this is how she's going to die – 'if', still a great big 'if' – then it's nothing like she'd imagined. Not that she'd imagined it often, she's not maudlin that way, but when she did she'd imagined long dusty roads or an ice age come early, civilization gone, her and a band of fellow survivors toughing it out as long as they can with a few books and a flute; not the school library on a normal day.

The footsteps haven't moved away. He's still outside. Keep

thinking about dystopian novels; frankly it's a bit embarrassing that the only way you could imagine your own death was to have the entire planet dying as well.

The door creaks. He's pushing it.

She wants to speak to Rafi; tries to believe it's really good that she can't because his last impression of her would be that she's not at all brave. And that might be stupid, but it's all he'll have to go on about her, and she wants him to remember them running through the woods this morning, even though she was wheezing like an old geezer in a tartan dressing gown, because they were happy and she was unafraid.

A book falls from the pile as he pushes against the door. The pile is budging. He must be putting his whole weight against the door.

Good that she can't speak to Dad too, because she'd break down and that would be awful for him, awful for her. She was quite calm on TV with lip-glossy Melanie, speaking normally, smiling even. He'll think that's how she feels, hopefully he'll think that.

There's a gap now, he's opened the door a tiny way.

Ed goes to the door and sits down with his back pressed to the books, using his body to shore up the barricade. Frank joins him, pushing back, and the door doesn't open any further.

A minute later, the footsteps walk away.

⋆   ⋆   ⋆

A young officer comes on to Rose's screen, one of Lysander's computer forensics team.

'A tweet's trending,' the officer says. 'It says the gunman inside the school is a psychopath. The news channels are picking it up.'

'Who tweeted it?' Bronze Commander asks.

'We're trying to trace the source.'

And the question they're asking, but not out loud, is if there is a leak inside the investigation? Is someone feeding information to the media? Rose hasn't met the majority of officers involved, but she trusts her colleagues; when kids' lives are at stake, she totally trusts them.

'Beth Alton has been held up because of snow,' Thandie says. 'There's a Portakabin ready for her when she arrives.'

'Tonya, the secretary inside Old School, is on the phone,' George says. 'A kid in her class has seen the tweet.'

⋆　⋆　⋆

Matthew's office is getting colder, the wind blowing in even through the shuttered windows. Neil has received another email from Frank in the library; the gunman tried to push his way in, but after one minute gave up.

One minute never used to seem long to Neil, the difference in the softness of a boiled egg, but now he knows how long each of the sixty seconds lasts when there's a gunman the other side of the door, as if he's taken control of time and stretched it.

Neil fears that next time he won't give up; that he'll shoot the kids against the door, because they won't move. They might be vomiting they're so frightened, he knows that's what's happening in the library, but they're still against the door.

How much time can Neil give to the children if he goes out and tackles the gunman? He will be shot, so how much time? And if it's a minute or two, will they feel long minutes to the kids? Because if they did, then it would be worth it. Or would the horror at seeing their deputy head lying in the corridor, like a betrayal in its own way, Neil thinks, would that contract the time they had left to them?

His phone rings and he answers it.

'Mr Forbright? It's PC Beard. I've just heard from Tonya in Jacintha's classroom. There was a tweet and it's all over the internet. The gunman in your corridor is a psychopath.'

The word chills Neil because he knows what it means, wishes he didn't, wishes his Kindle wasn't full of books on psychopathy, but he'd become fascinated by people at the other end of the mental health spectrum from himself. Because while he's felt fearful of life, as if missing a layer of skin, too empathetic, too sensitive, without enough confidence to steer a course through life, psychopaths have huge egos and are ruthless, many becoming captains of industry, valued for their lack of empathy and utter self-belief, and if they are murderous have no compassion.

'The police officers in charge of all this have said they cannot comment,' PC Beard says. 'Which is protocol and there's very good reasons for that protocol, but I'm afraid it means it's true, otherwise they'd have denied it.'

'Do the kids in the library know?' he asks. 'Has Tonya told them?'

'No. She thought it best not to.'

'Good.'

Frank is saving the data on his laptop for emails, he won't be searching the internet.

'You told me earlier that the corridor bends?' PC Beard says.

'Yes.'

'Is it a sharp bend?'

'Like an L-shape.'

'So, if he went past the bend towards the front door, everyone along your bit of the corridor would be out of his sight?' PC Beard asks.

'Yes, but—'

'And that means everyone in the library and in Jacintha's classroom, Tonya and Donna and all the children in there, they'd be out of his sight too?'

'Yes, but he just walks up and down our part of the corridor. He doesn't go towards the front door, doesn't go that far.'

'All right, we need to come up with a plan,' PC Beard says. 'Do you have the phone number of a teacher in the theatre? I'll need to let them know.'

'I'll text it to you.'

He'll send PC Beard Sally-Anne's number, humour him, but there is no way for any of them to escape.

He listens to the footsteps that have new menace now, and thinks of the experiment when people were given flashcards with the words *Murder* and *Rape*. Normal people were disturbed, their brain's amygdala lighting up, but the psychopaths' remained dark. Then they were shown graphic photos of murder victims. The psychopaths' amygdalae were still dark but their language centre was activated as if they were analysing the emotions instead of experiencing them. The man in the corridor has no connecting humanity.

★　★　★

There are no windows in the theatre so no sign of the storm outside, but despite the central heating the temperature is dropping. On stage, the kids have put on cardigans and hoodies over their hessian tunics as they rehearse. They've been forgetting lines and missing cues, and then they go back to the start of the scene, determined to get it right, as if by getting it right they can achieve some kind of control.

Sally-Anne comes up to Daphne.

'There's a policeman in the gatehouse,' she says. 'PC Beard. He wants to get everyone in Old School to us in the theatre.'

'Does he know how he'll do that?'

Sally-Anne shakes her head, as Daphne knew she would, because those children and staff can't get here without being shot by Victor Deakin.

'He says Victor Deakin is a psychopath,' Sally-Anne says. 'The real thing.'

When Zac said Jamie thought Victor was 'a psycho', Daphne had thought he meant it in a slangy way, like on the telly when anyone who's strange and unbalanced is a psycho.

'I just googled it,' Sally-Anne says. 'Here.'

And it's almost funny that you can google the mental state of a gunman in your school. Daphne skims the results:

... they hide among us ... ruthless, callous and superficially charming ... master manipulators ...

Another article:

Psychopaths are able to display emotions they don't feel . . .
everyone around them is convinced that those emotions are real. . .
they lack remorse . . . It's difficult to spot a psychopath . . . they
can look actually like they're more genuine than other people . . .
most people don't have to fake emotions all the time, so they
don't have any practice at it. But someone who doesn't feel these
emotions will have practice at faking them.

Daphne remembers that she didn't like Victor when he
arrived in Year 11, he hadn't charmed her then. When did he
start to charm her? When did he know how to play her? Or
rather, when did she teach him how to play her?

*They hide among us. Fake emotions all the time. Practice at faking
them.*

Oh dear God, what has she done? All those notes she gave him
that he was so brilliantly quick to pick up: she *taught* Victor to
mimic emotion. She coached him on how to appear like a normal person, a regular teenager, to dissemble convincingly.

On stage, Miranda is playing Lady Macbeth as a sex kitten,
pretty much how she'd play any part she was given, even in
these circumstances.

> 'Come, you spirits
> That tend on mortal thoughts, unsex me here
> And fill me from the crown to the toe top full
> Of direst cruelty; make thick my blood,
> Stop up the access and passage to remorse . . .'

She'd cast Victor, her star pupil, as Macbeth but if he is anyone
he is Lady Macbeth, not like sweet, implausible Miranda, but
right from the start ruthless, manipulative and wicked.

'I'll stand by the doors, wait for them,' Sally-Anne says.

She leaves and Daphne feels suddenly very alone, maybe

because she cannot share Sally-Anne's hopefulness or because guilt cuts you off from other people.

On stage, Miranda as Lady Macbeth continues.

'Come, thick night,
And pall thee in the dunnest smoke of hell,
That my keen knife see not the wound it makes,
Nor heaven peep through the blanket of the dark,
To cry, "Hold, hold".'

It's like she's trying to become a psychopath, pitiless and without remorse, as she pumps herself up to murder, but Victor doesn't need to try.

And she realizes this play isn't about getting titles and a crown and palaces, but about seizing raw power; something Victor has right now.

What will he do to everyone in Old School? What has he done to Jamie?

She wants to tell them all that she should have seen it, should have known or at least suspected; that it is her fault, because she helped him hide in plain sight.

★   ★   ★

In the police Range Rover, Beth Alton sees press vehicles being turned back at a police cordon, but they are waved through and drive nearer to the school. There are dozens of parked emergency vehicles, police cars and vans and ambulances, fire engines too, why do they need fire engines? Overhead the sound of a helicopter, a blurry black shape in the sky. The police driver parks the Range Rover and tells her that Detective Inspector Polstein will be with her shortly. He escorts her towards a Portakabin.

The emergency vehicles have snow inches deep on their roofs

and covering the windscreens; the sound of creaking as the wind pummels against them.

She sees a woman in her early thirties walking towards her, just wearing a dress, not a coat or jumper even, but strikingly upright despite the fierce wind and snow, almost marching.

'Mrs Alton? Detective Inspector Polstein,' the woman says, holding out her hand, having to raise her voice above the wind. 'Rose. Let's go inside.'

'Have you found him?' Beth asks, and despite no indications for this she hopes that Rose will say, *Yes! And he's fine! And you can take him home with you.*

'Not yet,' Rose replies. 'We're doing everything we can.'

She opens the door of the Portakabin and ushers Beth in.

'The police officers at the leisure centre said you haven't managed to speak to Jamie?'

'No.'

'And he hasn't texted?'

'No.'

As Rose turns up a heater, Beth looks at the side view of her face, pale, almost ill, her slanting cheekbones, the corner of her mouth, no lipstick, and then she turns to Beth and her eyes look directly at her, and Beth wants to look away because she reads something there.

'I heard he used to be friends with Victor Deakin?'

Here it comes; this is why they want to talk to her. She'd hoped she was being paranoid, hoped against all logic that it wasn't because of this.

'Yes, but then Jamie broke off their friendship.'

'When was this?'

'October the thirty-first.'

She thinks of devils and monsters at their door; Victor's handsome human face.

'After the vandalism incident in Exeter?'

'Yes. He wouldn't take Victor's calls or Snapchats or anything.

Mike and I told him to do that. To break from him completely. And I think Victor might want to punish him.'

The snake let out from its cage.

'Up until the vandalism incident, was there anything that Victor did that—'

'No. He had us completely fooled. But I should have seen what he was like, should have suspected – I was even grateful to him for being friends with Jamie.'

'It's not your fault nor Jamie's that you thought Victor was genuinely who he appeared to be. Nobody saw what he was really like.'

She's kind, Rose Polstein; but what kind of mother is grateful to someone for being friends with their child? And maybe that's why she didn't look harder at him, because Jamie was lonely and she was too busy being grateful to find out who this person really was. She imagines driving Victor Deakin to the top of a cliff, the car teetering over the edge, and threatening to go over unless he reveals himself.

Right, Mum, like that would've helped.

I know, but . . .

I told you before, he had me fooled too and he was my friend.

Rose Polstein's pager vibrates and she looks at it.

'I'm sorry, I have to go for a little while. It should warm up in here in a minute.'

When Rose has gone, Beth opens the door again and cold invades the Portakabin but she leaves it open as if she'll hear Jamie or at least be closer to him. When he was at his last school, and so unhappy, she used to arrive early to pick him up, ridiculously early, like an hour or more, and stand by the gates to the school as if that made any difference to anyone, but she'd done it anyway.

Getting him drunk might have been easier, Mum, rather than the whole car-cliff-teeter thing.

★　★　★

Rose walks quickly back to the command and control vehicle, the wind slicing through her dress, the snow falling thickly on to her hair and shoulders. She's numbed with cold by the time she gets inside. Thandie wraps her own jacket around her and she's grateful.

Before talking to Beth Alton, she'd suggested sending another text with a direct question:

> Do you have Jamie Alton with you?

Dannisha had paged her to say Victor had responded.
'What's he said?' Rose asks.
Dannisha shows Rose Victor's response.

> ☺

Dannisha types:

> How is Jamie?

> ☺

> Is he ok?

> Having a fuckin blast man, a fuckin blast

> What do you mean?

> Need me to fuckin spell it out moron? He's my pal my wingman

14.

11.00 a.m.

Beth Alton goes outside the Portakabin, scanning for Rose Polstein, the wind blowing snow against her face and into her eyes. She sees a blur of movement, hopes it's Rose, but it's three police officers, wearing black and carrying guns, moving fast towards the school. Her mobile is in her pocket, so that it doesn't freeze or get wet and stop working; her fingers are tightly around it. The helicopter overhead beams a searchlight down and for a moment she is blinded, has to blink to see again.

She takes out her mobile and tries ringing Jamie, expecting it to go straight through to message again. But it doesn't! It rings and rings, and she thinks he's going to answer, that he'll hear her special ringtone and answer! But after seven rings it goes to message.

Rose Polstein is walking towards her through the snow, with that upright marching stance. Beth hurries to meet her.

'Jamie's phone's on! It just rang. Didn't go straight to his message.'

'Did he answer?'

'No. But it rang several times, seven or more.'

Rose Polstein's face is drawn like she's suddenly very tired.

'We think his phone was powered off or the battery was out until very recently,' she says. 'But now his phone's on again and we're tracing the location.'

Rose goes into the Portakabin. Beth follows her quickly inside.

'So you can find him; you can get him out!'

Rose sits down on a plastic chair and gestures to Beth to sit next to her but she doesn't want to sit down. She wants Rose to tell her how they're going to rescue him.

'Has Jamie been lonely?' Rose asks.

What does that matter? For God's sake, why are they even in a Portakabin while Jamie is out there?

'Has he ever been violent?' Rose Polstein asks.

'Of course not, why—?'

'Has he said anything to you recently that's been out of character or strange?'

'Why are you asking me these things?'

'Mrs Alton, I need to know.'

A conversation with Jamie, a real one from just a fortnight ago, creeping then pushing its way in:

'Jesus, just stop the questions.'

'I just want to know if you're okay at school, with friends and things, and—'

'Get the fuck off my case.'

'I'm worried about you, sweetheart, that you're lonely and—'

'Yeah, and what can you do about it? I'm not in fucking nursery school, Mum.'

She'd held on to the 'Mum', like a tiny thing at the end of a cruel sentence that still meant they had a connection with each other. Because the truth is that the Jamie she's been talking to in her head, well, she hasn't heard from that boy for nearly six months; that long since she went out with him in the car on the farm track, teaching him to drive, longer since they went to visit St Andrews; all those words and phrases of his taken from six months ago and earlier.

He doesn't mean to hurt her though, she knows that; he still thinks mothers are unassailable. And her lovely boy is there, but hidden inside the bolshie teenager. And she has proof of that because at Halloween she and Mike had talked to him and he'd listened to them, had agreed not to see or talk to Victor again; he'd minded what they said and taken their advice.

But then he'd retreated back into his surly shell, a camouflage to disguise unhappiness. And it's just being a teenager, for heaven's sake, unknotting the apron strings, and loads of mothers complain about it, their loving little boys, the girls too, becoming rude teenagers, and it's worse when you've been particularly close, like her and Jamie. And yes it can feel like a stranger has arrived in your child's body. But her beloved boy is still there. And later, after this terrible thing is over, they'll be reunited, hugging, and she'll be crying, *heart soft as a baby bird, Mum*, and they'll be close again.

'Victor and Jamie have been WhatsApping, Snapchatting and phoning each other; over the last few weeks, they've spoken more than a dozen times a day.'

'I don't understand.'

'We've gathered information on Victor's phone and Jamie's too. And we have phone calls logged between them, as well as messages, including earlier this morning.'

Rose Polstein's face is close to hers, looking at her with sympathy that is damning her son.

'No, there must be a mistake.'

'I'm sorry, there isn't a mistake.'

Rose Polstein is wearing a corduroy jacket that's too tight, though it's too wide at the shoulders; focusing on her clothes not what she's saying because her words are appalling and absurd.

'We think that Jamie shot Mr Marr,' Rose Polstein says.

'No. You're wrong. Totally wrong.'

She's pregnant, Beth realizes, maybe five months. That's why the jacket's too tight, why does she realize that now? Rose Polstein's left hand has moved to her tummy, unconsciously protecting the baby. Against who?

'You can't have any proof,' she tells Rose Polstein. 'Because it's not true. Jamie would never hurt someone.'

Rose Polstein's pager bleeps and she turns from Beth to read it.

I'm phoning you again, Jamie, and my hands are shaking but I just need to press one button, because you're top of my favourites.

She says your mobile phone has been traced to outside the pottery room.
She says you're holding a gun.
She says there are children inside.
Pick up, pick up, pick up.

It goes through to message. 'Hey, it's Jamie, leave me a message.'
The same message he's had for over a year.

'It's Mum. Please call me, sweetheart, please. Please.'

'Do you think he can be negotiated with?' Rose Polstein asks.

'Yes. Of course! If it's Jamie, which I can't believe, but even if it is really him he won't fire the gun. I don't know how Victor got him back as a friend or persuaded him to frighten people but he won't be able to make him actually hurt anyone. He's not that powerful. No one could make Jamie change that much.'

From kind to violent; from a boy who's lived inside her body and heart and head and home for over seventeen years, to some-one she has never met. He's been withdrawn for the last few months, unhappy, but not fundamentally changed. Not deep down. He's a gentle person, always has been, never rough even as a little boy. She remembers seven-year-old Jamie with an injured bird, demanding she take it to the vet. He'd brought it to her from the lawn, pulling out the bottom of his jumper to make a fabric sling for it, in case touching it with his hands frightened it.

'And he's turned on his phone,' she says to Rose Polstein. 'So if it is him, it means he wants to talk, doesn't it? If it's him it means he wants this to stop.'

★　★　★

Daphne hadn't wanted to tell the kids in the theatre about Jamie, but Detective Sergeant Amaal Ayari, the gentle bearer of ter-rible, terrible news once more, had said the police need any information the students might have. But no one has any infor-mation, none of them can really believe it. They'd chosen to carry on with the rehearsal, shock in their hesitant, quiet voices.

Daphne had been so worried about Jamie, feared he'd been harmed by Victor, and she thinks that he has been but not in the ways she'd imagined.

On stage, Miranda plays Lady Macbeth convincing Tim as Macbeth to commit murder; but even shaken teenage Miranda cannot take away the horror of these lines.

'I have given suck and know
How tender 'tis to love the babe that milks me:
I would, while it was smiling in my face,
Have plucked my nipple from his boneless gums
And dashed the brains out, had I so sworn
As you have done to this.'

Right, enough is enough; Daphne gets up on to the stage. 'Okay, everyone. Let's decide if we really want to carry on with this.'

'She's a psycho bitch,' Tim says.

'Why doesn't he see that?' Caitlin asks. 'She's said she'll bash a little baby's brains out. Her own baby. While it was breastfeeding. Jesus.'

'How did he persuade Jamie? How the hell did he do that?' Josh asks.

Daphne also cannot understand how Victor could persuade gentle, shy Jamie to be part of something this wicked.

'There's the witches,' Tracey says, in her witch costume, so clearly aware of the power of the witches. 'They kind of started this too.'

'But Jamie doesn't have any witches,' Tim says. 'Does he, for fuck's sake?'

'We don't know that,' Tracey replies.

'He had a crush on me and I knew about it,' Antonella says. 'I wasn't kind to him, if I had been kinder maybe . . .'

'Not your fault, Antonella, half the school's got a crush on you,' Tim says. 'And nobody else teams up with a gunman.'

Zac looks up and Daphne sees he's crying. 'If I'd stayed his friend . . .'

'No, absolutely not,' Daphne says. 'This is nothing to do with you, Zac.'

Although if warm-hearted Zac had still been his friend, then maybe everything would be different.

'I think we should keep on rehearsing,' Tim says, and people are agreeing with him.

'Are you sure?' Daphne asks.

'I think it helps make sense of things,' Caitlin says.

Perhaps they also see this first act as being about how a murderer is made; the creation of a diabolical pair.

'Right then, we'll keep going, but we'll stop whenever you like. Any of you. If it gets too much.'

'We'll have to stop before we get to the Macduff children scene, won't we?' Tracey says.

Daphne nods.

'You're sure they're okay, Anna and Young Fry?' Josh asks.

'They're safe,' Daphne says. 'Evacuated with everyone else in New School.'

As they get on stage, ready to resume the rehearsal, Daphne thinks again about Lady Macbeth's psychopathic violent rant, and then in walks Macbeth, her poor sap of a husband. And what does he say to this woman, who's asked for night to hide her crime from heaven? *My dearest love.*

She thinks Jamie believes Victor cares about him.

★   ★   ★

Rose Polstein looks at the feed from the police surveillance UAV above the pottery room. Through the dense snow she can just make out the shape of Camille Giraud at the window. They now know that the gunman in the black balaclava, pointing his semi-automatic at the window, is Jamie Alton. Police imaging specialists, monitoring footage of Jamie Alton, say that for a few seconds he fiddled with something in his left cargo trouser pocket, while his other hand kept a finger on the trigger of the semi-automatic, braced against his shoulder. They now realize that he was powering up his mobile or putting in the battery. His two-way-radio antenna still protrudes from a right-hand pocket.

Rose wishes their suspicions had been unfounded but from the beginning of this every missing student had to be seen as a potential perpetrator as well as a victim. It was why she asked for Beth Alton to be brought here, so she could speak to her face to face. Officers met the father's train and are questioning him; at Warwick University police are talking to the older brother. They have also been talking to evacuated teachers and a team was ready and waiting to go into the Altons' house. So far they've found a journal hidden under his mattress which they have scanned and sent across, but no weapons; a computer forensics expert Rose hasn't worked with before is searching Jamie Alton's computer.

The FBI use the term *dyad* for killers who jointly carry out a crime. After the Columbine attack by Eric Harris and Dylan Klebold, the phenomenon has been researched extensively. Those two teenagers were not the bullied outcasts or members of a gang as originally portrayed by a frenzied media but, Rose believes, a psychopath and a depressive with lethal toxicity as a pair. The chance of such a dyad coming together must be infinitesimally tiny, all those coincidences and fateful small decisions.

She turns to her team. 'Okay, we don't know for definite Jamie's movements this morning because his mobile battery was out, but we now have a plausible narrative. Victor Deakin knew he couldn't come into the school unnoticed, he'd been expelled, but Jamie Alton could. He left the theatre this morning at 8.15, ostensibly to get props from the CDT room, but instead came into Old School. He was just another student at the school so didn't attract any attention. He was probably carrying a sports bag or a rucksack, something big enough to hide the guns.'

'The rifle's long, would stick out,' Thandie says. 'So he camouflaged it; a cricket bat cover maybe or rolled-up sleeping bag. And no one would take any notice because kids at a school like this are always going on D of E expeditions and the like. Or they'd just think he was fetching props.'

Rose nods. 'He's also got a balaclava and combat clothes in there,' she says. 'And a two-way digital radio to talk to Victor Deakin. He slips into an empty room in Old School. He puts on the clothes and balaclava, turns on the digital radio.

'The school goes into lockdown and he waits for his head teacher. And up until this point he's behaving very weirdly, extremely worryingly, but not yet violent; not yet abhorrent. He could simply be under Victor's influence up until now, undertaking his orders. But then he came out of that room and he shot his head teacher. He crossed a line into attempted murder. And we need to understand why, because that's the only way we're going to be able to predict what he'll do next, and if we can negotiate with him.'

'He knew Victor Deakin was coming to check up on him?' Dannisha suggests. 'You said that earlier.'

'Yes, and I think that's a part of it – remote coercion by Victor – but not all of it.'

'Do you think Victor deliberately chose him?' George asks.

'Yes.'

Because this toxic, catastrophic friendship wasn't random on Victor's side. Fate might have served up Jamie Alton at the same school as him, but she thinks Victor befriended Jamie and then somehow persuaded him to be his partner in the attack.

'I think Victor could well have tried to recruit other people first,' she says. 'A teacher saw him with Malin Cohen, maybe Malin refused.'

At Columbine High School, Eric Harris was turned down by other students before he found lonely, depressed Dylan to be his sidekick, a boy named after the poet Dylan Thomas, from a family where even toy guns weren't allowed; a gentle boy who made his mother origami birds.

★   ★   ★

There's a young male police officer in the Portakabin with Beth. She's on the phone to Mike, who is in a police car.

'To start with, they thought he might have been hurt by Victor or was his prisoner,' Mike says. 'But even then they were asking me these odd questions, like if he had a grudge against anyone, if he'd ever been violent. Violent. Jamie, for God's sake. And now they're searching the house. They asked me if it was safe. If there were booby traps. Jesus Christ.'

Beth thinks of her kitchen with the police in it; their breakfast things still piled up in the sink. Jamie hadn't eaten breakfast, had left early, rushing out to a waiting car, a friend giving him a lift this morning he'd said, not saying which friend, and she'd just been pleased and didn't pry. She called goodbye, but not I love you, because she's become wary of doing that, worried about getting it wrong. But she's done everything wrong. Because with a different mother, this wouldn't be happening.

She looks through the windows of the Portakabin, as if something will change, make all of this different, but there is just thick snow.

She has to face the truth, has to do that, because it's all her fault. She didn't know that Jamie had taken Victor's calls again; that Victor had somehow clawed his way back into Jamie's life. She didn't see how lonely and unhappy Jamie must have been; didn't prevent Victor from doing this to her son.

'We just need to talk to him,' Mike says. 'He wants to talk to us. Doesn't want to be doing this.'

'I know.'

It's intensely comforting to have another person who knows Jamie like she does, who's known him since he was a six-pound-two-ounce scrap of a baby, who knows that he is good.

200

'I've told them he'd never hurt anyone,' Mike says. 'I told them it's Victor behind this, not Jamie. Check again.'

They both hang up as they did a minute ago to check that Jamie hasn't phoned or texted while they've been talking, knowing that he hasn't, knowing that their mobiles would beep and vibrate if a call or message was coming through, but not trusting the knowledge.

Mike rings back.

'Nothing,' he says.

'No.'

'I told them he never even had toy guns, just the Nerf ones with the foam bullets, and water pistols, Super Soakers, and that's nothing like boys who want air rifles and BB guns or toys that look like the real thing. I told them it was Victor who'd have made him hold one. I told them he doesn't even play violent Xbox games; he likes that building-cities one.'

'And he likes drawing too,' Beth says.

Beautiful intricate pictures. But it feels indulgent to her, this conversation, as if they've been good parents.

'The police asked me if he's depressed,' Beth says.

'He wants an eighteenth-birthday party and he wants to do really well in his exams, that's not being depressed.'

'I think that might just be a brave front,' Beth says. 'Maybe for us. I don't know if he is or not.'

She thinks sadness and loneliness led him back to Victor, and then Victor did something terrible to him.

'I think it must've been Victor who turned him against us, made him even more isolated,' she says.

'He didn't turn against us.'

'He doesn't talk to us any more, Mike. He hasn't spoken to me, not really, not properly for almost six months. Hasn't taken my calls when I ring him at school. Most of the time, he doesn't even come out of his room.'

'He spoke to us after that thing in Exeter at Halloween; we were up half the night talking, just like we always used to.'

201

'But it was us talking, he was just listening.'

'He spoke to Zac.'

'Not for long. A few minutes maybe.'

And it sounded like he was laughing but his face wasn't smiling, just pretending to. But she'd believed he was fine, that it would all be all right, because she'd wanted to believe that.

'He'll talk to us now. He'll want to talk to us.'

'But what if he—'

'They'll shoot him, Beth, if we can't talk to him.'

'No. They can't. He's not going to hurt anyone.'

'I know that, darling. But the police don't know him, don't know us. Check again.'

★   ★   ★

Snow is blowing inside the command and control vehicle, George's shoe wedging the door open, but only the cold air stops Rose's nausea. Still wearing Thandie's jacket, she is gradually appropriating her team's clothing.

Rose knows that for the kids and staff trapped inside the school, the confined space will be getting smaller; quiet sounds will have a new volume as the world constricts around them. But at the same time this event is expanding with increasing numbers of police and counterterrorism officers, journalists and cameramen not only in the UK but all over the world covering the story live on TV screens, radio and internet news where social media brings it to an ever-growing audience.

Neil Forbright has told them that Victor Deakin tried to get into the library but gave up; Rose thinks he got bored, or was toying with them, and fears he'll try again.

They haven't yet been able to talk to Victor Deakin's parents; the police in Chile are trying to locate them but Rose thinks this may well be over before they are found. Matthew Marr told them about the rape fantasies and she thinks the violence and hubris probably fitted with personality traits they'll have seen in him since childhood. But surely they wouldn't have gone away on holiday if they had any inkling he could do something like this? No, he's most probably been on model behaviour for months, convincing them that Matthew Marr exaggerated what he'd done, that the childhood behaviours that worried them were now a thing of the past, that he's been keeping all his psychology appointments.

'Still nothing on the Deakin parents?' she asks Amaal.

'No. And Jamie Alton still isn't answering his mum or dad.'

'You'd have thought the parents would have noticed, wouldn't you?' Thandie says. 'I mean, what the hell are these parents doing?' Another thump to the punchbag.

But Rose feels compassion for Beth Alton: from what she's seen, she's a loving mother who doesn't deserve what's happening to her. And she feels sympathy for Victor Deakin's parents too, until there's evidence to the contrary, because Victor is adept at concealment and because a psychopath's brain is made that way. Yes, an abusive childhood can exacerbate it but it doesn't cause it. She remembers the case of a five-year-old girl calmly and repeatedly trying to flush a kitten down the loo, witnessed by her horrified mother. Later the little girl had just as calmly denied it. She doesn't know what kind of parents the Altons or the Deakins are, all of that will be found out after this, the details analysed every which way, but she does know that whether deserved or not, for the rest of their lives they'll be blamed for what's happening now. We're not a 'sins of our fathers' century, she thinks, but 'sins of our children'. Sometimes she has a terror of motherhood. She thinks of her scan earlier this morning, watching the second heart beating inside her body; the realization that from now on she'll always have two heartbeats.

What the hell are these parents doing?

Get a grip, Rose, it's not normal to worry like this. Normal pregnant women worry about folic acid and pelvic floor exercises. Get a grip and just focus on your job.

On screen, a briefing begins, led by Bronze Commander.

'Visibility is atrocious and it's impossible to monitor the sky,' Bronze Commander says. 'It's too risky to assume that we're not being watched. So our marksmen are still keeping their distance. As I said before, if they fire from that range they risk only wounding Alton, giving him time to shoot and inflict multiple civilian casualties before taking him out. Where are we on negotiation?'

'Jamie Alton's mother and father are attempting to phone him,' Dannisha says. 'But he hasn't answered.'

'UAV footage shows he hasn't taken his phone out of his pocket,' a UAV operator says.

'So why's he switched it on?' Bronze Commander asks.

'One of two reasons,' Rose says. 'He switched it on just after Victor told us that Jamie was his wingman. Victor knew we'd be able to trace the mobile number. He may have told Jamie to prove what he'd just told us.'

'Via the two-way radio?'

'Yes. Or, more optimistically, Jamie has turned on his phone because a part of him wants to talk to his parents, or to us, to be dissuaded from going any further.'

'Do we know why he's doing this? Does he have a grudge?' Bronze Commander asks.

'Not as far as we know,' Rose says. 'Nothing against Matthew Marr or the other teachers, nor with other students. There's very little bullying and no jock culture at the school. It's possible that he shot Mr Marr for expelling his best friend, pushed on by Victor, but it doesn't explain pointing a gun at a room full of children. There's nothing to suggest that he's psychotic and he's never been violent before.'

Jamie's been lonely, but no one has called him a loner. He might have felt left out, but he's never done anything aggressive, never hurt anyone, never even said mean things that students or teachers have reported. The diary found in his room has nothing violent, but is filled with intricately coloured drawings and romantic poems.

'I think that he was lonely and depressed, and that made him easy prey for Victor Deakin,' she says.

Teachers had noticed him becoming withdrawn and two had been concerned enough to talk to him about depression, but Jamie denied it. He was bullied at his previous school, according to his tutor, and that could have later caused teenage depression. His tutor had asked the school counsellor to see Jamie last term, but Jamie had failed to keep any of the appointments.

'We need to find out why Jamie has become violent,' she says. 'I don't think Victor Deakin's influence alone can make a previously unaggressive boy into a killer. There's something else in play.'

She tends to agree with his mother that a single person, even psychopathic highly manipulative Victor Deakin, doesn't have that kind of power.

'Once we know why he's become violent,' Dannisha says, 'then we will know if we can negotiate with him and how to do so.'

'Has your opinion of Victor Deakin remained the same, Detective Inspector Polstein?' Bronze Commander asks.

'Yes, a brutal psychopath and the orchestrator of the attack, and also wanting to orchestrate how it's covered by the media and how we investigate it.'

Rose thinks everyone in the briefing probably imagines Victor-the-brutal-psychopath as darkly malevolent but Rose sees him as a surfing, base-jumping DJ, a party guy, a prankster with Rohypnol in his pocket and a brick in his messenger bag, and hey! a semi-automatic in the kit bag, and he's having a blast, man, a fucking blast! And all the more terrifying because of it.

'What about a third shooter on site?' Bronze Commander asks.

'Our surveillance teams haven't found anybody else,' an officer says. 'But the school's extensive grounds are mainly woodland, much of it very dense, and the weather is making our search almost impossible.'

'There was a student on TV earlier,' Bronze Commander

says. 'She saw a glint coming from the high ropes course in the woods just before 8.20 which might have been binoculars.'

'If so, it doesn't mean it was a third man,' an officer says. 'Most probably Deakin keeping watch.'

'A scramble though,' Rose says. 'For Deakin to see PC Beard's car and then get in position to take the shot.'

'But doable,' the officer says.

Rose nods, yes, doable.

'Let's run the rest of that scenario,' Bronze Commander says. 'Victor Deakin shoots at PC Beard from the woods and then follows the head teacher. He sees there are children in the pottery room. When Jamie Alton has shot the head teacher in Old School they swap places. It's Jamie Alton who goes to the Junior School building where Basi Bukhari sees him. Junior School has been evacuated but Alton knows about the young children in the pottery room from Deakin. He goes to the pottery room, where our drone picks him up.'

Rose has been considering this scenario and she thinks it potentially has flaws.

'It's tight,' she says. 'For Alton to swap places with Deakin and then get from Old School to Junior School in the time. The head teacher was shot at 9.16, Rafi thinks Basi saw a gunman at 9.30.'

'But again it's doable,' an officer says. 'Even if Alton spent five minutes swapping over, he'd still have had nine minutes to cover a mile, which is fine for someone reasonably fit even in snow.'

'Yes, but I think the shooter Basi saw must have searched Junior School first and found nobody before he started randomly shooting at a window in a rage.'

'Then maybe the swap-over was quicker and he ran faster, or he simply fired for the hell of it without searching first,' another officer says.

Rose hopes they're right and there's no third gunman.

Lysander comes on to the screen; he doesn't bother with preliminaries.

'Deakin's been on the dark net, using Tor,' he says.

The so-called 'onion' router, because of its layer-within-layer of complex encryption.

'He visited a site which has Russian PKM machine guns for sale but didn't buy from there,' Lysander continues. 'He also spent time on a site called "How to Make Your Gun Shoot Like It's Fully Automatic – in One Easy Step" and "Fire-Power Enhancement", which sells the necessary equipment. Using bitcoin he made a payment to "Fire-Power Enhancement" for an amount that would equal two sets of the equipment.'

'Send out an alert to all units that we think both gunmen have converted their guns into fully automatics,' Bronze Commander says.

In the Las Vegas massacre, Paddock's converted semi-automatics fired 800 rounds a minute.

In effect, they have machine guns.

15.

11.10 a.m.

In the library, Frank is next to Ed, their backs against the books and the door. He hasn't tried pushing it again, perhaps he won't try again. Please let him not try again.

It's funny, up until today Frank and Luisa have never been close, not in the way that twins are meant to be, no secret language, nothing like that, but earlier she emailed him that she loves him, which she's never said before, or anything like it. He's always thought Luisa was embarrassed of him; perhaps she still is but it doesn't matter.

He thinks the footsteps are outside Mrs Kale's classroom and feels guilty for his relief that they're not outside the library door, tries to justify his relief as knowing that the English classroom has desks as a barricade, so more protection than they do, but knows that isn't the truth.

Hannah is with Mr Marr, stroking his face lightly, and Frank can tell she feels useless, that she thinks stroking his face isn't helping, but if it was him he'd like it, and not only because it would be Hannah doing it, but because another person's touch is comforting, and he thinks Mr Marr can feel the kindness in it.

When Luisa and people in the theatre emailed them questions about Mr Marr, they said that he's injured but will be okay, because they need to believe that.

A new email on his laptop from Benny in the theatre.

'Benny's spoken to Rafi,' he says and his voice is startling to himself and to everyone else in the library because no one has been talking and if they do so it's in whispers.

'He wanted Rafi to come to the theatre, but Rafi said he couldn't. Said his little brother's missing.'

'Basi wasn't evacuated?' Hannah asks him and he wants to lie to her but can't.

'No, he wanted to be with Rafi, so Rafi's in the woods on the way to find him, but he's lost.'

In his semi-consciousness, Matthew Marr hears Frank talking about Rafi and Basi and fear jolts him, adrenaline coursing through him.

His mind flicks through images: Scylla and Charybdis, the Cyclops, the drowned men and their wooden Ithacan ship; he remembers talking to Rafi about Odysseus's voyage, comparing it to Rafi and Basi's journey, their Circe the broker in Syria who said the route was safe.

But those dangers are past. New dangers now.

He'd thought they'd been evacuated but they're in danger and it's linked to Victor and the diary and to a word spoken in the corridor.

Rafi told him about a devil in the Quran called Iblis, with immense hubris, but whose only power is to cast evil suggestion into men's hearts. Why is he thinking of Iblis?

He sees the day with the blue sky, Old School bright with flowers, a bird calling.

He doesn't know what this day means, but he sees the darkness surrounding it and it's hiding something.

He feels someone gently stroking his face, and forces himself to go into the darkness, further and further, and it brings him to the school corridor with the photos of boy soldiers.

It's darker than normal, the lights are switched off, the corridor dim. Hannah is with him; she was waiting for news of Rafi, maybe about to go and find him because she loves Rafi too. He's talking to the policeman in their gatehouse. Tobias is next to him and he's trying to hurry Tobias along.

A door closing.

Which door? Must be the door to the drawing room, which he thought was empty.

Footsteps in the corridor behind them.

Hannah goes into the library, but Tobias isn't moving.

The footsteps continuing, getting closer.

A click. The cock of a gun.

He makes Tobias go into the library.

He turns to face the man behind him.

A balaclava covering his face. He's pointing a rifle. Another gun, like a machine gun, strapped to his chest. The rigidity of hatred, so that the guns and his hate are the same. He takes a step away from the gunman, his back against the wall; by his head is the display case of medals.

'Please,' he says, dropping his phone, betraying his fear. 'Talk to me. Tell me why you're doing this.'

'Collaborators!'

Jamie Alton's voice.

Stillness, time waiting.

The subtle press of a trigger.

The bullet travelling faster than its own sound.

Collaborators

Shrapnel made of gallantry.

Collaborators

Those boys dying so that this wouldn't happen.

The benevolent order of things destroyed.

He was outside Old School seven months earlier, the sky a perfect china-blue above him, the front of the building bright with white and purple clematis flowers, the call of a pied flycatcher; summer term, the start of the second week. That morning Olav Christoffersen had told him what he'd decrypted on Victor's laptop, shown him the journal, and he'd instantly expelled him.

Jamie Alton came up to him, distraught, tears streaming down his face.

'Please let Victor stay. Please.'

But he couldn't possibly do that.

'It's not his fault his dad lost their money,' Jamie said. 'You have a bursary fund, use that to pay his fees.'

So that was the story that Victor was spinning.

'They don't look poor,' Jamie said. 'But their cars are on HP and the house is already remortgaged.'

'Jamie—'

'You pay for the Bukhari brothers, so why not Victor?'

'This is nothing to do with money, Jamie. I can't have him in the school. He's done something wicked.'

'He told me you'd come up with something. An excuse. Why should the Bukhari boys be here instead of him?'

'Jamie—'

'He said you'd rather pay for fucking Muslims to be here but not one of your own! They're not even English! Don't belong here!'

And he heard Victor's voice in Jamie's, in this boy who was normally gentle and quiet.

'Like I said, this isn't about fees. He's done something unforgivable. You need to stay away from Victor.'

He'd attempted to comfort him, at one point trying to put an arm around him, but Jamie, silently tearful, had shaken him off. He'd just expelled his only close friend and at that moment he hated him. But Matthew didn't think that would last. And without Victor at the school Jamie would surely rekindle his old friendships and make new ones.

And he hadn't really thought Jamie needed to stay away from Victor, because even if Jamie wanted to continue the friendship he was certain that once Victor left the school he'd leave younger, shyer, more innocent, less clever Jamie behind him. A belief based on twenty-five years of teaching young people that was appallingly wrong.

They'd stayed friends; and the crying boy in April, loyal to a vicious older boy, vulnerable to him, had been turned into the man in the corridor, rigid with hatred.

The school is being attacked for taking in Muslim refugees.

But surely they'll just target him, please God let them just be violent towards him.

★　★　★

Despite the open door, the command and control vehicle feels more cramped to Rose, people's breath and body odour close up against her. It's now been two hours and twenty-eight minutes since the first shots at the police car; one hour and fifty-seven minutes since the head teacher was shot. Victor hasn't pushed at the library door again but she fears he will.

Lysander and Stuart, senior officer in counterterrorism intelligence, come on to the screen. This briefing is going to all senior officers.

'On the dark net I have uncovered multiple communication channels between Victor Deakin and Jamie Alton and an organization called "14 Words",' Lysander says. 'They are both members of this organization.'

'14 Words is a white supremacist terrorist group,' Stuart says. 'Its name refers to the fourteen words: "We must secure the existence of our people and a future for White Children." It calls for "White Jihad". Its particular hatred is against Muslims.'

'The girl whose drink Victor wanted to spike with Rohypnol is Muslim and the vandalized shop is owned by a Muslim couple,' an officer says.

'How many Muslim students and teachers are still at the school?' Bronze Commander asks.

'Just Rafi and Basi Bukhari,' another officer replies. 'Five Muslim students were evacuated from New School and two from Junior School.'

'Why shoot the white head teacher and terrorize non-Muslim children and staff?' Bronze Commander asks.

'As well as hating Muslims and other non-whites for, as they see it, polluting the gene pool,' Stuart says, 'the group has also threatened liberal journalists and MPs and others who they think condone the eradication of the white race. In this case it's a school taking in Muslim refugees. In their eyes, the staff and pupils are collaborating in white genocide.'

'Even seven-year-olds?'

'Probably. And they'd want to punish the parents too.'

Rose thinks of Jo Cox, the white MP and advocate for compassion towards Syrian refugees who was murdered by a white supremacist terrorist.

'14 Words was formed as a splinter group from National Action, a neo-Nazi group banned for being a terrorist group in the UK in 2016,' Stuart Dingwall says. 'It is affiliated with Scottish Dawn and NS131, banned under UK terrorism laws in 2017. It has links to far-right terror organizations in the USA, Europe and Australia, several of which have planned or carried out terrorist atrocities.'

The more Rose found out about this school which, like so many others in the UK, has the freedom to worship whichever god you want, or none, has openly gay teachers and multicultural liberalism, the more she's feared it could be a target for terrorists, both white supremacists and Islamic State, with their shared hatred for inclusivity and tolerance. 'Our people'; you cowardly inadequate bastards have so much in common.

And it makes her furious because the school has a fantastic kind of innocence, if innocence is openness uncorrupted by prejudice, and she admires whoever fought for it because you don't get this thoughtless tolerance without people taking risks, putting themselves on the line. Who was the first teacher to openly declare she was lesbian to the kids and then give them their geography homework? (Though in a school like this they probably don't believe in homework.) And now a school that should represent a microcosm of the UK, diverse and tolerant, is being punished for it.

'Since the end of June, Jamie Alton has had an online alias:

"Aryan Knight",' Lysander says. 'Using the alias Aryan Knight, Alton started interacting with 14 Words in August. Deakin was already a member of this terrorist group and the initial traffic between 14 Words and Aryan Knight was on Deakin's computer on the dark net.

'14 Words sent Alton links to white supremacist forums, blogs and propaganda videos. I'll send you the details. As well as the online interface, I am pretty certain there were also face-to-face meet-ups, using codes for places and people.'

Usman Pabey, a young IT forensics analyst, joins the briefing.

'I've been working under Lysander's direction. At the beginning of September, Alton increased the security on his own laptop. By the end of September he was having near-constant interaction with 14 Words on his own computer as well as Deakin's, at one point receiving up to forty messages a day from them.'

'So we can pretty much chart a textbook radicalization process,' Stuart says.

'Radicalization explains how Victor Deakin persuaded Jamie to join him in this attack,' Rose says. 'Victor would have groomed him first and he was lonely, probably depressed, so vulnerable to radicalization.'

Beth Alton was right, Victor alone wouldn't have been powerful enough to utterly change her son. Victor needed an organization to get Jamie to cross a line into murder and be a wingman for his attack. It was probably Victor who came up with the *nom de guerre* 'Aryan Knight' for Jamie.

'14 Words vet all new recruits,' Stuart says. 'They're paranoid about being infiltrated. Alton would have had to have a personal recommendation by Deakin.'

'A week ago, Twitter, YouTube and Instagram accounts were set up in the name Aryan Knight,' Usman says, 'with the banner "100%" or "18"; so far there's been no activity but we're monitoring the accounts.'

'100% means pure Aryan blood,' Stuart Dingwall says. '18

corresponds to the first and eighth letter of the alphabet, which are the initials of Adolf Hitler.'

'How does this affect negotiation with Jamie Alton?' Bronze Commander asks.

'Negotiating with a radicalized terrorist is extremely difficult,' Dannisha says. 'Sometimes impossible. We are up against intensive brainwashing. We don't know how extensive.'

Rose looks at the screen that shows the pottery room; it's snowing too hard to see anyone at the window. What would she say to Camille Giraud if she could speak to her? Could she tell this sensitive, brave art teacher that they can get her and the children safely out?

Only if there is something left of the boy Jamie Alton used to be; only if they can talk to that boy. Jamie did apparently break away from Victor Deakin on the 31st of October. Did Victor instruct Jamie to say he'd broken off their friendship? Ask him to broadcast that he thought Victor was a psycho? It would be safer for his plan if nobody linked the two of them, if there was no reason for anyone to watch Jamie in the run-up to the attack. And Halloween, with its devils and ghosts, masks and disguises, is a date Victor would have chosen to deceive people; there's a vicious playfulness to it.

But maybe on that one evening Jamie saw Victor for what he really is and tried to go back to his parents, to his old friend Zac, his liberal school and family tugging him back to the boy he used to be. And perhaps a part of that 'old Jamie' remains and he can be reasoned with and he'll let the children and their teacher go. But she fears it's unlikely.

'Detective Inspector Polstein?' Bronze Commander asks.

'I think our chance of getting through to Jamie Alton, that there is anyone left to get through to, is very small.'

'Have we been able to establish any communication?' Bronze Commander asks.

'He hasn't answered his phone to his parents or to us,' Dannisha says. 'His mother has a special ringtone; if his ringer is on he'll know it's her calling.'

'Get the parents to keep on trying, and we do too,' Bronze Commander says. 'What about Victor Deakin? Does belonging to this terror organization tell us anything more about what he intends to do?'

'Being a member of a white terrorist organization might be good news in one way,' Stuart Dingwall says. 'As Inspector Polstein said, Deakin is intelligent enough to know the police will shoot him dead if he opens fire. Unlike radical Islamist terrorists, where suicide is frequently part of the plan, far-right terrorists often aim to survive.'

Rose knows he's right; the Michigan State University report confirmed it. And you only have to think of far-right terrorists in the dock following an atrocity: the murderer in Pittsburgh, the murderer in Charlottesville, the murderer of scores of young people in Norway raising his – very much alive – arm in a Nazi salute.

'Victor won't die for any cause other than himself,' Rose says. 'And as I said, psychopaths rarely commit suicide. But he could still want to go out in what he sees as a blaze of glory.'

'And he's still waiting to build up an audience?'

'Yes. Perhaps he's waiting for the USA to wake up. It's 6.13 in New York.'

'Do you know why Deakin joined 14 Words?' Stuart asks.

'I think he wanted to use them to radicalize Jamie Alton, so he'd have an accomplice,' Rose says.

'And access to weapons,' Stuart says. 'He bought the guns himself, but this terrorist organization probably found him a dealer. More than that, like Generation Identity, they send UK recruits to military-style anti-Islam training camps in Europe. Deakin has been out of the country twice in the last six months, but Alton hasn't. So Deakin, perhaps others, trained Alton.'

'And has Victor Deakin been radicalized too?' Bronze Commander asks.

'I doubt it; he just found a natural home,' Rose says. 'A white supremacist terror organization fits a Caucasian narcissistic psychopath. But this terror group are using him too, to carry out this attack for them.'

Very useful to have a psychopath, a man utterly devoid of conscience, in your ranks; all the most ruthless paramilitary groups have them; they crawl out of the woodwork whenever a terrorist organization goes recruiting.

'Does it help us negotiate with Deakin?' Bronze Commander asks.

'I think he has already decided what he wants to do,' Rose says. 'If he reads our texts, even if he talks to us, he's not going to change his plan.'

While the discovery of 14 Words is relevant, and deeply worrying, for Jamie Alton and for the children held captive by him in the pottery room, it doesn't tell her more about Victor Deakin.

Lysander comes back on to the screen.

'We've tracked the tweet about Victor Deakin being a psychopath to 14 Words, through a variety of aliases; they used automated high-volume retweeting to get it trending.'

Rose already thought 14 Words knew Victor was a psychopath, probably top of his desirable qualities, and that Victor himself is proud of who he is.

'But why?' Bronze Commander asks. 'To increase the terror?'

'That's the logical conclusion, yes,' Rose says.

'And did nobody they know suspect terrorist involvement?' an officer asks.

'Victor Deakin is a psychopath so a skilful liar,' Rose says. 'And Jamie was probably coached on how to stay below everybody's radar. It's significant that he used an alias and to begin with, his interface with this organization was done on Deakin's computer, before he upped the security on his own computer. And with Jamie's previous personality, by all accounts an unaggressive, thoughtful boy, I doubt people had any reason to suspect, even people close to him.'

'I agree,' Stuart says. 'Unfortunately for us, members of 14 Words are not skinheads with white power tattoos or any other obvious signs of their beliefs. They are younger, tech-savvy, and have made themselves deliberately hard to detect.'

The part of the screen that showed Lysander's face now only shows the top of his head as he bends to work on Victor's computer, while he continues the briefing.

'There are levels of encryption we haven't been able to access on the 14 Words dark website,' Lysander says. 'We think they're hiding posts or messages, and possibly transactions. Instead of using 1024-bit RSA encryption keys they're using ED-25519 elliptic curve keys.'

'Can you decipher any of it?' Bronze Commander asks, Rose thinks unnecessarily since Lysander will be doing everything humanly possible; Bronze Commander can't have worked with him before.

'Everyone's doing their damnedest,' Lysander says.

'The significance of belonging to a terrorist organization isn't only in the way the two gunmen are going to behave and whether or not we can negotiate,' Stuart Dingwall says. 'It's that belonging to this group means they have a terrorist organization behind them, one that we believe is highly efficient and skilled. We've just seen that in their sophisticated use of bots on Twitter. It's likely that if they have a drone, it's of military grade so can withstand these conditions, and is being operated by someone away from the campus.'

This makes sense to Rose; they've had reports of Victor's footsteps walking up and down almost continuously, so although Victor would probably enjoy using a surveillance drone, it would be hard to do so at the same time as terrorizing everyone in Old School.

'Belonging to a terror group also makes it more likely that there's another gunman on the school grounds,' Stuart says.

'Deakin and Alton are part of the conspiracy to keep him secret?' Bronze Commander asks.

'If he exists, yes,' Stuart replies.

'Any sign of a third gunman?' Bronze Commander asks.

'Surveillance UAVs and helicopters haven't found anything,'

an officer reports. 'But in conditions like this, and with a campus this size, that doesn't mean very much.'

'If there is another gunman,' Stuart says, 'he's likely to be a senior member with paramilitary training; he would know how to keep out of sight.'

'Do we know the whereabouts of Rafi and Basi Bukhari?' Bronze Commander asks.

'We think Basi is in the Junior School building and I'm pretty sure Rafi went to find him,' Rose says.

The briefing ends.

A few moments of hush in the room and they can hear the storm outside the open door.

Rose tries to ring Rafi, but he doesn't answer.

★   ★   ★

The vicious icy wind whips against Rafi's face. He's running through bracken up to his thighs, heavy with snow, but he may be running in the wrong direction. It's snowing more heavily and he still cannot find the path, cannot orientate himself.

He remembers clinging on to Basi's T-shirt on the beach in Egypt so they wouldn't be separated. Next to them a little girl's father blew up armbands as if she was going in a swimming pool. Hours later, they'd had to wade through the sea in the dark to get to the boat. Basi was quickly out of his depth. Rafi tried to hold him up above the waves so that they could reach the boat, but he wasn't strong enough or tall enough, and it was getting too deep to keep Basi's face above the water.

★   ★   ★

The door creaks like someone is pushing it, but it's the wind, Ratty, just the wind, that's all, and there's nothing to be frightened of, and when Rafi gets here he'll make them laugh, really he will.

When they were near to Italy, men wearing big white hoods got on to their boat with masks over their faces and white suits and gloves, and he thought they were exterminators, and started crying, just like he is now, all crouched down in a boat just like now, but Rafi said: '*Look, Little Monkey! They've sent astronauts from Planet Almiriykh to welcome us!*' And then they really did look like astronauts.

Creaks are closer to him, but it's just the canoes on their hooks because the wind has got in through the door and is pushing them, that's all it is. Not the man in the dark.

There was this other time, they were all really cold and wet, even colder than he is now, and a man had got on to the boat and given them thin metal crumply blankets and he'd wanted a real blanket, soft and heavy, with Mama tucking it around him, and then Rafi said, '*Basi, we're a box of chocolates,*' and that's what they looked like, all crammed into their boat with the gold wrappers around them.

16.

11.16 a.m.

Rose pulls Thandie's jacket around her as she walks from the command and control vehicle towards the Portakabin; squalling wind tunnels of snow between the lines of parked emergency vehicles. Now they know that it's a terrorist attack, the government will be involved and potentially the military. COBRA, a crisis response committee headed by the prime minister, will be convened. This event is again escalating and expanding.

And she thinks there are others involved too, secret and hidden, because when Bronze Commander asked Lysander if he could access the terrorists' encrypted material on the dark net, Lysander had said, *'Everyone's doing their damnedest'*; she doesn't think he was only referring to his computer forensics team. There's a rumour that Lysander used to work for GhostSec, an offshoot of Anonymous, which attacks ISIS websites on the dark net and is believed to have thwarted several potential terrorist attacks; the rumour also goes that Lysander was personally responsible for replacing an ISIS website with an advert for Prozac; she's never heard him joke so thinks it unlikely. She does believe that he took down close to a hundred child pornography sites. And she's heard that some people living in totalitarian regimes, who use the dark net to publish and read uncensored news, track child abusers and terrorist organizations. She imagines them all hunting in the dark net to help the children and staff at the school. Victor Deakin won't have taken into account Lysander and his army of ghosts.

She opens the door of the Portakabin. There's a young

negotiator sitting with Beth Alton, one of Dannisha's team who will advise Beth on what to say to Jamie, but Jamie still hasn't answered Beth's calls. Rose sits down next to Beth, but Beth looks away from her and presses a number, one button because Jamie is in her favourites, top of the list. Rose wonders how many times she's tried to phone him now.

'Does Jamie ever go out on his own?'

To meet terrorists; to be trained.

'Sometimes. A film or shopping. And for long walks, he likes walking.'

'Do you know where he goes on his walks?'

Beth shakes her head; her call goes through to message.

'It's Mum again, please call me or Dad, sweetheart, please.'

'Jamie is using a different name on some social media accounts, do you know anything about that?'

Beth looks at her, with relief she thinks.

'Yes. J-Me. Zac thought of it, capital J and then me. J hyphen me.'

'A different one. For the last five months, he's called himself Aryan Knight. He has email, Instagram, Twitter and YouTube accounts in the name of Aryan Knight.'

'That can't be Jamie. I mean, why would he want to call himself something like that?'

She seems unable to take in this alternative name, this alternative son.

'Have you ever heard him use that name? Or refer to it in any way?'

'No. It's not Jamie. It's—'

'What about the number 18 or 100%?'

Beth turns away from her.

'Have you heard him say either of those numbers to anyone?'

'No.'

'But you recognize them?'

'He wants to do well in his exams, to get full marks. And he wants an eighteenth-birthday party.'

'Did you ever hear him talking to anyone else about this party?'

Beth is silent.

'Has he said anything about 14 Words?'

'What do you mean, fourteen words?'

'Maybe you heard him on the phone talk about—'

'No. I don't understand. What does it even mean?'

'It's a white supremacist terrorist group. Jamie is a member.'

Beth shrinks backwards as if Rose has hit her hard across her face.

'No. You've got it all wrong. He'd never be a part of something like that. He's not like that. Jamie's not racist, doesn't hate people.'

The same certainty with which she said he would never be violent.

'Our family aren't like that, or our friends,' Beth continues. 'And he goes to this school, this tolerant, liberal school.'

'I think Jamie's been depressed and lonely, and I think they preyed on that, Victor and then this group. I think Jamie was groomed first by Victor then by this terrorist organization. They would have made him feel noticed; wanted. And they gave him a cause, made him feel important and valuable. This is how these organizations work. A group like this exploits vulnerable young people.'

'You're saying he's been radicalized?'

'Yes.'

'But that's Muslim teenagers going off to join ISIS or girls going to marry fighters in Syria, it's not a boy like Jamie.'

As if she can disprove the fact of it by arguing against its probability.

'He's pointing a gun at a building full of children,' Rose says.

'But he won't hurt them.'

'Can you be sure?'

'Yes. It's this group and Victor who are making him do it.'

'No one is standing there making him do this, Mrs Alton.'

'But they are, they've got inside his head, that's what you're saying. That they've radicalized him.'

Beth has understood.

223

'Yes, and I need to know if any of the old Jamie is there.'

'Of course he's still there. Of course. I've seen that all along, even when he's been difficult – I've seen the old Jamie too. And he'll want this to be stopped. I just need to talk to him.'

Rose prays that she's right, and that if she is, Jamie answers his phone.

Her beloved boy, a terrorist; a white supremacist. Everything good broken apart.

You were drowning and I didn't even see, didn't rescue you. I let Victor pull you down deeper. I'm so sorry, sweetheart.

All the things she'd worried about, but then dismissed earlier – not having good friends who care about him, his low self-esteem and being unconfident, having his heart broken – are desperately, vitally important because they made him vulnerable to Victor and this appalling group. Antonella wasn't even a girlfriend, he made that up because he was so sad and lonely and wanting love, and that made him defenceless too.

And she didn't see. Happening to her boy, right there in front of her, and she didn't see.

They were trying to brainwash him, strip out who he is, but they haven't managed it, they haven't. Because Jamie is still there. Yes, he's changed in the last few months, beyond recognition from her boy, yes, that's true. He's barely spoken to her or Mike. Halloween was the last time he spent an evening with them. He doesn't want to eat with them, makes himself sandwiches to take to his room, and even his posture's changed; he's hunched and stiffer. He doesn't meet her eye when she talks to him. But then, out of the blue, he'll make her a cup of tea in her special mug, for no reason, or suddenly smile at her, and the other day, driving to school with Radio 1 on as usual, Wolf Alice came on, a band they both like, and he'd said, 'Hey, Mum . . .' so she'd know to listen.

These moments are spread out, weeks between them some-times, not all the time like they were six months ago, and they're tiny things, but they matter because they're signs that her son is still there; Jamie, who'd never hurt anyone, doesn't hate anyone, and he wants this to stop.

She calls him again and it goes through to his message, the same message he's had for over a year, and his voice sounds so young and friendly.

'Hey, it's Jamie, leave me a message.'

'It's Mum, please ring me, sweetheart, please.'

She hangs up and waits.

What did they do to you, Jamie?

      ★   ★   ★

1 IN 5 BRIT MUSLIMS' SYMPATHY FOR JIHADIS – *Sun*

MUSLIMS TELL BRITISH: GO TO HELL!! – *Daily Express*

MUSLIMS 'SILENT ON TERROR' – *The Times*

JIHADIST KILLERS ON OUR STREETS – *Daily Express*

**HUNDREDS MORE UK MUSLIMS CHOOSE
JIHAD THAN ARMY** – *The Times*

MUSLIM SCHOOLS BAN OUR CULTURE – *Daily Express*

**NOW MUSLIMS GET THEIR OWN LAWS
IN BRITAIN** – *Daily Express*

PM: UK MUSLIMS HELPING JIHADIS – *Daily Mail*

BRITAIN GOES HALAL – *Sunday Mail*

GIVE US FULL SHARIA LAW – *Daily Express*

MUSLIMS TELLS US HOW TO RUN OUR SCHOOLS – *Daily Express*

SNIFFER DOGS OFFEND MUSLIMS – *Daily Express*

RAMADAN A DING-DONG – *Sun*

FURY AT POLICE IN BURKAS – *Daily Express*

STRANGERS IN OUR OWN COUNTRY – *Daily Express*

BOMBERS ARE ALL SPONGING ASYLUM SEEKERS – *Daily Express*

MUSLIM THUGS AGED JUST 12 IN KNIFE ATTACK
ON BRIT SCHOOLBOY – *Daily Star*

ASYLUM: YOU'RE RIGHT TO WORRY – *Daily Mail*

MUSLIM PLOT TO KILL POPE – *Daily Express*

THE SWARM ON OUR STREETS – *Daily Mail*

CHRISTMAS IS BANNED IT OFFENDS MUSLIMS – *Daily Express*

BBC PUT MUSLIMS BEFORE YOU! – *Daily Star*

MUSLIMS FORCE POOL COVER-UP – *Daily Express*

CALAIS CRISIS: SEND IN THE DOGS – *Daily Mirror*

THEY WANT US TO BE ISLAMISED. THEY DESPISE
OUR COUNTRY AND OUR VALUES – *Daily Mail*

THOUSANDS OF ISIL FIGHTERS COULD USE MIGRANT CRISIS TO
'FLOOD' INTO EUROPE, NIGEL FARAGE WARNS – *Daily Telegraph*

CHRISTIANITY UNDER ATTACK – *Daily Mail*

JUST WAIT . . . ISLAMIC STATE REVEALS IT HAS SMUGGLED THOUSANDS OF EXTREMISTS INTO EUROPE – *Daily Express*

SHOCK REPORT: ISIS FIGHTERS HAVE ENTERED UK POSING AS MIGRANTS & WILL STRIKE NEXT – *Daily Express*

'And so on and so on,' Thandie says to Rose. 'Victor was emailing Jamie pages of national newspapers in May.'

It would have been around him for years, Rose thinks, this soft hatred, this precursor to radicalization – Muslim bans in America, Trump all over the news, hate headlines in newspapers – but this boy is from a liberal family, attends a liberal school, doesn't read those kind of papers, so Victor sent them to him.

'Jamie started using the Aryan Knight identity the last week of June, didn't he?' Rose asks and Thandie nods.

'The same week that his diary had "It's over" about Antonella,' Rose says. Not that anything had ever happened so presumably the day he realized this make-believe romance wouldn't ever become real. Victor probably made that crystal clear to him. Rose wonders if Jamie was clinging on to his romantic fantasy as a bulwark against Victor, a bulwark flimsily made of flowers and hearts, two dimensional and beautifully coloured in, that came crashing down. Perhaps at the same time his friend Zac didn't want him around and Jamie felt abandoned by both him and Antonella. And then Victor chose him. And yes, he did weird shit, had behaved badly, but could convince Jamie that he was his friend.

'By August, he was spending time on far-right vlogger sites, Facebook groups and websites,' Amaal says. 'Britain First, the English Defence League, Breitbart, the Anti-Islam Alliance, Knights Templar International, Generation Identity, the list goes on; all viciously anti-Muslim and all legal or legal until recently. A few weeks later he joins 14 Words.'

*   *   *

In the theatre, they have stopped the rehearsal.

'What does 14 Words even mean?' Tim asks but Daphne can't answer him.

'I googled it,' Joanna says, and she reads: ' "We must secure the existence of our people and a future for White Children." That's fourteen words.'

'Fuck's sake, that's the most stupid thing I've ever heard,' Antonella says. 'Cretinous fuckers.'

'But Jamie barely knows Rafi, let alone hates him,' Josh says. 'They've always been in different tutor groups. They had, what, one PSME class together?'

'And Victor wasn't even in the same year as Rafi,' Tracey says.

'He was in the theatre with him, at the auditions and first read-through,' Miranda says.

'But they didn't argue or anything. I don't think they even spoke,' Tim says.

They are trying to make sense of it, Daphne thinks, but there is no sense to be made of it.

'Rafi still isn't answering his phone,' Benny says, looking terrified, all that teen-boy banter between him and Rafi covering a depth of love.

'Probably to preserve the battery, being sensible,' Daphne says.

It's what she's been telling herself over and over since she heard.

'What if Rafi can't find Basi?' Miranda asks. 'Or they find him first?'

No one replies.

'So, they're the witches,' Antonella says. 'These 14 Words fuckers.'

And they are getting back on to the stage, Tim picking up two bloody daggers, to resume Act Two, Scene Two, and Daphne understands that this is their way of standing up to terror.

★ ★ ★

In the Portakabin, Beth feels faint and wants to black out and then she'll come to in her old life where she's in Waitrose and Jamie is at his school's dress rehearsal.

Again and again he doesn't answer his phone.

Another police officer has come into the Portakabin, and she can tell that this young athletic woman blames her and she's right to blame her because with a different mother this wouldn't be happening to him; and she'd give him up – give up his baby-hood and childhood, every day of him – give him to another mother if it stopped this.

She asks the athletic police officer if she can have a photo of Jamie today. She pretends, to herself as well as the police officer, it's so she can look at the photo and see that there's something of her boy in it and she'll know for sure that they can talk to him. But truthfully she has this hope, a lifeboat as her family drowns, that she'll look at the photo and it will all be a mistake, the wrong person, it won't be Jamie at all.

* * *

Thandie comes into the command and control centre, her hair and her jumper covered in snow, and Rose realizes that she's still wearing Thandie's corduroy jacket. She takes off the jacket and puts it across Thandie's shoulders.

'Beth Alton wants a photo of him,' Thandie says. 'Bit late to take a good look at him now, isn't it?'

Another hefty thump to that punchbag; Rose catches Dannisha's eye, both older women thinking Thandie harsh, because what could Beth Alton have seen? Jamie didn't shave his head, lace up his DMs and go on a white pride march; he's a floppy-haired, Converse-wearing kid who's doing props for his school play. There should be sacraments of evil, Rose thinks, showing outward visible signs of an inward invisible wickedness, so that parents would see the signs and stop their kids being groomed by white supremacists or ISIS or any other terrorist group.

But Beth Alton suspected nothing because everything is hidden. The searches on the Deakins' and Altons' houses haven't found bookshelves in the gunmen's bedrooms full of neo-Nazi literature and CDs of white supremacist music. Because *Mein Kampf, The Turner Diaries, Building a Whiter Brighter World, Angry Young Aryans*, Blue Eyed Devils and their ilk are invisible on Kindles, iPods and smart phones. And the time has long since passed when there was a household phone in a hall or sitting room, where eavesdropping happened as a matter of course, and parents had an inkling of what their children were up to, what they were thinking.

Thandie prints out two stills from UAV footage and leaves.

★ ★ ★

The young athletic woman police officer opens the door wearing the corduroy jacket that Rose Polstein was wearing earlier, because they are still in a life where you lend a friend a jacket.

She hands Beth a large envelope and Beth asks if she can be alone.

When the Portakabin is empty, she takes two photographs out of the envelope. They're large, like those professional family ones with the white background, everyone smiling and dressed in brightly coloured clothes, draped around each other; they have one in the hall – her and Mike and Theo and Jamie.

The first photo is of a man in army combat clothes with ammunition slung round him, holding a big gun; there's a building in front of him. The second photo is a close-up of the man's face hidden by a black balaclava.

She tries to imagine Jamie's voice, what he'd say to her. She didn't have to try before, it was remembering and daydreaming, a kind of empathetic talking.

All she can see are his eyes in the cut-out holes in the balaclava, the same hazel as Jamie's eyes, with thick lashes, the same eyelashes.

This isn't you, Jamie. It can't be.

What do you know, bitch?

You wouldn't do this. You're kind and gentle and—

What the fuck do you know?

The same eyes but Jamie has never looked at her like this, never looked at anybody like this.

I want to talk to my boy . . .

Still think I'm drowning, bitch? With a fucking gun in my hand?

Where's Jamie?

Fuck you, cunt.

Who are you?

17

11.23 a.m.

The photos are on Beth's lap; they're slippery and she has to hold on to them to stop them skidding off. She wants to let them go, let them slide to the floor.

She makes her fingers hold the photos and her eyes look at them.

This gunman can't be Jamie.

He isn't Jamie.

They've told her that he is.

No.

She faces the gunman who isn't Jamie, she's right about that, appallingly right; because her son was being killed in front of her as she took him tea in the morning, drove him to school listening to Radio 1, kissed him goodbye. She imagines him abducted and murdered; a stranger substituted.

His loving voice she's heard in her head all through this is the voice she's been longing to hear for months, but it had fallen silent.

She remembers those spread-out small incidents when Jamie appeared for a few moments; a smile, a cup of tea, Wolf Alice, *Hey, Mum* – those brief moments were the ghost of her son.

She looks at the full-length photo of the gunman in army combat clothes with ammunition slung round him, pointing a gun at the building in front of him; the pottery room.

Rose Polstein comes in.

'You said there are children inside?' Beth asks and her voice sounds like it belongs to a woman she's never met.

'Yes. A class of seven-year-olds.'

The Postman Pat van; the young father with the toddler in the corridor of the leisure centre, his white face. She can place his face now, one of the 'elect' parents as she'd thought of them, leaving the cafeteria while the other parents were waiting; but they are the parents of the children in the pottery room.

She remembers looking inside through the clear Plexiglas wall along the corridor then hurriedly looking away; because the fear and anguish was too nakedly shocking. A pregnant mother sitting on the floor rocking to and fro, and nobody going to her. Remembers how the terror in that room seemed to bulge out the walls.

'I can't talk to him,' she says to Rose Polstein. Him, not Jamie, because it's not Jamie standing there with a gun.

Rose Polstein takes her hand. Beth can't look at her, just feels the other woman's fingers pressing around hers.

'Nobody can talk to him,' Beth says. 'Because no part of Jamie is left.'

The words taste metallic in her mouth, the same taste she had in the first three months of pregnancy.

'I can't stop him shooting the children.'

She says this not because she's brave and selfless, not because she's thinking about other people's children and saving them, but because if those young children are killed, even the memory of Jamie, the seventeen years and two months when he was still her boy, before he was abducted and killed, will vanish; the beautiful soul of him will be lost. Dead, he can still be Jamie; can still be loved.

Rose Polstein has taken her hands into both of hers, as if Beth is slipping down a cliff face and she's trying to hold on to her, but surely Rose Polstein wants to rest one hand on her bump, check that her baby is moving; this new innocent beginning, a *tabula rasa*, which once Beth had too. For a few moments, the time for the midwife to hand him to her, Jamie had been the newest person in the world.

'I think Jamie was killed by Victor and these terrorists a long time ago,' she says. 'But nobody noticed. I didn't notice.'

233

She remembers the dead bird in the makeshift stretcher of Jamie's jumper. She remembers the feathers, smooth under her fingertips, and Jamie's tears.

'*Take him to the vet, Mum, please, please, you have to make him better.*'

'*He's already dead, Jamie.*'

'*No, he isn't dead! Look at his feathers. His feathers are still alive!*'

It hasn't hit her yet, what's happening, what she has made happen. But she knows what's coming, she does; the hell that she's sliding and falling towards.

⋆   ⋆   ⋆

Rose is giving an on-screen briefing to Bronze Command and other senior officers.

'Jamie Alton's mother says that she can't reason with him, even if she can get through to him. She thinks he's been entirely radicalized; that her son no longer exists. There is no chance of negotiation.'

As she speaks she looks at the live drone feed, watching the gunman in the balaclava and combat clothes, once Jamie Alton, facing the pottery room; his converted semi-automatic against his right shoulder, his finger on the trigger which will shoot fifty bullets in three seconds.

Camille Giraud is just visible at the window; maybe she's trying to talk to Jamie Alton or is back at work putting in her clay tiles. Both are futile. Perhaps Camille already knows that, but cannot bear feeling as useless as Rose does right now.

Lysander comes on to the screen.

'A heavily encrypted announcement on the dark net has been accessed. I'm sending it to your screens. Presumably it was meant to be about the children in Junior School but is now applicable to the children in the pottery room. It was scheduled to be released at 12.20 p.m. today on to Aryan Knight's Twitter and Instagram accounts.'

He sends through the announcement.

I am Aryan Knight.
When you read this I'll be firing until they take me out.
Cliff Heights School took in Muslim scum.
Doesn't matter how young the cucks are, they're traitors
    because their libtard parents are traitors.
This is a warning.
Collaborators in white genocide will be punished.
Put your own first.

When you read this, I'll be firing. The announcement was pro-grammed to be released at 12.20 p.m. It's now 11.26 a.m. They have fifty-four minutes to rescue the pottery-room children and their indefatigable teacher. It's a respite from the immediate pressing danger and gives them a chance. Around her, Rose sees her team's and Dannisha's relief and breathes out before she realizes she'd been holding her breath.

'We have fifty-four minutes to kill Alton and rescue the children and their teacher,' Bronze Commander says to all the unit commanders listening and watching this. 'Unless we're seen, in which case, he opens fire. So we make sure we're not seen. We find any terrorist drone and take it down. Yes, visibility is atrocious, but we have a window of opportunity. So we hunt hard. We take their drone down and then we close in and shoot him dead.'

Shots to his medulla oblongata, so there's no involuntary muscle movement, so his finger won't press the trigger.

'Will they know we've seen this?' Bronze Commander asks Lysander.

'No, there was an alarm on it, but the ghost— the person who found it lives in a totalitarian regime, she's good at not tripping alarms and hiding what she's up to. Though I very much doubt Alton thought anyone would get close to accessing it with that level of encryption.'

Rose thinks again about the timing of the announcement: 12.20 p.m. UK time is 7.20 a.m. on the east coast of America – timed to grab headlines on US primetime breakfast shows.

'Anything more on a third terrorist?' Bronze Commander asks.

No one in the briefing speaks, which is good, Rose thinks, because hopefully he doesn't exist and Rafi and Basi are safe.

*   *   *

Beth Alton sits in the Portakabin, waiting in a six metre by three metre hell for her son to be killed. Because of her.

'They'll shoot him, Beth, if we can't talk to him.'

She needs Mike to know about the children in the pottery room, their parents waiting; needs him to see these photos; to catch up with her to the point where you know that your son is already dead; that there are ways of being killed and remaining alive; that you want him to be killed so that he can still be loved.

She is aware of the jeans she put on this morning, the socks and the bra and pants and shirt and jumper, which belong to a different woman, as if she is wearing a dead woman's clothes.

She woke up this morning loving Jamie more than anyone else on this earth, would gladly have died for him, still would. She has a physical yearning for him, back to when he was little and wanted her as only a mother can be wanted; such a physical thing, parts of you that aren't loved by a husband or lover; small arms around your leg, your waist, your hair stroked and tugged, your lap climbed into. She wants to kiss his cheek, stroke his forehead, gather him up into her arms.

She looks down at her lap, at the enlarged picture of Jamie's face, covered in the balaclava, looking at his eyes in the cut-out holes.

Who is this person?

I don't know, Mum.

He doesn't even look like you, not when you look really closely.

The mask makes things a bit difficult, Mum.

But I can see the eyes. They've blown the photo up really big. The eyes are the right colour and shape, I can see the eyelashes too. You've always had such beautiful thick eyelashes. But they're not your eyes.

No.

He's talking to her again and his voice in her head isn't delusional; imagined, yes, but not mad. It's the Jamie he was six months ago, her son that she loves, the teenager he should be now.

This man is going to shoot children, Jamie.

I could never do that. Never.

I know that. It's like you were possessed. Like the devil came into your body and took it over.

Mum, that's really crazy talk.

Yes. Bit crazy. But it's true. In the old days—

The olden times . . .

Yes, people believed you could be possessed by the devil. It wasn't a person's fault that the devil got inside them.

And you could have an exorcism?

Yes. And the devil was cast out.

And you'd be back to your old self again.

Some countries still do believe that.

But not in the UK in the third millennium.

No. They're going to shoot you. Because of what I said.

It's not me they're shooting, Mum. You know that, right? You keep telling yourself that but you really need to know that. You must tell Theo and Dad too. You're crying.

Yes.

Heart soft as a baby bird.

I lost you, Jamie, and I didn't even know.

I was getting lost too.

Didn't even know to look for you.

Have you found me now?

★

Will they let her hold him when they've killed him? She imagines his soul free again.

★   ★   ★

The library is shrinking around Frank. They've made a toilet area in one of the library alcoves, with two waste bins for pee, one for vomit, and the smell is putrid. He and Ed with their backs shoring up the books barricade, and Hannah by Mr Marr, have a bin liner because they cannot get to the toilet alcove. The gunman – they long ago stopped calling him by a name, because it's wrong for him to be allowed a name that was on a class list and a rehearsal schedule and a locker, he doesn't deserve a name – the gunman hasn't tried pushing the door again, not yet. His footsteps have remained outside Mrs Kale's classroom, having a cigarette outside their door now. Desks as barricades. They'll be okay. Please let them be okay.

Hannah is just a foot or so away, in touching distance. Mr Marr keeps losing consciousness but then his eyelids jerk open again, staying with them.

There has been a spate of emails from people in the theatre, all outraged that white supremacists have come into their school and attacked them, because of Rafi who is their friend, because of his little brother. There's so much spirit in their anger, Frank heard it in their emails and he envies it. They are still rehearsing *Macbeth*, taking a stand against people who they call 'cretinous fuckers' and liken to witches. No one in here has called them 'cretinous fuckers' or likened them to witches; fear has tired them out too much to come up with such energetic words and analogies.

He thinks the footsteps have turned them into different people to their friends in the theatre, to his twin. Fear and imprisonment have eroded who they are. It's not just that the people in the theatre are safe – just! – but they have phone chargers and loos, and they might seem like small things, but they aren't at all small.

When they found out about 14 Words, Hannah was sick in their bin liner. She's as white as a sheet; a ghost.

Rafi has to be okay, has to be. The woods are huge and they won't find him. It's still better that he's outside than here in the library. But she imagines white supremacists hunting him down through the trees, Basi too, and it's all her fault. If it wasn't for her, Rafi and Basi would have got on a boat; if he hadn't come back for her they'd be safe.

★ ★ ★

Through the snow and the trees Rafi has spotted a light coming from Junior School and he's running as fast as he can through the woods towards it, the cat-'o-nine-tails wind whipping harder, the freezing air going deep into his lungs. He'll get there soon and then Basi will be okay.

Basi had been a little angel as a baby, it was Rafi who was colicky with crying fits and screaming sessions. He'd made up for it by being the good boy; the easy child. But Basi the angel baby became naughty and disobedient, *Qarrad Saghir* – Little Monkey. On the Journey the last part of that little boy had disappeared.

But recently Rafi's seen small signs of him again: a smile so wide his little teeth shone; a giggle that sounded like hiccups; last week Rafi saw him skip, a two-steps-only skip but a new rhythm. He still wets his bed and their foster mother is really kind about it, but Basi can't be comforted. It started on the Journey, Basi asleep on the side of the road; a stain on the tarmac, the smell of it, and he woke up shaking with cold and cried because there were no dry trousers and pants and because he was ashamed. Dr Reynolds has told Basi that many refugee children Basi's age routinely wet the bed. 'You're a casualty of war, Basi,' he said, man-to-man; but Basi is still mortified.

Rafi reaches the wire-link fence round Junior School; the playground is deep in snow, everything different and strange. His phone has kept vibrating with calls: Benny and his foster parents – loads of times, as soon as they found out – and other friends and Rose Polstein, but he didn't answer because how can any of them help him? And because he needs to conserve his phone's juice for when he finds Basi. Rose Polstein has also texted him, telling him to ring her urgently, but she'll just want to know that he's hiding and he can't, not till he's found his brother.

The lock on the gate is broken and he walks through; no sight or sound of children, just the wind making the swings rock and the slide creak. He sees the hardback book on a swing, protected by the pirate ship canopy, a book of fairy tales, the jacket illustrated with woods and snow falling. He notices there's a label attached – *For Basi Bukhari* – and remembers how kind everyone has been to Basi, giving him toys and clothes and books, and generous to Rafi too – a total stranger gave him a guitar, which he's learning to play. When he sees Basi's book he remembers all these strangers' kindnesses; when they arrived, there'd been welcome banners, like arms stretching open.

He picks up the book to take to Basi and sees a wire. He throws it. The book explodes, birds startling out of the trees, and his right leg is alight with pain.

There are pieces of metal and burns through his jeans, a jagged piece of metal deep in his thigh. Feeling dizzy and sick, he takes hold of the larger piece of shrapnel and tries to pull it free of his leg, but it won't come out. The startled birds have gone back to the trees but the air still hums with the shock of it.

* * *

Police surveillance UAVs are hunting for any terrorist drone over the pottery room. They have fifty minutes till Jamie Alton opens fire.

Lysander comes on to the screen.

'We've deciphered a post Victor Deakin wrote on the 14

Words website, a month ago, which wasn't so heavily encrypted. I'm sending it to you now.'

Rose reads: 'The only good Muslim is a dead Muslim. If you're a Muslim I'm going to enjoy shooting you in the head.'

Her first reaction is anxiety for Rafi and Basi Bukhari, their vulnerability stripped raw; but worrying about them won't help them, do your job.

Victor taught himself ancient Greek and Latin for fun, so why's he using such basic language?

She phones Stuart Dingwall in counterterrorism.

'Stuart? Rose. You got the post? This doesn't fit with Deakin.'

'No, he's copied it from a white supremacist called Patrick Stein.'

And that's also strange, because why would Victor, a narcissistic psychopath who feels god-like, copy anyone?

'What can you tell me about Stein?' she asks.

'Part of a terrorist organization in the US called The Crusaders, who planned to attack Muslims. Hold on, I'll bring it up. Yes, their plot was uncovered by the FBI in October 2016; it was less than a month before the presidential election and it didn't get a great deal of news coverage even in the US.'

But Victor Deakin saw it and must have followed it closely to be lifting words from Patrick Stein.

'They saw themselves as "patriots resisting a Muslim takeover of the United States",' Stuart continues. 'They planned to massacre as many Muslims as possible, who they called cockroaches.'

★ ★ ★

The door to Junior School has been shot off its hinges, lying on the ground covered in snow. Rafi goes inside but doesn't call out Basi's name, in case a gunman is in the building; in case Basi replies and gives his hiding place away.

He goes along the corridor, lined with shelves full of children's books. His injured right leg is making him nauseous. He wants to try pulling the metal out again, to stop the burning pain, but then he'd bleed more and the man might see the blood; would find him, would find Basi.

He goes into Basi's classroom and for a shocking, gut-wrenching moment thinks that there are children lying on the floor, but it's scarecrows, just scarecrows in children's clothing. Snow is being blown by the wind through the shattered windows on top of the mangled scarecrows and shards of glass. The rage of the gunman is a presence in the room.

He searches for Basi, looking in cupboards, under desks, going into every classroom and Mr Lorrimer's office too. No sign of him.

There must've been a reason he'd thought Basi was inside Junior School, but he can't remember the reason, his brain too unfocused with pain.

He goes back outside into the snow.

★   ★   ★

Thandie passes Rose a phone. 'It's Rafi Bukhari. Basi isn't inside the Junior School building. And he's been injured.'

As she'd thought, he hadn't done as she'd told him and hidden and stayed safe.

'Rafi, it's Rose Polstein . . .'

To start with she can only hear the wind and then she makes out ragged breathing.

'Rafi? Are you badly hurt?'

'I don't know where Basi is. There was a bomb meant for him.'

'What kind of bomb?'

'An IED in a book, there was a label with Basi's name on it in the playground. *Grimm's Fairy Tales*, I picked it up. Saw a wire and threw it. The book exploded. Fuck. Fuck. Sorry.'

'It really hurts?'

'I'll be okay. It was there this morning on a swing, I saw it. He must have left it there this morning.'

And if a different child picked it up that was okay because collaborators will be punished.

She turns to Amaal. 'Tell counterterrorism. And put out an alert to all officers that there could be IEDs; anything could be a booby-trapped bomb.'

She goes back to Rafi, hears the wind howling around him.

'I thought there was someone following me earlier. He might be after Basi.'

He's having to shout, but as if it's hard, as if pain has taken strength from his voice.

'Where did you see this man?'

'I didn't see him, just heard him, in the woods. And near Old School. But then I lost him. I might have imagined him.'

She doesn't hear him the first time and he has to repeat it, and she thinks this conversation is exhausting him.

'Can you tell me what you heard?'

'Thought I was just being crazy. An anorak rustling and a couple of times I heard a twig snapping.'

He pauses and in between the strong gusts of wind she can hear the boy's fast uneven breathing around his pain.

'The thing you need to know,' he says, 'is that I have hyper-vigilant PTSD, with paranoia and psychosis. It was a real IED in a book for Basi, but the person behind me might not have been real. Most likely wasn't, but I thought you should know, in case, for Basi. Even though I'm not reliable.'

'You got all the children in Junior School to safety, hyper-vigilant PTSD or not. I think you're pretty damn wonderful actually. When was the last time you thought this man was behind you?'

'Not sure. Just after ten.'

At that time, Jamie was in position outside the pottery room, Victor inside Old School. So, if Rafi didn't imagine him, this is evidence of a third terrorist here at the school.

The wind drops and there's a moment of stillness at the other end of the phone.

'Why would anyone want to hurt Basi?' Rafi asks.

'I'm so sorry, Rafi, the people attacking the school are white supremacist terrorists. They are wicked people, shameful people. Please hide. We'll find Basi as soon as we can, I promise.'

★   ★   ★

Basi is hated. He is hated. They are why the school is under attack.

He limps towards the gate out of the playground, the shrapnel working its way deeper into his leg.

Hated.

He tries to run over the thick snow towards the gate but a hole opens up – their worst hole – and it's snowing in Aleppo.

Five-year-old Basi is asleep on a beanbag and hasn't seen it's snowing, but Rafi's watching out of the window, waiting for Baba and Karam to come home. They were taken by Assad's men two days ago, to the airport, they think, but nobody knows; whispers that there are torture cells under the airport, whispers that burn his ears as he just stands and waits. Mama pacing and pacing and not sleeping, not for two nights.

A loud noise on the street wakes Basi. Rafi sees a truck pull up but Basi only sees that it's snowing and is too excited about the snow to remember to stay inside and runs out.

Think of a face, quickly think of a face. The old man on the boat, his beard with salt in it, smelling of vomit and urine and excrement, as they all did. He'd been a judge and talked to Rafi about being a lawyer before that, and before that a student as Rafi would be one day. He'd talked to him about art and architecture and literature and philosophy, all through that first terrible night on the boat, as if Rafi was his equal, as if he wanted to have a proper conversation with him; and in the morning, he gave Basi his last lemon, because lemons help with seasickness.

He's back in Junior School's playground, each step sinking into the snow.

But still he sees his father and brother lying on the road, snow falling on to them, and he cannot blink it away. Will never be able to blink it away.

Last term his English class read *King Lear*. '*Enter Gloucester his eyes put out.*' Mrs Kale saw his reaction and must've guessed something and was kind, but he was glad there was that same violence in the play, wanted it pinned down and examined for what it was. He'd understood then why Baba quoted from playwrights and poets: he was using great culture to articulate the opposite of culture. '*Did Heaven look on, and would not take their part?*'

He left Mama in that terrible place. He hasn't spoken to her since he and Basi were in Egypt, over two years ago. He doesn't know if she's still alive. Mr Marr and various charities have tried to find her but no one has been able to.

Daphne wanted him to play Macduff or Young Seward in *Macbeth*, but he asked to play the part of Fleance, because he is the one who runs away.

*   *   *

A violent gust of wind rocks the command and control vehicle as if they are momentarily on water. Police UAVs are looking for Basi, and a helicopter pilot is determined to search, but the area where he could be is huge and visibility appalling.

Rose is part of an on-screen briefing.

'How badly has Rafi been injured?' Bronze Commander asks.

'He says he'll be okay,' Rose says. 'I think he's being brave. Medics are on standby for when we can get to him.'

'Bombs in fairy stories, what in hell are we dealing with?' Bronze Commander asks.

'Islamic State hid bombs in copies of the Quran when they left Ramadi,' Stuart Dingwall says. 'Left them lying in the street; and there were bombs in booby-trapped books in a village near Mosul. They also planted IEDs in teddies and dolls.'

The cowardly inadequate bastards are copying each other.

'Did anyone see it being left?' Bronze Commander asks.

'No, but we think it must have been this morning when parents dropped off their children,' Stuart says. 'Lots of people going in and out, siblings too. Jamie Alton or Victor Deakin could have posed as an older brother. Junior school staff would never have met Victor so wouldn't know to be suspicious. And his mother's Mini is parked in Junior School car park.'

'Rafi thought he heard someone coming after him,' Rose says. 'After ten, when Jamie Alton was outside the pottery room and Victor Deakin was in Old School. Rafi has delusional PTSD, so he doesn't trust himself to be reliable. He says he managed to lose him.'

Lysander comes on to the screen.

'We have decrypted some of the transactions on the dark net made by 14 Words. They bought a Ruger MKII with Outback II Suppressor and subsonic ammo. They also bought a pair of Steiner military series binoculars. There are other items more heavily encrypted that we can't decipher.'

A man dressed in the distinctive grey combat uniform worn by counterterrorism specialist firearms officers, CTSFOs, joins the briefing. He introduces himself as Safa Rahman. His snowy facemask and goggles have been pushed off his face, a link between their removed environment of screens and computers and what is physically happening at the school.

'Steiner military binoculars are used by armed forces, often for perimeter and border patrols,' Rahman says. 'They're sophisticated and powerful, sharp images and a wide field of view.'

'The binoculars that the girl on TV saw glinting at the top of the high ropes course,' Bronze Commander says. 'And the guns?'

'They've been shopping for the quietest weaponry out there,' Rahman says. 'The Ruger MKII with a suppressor, a silencer, is about as quiet as you can get. The subsonic ammo means that the bullets don't break the sound barrier, so are virtually soundless.'

'So, if there is a third man out there, he's using a gun that we can't detect,' Bronze Commander says. 'But Jamie Alton is flaunting his gun and Victor Deakin must know we think he's got a similar weapon to Alton's. Okay, so they don't know we've found out their semi-automatics have been converted into fully automatics, but they haven't been discreet about their weapons.'

Rose agrees and thinks that even the rifle shots at the beginning of the attack were part of a game, rather than any attempt at concealment.

'Locating a shooter with that kind of gun and suppressor and bullets is bloody hard, if not impossible,' Safa Rahman says. 'I'd say this guy doesn't want us to take him out.'

'We don't know for sure yet whether there's a third man,' Lysander says; he looks pale and Rose likes him for this leak of emotion, because he's afraid for Basi and Rafi, as she is, and doesn't want this third man to be definite.

'Detective Inspector Polstein, what do you think?'

'My guess is that if he exists he's not malleable like Jamie; nor does he want to go out in a blaze of murderous glory if that's what Victor is planning. I would imagine him to be older. He wants to kill Muslims, punish the school and live.'

'We should run the scenario,' Bronze Commander says. 'A third man on campus could have acted as lookout up on the high ropes course this morning, using the military binoculars.'

Rose thinks that even if there was a third man up there this morning, Victor Deakin was probably up there as well at some point, surveying the school from high in his eyrie; he'd have enjoyed the feeling of elevated power. But he'd have also got bored, probably wouldn't have hung around being lookout.

'The third man's job would be to watch for the police arriving,' Bronze Commander continues. 'He watches the road and drive up to Old School, which are in the opposite direction to Junior School, half a mile away, so he doesn't see the junior school children evacuating. Meanwhile, Victor Deakin is on the ground. The third man alerts Deakin when the police car is coming so that he can take the shot.'

If this is the case, Rose thinks, then there was no scramble. No flaws.

'The third man, still up the high ropes, sees the head teacher leaving Old School,' Bronze Commander continues. 'He goes after him. But the head returns to Old School and their original plan can go ahead. Then what does he do?'

'As well as being lookout, he'd have a second job,' Stuart says. 'To murder Basi and Rafi Bukhari. The other children and teachers are collaborators but the object of their hatred is Muslims. So he goes to Junior School. A lone police constable who's been shot at won't go after him, and it'll be a while before more police arrive, so he won't be caught. I think he wants to kill Basi Bukhari first, as a message.'

'But the Junior School building is empty,' Bronze Commander says. 'He doesn't see the children from the top of the cliffs, doesn't know they're sheltering underneath. He thinks Basi Bukhari has been evacuated along with the others. He shoots up a classroom in a rage, not knowing Basi is watching him.'

'And then he hunts for Rafi,' Stuart says.

'My guess is that he went back up the high ropes,' Bronze Commander says. 'Used his military-grade binoculars and spotted him.'

'It wouldn't be hard,' Safa Rahman says. 'Rafi was the only person moving, everyone else was in lockdown, and the snowfall wasn't yet that heavy.'

'But how did he know to look for Rafi outside?' Rose asks. 'How did he know that he wasn't in a building or evacuated?'

'We know at least one teacher on the beach phoned a colleague at the school and said Rafi had left the beach,' Stuart says. 'Rafi himself phoned a friend with that information, maybe more than one. So other staff and kids knew and information leaks. It's probably out there on the net, a news site or social media, and this organization will be scanning everything to do with the school, gleaning information.'

'Or he could have just got lucky,' Rahman says. 'He went back up the high ropes, keeping watch again, spotted someone moving in the woods and went after him. If he hadn't already seen it was Rafi Bukhari, he did when he got closer.'

'And then Rafi managed to lose him,' Rose says.

'But he knows that Rafi is out there, not protected,' Rahman says. 'And he's hunting for him now.'

Talking as if he exists because the scenario makes too much sense; it points, almost conclusively, to a third terrorist on the school campus. After the purchase of the silencer and subsonic ammo was discovered, there was little doubt, but now Rose thinks there's none. She needs to check anyway.

'With a suppressor and the subsonic bullets, would firing the gun make any noise?'

'Yeah, a bit,' Safa Rahman says. 'But hard to detect from any distance.'

'What sound would it make?' Rose asks, but she thinks she already knows.

'Like a twig snapping.'

*   *   *

Rafi limps through the blizzard, yelling Basi's name and waiting for Basi to call back, but there's just the sounds of the storm. His face has been cut by shrapnel, stinging as he wipes blood and snow away so his eyes are clear to look for his brother. Maybe Basi was outside Mrs Cardswell's classroom when he saw the gunman, maybe he's still there.

His phone vibrates, Rose Polstein, and he answers.

'Do you know something about Basi?' he asks.

'No, I'm sorry. Not yet. Rafi, you absolutely have to hide until it's safe. There is another terrorist in the school grounds who we think is armed. We think that you are a target.'

Rafi hangs up and tries to run round the side of the building to outside Mrs Cardswell's classroom, his leg so painful he gasps in snow.

But he'd have seen Basi when he was in her classroom earlier. Unless Basi was crouched down outside the window, hiding.

He reaches the outside of Mrs Cardswell's classroom; a

249

yellow life jacket is lying half buried in the snow under the window frame. Where's he run to? Which direction? But Basi's light shallow footprints have long since been filled in.

Rose Polstein wants to help, he rates Rose Polstein, but the police can't help find Basi, he was stupid to even hope that they could. They can't fly a helicopter in this snow, and even if they did, Basi would run away because helicopters drop barrel bombs. And if they send in police to look for him, Basi will hide from them, because of France, because they set dogs on him and a dog bit his cheek, and the policeman waited before calling the dog off. He's terrified of police.

He phones Mr Marr; he's wanted to talk to him all through this, since he first left the beach, but thought that he mustn't because Mr Marr has so many other kids to look after. In the camp, he'd thought about Mr Marr's kind face, remembered his thoughtful eyes and his reassuring voice and what he said, the promise he'd made, and even though Rafi didn't think he could, he'd kept it. And he's not a kind face in their memories but a loving man in their lives.

Mr Marr doesn't answer. He doesn't answer. Mr Marr would talk to him if he could. Pain is muddling his thoughts, taking up too much room in his head. Why isn't he answering?

But he can't worry about Mr Marr, not till Basi is safe, just like he couldn't worry about Hannah earlier, not till he'd got Basi to the beach, because he's not big enough to worry about more than one person that he loves at the same time, and later he will hate himself for that, but now he just has to find Basi.

He could be in the woods near to Junior School or further away if he ran for longer, or not in the woods at all but on the path down to the beach. And the snow is so dense he can barely see in front of him.

He stumbles and falls heavily, pushing the jagged piece of metal shrapnel deeper into his right thigh. The same leg that was broken in Aleppo when the building collapsed on top of him. He lies on the snow, panting, trying to overcome the pain and get up again.

He remembers Mama's slender fingers broken and bruised from digging for him, Baba's hands bloody, but both of them smiling like it was the happiest day of their lives as they pulled him free.

Baba is dead and he left Mama behind; nobody digging for him now.

Only him to look for Basi.

He gets up, dragging his injured leg behind him.

There's so much snow falling around him, like it's isolating him in his own tiny spot in the world.

*　*　*

In the shed the noises are getting closer. Basi takes his hands out of his anorak sleeves and puts them over his ears, but he can still hear the creaks and groans. He closes his eyes and remembers the noises of the sea at night, the boat creaking, the black sky raining wet darkness on to them, and you were so frightened and cold you didn't think anything good could ever happen ever again. Then Rafi turned on his laser pointer and shone it up at the darkness and made a magic shimmery tunnel of falling raindrops from their boat right up into the top of the black sky.

'It's all right. Don't worry. I'll come and find you.'

He must've told Rafi where he is; must've done.

*　*　*

Two minutes ago, the young police UAV operator with a headset under her hijab, who's been hunting for a terrorist drone in the relatively small space of sky above the pottery room, spotted a dark shape amongst the snow but it disappeared. They are taking stills from the footage and enlarging the image to decipher what she saw.

There's still time, Rose says to herself, thirty-eight minutes until Jamie Alton opens fire.

'The girl on TV, who saw the glint at the top of the high ropes course, does anyone know where she was speaking from?' Thandie asks.

'The library,' Amaal says. 'She was trying to get medical help for their head teacher.'

'Jesus,' Rose says. She has a sudden glimpse into one of many stories that are playing out simultaneously here and she feels again this sense that she isn't at the heart of things; that she is skimming surfaces and imposing metallic rationality but what is happening is human and extreme and she wants to leave this vehicle and go into the school itself. *Which will accomplish what, exactly, Rose? Bloody hell, stop being so self-indulgent and focus on what you're here to do.*

Rose's team and other officers have spoken to staff but none of them can give any information on 14 Words, none of them even knew of its existence, let alone that a pupil was involved. The police told them they had to keep the information about 14 Words confidential. 'But not from the kids inside the school, surely?' Neil Forbright had said to her. 'They deserve to know who is attacking them; to be trusted.' She'd told him that actually, yes, it did include them. But she thinks that the teachers as well as the kids are not used to being obedient, and she likes them for it.

An officer has spoken to the gardener who saw a possible intruder outside the maintenance shed but he couldn't give a description; the man's back was towards him, his hood up.

★   ★   ★

The stench in the library is stronger: vomit and urine; fear and captivity. The footsteps are coming towards them. They stop outside the door. They are all holding their bodies rigid and still, holding their breaths. Hannah joins Ed and Frank, sitting next to them, with her back to the books and the door, the three of them squashed together. She's worried about leaving Mr Marr but the main thing is to stop the gunman getting inside, because she thinks the first person he'll kill will be Mr Marr.

She feels a shove against her back, and she and Ed and Frank push back.

She thinks of people smugglers trying to shove Rafi and Basi down into the hold, where you would be drowned first or suffocated by the fumes of the engine, hundreds of them below deck. Rafi had held on to Basi and pushed back.

The door doesn't open any further.

He knocks on the door, *tap-tap*, like he's asking to come in; a joke.

Soon he'll realize it's their bodies pressing against the door and he'll shoot; *splashes of purple, a wrecked time machine, a smashed lighthouse lamp, and everything going dark.*

She thinks of Dad's arm around her and his voice, *Courage, mon brave*; and she must tell him that she's had him with her all through this, because they've been growing a little apart, not in big obvious ways, but in small important ways, and now she knows they haven't really grown apart at all.

If she's going to die, it's easier to think about Dad. No one can take away the time she's had with him, years and years together and memories and words handed down like watches.

But she and Rafi have only had four months and the gunman in the corridor and the ones she imagines in the woods, hunting down Rafi, could take away all the unlived months, secretly she's dreamt of years and ever after, and they could steal it all before it's even happened. She thinks of the people that they were this morning, running through the woods holding hands like two in-love young skeletons, bones touching, and *in love* was true, they were, they are, but there's no future round the bend in the path; no this afternoon, this evening, tomorrow, and all those days after that will disappear before she's lived them.

The footsteps leave, but he'll come back again.

★ ★ ★

Lysander starts an on-screen briefing.

'We can't get any further with the heavily encrypted transactions, not in the time that we have. But Usman's just got something.'

Usman comes on to the screen. Rose thinks that he is shaking. Bronze Commander and Stuart Dingwall have also joined the briefing.

'I've decrypted another time-delayed announcement,' Usman says. 'It refers to Victor Deakin and Old School. It's scheduled to go public on the Aryan Knight social media accounts at 12.00 midday today, twenty minutes before Jamie Alton's announcement. I'm sorry, it wasn't as heavily encrypted, I should have deciphered it faster. It's really bad.'

He turns the computer screen so they can all read it.

'Jesus Christ,' someone says.

The only fucking way this country's ever going to get turned around is if there's **a fucking bloodbath** and at 12.00 it's a **bloodbath in Old School,** in the library & classrooms, a nasty, messy motherfucker.

A lot of people are waking up in this country and smelling the fucking coffee and **deciding they want this country back from Muslims** and all you SJWs and snowflakes and libtards will wake up.

We might be too late, if they do wake up, but I think we can get it done. But it ain't going to be nothing nice about it.

When we go on operations, there's no leaving anyone behind. I guarantee when we go on this mission those little fuckers in Old School are going bye-bye. Before I leave this worthless place, I will kill.

I will die but I will become IMMORTAL.

They have fifteen minutes till Deakin opens fire in Old School.

'I tripped an alarm on the announcement,' Usman says. 'They know we've seen it.'

Rose sees that Safa Rahman in his grey combat uniform is talking hurriedly to other members of the elite counterterrorism armed unit and she imagines them fast-roping down from their helicopters through the skylights of Old School, bursting in through the windows, but the plans of the building haven't changed and the gunman is still in an interior corridor without windows or skylights to surprise him.

There are thirteen students in the library, and the badly wounded head teacher, twelve students and three adults in the English teacher's classroom, and Neil Forbright on his own. If Rahman's unit storm the building, how many will Deakin kill with his converted semi-automatic before they take him out? She cannot see how this will be accomplished without terrible loss of life.

Not your job. As she told Thandie, they have their job and they leave the armed units and everyone else to do theirs. Her role is to help find out who's doing this and why they're doing this. That's where she might have value, though she thinks there's precious little she can do now. Not her call to make.

Do your job.

She recognizes some of Victor's words in the time-delayed announcement: *Before I leave this worthless place, I will kill.* He's copied them from Eric Harris's journal, one of the two gunmen at Columbine High School.

'Do you recognize any of the message, Stuart?' Rose asks. 'He's lifted some of it from one of the Columbine shooters.'

'A whole load's taken from Patrick Stein again, with a few personalized tweaks,' Stuart says.

And it bothers her again, because it makes no sense that a narcissistic psychopath would use other people's words.

'14 Words have tweeted part of the bloodbath announcement,' Lysander says. 'Again it's via proxies and aliases. They're using bots to get it to trend.'

'Jesus,' Bronze Commander says. He takes a moment and his voice is calmer. 'We're taking it down?'

'Yes.'

But it will already be growing exponentially on the internet with humans now retweeting.

'Why are they making it public?' Bronze Commander asks.

'Maybe because they have nothing to lose now,' Rose says. 'They know we saw the timed announcement so they're trying to take back some ground. Or maybe they want it out there.'

'To create more terror?' he asks.

'Yes.'

★ ★ ★

In Matthew's office, Neil Forbright has received an email from Frank in the library. The gunman tried to get in again; then he knocked at the door, like a joke. He is no longer human to Neil but satanic; a demon hunting for souls. Psychiatrists can dress him up any which way in scientific terms but he is something evil, connected to times when the devil roamed the world and came knocking at your door. Only now he has a gun and the door is in a school with kids the other side. And it makes it worse, it does, the kids' courage.

Tonya has just sent him a link on his phone. He clicks on it. It's a tweet.

14 Words.abc @14words.bca
The only fucking way this country's ever going to get turned around is if there's A FUCKING BLOODBATH. At 12.00 it's a BLOODBATH IN OLD SCHOOL, in the library & classrooms, a nasty, messy motherfucker

His phone rings and he answers.

'Mr Forbright? It's PC Beard. Tonya's sent you the tweet?'

'Yes.'

'We need to go for my plan straight away. Tonya and the other adults in the English classroom agree.'

256

'But—'

'He probably won't spot me but even if he does, I'm just in a PC's uniform, even got the helmet. Not like the armed lot – he's more likely to laugh at me than start firing at anyone. I'll be Bobby the retro policeman to him.'

'Do the police even know about this plan?'

'I am the police, Mr Forbright. We have strict ways of doing things. Playing "ring the doorbell and run away from the gunman" isn't one of those ways. They would almost definitely try and stop me.'

'Because he'll kill you.'

'I'll be running away by the time he gets to the door. Not fast, my wife's roast dinners haven't made me a running machine, but there's plenty of bushes to hide behind. He'll chase after me for a bit, hopefully, and then he'll return to you lot, but you lot won't be there any more.'

'What if he finds you?'

'This is my community, my patch. And from what I know of your school, it's a special place, a smaller version of England; lots of different nationalities, any religion you like, nobody's fussed, takes in refugees – Sorry, going on. No time for that. But the thing is, I want to help. When you hear the doorbell, good and loud, that'll be me – as if anyone else will be ringing the doorbell.' He actually chortles. 'Tell everyone to wait for the doorbell, and then count, what do you think, to twenty? To give him time to get to the front door?'

'Depends how quick he is. Maybe fifteen if he's fast.'

'Yes, I think he'll be fast. Count to fifteen and then run like the wind to the theatre. I'll tell Tonya and you tell the kids in the library?'

'Okay.'

'You need to go with them, all right, son? They'll need someone they trust to be with them. I'll tell that lovely lady Sally-Anne in the theatre to let you in. She's been waiting.'

And this is what evil does, Neil thinks. It exposes your fear and cowardice, your vulnerability and your fragility, makes you confront your mortality; but it also finds courage and selflessness that amaze Neil. He thinks of white type on a white screen, the poem's beauty invisible until the background screen is turned black.

*　*　*

In the library, Hannah checks Mr Marr is breathing and he is, but so faintly that she needs to put her hand on his chest to feel it move. Ed and David are taking books away from the heaped barricade; Ed passes books to Frank, David to Esme, and then they carefully put them down on to the floor, trying to make no sound.

The book barricade dwindles.

The door is visible.

The footsteps are getting louder. They're coming towards them.

The footsteps stop outside the door. Does he know he can open it? One shove and he'll be inside.

She just wants to live so badly. Because it's all out there, Rafi is out there and university and all of it. And Dad needs her. He still thinks that she needs him more than he needs her, but it's changing, the pattern, the parabola, so she can't not be here any more.

The footsteps move away; he doesn't know he can open the door.

Ed and David pass the last of the books, Frank and Esme gently putting them down.

Everyone is taking off their shoes so they'll just be in their socks and not make any noise. Hannah's socks are still damp from running through the woods this morning. She takes off Frank's anorak, which rustles, and her bangles that will jingle; lots of the girls are doing that, dangly earrings too, just in case.

A loud long ring on the doorbell, sounding strange and echoey in the corridor.

The footsteps come towards them, they get to their door, they keep going.

He's gone past the door! He went past!

They start to count. They get to five.

* * *

Neil runs down the corridor towards Jacintha's classroom, fearing that the gunman will realize it's a trick and come back. Their part of the corridor remains deserted, the gunman doesn't yet realize.

He reaches Jacintha's classroom and opens the door, but only a few inches because there's a desk still up against it and behind the desk he sees terror blanching the faces of children and the three adults, and then the relief that it's him. 'Time to go,' he whispers. 'Quickly now.' And it's like he's asked them to jump off a cliff or stand in front of a firing squad, then Jacintha and Tonya quietly lift the desk and set it down softly away from the door; Tonya walks through the open doorway and the curse is broken and they all run through the doorway into the corridor.

* * *

They've counted to fifteen and it's time to leave the library. Hannah's hand is on Mr Marr's chest, he's still breathing. She looks at her socks and her wrist bare of jangling bangles; how can she leave him?

The door opens very quietly. It's Mr Forbright. He looks at Mr Marr and Hannah sees his shock and upset, his love for Mr Marr, and through his eyes she knows for a fact, though really she's known since he was first shot, that Mr Marr is dying.

'Everyone out,' he says. 'Quick as you can. Run. You too, Hannah. I'll come back for him, I promise.'

18.

11.54 a.m.

They hurry out of the library. Hannah sees her English class with Mrs Kale and they look sheet white and thinner somehow, as if they've been shrunk by this. Everyone is running towards the doors to the glass corridor in their socks; so quiet that they're barely breathing, so quiet you can hear the swish of a girl's long hair.

A loud creak as Mr Forbright opens the doors and they all tense. He holds the doors open and they run through.

Through the glass, daylight is like headlamps shining into your eyes. Snow has banked up, everywhere white, their school has changed entirely; and they are all sprinting towards the theatre, faster than they've ever run before. Hannah turns and sees Mr Forbright locking the doors behind them; still inside Old School.

Sally-Anne, waiting by the open doors in the foyer, sees kids streaming towards her along the glass corridor; for a few moments, she can't believe it's real because they are silent. As they get closer she can hear them breathing, sees that they're in socks, holding their shoes, a rustle as they run alongside each other and touch. In the middle of them, but not being touched, is Tobias, his hands pressing his shoes over his headphones. She ushers them in, patting shoulders and backs, shiny hair.

She hasn't told anyone else about the rescue plan because what if the gunman chased after everyone escaping from Old School along the glass corridor? Followed them here? The kids in the theatre were safer behind the locked doors to the auditorium, safer not knowing.

Last down the glass corridor are the staff, like sheepdogs, she thinks: Tonya, Matthew's punky secretary, and Donna, the matronly receptionist, and Jacintha. No one else coming down the corridor. No sign of Matthew or Neil.

'Is that everyone?' she asks.

'Yes,' Donna says. 'Neil said to lock the doors.'

Startled and moved by Neil's courage, she locks the doors; the Yale and the deadbolt.

The Old School kids are all in the centrally heated foyer, a great crush of them, but shivering as if they are in snow as the shock of it hits them. Some cannot move but just sit where they are. Hannah is covered in blood and just wearing a bra on her top half.

'Sweetheart?' Sally-Anne says to her.

'It's not mine, the blood.'

Sally-Anne takes off her cardigan and wraps it around the shivering girl.

'Everybody into the auditorium,' she says. 'Quick as you can.'

She opens the locked doors and helps the ones who are sitting to stand again and ushers them all into the auditorium. Once inside, she locks and bolts the security doors. No way can the gunman follow them in here.

*   *   *

In the library, Neil sits beside Matthew, holding his hand. Outside the library door he saw the shattered case of medals, but their students have reached the safety of the theatre. Soon the gunman will realize it was all a trick and come back but in the meantime he and Matthew will stay like this. And in the meantime is everything; it is the gap between terror and isolation and whatever is to come; it is the time in between, in this building, empty apart from the two of them, where love and kindness and friendship exist, and it can't be measured in minutes or hours, but moments in a lifetime. He isn't sure if Matthew is conscious, isn't sure if he can hear him, but is sure he can feel his hand.

★ ★ ★

They walk into the auditorium and Frank thinks it's like walking into normal life, back into a normal world. The theatre looks exactly the same and some of their friends are on stage, with tunics on, just like they are meant to be; because they are rehearsing just like they are meant to be rehearsing this morning. But as he gets closer he sees their faces are strange, painted green and brown.

Luisa is running at him, like she's flying towards him; she flings herself around him, his cool twin sobbing into his chest. And other people are hugging, a hug-a-thon all around him; it's the kids in the theatre giving the hugs, not shaking and sheet white like they all are. No footsteps, he thinks, and loos and phones and chargers. It hits him that they are safe now. Safe. He hugs Luisa back and his shaking subsides a little.

Hannah is in the changing-room loos. She takes off the teacher's cardigan. Her bra and torso are covered in blood. She'll wash off the blood and then she'll find a charger for her phone and call Rafi. He must be okay. Must be. Has to wash the blood off.

Everyone was so happy to start with, being reunited and being safe, and it was like their friends in the theatre were pumping energy and warmth into them.

She runs her bra under the tap, washing the blood off, but why is she doing that? She's not going to ever wear it again.

And then someone, she's not sure who, asked about Mr Marr and then they were all asking. 'Will he be okay? Will he make it?'

Frank said, 'Yes, he's conscious and he'll be okay.'

'What about Mr Forbright?'

'He's staying with him.'

The most brave thing Hannah has ever seen.

All the library kids know Frank was lying about Mr Marr but also the reason, that he's protecting everyone who's been in the theatre until this terrible, terrible thing is over; and because they all feel guilty leaving him, Hannah especially because she's the one who was mainly looking after him, and nobody wants the people in the theatre to feel that bad too.

She tries to wash the blood off her skin, splashing water all over the place. In the mirror above the basin, she sees her pale body reflected back at her; her breasts look so naked, vulnerable and ugly with dried specks of blood. She wishes that she and Rafi had made love. He'd been the one who'd wanted to wait.

'Jesus, Rafi, you mean till we're married?'

'I don't want you to think you've made a mistake. I want you to be sure first.'

She should have just taken his clothes off and made love to him then and there. But she'd worried that it was Rafi who'd later think it was a mistake; that she was. And then he'd left the beach and come back for her. And she'd known that he would never think she was a mistake.

The specks of dried blood won't wash off; she tries to pick at them with her nail, the shock of it all hitting her now as she scrapes them off.

She's the reason he and Basi are in danger, because he loves her, and if he dies, if Basi does, it would be better if he'd never loved her, never even met her.

Antonella comes in. 'Hannah? Are you okay?' She sees the bloody bra at her feet, the red water in the basin. 'Jesus, you're hurt.'

'No. I'm fine.'

'Mr Marr?'

'Yes.'

'But Frank said he'd be okay.'

'He will.'

Colluding in the lie that they're all telling, till this is over.

'Frank said you used up all the charge on your phone calling the ambulance?'

'Yup.'

'Do you want to borrow mine?'

Hannah takes her iPhone, startled by the generosity.

'We have chargers, it's no big deal,' Antonella says.

'Thank you.'

'You won't get reception in here, only on the stage or right at the back of the auditorium. They're going to carry on with *Macbeth* in a minute.'

Hannah feels something like a laugh in her chest, really inappropriate but there it is, rising up.

'You're fucking joking?'

'Fucking not.'

Why did she never really like this girl before? She has a girl crush on her now, because of her lending her mobile and because she hasn't commented on her standing there with nothing on her top and because she said, 'Fucking not.'

'Hannah . . .?' Antonella asks.

'I'll be there in a minute,' she says, because she is shaking now, uncontrollably, and can't even get the teacher's cardigan back on again. 'It'll stop in a minute,' she says.

'It's okay,' Antonella says. 'Got nowhere I need to be for a while.'

★   ★   ★

Rafi is trying to run, the wind driving snow against him and into the abrasions on his face; he has to find Basi before the terrorist, but he doesn't know where to go.

The lights of Abu Qir harbour at night; in the darkness dogs are barking and men are shouting and they have to leave the beach and get to the boat again.

He knows now how deep the sea is, that Basi will be out of his depth and that he's not strong enough to carry him. He gives money to a man on the beach next to them, who's told him that he's an engineer like Baba; a strong, kind-looking man. The man promises he'll carry Basi through the water to the boat. Rafi splashes through the waves, having to swim by the time he reaches the boat. He hauls himself up and looks for Basi. The engineer is getting into the boat without Basi, and he sees that the man has dumped Basi in the water near the beach. Out of his depth, Basi is trying to swim to the boat but he can only do doggy-paddle. The people smugglers start the boat's engine, and Rafi is yelling at them to wait, yelling and yelling, but they don't turn off the engine. His phone is vibrating but it's part of the boat's engine, the whole boat vibrating, and they're going to leave Basi behind.

* * *

Hannah has joined her friends on the stage because it has reception and she's phoning Rafi but he doesn't pick up. Maybe he doesn't know it's her phoning because she's using Antonella's phone so she texts him.

> It's Hannah using Antonella's phone

She sends the text, then rings him. His phone rings five times and each time her heart beats faster, please let him be safe. He answers and she thinks he says something but can't be sure because all she can hear is the violent wind.

'Rafi? It's me. Can you hear me?'

* * *

Rafi is sitting on the snow, his hoody soaked through, his leg bleeding, pressing his phone against his ear.

'Are you okay?' Hannah asks.

Her voice is a pure warm thing among the wind and pain and isolation of the snow.

265

'Yes.' But she can't hear him so he raises his voice, 'Yes!'
Pressing his phone against his ear, holding her against him.
'Where are you?' he asks, having to shout above the wind.
Because surely she's at home with her father by now.
'I'm safe. Is Basi all right?'
'I'm going to find him.'

He's having to shout so Hannah can hear him and he had to shout when he spoke to Rose Polstein too, to be heard above the wind, but Basi had used his usual little voice when they spoke. It had been hard for Rafi to hear him but that was the wind where Rafi was, not Basi, because where Basi was it was quiet. He's inside. That's what he knew when he first talked to Basi, but didn't register it, not properly, just thought he must be inside Junior School. So, he must be inside somewhere near to Junior School and he will find him.

One hand presses his phone against his ear to hear Hannah better, and he makes out noises in the background, other voices.

'Where are you?' he asks again.
'The theatre. Don't worry, it's completely safe here.'
'But Frank said . . .'
'I asked him to lie, I'm sorry. I didn't want you putting yourself in more danger for me.'

'I love you,' he says but the harsh wind is gusting, screaming around him, so he has to yell, 'I love you!' He checks around him in case the terrorist has heard and is coming after him and imagines his love decimating hate, flattening it, no contest, the man turning into a phantom, a ghost in the snow. But Basi needs him and the terrorist is real and armed.

'I love you too,' she says and in the background he hears people cheering; someone even whistles, the way Benny whistles. 'They're rehearsing *Macbeth*,' she says. 'They're all a bit bonkers right now. You should be Young Seward, you know that, don't you? Find Basi and stay safe.'

He pockets his mobile.

She got Frank to lie to him about being evacuated. She was

266

protecting him, didn't want him to be in danger, didn't want him to be hurt.

All this time she's been digging for him.

The engineer was in the boat, leaving Basi in the water, and Rafi was yelling at the people smugglers as they started the engine, screaming at them, the boat vibrating with the engine, and they were cursing him, but he wouldn't stop yelling and then they turned the engine off and the boat was quiet and still and Basi was doggy-paddling towards them, Rafi calling to him in Arabic and in English, 'Come on, Basi, not much further, come on! Come on . . .!' and another man, an elderly man, was calling to Basi too, and then he and the elderly man, who later turned out to be a judge, pulled him in.

There's a boatshed, he remembers passing it earlier when he ran across the car park from the top of the cliff path; the only indoor place where Basi might be hiding. He will go to the boatshed and find him.

He thinks that a long time ago he was like a glass, a tall jug, he imagines, clear and transparent, made of invisible love – Mama's and Baba's and Karam's and Basi's – and he was filled with liquid running life, right to the brim.

Then a truck stopped – 'Enter Gloucester his eyes put out' – and he'd had to leave Mama behind and he'd been beaten and ashamed and frightened and he was a thousand pieces scattered on a snow-covered pavement in Aleppo, an Egyptian beach, the deck of a boat, a migrant camp.

But then he met a girl, loves this girl, and each of those thousand pieces know their way back to their place in the glass, the cracks in him kaleidoscopes of light.

★   ★   ★

In the theatre, Hannah feels again that flashing joy, euphorically happy, weightless with it. She walks up the steps to the back of the auditorium with her own phone which has enough charge now for one call.

She reaches the back of the auditorium, where it's quiet and gets a good signal. She dials.

'Hey, Dad? I'm in the theatre. I'm safe. Don't cry.'

It feels like a miracle to Daphne, all of them here and safe in the theatre. She thinks that for everyone in Old School the noise of his footsteps is still there – they've all told her about the footsteps – but now they are borrowing phones and chargers and they've been to the loo and they're with friends and teachers, all of them together in their school theatre, and they're about to watch a dress rehearsal of *Macbeth*, which is what is meant to be happening this morning, and the fact that one normal strand of the morning is continuing, and they are a part of it, takes them a little bit further away from the fear and the trauma.

Neil sent a message to say that Victor Deakin hasn't returned – hasn't returned! – so Neil and Matthew are safe too.

'Hey, Hannah,' Antonella says, calling to Hannah at the back of the auditorium. 'Text for you from Rafi. He says that Basi must be in the boatshed by Junior School. He's going to join him.'

'He'll be safe in there. Sheltered too,' Benny says, loud with relief, and Daphne claps her hands; she's not sure if it's because she's in a theatre that she's clapping – would anyone clap in everyday life at good news? Hannah looks like she could float, as if she isn't fully physically present.

'More good news,' Sally-Anne says. 'PC Beard's texted and he's safe. He's hiding in the woods.'

And now she wants to cheer; restrain yourself, Daphne.

Sally-Anne texts PC Beard and tells him where Rafi and Basi are. Maybe he can go and shelter with them until this awful thing finally ends. She doesn't want them to be on their own.

'Right then,' Daphne says. 'Shall we carry on?'

After they'd found out about 14 Words, fearing for Rafi and

Basi, the rehearsal had become frenetic and disorganized, some scenes left out, others abandoned, and before the arrival of everyone from Old School they'd reached the end of Act Three. The kids from Old School just want this rehearsal to continue, so even though Daphne's not sure how many of them will follow what's going on, they're going to start Act Four.

Benny again projects the huge photo of a bombed street in Aleppo on to the back wall of the stage: collapsed chalk-white buildings, black shadow spaces where rooms should be, whitened cables and wires trailing; no building left intact; nowhere left to run. Their desolate place.

Zac bangs a gong for thunder and Luisa strobes a bright light across the stage as lightning for the entrance of the three witches, the *instruments of darkness*.

Sophie, Tracey and Antonella stride out on to the stage. They are wearing the black balaclavas again and have put on the black sashes, but must have turned the sashes inside out, because now they have white supremacist symbols on them of a swastika and a raised white fist – most probably done with Tippex, Daphne thinks. The audience applaud; she hears Donna shout 'Brava!'

'People from New School are on TV,' Frank says, looking at his laptop.

Everyone looks at their screens, the theatre people sharing theirs with the library kids and the ones in Jacintha's class whose mobiles ran out of charge.

News sites and social media sites have footage of a coach and four minibuses, all with CLIFF HEIGHTS CO-ED SCHOOL 4–18 written on the side, and teachers' cars arriving at The Pines Leisure Centre. Someone at the leisure centre must have filmed this, sold it perhaps.

Daphne sees colleagues getting out of their cars, which are crammed full of children, and although she already knew they were evacuated, seeing it now makes it newly uplifting, because that really is the word for it, like watching this momentarily lifts her out of this appalling thing that's happening to their school. The kids too are buoyed up by this footage, their bodies less tense, voices lighter as they spot their friends.

'There's James and Maddy.'

'Sarah Jennings. Lucy Carver.'

'Look at the Year Eights, they're *strutting*!'

'Not all of them, some are in tears, look.'

'Where's Anna and Young Fry?' Josh asks.

Daphne looks for the two young children. It was the sixth-formers who nicknamed Davy 'Young Fry' because Davy loves his murderer's line, 'What, you egg? Young fry of treachery!' and they'd all got into the habit of asking where Young Fry had got to, which was often, as he has the knack of never being where he's meant to be. Last week Daphne had found him with the sixth-formers on an illicit fag break, though not himself smoking, small mercies; she's suspected his mother wanted him in a school play to wear him out.

'I found Anna fast asleep on my fake-fur coat last week,' Antonella says. 'Curled up like a kitten.'

Unlike her stage brother, who will one day make a fantastically exuberant Puck, Anna is a dreamy little girl, easily tired.

'I can't see any junior school class,' Josh says.

'There's no little kids there,' Caitlin says. 'They're all too tall.'

'They were doing art in New School this morning, right, Daphne?' Tracey says.

'Yes,' Daphne says. And she's certain of this because she had everyone's timetables to schedule the dress rehearsal. 'We'll see them in a minute, I'm sure.'

Everyone looks for young children on their screens; phone screens are too small so they cluster round people with iPads and laptops.

'Maybe they didn't go to art, maybe they were in Junior School and got out with the other children on the boats,' Antonella says.

'But I was going to pick them up from the art room in New

School,' Tracey says. 'In time for their cue. You emailed me, Daphne.'

They're going to other news sites, searching the footage for young children.

Daphne sees Tonya, the headmaster's secretary, and Donna, Old School's receptionist, looking very anxious, almost in tears.

'They're in the pottery room,' Tonya says. 'Anna and Davy, with their class. Matthew went to warn Camille when this first started.'

'They didn't get out?' Tracey says.

'I don't think so, no,' Tonya says.

The theatre is quiet, appalled.

'Surely Jamie, Victor even, won't go after young children,' Zac says.

'They probably don't even know they're in the pottery room,' Josh says.

Please God, let them be right.

★ ★ ★

The shape in the snow that was earlier spotted above the pottery room has been identified as a military-grade UAV. It seemed to have vanished but they reran their footage and tracked it dipping below the treeline and out of sight. They hope that the dense snow has got into its engine, that even though it's military grade it's crashed to the ground; but it could be waiting, hiding.

'We don't go in yet,' Bronze Commander says. 'We still have eighteen minutes till Alton opens fire. We need to make sure. Search again.'

Rose has often been under time pressure in her career, but time has always been digital before, not seconds as grains of sand running through an hour glass.

But the kids and staff from Old School are safe. Astonishingly, they are safe. And Victor Deakin hasn't returned. They're searching for him in the woods, but aren't hopeful of finding him in these conditions. They've tried phoning PC Beard but he must have turned his phone off – sensible when he's hiding in a woodland with a gunman on the loose.

Would they have stopped PC Beard's plan if they'd known about it? (And they only found out about it from the teachers once they were safely in the theatre.) She doubts it, because of all potential options, and she cannot believe there were any good ones, it surely carried the least risk to the kids.

She goes to the open door, needing the icy air and physical separation to think. She's still troubled by the language Victor used in the announcement about the bloodbath in Old School. Because why would Victor Deakin use words from a teenage attacker at Columbine, with no obvious motive beyond world fame, and a Kansas white supremacist terrorist with a hatred for Muslims? Maybe he couldn't be bothered to come up with his own words; taking the piss out of the organization he's supposedly killing for because he's superior to them; superior even to a supremacist group – only a narcissistic psychopath could go that far.

But there might be something important here: perhaps Victor Deakin thought they might decode his announcement about Old School – it wasn't as difficult as the Jamie Alton one – and left them a clue, as if this is a game; but she can't yet figure out what it is.

*   *   *

Rafi hardly has any strength left, his right leg barely able to support him, but he pushes himself on towards the car park and Basi in the boatshed.

I love you. Just three words that are the spoken soul of you, that make the unseen spine of who you are in the world. *I hate you* is only three words too but isn't enough; you can't say *I hate you* and leave it at that, you have to say why, but *I love you* are three words complete in themselves.

He checks behind, but cannot see anyone following him in the driving snow.

In the Dunkirk camp, he worried every time he returned to their shed with food that he'd lead men back to Basi. He'd told Basi only to answer the door to their knocking code but didn't tell him the reason he couldn't call out that it was him; that his fourteen-year-old's voice would also mark him out to the paedophiles. In the camp, he always had his hood pulled forward to hide how young he was.

He tries to run, but the snow is too deep and his right leg keeps giving way, so hobbling is the best he can manage; a fast fucking hobble but he will get to Basi.

★   ★   ★

In the theatre, Hannah's phone is charging in a floor socket next to her seat. They're all watching the dress rehearsal. Some of the audience don't really know what's going on, apart from people like her doing English A level, but they didn't want their friends to start over.

Her phone buzzes and she sees she's got an Instagram message from someone called Aryan Knight: a photo of the front page of the *Sun* newspaper.

1 IN 5 BRIT MUSLIMS' SYMPATHY FOR JIHADIS

It buzzes again with another photo of a newspaper front page.

MUSLIMS TELL BRITISH: GO TO HELL!!

Hannah shows her phone to Benny and Frank. More photos of front pages ping on to her phone.

MUSLIMS 'SILENT ON TERROR'

JIHADIST KILLERS ON OUR STREETS

HUNDREDS MORE UK MUSLIMS CHOOSE
JIHAD THAN ARMY

Daphne sees kids around Hannah and goes over. She looks at the Instagram photos on Hannah's phone and puts her arm around the girl's shoulders as more and more of them come on to her screen. Other kids are gathering around Hannah.

'Why are they sending us this bullshit?' Frank asks.

Daphne starts to say something then stops. But they are all looking at her, and this is the kind of school where the kids are included, treated as independent and responsible.

'We are being told why our school is being punished,' Daphne says.

Daphne has felt the kids' camaraderie as an almost tangible thing; the kids in the theatre pouring their energy and love into their friends from Old School, bonding them tightly together. But with these headlines something different is happening; the kids from Old School no longer look vulnerable but angry, all the kids now enraged that white supremacists are doing this to their school; to Rafi and Basi and Anna and Davy and Mr Marr; and she feels this fury as energy, a wild thing, that has nowhere to go.

★   ★   ★

Rafi is nearing the car park. The pain from his leg and the cold are making him shudder uncontrollably. He sees that blood has soaked through his jeans and is falling on to the snow. He has told Hannah Syrian folk tales and she's told him her fairy tales, part of their childhoods so part of themselves. He thinks of Little Red Riding Hood being followed by a wolf; Snow White being taken into the woods to be murdered; red and white, blood on snow, a breadcrumb trail.

He's so cold and tired that he finds it hard to lift his arms to take off his hoody. He manages to take off the hoody and then his shirt, his bare arms trembling. He wraps his shirt around his injured right leg, tightly despite pressing at the shrapnel, to absorb his blood so he won't lead anyone to Basi. He puts the hoody back on again but it is covered in snow, freezing against his bare skin.

He walks a few more paces towards the car park, but is too cold and exhausted to walk any further. He sinks down on to his knees and then he crawls through the thick snow towards his brother. His legs are becoming numb, his hands aching with cold as he crawls.

'*You should be Young Seward, you know that, don't you?*' Hannah said to him.

She knows that he admires Young Seward the most of all the characters, because he doesn't run away. '*Had he his hurts before?*' his father asks, when he's told his son is dead. '*Ay, on the front,*' the man replies. He died facing evil, not running away. He wants Baba to be proud.

His mobile buzzes and he thinks it's Hannah but it's an Instagram photo of segments of a newspaper, with the name Katie Hopkins.

Rescue boats? I'd use gunships to stop migrants

Show me bodies floating in water, I still don't care. Make no mistake, these migrants are like cockroaches. Bring on the gunships, force migrants back to their shores and burn the boats.

He is crawling like a cockroach but this journalist is wrong. He is not like a cockroach, he is like Young Seward. And he will reach Basi.

*　*　*

The shed is getting darker and the blackness smells of monsters, their mouths with rotting things inside, and they are going to

275

bite his face with their dagger-teeth. He hears them creeping towards him.

He didn't tell Rafi where he is.

He puts his hands over his mouth, trying not to make any sounds as he cries, but he hears moaning noises, like he's a little baby not a boy, but he can't stop.

Rafi won't be able to find him.

They're not monsters but a man with a gun. He pushes his fist into his mouth so the man won't hear him cry, but he's juddering and he's making the boat judder too, making it creak, and the man with the gun will hear him and shoot him.

There's no Ratty in here, nobody with him. His phone is open but it's dark and won't switch on and inside all his animals are starved.

★   ★   ★

In the theatre, everyone is looking at their screens; the news is reporting that one of the attackers is called 'Aryan Knight'.

'A fucking knight?' Frank says.

Knights are decent and brave; Arthurian knights and their quests, Chaucer's gentle knight on a pilgrimage, Rafi coming back for Hannah, and the gunmen are the opposite of everything that is decent and brave and gentle.

'He's trending on Twitter,' Luisa says.

'Probably not Aryan Knight himself,' Josh says. 'Probably needs both hands on his fucking gun.'

'It's just bots retweeting, not real people,' Antonella says.

But real people will be reading it now. Frank puts his arm around Hannah, trying to stop her shaking, as they read Aryan Knight's retweets:

Donald J. Trump @realDonaldTrump
Thank you to respected columnist Katie Hopkins of Daily Mail. com for her powerful writing on the UK's Muslim problems.

Donald J. Trump @realDonaldTrump
The politicians of the U.K. should watch Katie Hopkins of Daily
Mail.com on @FoxNews. Many people in the U.K. agree with me!

Donald J. Trump @realDonaldTrump
The United Kingdom is trying hard to disguise their massive
Muslim problem. Everybody is wise to what is happening, very
sad! Be honest.

Donald J. Trump @realDonaldTrump
In Britain, more Muslims join ISIS than join the British Army.

Donald J. Trump @realDonaldTrump
We must stop being politically correct and get down to the
business of security for our people. If we don't get smart it will
only get worse.

Donald J. Trump @realDonaldTrump
Just out report: "United Kingdom crime rises 13% annually amid
spread of Radical Islamic terror." Not good, we must keep
America safe!

         ★   ★   ★

There are fourteen minutes until Jamie Alton opens fire. A
police UAV operator has just spotted the terrorist's drone back
up over the pottery room.

'They're now retweeting Trump's retweets of Jayda Fransen,'
Stuart says. 'Deputy leader of Britain First.'

'We still can't stop it?' Bronze Commander's frustration is
evident.

'They've got software which is creating aliases very fast, as
fast as we take them down,' Lysander says.

'They've retweeted Britain First's response,' Stuart says.

Britain First @BritainFirstHQ
THE PRESIDENT OF THE UNITED STATES HAS
RETWEETED THREE OF DEPUTY LEADER JAYDA
FRANSEN'S TWITTER VIDEOS. DONALD TRUMP HAS
AROUND 44 MILLION FOLLOWERS! GOD BLESS YOU
TRUMP!

Rose remembers that the white supremacist murderer of the MP Jo Cox – mother of two young children, wife, daughter, sister and friend – shouted 'Britain First' as he killed her.

She wonders what would have happened to seventeen-year-old Jamie Alton if the president of America and mainstream newspapers hadn't fostered hatred against Muslims? Perhaps there would have been a brake on his mental deterioration and brainwashing; perhaps he would have had more of a chance against it. But there's no point now going down this path because it is too late.

Police attack drones are being launched to take out the terrorists' drone. Her team and Dannisha watch the screen, but she turns away.

Not your job.

She goes back to the open door, looks out at the snow. Victor has orchestrated all of it, she's sure of that, so it's Victor behind retweeting Trump. And that makes sense because even if Victor thinks him moronic, and she expects that he does, at least he's a world-famous wielder of immense power; but that's far from the case with Patrick Stein and Eric Harris, whose words Victor has appropriated.

Again, she wonders if Victor has given them a clue. But if he has, then he's confident they won't understand; that he can outplay them.

'The BBC's just got a message,' an officer says on screen. 'Pull back or we kill now. The message includes a YouTube link.'

He presses the link and YouTube footage plays, which must have been taken by the terrorists' drone. It shows Jamie Alton pointing his gun at the pottery room.

'It's been posted on to Aryan Knight's Instagram and YouTube accounts,' Usman says. 'We closed it down, but it had already gone viral.'

A man in a balaclava pointing a gun at children, of course it went viral. Victor has not only orchestrated the violence but also how it is shown; releasing this footage to heat up already febrile news coverage, guaranteeing airtime around the world.

★ ★ ★

In the theatre, they are all on screens watching a repost of Aryan Knight's YouTube video. Most kids are sharing, even if they have a working mobile of their own, because they want to be close to someone else. Daphne and Sally-Anne watch on Sally-Anne's iPad.

From high up Daphne sees their school, the snow falling, the beautiful woods, and then further in to see the pottery room where Anna and Davy are. It must be taken from a drone with a camera; but why?

The camera moves down through the falling snow. Through the branches of trees, she sees the pottery room's huge windows, with something filling them, tiles she thinks, but the snow is too thick to be sure. And then the drone turns and she is looking at a man in army clothes, his face covered by a black balaclava, ammunition belts looped round his body. His gun is pointing at the windows of the pottery room.

The large theatre is silent. Daphne has never heard it so quiet, even when she's been alone here. And in the quiet, all their phones and iPads play the sound of the wind outside the pottery room.

'Mr Marr is dying,' Hannah says. 'He's bleeding and he can hardly breathe, he won't be able to, not for much longer. Frank lied to protect you all, we all did, but I think you should know.'

On stage Caitlin, playing Lady Macduff, and Josh, playing Ross, start their scene, jumping ahead; perhaps they don't care or perhaps they can't remember – as if it matters.

'You must have patience, Madam,' Ross says.

'He had none,' Lady Macduff replies. '*His flight was madness . . . Our fears do make us traitors.*'

Little Anna is meant to be holding Lady Macduff's hand, Davy scampering around and not doing as he's told, while First Murderer waits in the wings, and Daphne must stop this rehearsal. She stands and gestures to Caitlin and Josh to stop but they ignore her. Normally she'd like it that they are not biddable, that the kids here think for themselves, are not in awe of authority – even kids like Caitlin who you'd think would do as they're told are not like that at all – but she really needs them to do as they are told now.

'*You know not whether it was his wisdom or his fear,*' Ross says and the audience are glued to the stage now, as if it really matters to them, as if a play can make any difference at all.

'*Wisdom? To leave his wife, to leave his babes,*' Lady Macduff says. '*His mansion, and his titles in a place from whence himself does fly?*'

Daphne goes towards the stage. 'Enough now,' she says, but Caitlin as Lady Macduff ignores her.

'*He loves us not,*
He wants the natural touch, for the poor wren,
The most diminutive of birds, will fight
Her young ones in her nest, against the owl.
All is the fear, and nothing is the love.'

'Please,' Daphne says, going to Caitlin, and putting her arm around her. 'Enough.'

19.

12.11 p.m.

A live feed from a police surveillance UAV shows the terrorists' drone above the pottery room and the police attack drones moving closer. Another police surveillance UAV gives a wider view. Through the snow, Rose can make out lines of police and counter-terrorism specialist firearms officers in their grey uniforms. For the first time, she sees how huge an operation the rescue is.

'We stay back till their drone is down,' Bronze Commander says. 'Then move in fast and take him out.'

A police attack drone moves closer. It shoots out a white net, a spider's web in the sky that's barely perceptible in the snow; the net wraps round the terrorists' drone and brings it plummeting to the ground.

'Move in,' Bronze Commander says.

Rose knows that Silver Commander, although off site, is linked into the briefing and will be providing leadership and direction to Bronze Commander.

The first surveillance UAV shows the grey-uniformed armed counterterrorism officers moving swiftly through the snow towards the pottery room.

It will take four minutes until they're close enough to shoot accurately. Nine minutes till he starts firing. There's enough time, Rose says to herself.

The snowfall has lessened a little and a second UAV shows Jamie Alton in more detail than Rose has seen before, his converted semi-automatic braced against his right shoulder, hand on the trigger, and then the camera turns to the pottery room and for the first time Rose sees Camille Giraud's face at the window.

Do your job.

Rose stands back at the open doorway, her face frozen by the wind and the snow, separating herself physically and mentally from everyone else. She has to focus on the thing that's been bothering her, examine it.

It's not just the question of why Victor, a narcissistic psychopath, would borrow language from other people less intelligent than himself, but another question that arises from it. What is the link between Patrick Stein, a terrorist who hates Muslims, and Eric Harris, a teenager whose agenda was world infamy? Alone in the cold doorway she sees the link.

She hurries inside, the knowledge brutal and physical.

'I think they have a bomb,' Rose says.

'Why? What makes you think that?' Bronze Commander asks, and he sounds angry but he looks appalled.

'Columbine was a failed bombing, so was Patrick Stein's plot in Kansas. That's the connection between Harris and Stein. That's why Victor's been using their words; like a clue.'

'Stein and The Crusaders had four trucks piled with ammonium nitrate,' Stuart says. 'The FBI uncovered the plot in time.'

'The attackers at Columbine had forty pounds of propane tank bombs, strapped to gasoline cans,' Rose says. 'Their homemade bombs didn't go off because of faulty wiring but they didn't have a terrorist organization behind them.'

Because now Rose knows why Victor joined 14 Words: not just to get himself a wingman and access to guns – he wanted to get his hands on a bomb.

'The heavily encrypted transactions that we can't decipher could well be the acquisition of a bomb or bomb-making materials,' Lysander says. 'The level of encryption fits with a paramilitary organization.'

'Deakin and Alton would have been trained in bomb-making by 14 Words,' Stuart says.

The small home-made bomb at the beginning was like the rifle shots, a misdirection of the vicious, destructive weapons they actually had; toying with them; a joke even.

'Victor's sent a text,' Dannisha says.

> Watch and learn motherfuckers

A taunt to Eric Harris and to Patrick Stein, Rose thinks. To all of them.

'The bomb is most likely to be in Old School, isn't it?' Bronze Commander says, and maybe he's right. Matthew Marr and Neil Forbright are still there, but everyone else has escaped to the theatre; in a coldly dispassionate numbers game, this isn't the carnage it would be otherwise.

'Victor Deakin must've brought the bomb into Old School with him when he swapped places with Jamie Alton,' Bronze Commander continues. 'Or Alton brought it in this morning as well as the gun, left it in an empty room.'

'The Columbine bombers had duffel bags that they carried into the school dining room,' Rose says. 'It needed two of them. And they also packed their cars with explosives. The Crusader bombers planned on trucks packed with explosives. It's bigger than something one man could carry on his own. I think he's boasting about it being bigger as well as succeeding.'

She has to get into Victor's head, predict what he would want, then how he'd accomplish it.

He'd want to bomb the place that was the most crowded, because he'd want maximum carnage and spectacle. That means he'd choose the place least likely to be evacuated.

Come on, Rose, think. Do better. This is Victor's masterstroke, his end game, unleashing hell.

He'd think of the place that would be safest.

The safest place in the school is the theatre.

And Jamie Alton, his pal on the inside, his wingman, is responsible for props.

'It's in the theatre,' she says. 'In a props room. Jamie Alton could have ferried explosives inside for weeks.'

'Tell them to evacuate,' Bronze Commander says. 'Tell them to run in all directions. We risk them being shot in the woods, but just get them out.'

It's against all rules of hostage evacuation but there are no other choices; again the devil driving.

Amaal is hurriedly phoning Daphne, Thandie phones Jacintha, George phones Sally-Anne, white-faced and shaking; other officers are phoning Donna and Tonya and the kids, they have all their numbers.

But nobody answers.

They try again and again.

Why've they switched their phones off? Because they're performing and watching a play? Jesus.

Officers are leaving messages to evacuate, but when will they hear their messages?

Again and again they try but still nobody answers.

'Victor's texted,' Dannisha says.

> **Columbine and Kansas – Amateur Hour**

Breaking with all protocol and rules, emergency vehicles are racing along the snowy drive towards the theatre despite the danger and the site not being secured; the devil driving but brave people trying to stop him. Rose cannot bear to look at the faces of her young team; to be responsible for what they may have to live with.

Police officers are getting out of their cars and jeeps and running towards the theatre to warn them. They'll be using megaphones but the theatre walls are thick and they are still too far away to be heard.

Another text from Victor:

> **BOOM!**

Live footage from a police surveillance UAV shows the theatre, a sturdy building in the trees. For a few seconds it is peaceful, snow falling on to the trees and the simple cedar-clad building.

The bomb rips apart the theatre, the percussive force exploding the walls and roof, hurling everything upwards past the treeline into the sky; then a fireball engulfs the whole of the remaining building, flames shooting up, the winter trees alight as the building collapses in on itself.

PART THREE

To be conscious is not to be in time
But only in time can the moment in the rose-garden,
The moment in the arbour when the rain beat,
The moment in the draughty church at smokefall
Be remembered; involved with past and future.
Only through time time is conquered.

T. S. Eliot, 'Burnt Norton', *Four Quartets* (1936)

20.

12.15 p.m.

Around Rose people stand in silent paralysis; shocked into stillness. She is no longer thinking or feeling, numbed, so that she is aware only of the plastic smell of the inside of the vehicle, as if they should be driving somewhere, instead of this terrible inert uselessness.

Bronze Commander comes on screen, his ruddy face ashen.

'We all face this, deal with this, later, we have no time now. No time. There are still children in the pottery room. We have young children in the pottery room. We move in now.'

A feed from a police UAV shows counterterrorism specialist firearms officers in their grey uniforms closing in through the woods on the pottery room, the black smoke from the burning theatre a quarter of a mile away hazing around them.

A second police UAV, close to the pottery room, shows Jamie Alton in the same position; converted semi-automatic pointed at the children, finger on the trigger. The UAV's camera turns towards the pottery-room windows.

'Stop moving!' Bronze Commander tells the counterterrorism firearms officers.

Victor Deakin is inside the pottery room.

He's looking out of the window, dressed in grey. He must have predicted that CTSFOs would be deployed; so even if he was spotted people would assume he was one of them. But he wasn't spotted. He left Old School as soon as the children and teachers ran to the theatre, went through the woods and then used the cover of the bomb – the noise and flames and shock, everybody's eyes turned towards the explosion – to get inside the pottery room.

Rose is explaining what he did to try to deflect her mind from what she's seeing, but her body shakes violently with the horror of it. Because what chance do they have to save any of the children now? Two men with guns that fire fifty bullets in three seconds; what chance for the children and their brave, indefatigable teacher?

'There's something moving,' Amaal says, looking at the feed from the first police UAV. 'Look . . .'

Through the snow and black smoke from the burning theatre, trees in the woods seem to be moving.

'Jesus, it's kids with trees . . .' Rose says.

'How many?' Thandie asks.

'Fifty? More? Must be all of them. Must be.'

★   ★   ★

There's a long line of them, students and teachers, and another line behind them, and Daphne feels tremendously, wonderfully proud of them all.

Whose idea was it? Daphne can't remember. It feels like it was everyone's idea, or at least when whoever it was suggested it everybody had grabbed hold of the idea and made it their own. They'd gone backstage and taken the saplings that were Birnam Wood. And then they'd left the theatre, holding their trees in front of them, walking through the snow to try to help the children in the pottery room. A minute later, a huge explosion behind them and they'd carried on walking, their ears ringing, the force of the blast rippling the trees; black smoke billowing around them, stinging their eyes and throats.

She tries to resist quoting from Shakespeare, that really wouldn't be helpful right now, Daphne. The last thing Frank needs, walking next to her, is a dose of Shakespeare at this point. Luisa is the other side of him and next to her is Benny and then Zac, and on the line goes, child after child; Tobias at the back, headphones on, marching too. She thinks about it though, the soldiers marching at the end of *Macbeth*, camouflaged with branches, Birnam Wood marching to Dunsinane Hill: good triumphing over evil. And really, is there any better image of goodness and courage than kids carrying saplings against bullets?

★ ★ ★

Up until a few minutes ago the children in the pottery room hadn't questioned Camille's game of house because for seven-year-olds playing is totally natural, pretending interchangeable with reality.

But then a man with a gun came in.

He is sitting, lolling almost, on one of the tables, their roof, and underneath Camille can hear them crying and whimpering and she's livid with an anger she's never felt before, white-hot rage, that this man can frighten children who have just made clay cats, dogs and a guinea pig for a make-believe house. This rage burns everything else away, so that all she is left with is love for the children and that is all that matters.

She has asked him, begged him, to let the children go. He didn't even look at her, let alone reply; as if he has nothing human at all inside him.

She looks out of the window to the man outside with the balaclava, his gun pointed at them. She's done this so many times, hoping to see police running to their rescue, but even if they are coming it's too late now.

Through the thick snow and smoke, she can see the flames from the theatre, far away.

The woods are moving through the snow and smoke. She blinks.

Trees are moving.

It can't be. The gunman lolling on the table has noticed because he gets up and shouts something at the gunman in the balaclava.

★ ★ ★

Watching the feed from the police UAV, Rose and her team see Victor Deakin coming out of the pottery room and he must say something to Jamie Alton because Jamie Alton turns. For a moment both men, holding their guns, are turned away from the children in the pottery room and towards the woods, looking through the snow and smoke at the kids and teachers they think are dead. The armed counterterrorism officers fire, killing them both.

★ ★ ★

Camille bends down and looks at the terrified children under the tables, her knees shaking as she crouches.

'You can come out of your house now. You're safe.'

She opens the door of the pottery room, with children clustered around her; all of them seem to be holding on to a part of her – her hands, her cardigan sleeves, her gilet. Anna is holding tightly to her skirt. Davy, his face tear-streaked, holds on to her wrist because her hands are already taken.

Police and men in grey uniforms are running towards the children, their hair and uniforms covered in snow and ash, and she sees that one of the men in grey is crying.

Beyond them in the woods, students and teachers are putting down small trees. She recognizes children that she's taught, Hannah and Frank and Tobias, and more police are with them; she spots Daphne and Matthew's secretary and Old School's receptionist.

The ambulance people have blankets that they wrap around the children and someone puts a blanket around her too, and she thinks it's not so much that she's cold, although she is suddenly terribly, terribly cold, but that it's symbolic of something good but she doesn't have the energy any more to think or even to stand.

★ ★ ★

Rafi has crawled halfway across the car park towards the boat-shed. He cannot feel his hands or his knees in the snow as he crawls, just the pain in his leg from the shrapnel. As he gets close to the shed, he thinks someone is watching him, following him to Basi; hatred wearing an anorak and cracking twigs, hunting them down.

He waits for the heavy snow to fill in his tracks, so that he won't bring danger to Basi.

A little while ago, he got a text from Hannah.

> We have left theatre. We r Birnam wood marching 2 Dunsinane. U were right about trees. Love u

A few minutes later he heard a huge explosion in the distance. But they were all out, they were in the woods. Safe. And then he heard shots. The police. Surely the police.

He looks around the car park, but the snow is too thick to see anything further than a foot away and the gusting wind camouflages all other sounds with its own.

*   *   *

He's crying and his legs are shaking and he just wants Rafi. He can't ever have Baba and Karam and maybe not Mama, not ever again, so he just wants Rafi; wants his arms around him, holding him tightly. But he fed his animals in his phone and he didn't tell Rafi where he is. He's stupid and he wees himself at night and Rafi's wrong, he's not brave as Basi Bukhari because Basi Bukhari isn't brave at all.

He hears a quiet *rat-a-TAT-tat, rat-a-TAT-tat*; so quiet he thinks he's imagining it. Then he hears it again *rat-a-TAT-tat, rat-a-TAT-tat*.

He gets out of the boat, feeling his way towards the door. He's bumping into things and once he trips but he gets to the door; he feels on the door for the rusty, creaky bolt and he finds it and then he pulls it back and opens the door.

Rafi's here!

Rafi comes inside and shuts the door and it's dark again; and in the dark he can feel Rafi's arms around him and he's all covered in snow.

He's really here!

Rafi puts on his phone and shines it as a torch around the shed and it's not dark any more. Rafi pushes the bolt across the door again.

'Are you all right, Little Monkey?'

'I thought you wouldn't find me.'

'Course I did.'

'There's a boat at the back, that's where I've been hiding.'

They go to the back of the shed together and they get in the boat. He has to help Rafi because of his poor leg, it's all bleeding and hurt, and his face is bleeding too but he's got a really big smile.

They're in the boat together and he hugs Rafi and hugs him, even though he's covered in snow, and Rafi hugs him tightly back. The light suddenly goes off.

'My mobile's out of juice,' Rafi says and it's like his phone is magic, like it knew it had to last just long enough till Rafi got here. Though Rafi has probably been careful, because he always makes sure he has enough juice to speak to Basi.

Rafi rubs his legs and then his arms, but he still can't get very warm, and Rafi can't give him a hot potato through his anorak so he gives his hands a hot potato.

Basi's hands feel like little ice blocks against Rafi's mouth as he tries to use his own breath to warm him.

'There was a bomb,' Basi says, his words hopping up and down with his shivering. 'I heard it.'

'Nobody was hurt. They were all outside pretending to be trees.'

'Really?'

'Yes.'

'It's funny we're inside a boat inside a shed, isn't it?' Basi says, his words still hopping up and down with his shivering, and Rafi knows he's been waiting to say this, hoping that Rafi wouldn't notice so that Basi can point it out.

'It's hilarious!' Rafi says.

Basi is shaking with cold and his laugh sounds different.

'Remember when I went blue?' Basi asks.

'Course I do.'

The third night on the boat from Egypt to Italy, no shelter on the deck. Basi turning blue with cold, all the children turning blue, as the rain hammered down over them. Everyone crammed up against the stern, pushing the boat too low in the water, nobody at the bow because of the huge waves. Rafi was terrified they were going to capsize and go into the violent sea so he got out his laser pointer, to shine if they capsized so a nearby ship would see them and rescue them, but there weren't any ships, the sea vast and empty and dark, and all he had was a laser pointer. Then he saw Basi watching him.

'Look, Basi!' and he shone the light up at the sky.

'You shone a laser pointer,' Basi says. 'You made the dark rain into a light tunnel!'

'I did.'

And then dawn had come finally, lightening the dark ocean, bringing some warmth; people sharing sea-sickness pills and lemons. A child pointed, and in the murderous sea dolphins were playing in the waves.

★   ★   ★

Beth Alton is being driven away in a police Range Rover to a police station, where Mike has also been taken. Press vehicles are parked half on the snowy verge, journalists with TV cameras line the road for what seems like miles. Cameramen run after the Range Rover but the police vehicle is too fast for them and they pass in a blur through the snow. Theo is being questioned by the police at Warwick University. He phoned her a few minutes ago, no longer a fledging adult but a distraught boy, and she must take care of him, make sure he survives this somehow, help him as she didn't help Jamie; and for a few seconds she resents Theo, that loving him means enduring what she feels now because she cannot kill herself; love for her older son must come before guilt and grief for her beloved younger child.

But the three of them, Mike and Theo and her, must keep intact who Jamie was, not what he was turned into; because they alone know that he was dead even if he seemed alive.

Like I was a kind of zombie, Mum?

Jamie . . .

That whole zombie thing was weird, loving someone one moment, then they die and become terrifying.

You still liked the zombie films though.

Only the funny ones with a cushion for jumpy-out moments.

They'll remember little details about him like him enjoying funny zombie movies, *Shaun of the Dead*, but not horror, he hated horror, and they watched them together because he was a boy who liked watching films with his mother, a cushion for *jumpy-out* moments. No one else will know that about him or want to know that about him.

The police Range Rover has to stop behind a car moving slowly in front of them, perhaps deliberately because there are lenses being pushed up against the car window, camera flashes going off, dazzling, so that she can't see properly, lights shimmering in rings. She closes her eyes and for a few moments there is a slippage in time; she has picked Jamie up from school as usual and she's driving him home.

★   ★   ★

Rose Polstein is walking towards Old School along the drive. Thandie has given her her jacket on permanent loan. This evening and into the night she and her team will be debriefing and doing the paperwork and although exhausted she thinks this will probably be a good thing for all of them; she'll be able to tell them she's proud of each of them and why. Emergency vehicles stream past, throwing up slush over her, but she wants to be physically present when she's had to be at a remove for so long, watching it all on a screen. Above her helicopters buzz through the snow.

By the old Victorian gatehouse, she sees a police patrol car, skewed at an angle off the drive, the windscreen shot. There's a splatter of yellow paint on the CCTV camera, just visible under the snow.

She's on her phone to Stuart Dingwall, who's in his Land Rover on his way to the boatshed. There's fifty armed police officers also on their way.

'How long till you're there?' she asks.

'Not long. The drive's just about passable with a four-wheel drive. That first copper on the scene, PC Beard, is probably with them already; a teacher with a tree told him where they were.'

'He won't be armed.'

'I think they're safe, Rose.'

'You're counterterrorism. You think the third terrorist is still after them. That's why you're going.'

'To be honest, it's a long shot. I don't think the third terrorist hung around after the bomb. I think he scarpered pronto. We've secured the perimeter immediately around the school but not the woods; too big, too porous. Relatively easy for him to escape. We'll get him though. These terror organizations aren't closed off from each other and they like to boast. So we'll find him.'

She remembers Stuart saying that 14 Words were paranoid about being infiltrated but thinks counterterrorism has managed that with another group. She thinks that's how he'll be found and his identity discovered. But she already knows his essential self – a cowardly inadequate bastard, the same as every other cowardly inadequate bastard terrorist. Counterterrorism don't want the media to give undue coverage to terrorism and she hopes the media won't puff him up with a name and a story, that they save the names and stories for the kids and teachers at the school, the police and counterterrorism officers and the helicopter pilot flying in the teeth of a blizzard, and their remarkable and different stories.

'Let me know how Rafi is?' she asks Stuart.

'Sure. There's paramedics. A whole convoy of us.'

She smiles and hangs up.

Three police officers were wounded by the blast as they ran towards the theatre, trying to get the kids to evacuate, but she's been told that their injuries are minor.

As she gets closer to Old School she sees groups of children and teachers with emergency personnel being loaded on to coaches. Some seem dazed, as if in a trance, early symptoms of PTSD starting – but alive.

She feels suddenly dehydrated and exhausted. And something else, that's subtler, and she knows that she is fundamentally changed from who she was before this.

She thinks about Rafi looking after his brother on a journey from Syria to England and then again today; the fierce responsibility of his love. She's never had to look after anyone, not outside of her job where her role is defined and limited. It's funny, since becoming pregnant she's looked at kids, wondering if her son will turn out like this one or dear God please not like that one, but when she thinks about Rafi Bukhari she wonders what kind of parent she'll be.

She sees a girl sitting on the doorstep of Old School, her long red hair bright in the snow, as if waiting for someone. A paramedic's blanket is wrapped around her. Snowflakes and tiny burnt fragments from the theatre fall around her. She must have charmed a police officer because she should be getting on to a coach, but Rose will let her be. Stuart said they'd secured the immediate perimeter around the school, so she's safe enough.

Rose walks past Old School and sees four fire engines; firefighters are hosing water on to the burning theatre; debris scattered through the trees. But culture isn't contained within a building, it is alive with beating hearts walking into the woods, holding their trees, doing a promenade performance of *Macbeth*. Bloody hell, these kids. Unbelievable. Fucking amazing.

The glass corridor lies on the snow in shards, reflecting the flames, and something bothers her.

★   ★   ★

They won't let Hannah go to the boatshed and find Rafi herself but the drive from Junior School and the boatshed goes past where she is sitting, so she'll see him soon. A young policeman checked her for weapons but she convinced him that she wasn't a terrorist, though he didn't need much convincing, he was smiling the whole time. Rules, he'd said. Right, she'd said.

She'll see Dad soon. He's waiting for her with her aunt and cousins and second cousins; *all rabbit's friends and relations*, a joke between them since she was about three. She's told him she can't leave till she's seen Rafi, and he understands. She didn't tell him that she also just needs to be alone for a little while, nobody talking or even breathing close to her, just her in the cold air with no walls, no footsteps; to feel her own space and inhabit the world again. She needs a bit of time to put the pieces of herself back together that the footsteps broke apart; *all the king's horses and all the king's men*. She will be put back together again, just not quite the same.

Dark snowflakes drift through the sky, falling mainly over the woods but some of them over Old School and her too; they must be pieces of the theatre – walls and roof and seats and stage and props burnt to almost nothing. She'd have minded much more if it was the library that was blown up. She feels a debt to books for being a barricade against the gunman and would have been upset if they'd been blown to smithereens and were drifting down over the woods; but then books are made from trees, so maybe it would have been a returning home, their heroines and heroes unfettered from the covers – a new unbound narrative. Weird, but Rafi will understand. How much longer till he gets here?

★ ★ ★

Rose hurries towards the Victorian gatehouse. She's radioed for assistance because she doesn't think it was luck for the terrorists that the kids and staff in Old School were all evacuated to the theatre, all of them meant to be blown up. She fears they were corralled in there. 14 Words is tech-savvy; sophisticated. What if the police were *meant* to decrypt the bloodbath threat? And just in case they didn't, 14 Words leaked that threat, and that Victor was a psychopath, in order to heighten the jeopardy, to create panic, so they all went along with the plan to run to the theatre?

She goes into the gatehouse. Other officers are with her. Shining a torch, they see drag-marks of blood and a police constable in uniform lying dead on the brick floor, shot in the chest, his police radio in fragments. Their torch shows his badge, 'PC Beard'.

Rose puts out an emergency alert. Officers are opening the door to PC Beard's car. A blanket is draped over the driver's seat covering the blood, but it has seeped through. They take the blanket away. From the amount of blood, it's clear PC Beard was shot inside the car. He was killed as he drove up towards the school at the very beginning of this.

She will mourn for a murdered colleague when her job is done. Think. What does this mean? She sweeps the beam of her torch around the gatehouse and sees a mobile phone in the corner, switched on and connected to an external battery pack; contributing to the lie that PC Beard was alive and in the gatehouse using his own phone. Was the third terrorist ever in here? People he spoke to thought he was and if he'd been outside they'd have heard the wind in the background. He was probably in the gatehouse for a short period of time, Victor and

300

him hiding the body, covering over the evidence, and then he phoned from the maintenance shed and maybe the empty Junior School, just putting the battery into his burner phone for the duration of each call so the police didn't pick it up. And now?

Surely he has escaped. He has consistently wanted to avoid being seen and captured; using a silencer, keeping hidden. He probably never even rang the doorbell, Victor just played a recording on his phone. But she imagines his rage as he spent two hours searching for Rafi, thinking Basi had been evacuated; his hate for the boys becoming stronger than his fear of being caught or killed.

Officers are using their hands to dig through the top layers of snow. They find tracks of blood, from the car to the gatehouse; and the CCTV camera covered in paint was blind.

Stuart Dingwall phones her.

'I just got an alert that you—'

'Are you with Rafi and Basi?' she asks.

'A school minibus has overturned across the drive. A branch was used as a lever. We're moving it now.'

★ ★ ★

Rafi and Basi are in the boat. In the dark Rafi can feel Basi's body gibbering with cold and he's worried that hugging Basi close to him is just making him colder.

A knock on the door of the shed. Rafi feels Basi's body stiffen with fear and tightens his arms around him.

Another *knock-knock* and the man knocking at the door is one of Assad's men battering at their door to arrest their father and brother or he is part of Daesh or a paedophile at the camp banging on the door of their shed; he is First Murderer or Second Murderer or Third Murderer in *Macbeth*, a man of violence without a name who lives in the dark, who will hurt a person you love, bringing the darkness with him, falling across something bright and good so that love has a shadow.

A friendly English voice calls to them.

'Rafi? Basi? I'm a police officer. My name's PC Beard, can you let me in?'

English police officers are good. Nothing bad will happen. He should trust him.

'You're okay now, sons. Let me in. You're safe.'

But something stops Rafi from getting out of the boat and opening the door; maybe because he'll have to take his arms away from his little brother who's so cold or because of his injured leg which means he doesn't want to move and a bodily knowledge of how much they are hated, and he remembers some people here see them as less than human; as cockroaches.

The sound of a twig snapping and another.

Dots of light appear in the door as the man outside fires. Basi doesn't know to be afraid, but Rafi uses his body to shield Basi, lying over him in the boat, because the man will get into the shed any moment. Terror is a black thing: the dead of night, the pitch of darkness; Baba and Karam's bodies in the snow.

The sound of gunfire, rapid and loud. Basi whimpers in terror. And there are men pushing at the door, opening it, and they're coming in and telling him and Basi to get out of the boat and that they're safe. But they're not. Nowhere is safe. He has his arms around Basi, just looking at Basi, protecting him, not looking at the people in the shed, not wanting to look at them.

And then he hears a woman's voice he recognizes. 'Rafi, it's Rose Polstein . . .'

He tries to get out of the boat but his hands are numb. 'It's okay,' he tells Basi. 'We can get out of the boat now.' He can't feel the sides of the boat and the pain in his right leg makes him dizzy.

People in police uniforms and grey uniforms are helping him and Basi out of the boat; and someone is putting blankets around him and around Basi, soft blankets, like picnic blankets, perhaps they've got them from their cars, and he sees a woman who must be Rose Polstein smiling at him, not wearing a police uniform but a dress and jacket, covered in snow.

Angels are bright still.

Benny would say, *Wow, man, you're so fucking deep*, and he'd say back, *Hey, bro', you're so fucking shallow.*

They're helping him into an ambulance, Basi coming in the same one, because they won't be separated.

He's right though, even if Benny would tease him, because against the men who live in darkness, there's Rose Polstein, who's shivering, and all these other people out in the snow, and Hannah and Mr Marr and Benny and his foster parents and his other friends and teachers and the people with welcome banners.

He holds on to love, will not fear its shadow.

★　★　★

They've promised her that the ambulance with Rafi and Basi will stop and let her in, 'like a bloody party bus', the police officer said, but he was smiling. The coach with the little kids from the pottery room is leaving and Hannah waves at them as they go. Her other hand holds her mobile. Daphne gave her Mr Forbright's number and she rings him. It rings and rings and she's afraid he won't answer, afraid of what that means for Mr Marr, and then he picks up.

'Hello?'

'Mr Forbright? It's Hannah.'

In the silence, she daren't ask about Mr Marr.

'We're on the way to hospital, Hannah.'

She thinks of her Gap T-shirt pressed into his foot and her hoody round his head, the best she could do, and wishes she'd had real bandages, wishes she'd known what to do to save him. Because even though he's in an ambulance with proper help now, she knows that he will die. 'Do you want to talk to him?' Mr Forbright asks.

'Yes.'

'I'll hold my phone next to him,' Mr Forbright says.

'Hey, Mr Marr, it's Hannah.'

She remembers holding his hand in the library, how even when he could no longer open his eyes she'd see them moving under his eyelids, letting her know that he was still with them.

'It was really brave what you did, getting Tobias and me into the library, not saving yourself. I didn't tell you that. I'm sorry. We're all safe now, Rafi and Basi too. Do you know about everyone leaving the theatre? There were loads of trees backstage, little saplings that you can carry, and we all took one. Daphne said, "Method act trees!" You can imagine how much she liked saying that, but she looked sick with worry too. And then we left the theatre by the fire-exit door straight into the woods.'

Dad says *Lead on, Macduff* as a joke, like when she needs to show him the right aisle in Sainsbury's to get Shreddies. But it wasn't *Lead on, Macduff* because no one was leading; they were all leading.

'Did you know that there's an oak tree in the real Birnam Wood which was alive when Shakespeare wrote *Macbeth*? Its trunk is rotten, but it's still alive and has branches growing.'

Frank had told her that, while they were walking with their trees in the snow, expecting to hear the shots, expecting to feel them.

'You were right, Mr Marr, love is the most powerful thing there is and the only three words that really matter are *I love you*.'

They thought they'd die, she's pretty sure everybody thought that, but in an energetic, crazy way – Butch Cassidy and the Sundance Kid, Thelma and Louise going over the cliff – more exciting and less self-centred than her dystopian scenario. But that wasn't right either, because they weren't just a pair, there were loads of them, a small army of teenagers and teachers, getting splinters in their fingers. They'd all been so cold, that's what she remembers.

'It was amazing, Mr Marr, it really was.'

Everyone shaking with cold so their trees shook too like another wind was going through them.

'We were Birnam Wood coming to Dunsinane Hill, marching to the beat of three words.'

*   *   *

In the ambulance, paramedics are asking Neil, who hasn't once let go of his hand, when he was shot, and Neil says, 'about three hours ago'. And Matthew Marr thinks *about* is not very exact, but life isn't very exact, nor time itself, come to that. It's been like a gift, these last three hours – plus a bit, he thinks it's plus a bit, thinks the gift erred on the generous side – a lifetime he might not have had if the bullet had hit his head and not the medals first. Now, exhausted, he is slipping away from the conscious world and it's a relief to give way to it. He thought he'd have regrets, that he'd get to the end of his life and think, *I should have married, should have had children of my own, I gave everything to the job*. But there are no regrets, or any he has are too piddling to take notice of, not when children turn into invincible trees and a man risked his life to hold your hand as you die.

Acknowledgements

I'd like to thank the following people, for whom thanks on a typed page really aren't enough:

Everyone who wrote books, gave interviews and made documentaries that helped my research for *Three Hours*. Among the books, the following were especially helpful: *The Lightless Sky: An Afghan Refugee Boy's Journey of Escape to a New Life in Britain* by Gulwali Passarlay; *The New Odyssey: The Story of Europe's Refugee Crisis* by Patrick Kingsley; *Human Cargo: A Journey among Refugees* by Caroline Moorehead; *State of Hate*, by the campaign group HOPE not Hate; *A Mother's Reckoning: Living in the Aftermath of the Columbine Tragedy* by Sue Klebold; and *Columbine* by Dave Cullen.

Graham Bartlett, former Chief Superintendent with Sussex police, and Police Commander for Brighton and Hove, for his generous help and guidance; any mistakes I have made are entirely my own.

My agent Felicity Blunt at Curtis Brown, whose generous enthusiasm when the novel was no more than twenty pages kept me writing and whose creative suggestions as it neared the finishing line made it far better; and Lucy Morris for her tireless help and advice.

Venetia Butterfield, my wonderful and inspiring editor, for her astute observations and passionate championing of this book.

The stand-out team at Viking for their many talents and hard work on this novel: Isabel Wall, Maria Garbutt-Lucero, Ellie Hudson, Ellie Smith, Karen Whitlock, Sara Granger, Anna Ridley, Georgia Taylor, Samantha Fanaken, Tineke Mollemans,

Ruth Johnstone, Linda Viberg, Guy Lloyd, Richard Bravery and Laura Bijelic.

The amazing people at Penguin General for reading almost overnight and believing in the novel from the beginning: Joanna Prior, Amelia Fairney, Katy Loftus, Mary Mount, Poppy North, Jack Ramm, Lindsay Terrell, Rosanna Forte and Grace Thornton.

I'd also like to pay tribute to the immensely talented and creative John Hamilton.

Deborah Schneider at Gelfman Schneider/ICM Partners for the best email I have ever received. Sophia Macaskill, Rose Pierce, Nadia Mokdad, and the marvellous Alice Lutyens and Kate Cooper, at Curtis Brown.

The staff and pupils at Frensham Heights School, a progressive school in every good way. The staff and pupils at More House School, who kindly allowed me watch their lock-down drill. Anna Ledgard for her generous help in my research.

And the people without whom I couldn't write:

My sister, Tora Orde-Powlett, who is unfailingly supportive and fantastic; the best of sisters.

The great friends who are still my great friends despite me being absent most of the time I was writing *Three Hours*.

My parents Kit and Jane Orde-Powlett, who have always believed I could write and continue to do so, even when I think I'm stuck.

Last, but most of all, my husband, Martin, and my sons, Cosmo and Joe. My conversations with Cosmo informed and shaped much of this novel, Joe's explanation that editing is like cutting off the head of the hydra meant I sat down at my desk prepared to do battle and Martin, the rock in my life, for whom words will never be enough.